ONE DEADLY LIE

A DCI DANNY FLINT BOOK

TREVOR NEGUS

INKUBATOR
BOOKS

Published by Inkubator Books
www.inkubatorbooks.com

ISBN (eBook): 978-1-915275-26-4
ISBN (Paperback): 978-1-915275-27-1

PROLOGUE

6.00pm, 10 October 1974
Carrington Lane, Calverton

The group were all huddled around the Suzuki 250cc trials motorcycle. The machine was old and battered, but it was still a source of great excitement and trepidation to the gathered youths. None of them were sure where the bike had come from, but it had given them hours of fun, tearing across the open fields one at a time. Topping it up with two-stroke petrol from the green plastic can after every hair-raising trip across the grass.

Standing on the periphery of the group were two brothers. They were identical twins, and at fourteen years of age they were a couple of years younger than the other lads there. They were the only two who hadn't yet ridden the motorcycle they had collectively nicknamed 'The Death Machine'.

The brothers were so identical that no one was ever quite sure who was who. They were tall and gangly, like a lot of other youngsters, and had the same amount of teenage acne on their faces. They both had the popular crew cut hairstyle and always dressed the same. The clothes they wore were cheap and bought from catalogues. It was something they both hated but could do nothing about, as their overbearing mother still purchased all their clothes.

If there was a difference at all in the twins, it was their confidence.

Solomon Peleg was shy and reserved. He was far more studious than his brother, who was two hours younger than he was. Considered to be the brighter of the twins, he always did well at school.

His brother Saul was completely different. He was brash, very loud, and his confidence was at times almost arrogance. He excelled at sports but struggled with other lessons. He was by far the more popular of the two brothers.

One of the older youths shouted, 'Come on, Solomon! There's only you and Saul who haven't had a go.'

Solomon was terrified of the lethal-looking motorcycle but didn't want to show that fear in front of his peer group. He feigned nonchalance and replied, 'Nah, I'm not bothered.'

Somebody at the back of the group started making clucking noises, imitating a chicken.

Immediately Saul said, 'Come on, Solly, I'll do it with you. You ride, and I'll sit on the back.'

Solomon shook his head. 'No thanks, bruv.'

Again, the derision started among the group. Saul moved in close to his older brother and whispered, 'Come on, Solly. You've got to do this, or they'll fuck us off!'

Reluctantly, Solomon sat astride the big yellow motorcycle. His brother confidently jumped on behind him and gripped his waist.

'Don't be scared,' Saul murmured behind him. 'It'll be fine. We'll just go once around the field.' He then shouted confidently for the group to hear, 'Start it up, bruv!'

Solomon stamped down hard on the stiff kickstart, and nothing happened. Hoots and howls of laughter rang out.

'Twist the revs as you kick down!' Saul shouted.

Solomon tried again and gave the twistgrip of the throttle a sharp turn. This time the machine roared into life. He gripped the brake and kicked the motorcycle into first gear before releasing the brake slowly and increasing the throttle.

The motorcycle roared into life and sped across the field. He stamped down on the gears, and the machine went even faster. Saul's arms were around his waist, holding on tightly, and he was terrified and exhilarated in equal measure. Slowing down, he began to turn the motorcycle and eventually came to a complete stop at the other end of the field.

'That was brilliant!' Saul whooped above the noise of the engine. 'Let's give the lads a show now. Get it going flat out, Solly.'

'I don't know. It's hard to steer when it's going fast.'

'Don't be such a soft shit!' Saul clapped a hand on his brother's shoulder. 'Come on, let's go.'

Revving the machine loudly, Solomon stamped down and selected first gear, then opened the throttle. As they raced across the field back towards their friends, Saul suddenly stood on the footrests behind him, gripping his brother's shoulders tightly. Solomon yelled above the noise of the powerful engine, 'Sit down! I can't control it!'

Saul ignored his brother, showing off to their friends. He let out a rebel yell and held his arms out, leaning into the back of his brother with his thighs to maintain his balance. The motorcycle was now flying at top speed across the grass.

Suddenly, the front wheel dipped into a gully and threw Saul off balance. His weight shifted into Solomon's back, who lost control of the handlebars. In a flash, the front wheel slid from beneath them, catapulting them both high into the air.

Solomon landed on his side and rolled over and over, all the air knocked from him. When he came to a stop, he was dazed and gasping for breath. His ribs and left leg ached, but he didn't think anything was broken.

Saul had been completely flipped up into the air. He did a full cartwheel before landing heavily on the small of his back. He bounced once and came to a stop, groaning loudly. Something snapped in his back as he landed. His legs felt strange. Gingerly, he tried to stand up.

His legs were a little wobbly, his head was throbbing, and he felt light-headed. Unable to stop himself, he collapsed back to the floor.

Dashing over to his brother, Solomon yelled, 'Get an ambulance!' One of the watching youths started to run towards the telephone box on nearby Carrington Lane. 'Stay calm. Where are you hurt?'

Saul opened his eyes. 'I'm okay. I just feel a bit weird. My head hurts.'

'Just lie still, bruv. There's an ambulance on its way; we'll get you checked out at the hospital.'

The oldest youth in the group came over and picked the wrecked motorcycle up. 'The other lads are going to stay here until the ambulance comes,' he said. 'I'd better get rid of this thing; I nicked the fucker from Lowdham last night, and you don't need to be dealing with all that shit as well.'

Solomon looked up at the older boy. 'Thanks, Matt.'

'Is he okay?'

'He's fine. He's just banged his head, that's all. He'll be okay once the hospital has checked him over.'

'He's a fucking nutter!' Matt spluttered. 'Did you see him standing up? Crazy!'

'Tell me about it.' Solomon glanced back at his brother. Saul had closed his eyes, his face pale. 'Get rid of the bike. I can hear sirens coming.'

1

3.00pm, 21 July 1987
Woodthorpe Grange Park, Sherwood, Nottingham

Danny Flint stopped the car and showed his warrant card to the uniformed officer at the gates, who immediately wrote his name in the scene log he was maintaining.

'Everyone's rendezvousing in the main car park,' the young officer told him. 'Just follow the drive, sir.'

Danny raised his hand in thanks and drove into the car park of Woodthorpe Grange Park. He could see the other CID cars and the plain white Scenes of Crime vans already parked up near the café. Being in the park again stirred up some wonderful memories for Danny. His father had brought him here when he was a youngster. Woodthorpe Grange Park was beautiful. Dominated by the stone, two-storey Victorian manor house, it had picturesque gardens, wide-open spaces for ball games, and an established pitch and putt golf course. There was also a little café housed within the ground-floor rooms of the manor house. The first floor contained administration offices used by Nottingham City Council.

His father's love of golf had been his reason for bringing a young Danny here. He had used the pitch and putt course to try to encourage his son to play the game.

Danny parked his car next to the other police vehicles and got out, the memories fading as quickly as they had arrived. He scanned the car park and saw Detective Inspector Tina Cartwright talking to Tim Donnelly, the head of the Scenes of Crime team. Both were already dressed in the pale blue, full forensic suits.

As he made his way towards them, he could see DC Jagvir Singh and DC Helen Bailey talking to two young lads. The boys looked to be in their early teens.

'Afternoon, boss,' Tina said. 'This seems a bit of a strange one to me.'

Danny was handed a forensic suit and overshoes. As he slipped them on, he asked, 'Have you only got two DCs here with you?'

'No. Rachel's inside the café, talking to the staff.'

'Where's DS Harris?'

'Lynn phoned in sick this morning, with a stomach bug.'

'That's not great when we're already a DI down.'

'I spoke to Lynn; she thinks it's just food poisoning and expects to be back tomorrow.'

Danny sighed. 'Well, that's some good news at least. Anyway, you said this was a strange one. In what way, Tina?'

'The deceased is a middle-aged female. There doesn't appear to be any disturbance to her clothing, which may rule out sexual assault as a motive. Her handbag, purse and contents don't appear to have been touched, which rules out robbery.'

'Which leaves us with a possible domestic situation,' Danny interrupted. 'Do you know who she is yet?'

'We have a name. A Blockbuster Video card in her purse has the name Ms Angela Billson on. Obviously, we haven't been able to do much with that yet.'

'Who found the body?'

Tina pointed across the car park to the two teenagers talking to the detectives. 'You see the blonde-haired lad? He hit his golf ball into the thick bushes. As he was searching for his ball, he literally stumbled across the victim. Both the boys are only thirteen. Understandably, they're a bit shaken up.'

'Don't keep them here too long, Tina. Obtain their full details and a basic story of what they did, where they went, if they touched anything, etcetera; then get Jag and Helen to take them home. They can get full written statements from them in the comfort of their own homes, with their parents at their side. Let's try to make the whole process for them as least traumatic as possible. As you say, they've already seen something no one should have to see.'

Tina nodded.

'Have you called out a Home Office pathologist yet?' Danny continued.

'Yes. Seamus Carter's on his way. He was travelling from Retford, so he shouldn't be much longer.'

'Any obvious cause of death?'

'The victim's lying on her back. There's some bruising I could see around her throat. So strangulation's a possibility.'

'Okay. Well, let's wait for Seamus to arrive, and then we'll all go to the scene together. Go and speak to Jag and Helen and arrange for them to take the boys' statements, please.'

As Tina walked across the car park towards the detectives, Danny looked at Tim Donnelly, who had so far been silent. 'Any thoughts, Tim?'

'On first viewing, this looks like a classic deposition site to me. My professional first impression would be that she was killed elsewhere and dumped here, to hide her. Had the kid not smashed his ball so deep into the undergrowth, she wouldn't have been found for a long time. She was very well hidden.'

A dark blue Volvo estate car arrived in the car park. The tyres locked on the loose gravel as it was brought to an abrupt halt.

A huge bear of a man with a bushy, unkempt beard got out of the driver's seat. He was followed by a slim, red-haired woman.

Seamus Carter strode across the car park, his long legs devouring the distance, while the woman scampered behind, carrying the black leather grip bag that contained the pathologist's equipment.

Danny half smiled and said, 'Good afternoon, Seamus. I hope you're well.'

Carter's Irish brogue filled the air as he boomed, 'I'm fine and dandy. Thank you, Danny.' He gestured to the woman at his side. 'Let me introduce you to my esteemed trainee. This wonderful, bright, young woman is Brigitte O'Hara. Like my good self, she's from the Emerald Isle and will one day, also like myself, make a superb pathologist. Let me tell you Danny, there isn't much I can teach this one.'

Danny gave Brigitte a brief smile. 'Nice to meet you, Brigitte.'

The young woman smiled confidently in response and handed a forensic suit to Seamus before donning one herself.

When suitably attired, Seamus said, 'Let's go and have a look, shall we?'

Led by Tina, the group made their way along the line of police tape through the dense undergrowth until they found the deceased.

As Tina had said, the woman was lying on her back. Her arms were by her sides, as though they had been placed there, and her legs were together. She was wearing black leather calf-length boots, blue denim jeans and a pink lamb-swool sweater. None of her clothing looked like it had been disturbed. She had short blonde hair cut in a pixie style. Apart from a few cuts around her cheeks and nose, possibly caused by small forest creatures scavenging, there were no visible marks of violence on her face. Her eyes were half open, and her mouth had been forced open by a swollen tongue that now protruded through her teeth.

Seamus spoke into a Dictaphone that had been handed to him by the efficient Brigitte. In a matter-of-fact tone, he said, 'The deceased is an adult white female. Late thirties, possibly early forties. Approximately five feet three inches tall, medium build. Clothing appears intact. No obvious signs of sexual assault.'

He crouched down and closely examined the dead woman's throat.

'This bruising looks consistent with manual strangulation. The way the tongue is presenting also supports that initial theory. I'll know for sure at the post-mortem examination.'

Danny said, 'How long do you think she's been here?'

'Brigitte will do the temperature readings in a second, but my best guess would be she hasn't been here that long. Possibly as recent as last night. I'll be able to give you a better idea after the temperature readings have been done.' He looked at his trainee. 'Can you do those for me, Brigitte?'

The young trainee agreed and reached into the bag.

'There's nothing more I can tell you now, Danny,' Seamus said. 'I'll stay here and work with Tim to get the relevant samples and photographs of everything. Have you made arrangements for removal yet?'

'Not yet,' Tina replied. 'How long will you need?'

Seamus looked at Tim. 'What do you think? An hour or so?'

Tim nodded. 'Better make it two.'

Tina looked at her watch; it was now three thirty. 'Okay, I'll arrange for the undertakers to be here at five thirty. City Hospital for the post-mortem?'

'Yes, please,' Seamus confirmed. 'Let's say six thirty for the post-mortem. Is everyone okay with that?'

Danny agreed and then made his way back to the car park with Tina, leaving the pathologist, his trainee and Tim Donnelly to work the scene. As they walked out of the undergrowth, they passed by Scenes of Crime staff.

Danny was deep in thought. He felt calm and began to process all the information he'd been given. His thoughts were already focussing on the most important, crucial enquiries that would need to be done.

As they got out of the forensic suits, they were joined by DC Rachel Moore.

'What's going to be your priority enquiries, Tina?' Danny asked his colleague.

Tina thought for a second. 'First priority is to research the name Angela Billson and confirm the identity of our victim. We need to establish an address for her as soon as possible, as that could be the actual murder scene. I want to do a full search of the deposition area this evening, as soon as the pathologist has finished and the body is removed. We still have plenty of light, so I want a section of the Special Operations Unit here on standby, ready to do a full fingertip search.'

'Good.' Turning to Rachel, he said, 'Have you checked for any security cameras in the car park?'

'I have. The only camera is focussed on the front door of the café; there's nothing that faces the car park. The gates are habitually left unlocked throughout the summer months. I've seized the video from the camera and will be viewing it right through, back at the office. It may at least pick up some headlights if any cars were driven into the park after dark. The woman who runs the café says the car park is extensively used by courting couples at night. She told me that some of the things she finds here in the mornings are disgusting.'

'That's interesting. That could open a whole new possibility for motive. Do the usual checks for other CCTV in the area too, on the approaches to the park gates. When the Special Operations Unit arrive, work with their sergeant and do a preliminary street search, ready for the house-to-house enquiries.'

Rachel nodded. 'Will do.'

'Stay here and manage the scene,' Danny said to Tina. 'I'll join you at the City Hospital at six thirty for the post-mortem. I need to get back to the office and start preparing for a full unit briefing later this evening, after the post-mortem. Anything else you can think of?'

'No, I think that's everything. Rachel's already got a list of the staff who work here, gardeners, waitresses, etc.'

'Okay. I'll get Fran Jefferies to make a start on researching the name Angela Billson. See you at the hospital later.'

Danny got in his car and drove back down the driveway, pausing at the gates so the uniformed officer could sign him out of the scene. As he drove out of the city back towards Mansfield, his thoughts turned to wondering exactly who Angela Billson was. Was she a mother, a sister, a daughter, all those things?

He felt the same burning desire he always felt when there was a murder. An overwhelming need to find out exactly what had happened to her, and to find the person who had snatched her life away.

2

6.30pm, 21 July 1987
City Hospital, Nottingham

I t didn't matter how many post-mortems he went to,
Danny didn't think he would ever get used to the smell
of formaldehyde and the brightness of the artificial
lights in the examination room. He squinted as he walked in,
followed by DC Nigel Singleton, who would be undertaking
the important role of exhibits officer. It would be the young
detective's job to ensure that every exhibit taken from the
deceased was bagged and labelled correctly. He would be
assisted in this task by two Scenes of Crime officers, who
would also take photographs and make a full video recording
of the post-mortem.

Already waiting in the room were Tina Cartwright,
Seamus Carter and his assistant Brigitte O'Hara. The trainee
pathologist would also take photographs and generally assist
Carter so he would have all the information required to make
his written report.

As Nigel Singleton made ready the various sizes and types of exhibit bags he would need, Tina addressed him, 'As soon as you're ready, Nigel, I'll ask Brigitte to make a start undressing the body.'

Singleton looked slightly flustered. 'I'm ready now, boss.'

Tina nodded to the trainee pathologist, who slowly began to undress the body. Photographs were taken by the Scenes of Crime officers as each individual garment was bagged and labelled ready for forensic testing. It was a careful process that demonstrated a great deal of professional skill, as well as courtesy for the deceased.

Finally, the body was naked, and Seamus Carter began the post-mortem. Fingernail scrapings were taken and exhibited, followed by head and pubic hair samples. Brigitte then took swabs from all the body orifices. These swabs were also bagged carefully by Scenes of Crime officers, while Nigel Singleton filled in each corresponding exhibit label.

Speaking into his Dictaphone as he worked, Carter then made a full visual inspection of the deceased, concentrating on the area around the neck, internally examining the area around the bruising. After ten minutes, he called Danny over. 'You need to see this, Danny. The woman was killed by manual strangulation. If you look closer, you can see where the hyoid bone has been broken. This takes quite a lot of force, so whoever did this did it deliberately. It cannot have been done by some freak accident. This was caused by prolonged and severe pressure. It's definitely murder.'

'Okay. Is this what you would normally find?'

'Sometimes we do. It's just an indication of the level of force used and the sustained nature of the assault. In nature, it's how a big cat would kill a wildebeest. Its jaws clamp on to the area containing the hyoid bone until it snaps. The animal is then suffocated because of the continued pressure and the weight of its own tongue, which is no longer being supported by the hyoid.'

Danny could have done without the graphic description and stepped back from the examining table.

Forty minutes later, the entire examination was complete. The body of Angela Billson, if that was who she was, was no longer recognisable. The extensive post-mortem had been thorough and invasive. It would be left to the mortuary technicians to repair the necessary damage caused.

'Have you obtained all the samples you need for a full toxicology report?' Danny asked.

'We've got samples of everything we need, thanks.'

'Okay. So what's your preliminary report?'

'As I said before, it's definitely murder. She was strangled to death. I would estimate the time of her death as sometime yesterday evening, between the hours of six o'clock and ten o'clock. I can't be any more specific than that. There are no indications of sexual assault; obviously we've taken swabs to confirm this. I can find no other marks of violence other than some very faint bruising around the wrists. This could have been caused when the body was being moved. The woman appears to have been a healthy individual; there were no underlying health issues.'

'Can you tell me anything about her killer?'

'Other than the fact that whoever did this is a relatively powerful and strong individual, not really. It's over to you, Detective. I'll write up my full report as soon as the toxicology reports are in. Brigitte has taken full sets of fingerprints and will do a full dental chart, to assist with identification, should you need them.'

Danny said quietly, 'Thanks, Seamus. See you soon.'

'Undoubtably. Take care.'

'Anything else you want to know, Tina?' Danny asked.

'No, thanks.'

He turned to DC Singleton. 'Nigel, I'll travel back with DI Cartwright. Get back for the briefing as soon as you've finished up here, okay.'

The young detective nodded. 'Will do, boss.'

Danny and Tina walked out of the hospital to the car park. As she unlocked the door, she said, 'How did Fran get on with researching the name?'

'I left her working on it. Hopefully, she'll have some news when we get back.'

'The Special Ops lads were busy doing the search at the scene when I left. Their sergeant is going to phone in anything they find. He wants to work until the light goes. He thinks they'll be able to finish the allocated search area this evening.'

'That's good. Did Rachel make a start on the house-to-house mastering?'

'Yes. She was on top of that and is doing a preliminary CCTV scan at the same time.'

'It's another ten days before Rob's back from his annual leave. Are you going to be able to manage this enquiry along with your current workload?'

'It shouldn't be an issue, boss; my team are relatively free now, and I know Rob cleared the decks with his staff before he took his fortnight-long holiday.'

Danny knew that the MCIU functioned best when both of his detective inspectors could work a case in tandem, utilising their staff and expertise to the maximum effect. So the loss of Rob Buxton, albeit temporarily, at this time would be keenly felt. There was never a good time to take a holiday, but it was crucial his staff were allowed time off, to recharge and reenergise.

'That's great. Don't forget, I'll always be on hand to

bounce things off, and to get stuck in as well. First and foremost, I'm still a detective.'

She smiled. 'Thanks. I'm sure we'll cope between us.'

Danny returned the smile and said, 'Let's get back and get the troops briefed.'

3

8.30pm, 21 July 1987
MCIU Office, Mansfield Police Station

The briefing room was already full when Danny and Tina walked in. The general noise, created by several different conversations all being held at once, ceased immediately, and the room was silent.

'Thanks for staying on tonight,' Danny began. 'Let's get this done quickly. I want everyone back on duty tomorrow morning to continue enquiries at seven o'clock. Tina, can you give an overview of what we know so far, please.'

'Okay, everyone. The body of a white female in her mid to late forties was discovered in the undergrowth at the Woodthorpe Grange Park pitch and putt course earlier today. The body was fully clothed, and there were no signs of any sexual assault. This has subsequently been confirmed at the post-mortem. Found in the jeans pocket of the deceased was a small, red leather clasp purse. Inside the purse was thirty-five pounds, in Bank of England notes, and some loose change. There was also a Blockbuster Video membership card in the name of Angela Billson, and a Yale key that looks like a front door key. DC Jefferies will give us an update shortly on enquiries into the full identity of Angela Billson. The fact that there was no sexual assault and valuables were still with the body could rule out robbery or sex as a motive, but we should all keep an open mind.'

She paused to let that last statement sink in. Just because something appeared to be so didn't make it fact.

'The deceased was found by two teenagers who were playing the pitch and putt course,' she continued. 'They stumbled across the body as they looked for a ball. They have both been taken home, interviewed and statemented. I will update everyone on the content of those statements tomorrow. Access to Woodthorpe Grange Park is open to the public after the hours of darkness. Preliminary enquiries have revealed that the car park is extensively used by courting couples. I want extensive enquiries carried out over the next few days to try to identify people using the car park for this purpose. There is CCTV that covers the café; this may give us times when vehicles came into the car park, although it won't give details of the vehicles.'

Once again, she paused. 'Any questions so far?'

The room remained quiet.

'The post-mortem has revealed that the cause of death was manual strangulation. There were no other marks of violence found on the deceased. The pathologist has cautiously given the time of death as between six o'clock and ten o'clock on the night of the twentieth, so around twenty-four hours ago. This will be treated as a murder enquiry.'

'Thanks, Tina,' Danny said. He looked at DC Fran Jefferies. 'Right, Fran. Do you have any updates for us on your research into Angela Billson?'

'I contacted Blockbuster Video using the number on the card, but it rings directly into their head office in Buckinghamshire. I passed over the membership details, and someone from their customer service team will be contacting me first thing in the morning, with the details of Angela Billson. From their records they will be able to provide us with a home address.'

'What time do they start work tomorrow?'

'Nine o'clock.'

'Right, I want you to call them at nine o'clock sharp. It's imperative we get that address as soon as possible. Woodthorpe Grange Park is quite obviously a deposition site, so we're still looking for a murder scene, and that could well be this woman's home address.'

'Yes, boss,' Fran replied.

'Anything else?'

'I did a name check on the Police National Computer. There are two Angela Billsons shown as being reported missing from home. One is in Merseyside and the other in Dorset. Both women are in their early twenties, so I think it's safe to discount them, judging by the description of our victim.'

'I agree. Which makes it even more important that you follow up with Blockbuster first thing tomorrow.'

'I'll be on to them straight away, boss.'

'Rachel,' Danny said to DC Moore, 'how did you get on with mastering the house-to-house enquiries?'

'I worked with Sergeant Turner from the Special Operations Unit to index all the surrounding streets that could be covered, depending on how far you extend the parameters. Woodthorpe Grange Park is surrounded by housing on all four sides. We concentrated initially on the side that affords access into the park. There's a large area of housing on Woodthorpe Drive, as well as housing estates that access onto Woodthorpe Drive. The house-to-house enquiry is going to be quite extensive.'

'Thanks. Good work today. Come and see me and the DI after the briefing, and we'll decide on the areas we want to cover first. Did Sergeant Turner indicate if the Special Operations Unit can provide any staff to undertake the house-to-house?'

'I asked the question, and he thinks they'll be able to provide two full sections for the next three days. He will confirm that in the morning after he's checked their commitments for the remainder of the week.'

'That's excellent. I understand you did a basic scope for any other CCTV as well. Any joy?'

'Not really. But it was an extremely basic scope, and the light wasn't the best.'

'Okay. Phil,' Danny said to DC Baxter, 'I want you to undertake the CCTV enquiry. Start trawling the surrounding streets, from first light tomorrow. There will be private cameras out there somewhere. I'm looking for vehicles in and around the area between eight o'clock on the night of the twentieth and five o'clock on the morning of the twenty-first. I don't think there's any way the offender could have placed the body in that location during daylight. It must have been done under the cover of darkness.'

Phil Baxter scribbled the time parameters in his notebook. 'Got that. I'll also make enquiries with the bus companies. Some of the cabs in their vehicles are fitted with cameras now.'

'Thanks. I want everyone back on duty at seven o'clock. We have plenty of overtime capability on this enquiry, so don't make any plans for the next few days. Top priority will be to establish an address for Angela Billson. Once that's done, we'll need to do a full forensic search and establish exactly who our victim was. The enquiries will come thick and fast as soon as that's done, so there will be plenty of work to do. Tina, Rachel, let's have a chat in my office. Thanks, everyone.'

The office erupted into conversation as the individual detectives all started to discuss their various enquiries and what tomorrow may bring.

Danny closed the door of his office. 'Rachel, I'd like you to stay on the house-to-house enquiry and work alongside Sergeant Turner and his team. The area I want to initially focus on is the stretch of Woodthorpe Drive between Mansfield Road and Mapperley Tops. Incorporate the main roads off Woodthorpe Drive along that stretch, as well. That will be more than enough to get started on. I'll leave you to organise the relevant maps so we can monitor progress in the office. Any thoughts, Tina?'

'Only that I think that area alone will be a huge undertaking.'

'It will, but it's manageable if we have the Special Operations Unit with us for the full three days. Are there any plans for the council to close the park at night now?'

'Not that I'm aware of,' Tina replied. 'Why?'

'I think we need to be proactive in establishing exactly who's frequenting that car park at night. I'd like to place two detectives in the café after closing time at night, to take numbers of vehicles using the car park for the next week. Once we have the numbers, we can carry out follow-up enquiries to trace the owners. We can then find out what they were doing there, and if they were there on the night in question. I want you to get a couple of volunteers to work a week of night shifts in the café.'

'Okay. I'll go and sort that out now before everyone leaves. The two doing the night shifts won't need to be on duty at seven o'clock tomorrow morning.'

'Thanks, Tina.'

The two women stood and went back to the briefing room.

Lost in his thoughts, Danny stared at his enquiry log, focussing on the name he had written down at the top of the page. Angela Billson.

He closed his book, stood up and slipped his overcoat over his jacket, his mind full of unanswered questions. Who was Angela Billson? Who was the person who had brought about her untimely death? And why?

He walked into the main briefing room, which was now empty except for Tina Cartwright talking to DC Simon Paine and DC Sam Blake, the two detectives who had volunteered for a week of long, boring night shifts.

4

3.00pm, 6 August 1978
Royal Courts of Justice, The Strand, London

At the back of the court, the barrister spoke in hushed tones to Jacob and Rebecca Peleg. He was upbeat and confident that he had proved, beyond doubt, that the junior doctor who had initially treated Saul for the injuries he sustained during the motorcycle crash had been negligent in his care. The court case had seemingly taken an age to get to the high court, but now they were finally within touching distance of a verdict.

The evidence given by Dr Salisbury had been an honest and damning indictment of the scandalously long hours junior doctors were expected to work in critical care.

When the injured Saul Peleg had first been brought into the City Hospital in Nottingham, he was on a spinal board, and his neck was in a brace as a precautionary measure. His brother, Solomon Peleg, had also been brought in on a stretcher but without the complications of a possible neck or spine injury. After both boys had waited in the same cubicle for forty minutes, an exhausted Dr Salisbury *had begun his examination of them both. By the time he started his examination, he had already been on call for fourteen hours.*

Very carefully, he had removed the neck brace and begun his examination of Saul Peleg. To assist in this, he loosened all the straps on the spinal board.

Five minutes into his examination of Saul, a nurse had rushed into the cubicle and shouted that there was a code red emergency in one of the adjoining cubicles. An elderly patient had gone into cardiac arrest and had stopped breathing.

Dr Salisbury had rushed to the nurse's assistance and began doing CPR until the cardiac crash team had arrived. He stayed working on the elderly patient alongside the crash team for another forty-five minutes. His swift, decisive intervention had undoubtably saved the old woman's life.

Feeling exhausted, he had then returned to the cubicle that contained Saul and Solomon Peleg. With an uncharacteristic lapse of concentration, no doubt brought about by fatigue, Dr Salisbury momentarily forgot the injury that Saul had presented with and turned the boy over onto his front. As he was moved, Saul Peleg had yelled out in pain. From the moment he had felt that sharp excruciating pain in the small of his back, Saul Peleg no longer had any feeling in his legs.

Subsequent specialist examinations and scans revealed that there had been a partial fracture of one of the lower vertebrae in Saul's back, caused by the initial motorcycle accident. The twisting action created when Dr Salisbury had turned the boy over had resulted in the spine fracturing completely. The fractured vertebrae had then severed the spinal cord between the L2 and L3 vertebrae in the teenager's lower back. The paralysis was instantaneous and permanent.

As well as the loss of the use of his legs, the injury would have other massive life-altering implications. These had all been presented in open court. The lack of control over his bladder and bowel movements. The possibility of never being able to be a parent. All these matters and others, such as his mental health, had been discussed by the barristers in open court.

On more than one occasion, Saul Peleg found himself squirming with embarrassment as such personal matters were spoken about in the open forum.

The court would consider the long hours worked by the junior doctor as justifiable mitigation. There could be no doubt that the fault of the devastating injury suffered by the boy was caused by the Health Trust and its unrealistic expectations of junior staff. Any damages that were awarded would come from the Health Trust and not the doctor involved.

Now as they waited for the return of the three judges and their verdict, Saul and Solomon Peleg sat in stony silence at the front of the court. Saul in his wheelchair, his wasted legs now covered by a tartan blanket, and Solomon on the hard wooden bench seat next to him.

'Are you okay?' Solomon asked.

'What do you think, Solly?'

'Will you ever tell mother what really happened that day?'

'Do you want me to?' He indicated his wheelchair. 'Don't you think being in this contraption for the rest of my life is punishment enough?'

'But she blames me. She's always blamed me.'

Saul shrugged his shoulders, one of the few movements he could still do. 'I don't want to talk about it. I don't care who she blames.'

The barrister and the boys' parents returned to the front of the court and sat next to the sullen twins. The barrister gave Saul a greasy smile and said, 'The judges are coming back now. I think they'll find for us.'

Again, Saul shrugged his shoulders and said in a sarcastic tone, 'Whoopee do.'

Rebecca scolded her son. 'Saul, remember your manners! Mr Etheridge has worked hard for you. Show some respect.'

Saul looked away.

The three judges walked in and sat down.

The judge sitting in the middle announced solemnly, 'In the case of Saul Peleg verses the Nottingham Trent Health Trust, we find for the plaintiff and award damages of one million seven hundred thousand pounds, to be paid by the Trust for the irreparable injury sustained by Saul Peleg when he was in the care of the Nottingham Trent Health Trust. This award considers both the extent and permanence of the injury, as well as the age of the plaintiff, who will need to be supported by this award for the rest of his life. We also grant the Health Trust twenty-eight days in which to lodge any appeal, both in the finding and the level of damages awarded.'

The barrister gave Mr and Mrs Peleg a huge smile. 'Congratulations. I've already spoken to the barrister representing the Health Trust, and she's indicated that any award below two million would not be contested.'

'When will the money be given to Saul?' Rebecca asked coldly, not returning his smile.

'We will still have to wait the twenty-eight days. Then the money will be paid into an account of your choosing. As Saul's parents and legal guardians, you should establish a trust fund to put the money into. This will safeguard it should anything happen to either you or Mr Peleg. It will always require Saul's consent to access it. This will safeguard his future. I will assist you to draw up the legal papers to set up the trust. I hope this money will help Saul to continue to live a full life despite his devastating disability.'

The family then left the courtroom and made their way through the ancient building. Jacob Peleg walked behind with Solomon, while Rebecca pushed Saul in his wheelchair down the ramp and out onto the pavement. A television news crew were waiting outside for them, there to cover the story for the local East Midlands news.

The family left the barrister to speak on their behalf and hailed a taxi to take them to St Pancras Railway Station, where they could catch a train to take them back to Nottingham. As usual, Rebecca only spoke to Saul on the return journey, choosing to totally ignore both her husband and her other son. It was as if they no longer existed. All her energy was now devoted to looking after Saul's every need.

5

9.05am, 22 July 1987
MCIU Office, Mansfield Police Station

Danny was sitting in his office with Tina, discussing the enquiries they had already set in motion that morning. DS Lynn Harris had returned to duty after her short bout of sickness. She had been sent to Woodthorpe Grange Park to finalise the arrangements for the two detectives who would be using the Victorian manor house at the park to conduct observations on the car park overnight.

DC Moore had already travelled to the park to liaise with Sergeant Turner of the Special Operations Unit. They would commence the house-to-house enquiries on Woodthorpe Drive and the surrounding streets that morning and continue with them for the next three days.

Both Danny and Tina kept glancing into the main office, watching DC Jefferies talking on the telephone. The two senior detectives knew she was talking to the customer service department of Blockbuster Video. They were both hoping the detective would be able to obtain the full details of Angela Billson so they could move the enquiry forward.

Danny had placed Tim Donnelly and a full contingent of Scenes of Crime officers on standby. They would perform a full forensic search once a home address for Angela Billson had been established.

Fran Jefferies finally put the telephone down and walked to Danny's office door. He had seen her coming and opened the door as she approached.

'Well?'

'According to Blockbuster's records, Angela Billson's home address is 22 Cross Street in Arnold. I've done some quick preliminary checks with the voters register, and the only person shown at that address is Angela Billson. The address is a two-bedroom town house, not far from the White Hart pub.'

'That's great work. I want you to keep digging on the address and into Angela Billson. See what else you can find out about her.' He turned to Tina. 'I'll contact Tim and get him and his team travelling to Cross Street. I think we should visit the address first, just in case Angela Billson is still alive and has lent her video card to someone else.'

Tina nodded. 'I'll get the Yale key that was in her purse and grab some car keys.'

Danny picked up the telephone, dialling a number from memory. 'Tim? It's Danny. The address for Angela Billson is 22 Cross Street in Arnold. We'll meet you there. Tina and I will go to the property first and will then call you in.'

6

9.45am, 22 July 1987
22 Cross Street, Arnold, Nottingham

The two Scenes of Crime vans were already parked on Cross Street when Tina and Danny arrived. They walked across to the first van to speak to Tim Donnelly.

'Thanks for getting here so promptly. I just want to make sure that we don't give someone an almighty fright. It could be that Angela Billson's alive and well and has either lost or lent out her Blockbuster card.'

Tina added, 'We'll know soon enough. If there's no reply to knocking, I'll try the key that was in the dead woman's purse. If it fits the door, I think it's a fair bet that the deceased is Angela Billson.'

Tim nodded. 'I'll wait here for your call.'

Danny and Tina walked across the street to the two-bedroom town house. The postage-stamp garden at the front of the house was neat and well-kept. The paintwork of the window frames looked in pristine condition.

Danny knocked loudly on the hardwood door. He tried twice more, and when there was still no answer, he peered through the letter box. The door opened onto a hallway with the stairs immediately to the left. All the internal doors were closed, but the hallway looked tidy with no signs of a disturbance.

'Try the key,' he said to Tina.

Tina slipped the Yale key into the lock. She did a quarter turn to the right and pushed the door.

The door opened.

Danny stepped forward and shouted into the silent house, 'Mrs Billson, Are you home?'

There was no reply.

Danny spoke into his radio. 'Tim, there doesn't appear to be anyone home, and the key we found on the body has opened the door. Can you come forward now and bring us both a forensic suit so we can enter the property as well.'

'Will do.'

As soon as they had donned the full forensic suits, over-shoes and gloves, Danny and Tina walked into the small property. The first door off the hallway opened into a living room. It was very clean and comfortably furnished. There were no apparent signs of any struggle. A photograph on the television showed a woman, with an older man and woman. Danny recognised the younger woman as the deceased.

He looked at Tina. 'What do you think?'

'That's definitely our victim,' she agreed. 'The other two could be her parents?'

'Possibly. Let's have a quick look in the other rooms before we leave Tim and his team to do their stuff.'

Every room they went in was the same. It was spick and span. In life, Angela Billson had obviously been a very neat and organised person. There were no dirty pots in the kitchen, and the bed was made in the main bedroom. There were no signs of a struggle in any of the rooms. Danny doubted that anything ominous had happened here.

'It doesn't look like the murder scene to me,' he said to Tim, 'but I could be wrong. I want you and your team to go over it with a fine-tooth comb. If there's something here, I don't want to miss it. Anything you find that will help us with her family, associates or work, I want to know straight away, please. Don't wait for a debrief; give me a call on the landline.'

'Will do.'

'I'll get a couple of detectives down here now. They can start making enquiries with the neighbours while you examine the premises.'

Danny and Tina got out of the forensic suits and made their way back to the car. Once inside the car, Tina spoke on the radio, instructing DC Jeff Williams and DC Nigel Singleton to attend immediately and commence house-to-house enquiries on Cross Street.

'While we're here,' Danny said, 'let's go to Woodthorpe Grange and see Rachel. We need to let the house-to-house team know that we've now almost certainly identified the victim, and we'll need to find somebody to do a formal identification as soon as we can. After we've spoken to Rachel, we can see Lynn and check that everything's in place for the night-shift detectives and that they have all the access they'll need. I know the council can sometimes be obstructive when it comes to allowing the police to do observations from their premises. Lynn may need a bit of added clout behind her request.'

Tina started the car. 'Let's hope Fran's found more information on Angela Billson that will help us with a formal identification.'

'If she doesn't, I'm sure Tim and his team will find something at the house. Let's go.'

7

.45am, 10 June 1980
2 Fairview Road, Woodthorpe, Nottingham

The house on *Fairview Road was stunning. Set back from the road, near to the junction with Woodthorpe Drive, the house boasted five spacious bedrooms and two sepa-rate lounges, a dining room and a large, fitted kitchen.*

The most important aspect of the house had been the extensive work, commissioned by Rebecca Peleg, to totally adapt the house for use by her disabled son, Saul.

After receiving the seven-figure compensation payment from the Health Trust that had been found liable for her son's medical negligence claim, Rebecca had been determined to spend the money in a way that would enable her son to live a fulfilled, settled life. She also wanted to ensure he had an element of luxury in the house, where he would spend the rest of that life.

Everything had been altered to suit Saul. Every door frame had been removed and widened to allow access for his custom-made wheelchair. The entire ground floor had been made one level, and all the carpets had been replaced with hardwood floors. A lift had been installed to allow access to the first-floor bedrooms, and a specialist wet room area, with a hoist into the bath, had been built alongside Saul's bedroom. The kitchen had been modified so that all the cupboards and work surfaces were accessible for him as he sat in his wheelchair. The hob was adjustable, so he could cook his own meals if he wished. The garden had also been altered massively to allow wheelchair access out into the manicured back garden.

The notion that the rest of her family would also benefit massively from the move from their cramped, semi-detached house in Calverton to the stunning detached house at Woodthorpe genuinely never entered her head.

A large proportion of the settlement money had been placed into a separate account. This money would be used to pay for the continued private medical care that would be required to manage Saul's bowel movements. This was vital. Failing to do this could eventually lead to bowel problems, renal failure and death. The private medical company they had commissioned was expensive but the best. The specialist who came to see Saul at the house had quickly established a routine where his patient's bowels would be cleared every other day. It was a combination of diet, medication and fluid intake that enabled the two-day regime to be successful.

Rebecca had taken it upon herself to manage her son's bladder incontinence. In the beginning, she would insert the catheter every four to six hours herself, to fully empty his bladder. As time went by, she patiently instructed Saul how to do this very personal task for himself. He had quickly mastered the procedure.

Her only motivation, her entire reason for being to the detriment of everything else, was now the welfare of her twenty-year-old son Saul.

It was this obsession with her disabled son that had finally forced Jacob Peleg to write the letter, which now sat unopened on the kitchen table, to his wife.

Rebecca had risen early. She had been surprised to find that her husband hadn't slept in their bed. She had walked downstairs to the kitchen and found the letter. In no real rush to open the letter and read the contents, which she could half guess at already, she made herself a cup of strong, black coffee.

After taking a couple of sips of the hot beverage, she grabbed a butter knife from the drawer and slid it into the envelope to open it.

Her husband, Jacob, had always been a man of few words, and the letter echoed that fact. It was very brief and to the point. It was also brutal in its damnation of her neglect and rejection of him.

He had written that he could no longer remain in a house that wasn't a home. Where there was no love, there was no home. He had left to find a new life, where he could be with somebody who cared about his very existence.

There was no apology for going. It was all very matter of fact.

Rebecca screwed up the letter and hurled it into the waste bin. She would not mourn over a man she had stopped loving years ago. He would be no great loss to her and Saul, either emotionally or financially. The high court settlement had seen to that. She would tell her sons when they got up, later that morning, that their feckless excuse of a father had left them for good. She knew that Saul would not miss his father, but Solomon was different. He had remained close to his father and would be devastated that he had left so abruptly.

Rebecca smiled to herself. She thought their father's disappearance could be just the nudge that Solomon needed to also leave the family home. Seeing his face every day was a constant, painful reminder of why her precious Saul had been so horribly damaged.

Solomon was a reckless idiot. His thoughtless actions had ruined his brother's life. Even now he showed no contrition and still insisted that the accident had been Saul's fault. It was despicable of him to try to blame his brother for what had happened. She would make it clear to Solomon that at twenty years of age, maybe it was time he started to build his own life and, like his father, move out of the family home.

As far as Rebecca was concerned, Solomon was a scrounging layabout, who drifted from dead-end job to dead-end job. When he wasn't in work, he would idle away his days at the house. He contributed nothing. It was pure laziness. She knew that he had always been a bright boy, who could have made something of his life. Instead, he chose to be idle and sponge off his brother's money.

Well, not for much longer, she would see to that. It had only been the presence of her husband that had prevented her from throwing her good-for-nothing son out before. Solomon would now either shape up and get a worthwhile job, or he could leave the family home.

The choice would be his.

The twin brothers hardly communicated anymore. There was a mutual loathing that Rebecca had allowed to fester. She knew that Saul would not object if his brother left the family home. He would probably be glad he had gone.

If all went to plan, it would be just the two of them left. Rebecca and her darling son, Saul.

Truth be told, it was what she had always wanted.

8

11.00am, 22 July 1987
MCIU Office, Mansfield Police Station

D anny was sitting in his office, preparing a press release. Confirmation of their victim's identity had come from Tim Donnelly during the search at Cross Street. A passport bearing the victim's photograph and identity details had been found, as well as an address book with details of family and friends.

The passport had details of who to contact in an emergency. When DC Fran Jefferies had cross-referenced this information with names in the address book, she had been able to establish that Angela Billson's next of kin was her older brother, Dennis.

Dennis Billson still lived in the city, at Sneinton. It had been a simple task for Fran Jefferies to arrange for uniform officers from the local police station to visit the brother's address and deliver the bad news in person. Dennis Billson had been understandably shocked at the news, but he had agreed to attend the City Hospital mortuary at eleven thirty that morning to carry out a formal identification.

The police officers who had delivered the devastating news would be bringing Mr Billson to the mortuary. Tina would meet him there to conduct the formal identification.

The telephone on Danny's desk rang. 'Hello, DCI Flint.'

'Sir, it's the control room. Am I right in thinking that the murdered woman found at Woodthorpe Grange Park has now been identified as Angela Billson?'

Danny recognised the voice as Inspector Hopley. 'Yes,' he replied. 'We've managed to confirm it this morning. Her brother's on his way to make a formal identification at the City Hospital right now. Why do you ask?'

'A young copper at Hyson Green has just done a PNC check on a vehicle that's apparently been abandoned on the Forest Recreation Ground. The vehicle he checked is a Mini Metro. It's not reported stolen, but the registered owner is Angela Billson. Her address on the Police National Computer is 22 Cross Street at Arnold. Is that the same woman?'

'Yes, it is. Contact the officer, and tell him not to touch the vehicle, but to remain with it. I'll see him there in twenty minutes.'

'Will do, sir. The vehicle was abandoned on one of the top walkways, near Forest Road East.'

'Thanks, Ian. Good work putting the two together.'

'We aim to please, sir.'

Danny put the phone down, grabbed his jacket from the back of his chair and walked out into the main office. DC Jagvir Singh was at his desk, busy working on a report.

Danny said, 'Is that urgent, or can you get back to it?'

'It will keep, boss. What's up?'

'The control room have just informed me that a beat officer at Hyson Green has located a vehicle registered to

Angela Billson, apparently abandoned on the Forest Rec. He's staying with it until we get there.'

DC Singh grabbed his coat. 'I've got car keys. Which end of the Forest Rec is the car?'

'I'll tell you on the way; let's go. Have you got protective clothing in the car?'

'In the boot as always, boss.'

'Good man.'

Twenty minutes later, DC Singh slowed the car to a stop on Forest Road East. As Danny got out of the vehicle, he could see a uniformed officer standing on the top walkway next to a burgundy Mini Metro.

He glanced over his shoulder and saw the boarded-up garages that contained the entrance to the caves where DI Brian Hopkirk had died. Surprised at the rush of emotion that engulfed him, Danny swallowed hard and managed to say, 'Grab some gloves from the boot, Jag.'

The two detectives then walked down the grassy bank onto the concrete walkway.

Danny took out his warrant card. 'I'm DCI Flint,' he said to the police constable, 'from the MCIU. Is this the car that's registered to Angela Billson?'

The cop looked at the ID. 'Good morning, sir. Yeah, this is it. It just looked out of place, so I thought I'd better check it on the PNC. I thought it was nicked.'

'I'm sorry, the control room never gave me your name?'

'It's PC Evans.'

'Good work, PC Evans. Have you touched anything?'

'I touched the driver's door handle to see if the vehicle was secure. When I found it was unlocked, I radioed in the check. The control room informed me that the vehicle wasn't stolen, but that I wasn't to touch anything else and to remain with the vehicle until you got here.'

'So nothing's been touched inside?'

'No, sir.'

'Excellent. Did you see anyone loitering near the vehicle as you approached it?'

'No, sir.'

Without touching the glass, Danny peered into the back of the car. On the back seat he could see a maroon-coloured cagoule, with a hood.

Danny gestured to DC Singh. 'Jag, get on the radio and arrange for the vehicle examiners to attend and do a full lift on the car. I want it taken to the forensic bay at headquarters. Then contact Tim Donnelly and let him know that this will be his next job. I want this vehicle subjected to a full forensic examination. Our killer might have potentially brought the vehicle here, so forensically, this could be a huge opportunity for us.'

'Will do.'

DC Singh walked back up the hill to the car, to arrange the full lift. He returned five minutes later.

'Vehicle examiners can be here in the next twenty minutes, boss.'

'That's great.' He glanced around the location where the vehicle had been abandoned. There were no houses over-looking this part of the recreation ground, and no cameras in the area.

Danny addressed PC Evans. 'Which entrance would the driver have to use to abandon the vehicle here?'

'There are two entrances they could have used, sir. Either the entrance at Mount Hooton Road, or through the gates at Mansfield Road.'

The vehicle was now facing in the direction of Mansfield Road.

Danny examined the grass either side of the narrow concrete walkway. There were no signs in the soft earth that the vehicle had been turned around.

'If the vehicle had been driven in through the Mansfield Road gates, would it have to be turned around here? Or is there a wider turning circle somewhere?'

'The walkway runs in a straight line from one end of the recreation ground to the other. Its main purpose is for the Goose Fair – the stall holders all set up along this walkway. If the car had been driven in from the Mansfield Road entrance, it would have to be turned around somewhere along the walkway to finish up facing in this direction.'

'Thanks. Can you wait here, please?'

'Jag, I want you to walk from here to the Mansfield Road entrance and see if you can find any tyre tracks where this car might have been turned round. I'll go down to the Mount Hooton Road entrance and do the same.'

Fifteen minutes later, Danny and Jag were back at the car; neither had found any tyre tracks.

'Jag,' Danny said, 'I want you to stay down here today and concentrate on finding any CCTV you can, in and around the area of Mount Hooton Road. We roughly know the time frame when the vehicle would have been left here. Let's see if there's a camera somewhere that's captured it being driven here. I'll travel into headquarters with the vehicle examiners and arrange a lift back to Mansfield from there.'

As the vehicle examiners rolled through the Mansfield Road entrance, with their full-lift tow truck, Danny smiled to PC Evans. 'Good work this morning. Do you check this area for stolen vehicles every shift?'

'Whenever I'm on a day shift, yes, sir. It's a regular dumping ground for nicked cars.'

'Were you on duty yesterday?'

'I was, and I know what you're going to ask next. Unfortunately, the answer is I didn't check it yesterday. I was giving evidence at the Magistrates Court, so I wasn't on my beat. Sorry, sir.'

'No need to apologise. You can resume your foot beat now, and thanks again for doing a professional job this morning.'

'No problem, sir.'

Confirmation from the officer that the vehicle had only appeared overnight would have been the icing on the cake, but Danny was still jubilant. He felt confident that a full forensic search of the vehicle would provide something evidential.

9

8.00pm, 22 July 1987
MCIU Office, Mansfield Police Station

Danny and Tina sat at the front of the gathered detectives in the main office at the MCIU. It was time to evaluate how the case had progressed and to get feedback from everyone involved.

Finding the victim's car so soon, and undamaged, had been a major positive in the investigation. Danny was waiting for Tim Donnelly to arrive before starting the debrief. He had phoned half an hour ago to say that the examination of the vehicle was almost complete. He had been non-committal on the telephone, but Danny was still hopeful there would be forensic evidence gained from the interior of the car.

The dour expression on Tim Donnelly's face as he walked in, however, scuppered any thoughts of a significant break-through.

Danny started the debrief feeling a little deflated. 'Okay. Now we're all here, let's make a start. I know it's been a long day for everyone, but we've made some progress. Tim, if we could start with you and the search of the victim's home address.'

Tim coughed once and said, 'We've carried out a painstaking search of the property, which is a two-bedroomed town house on Cross Street in Arnold. I'm satisfied this property is not the location where Angela Billson was killed. We've taken numerous fingerprint impressions from all over the house, and these have yet to be checked. There were no signs of a struggle anywhere in the building, and nothing to suggest foul play at that location. We must caution these findings with the injuries sustained by the deceased. Those injuries mean that we were never going to find blood splashes or large amounts of other bodily fluids. All the bedding has been seized for forensic testing, to ascertain if there had been any recent sexual activity. The bed had been fully made, and there were no apparent stains. But we will subject the bedding to a full forensic examination anyway.

'On a more positive note, we've found documentation that fully identifies our victim. This has already been used to facilitate the formal identification earlier today. What we've also found this afternoon was documentation that shows our victim was employed as a health visitor, working out of the Bestwood Park Health Centre.'

Tina Cartwright interrupted, 'The health centre was closed when we received this information. It will form the main thrust of our enquiries moving forward.'

'Thanks, Tina,' Danny said. 'Tim, if you'd like to continue – how did you get on with the victim's vehicle?'

'It's bad news, I'm afraid. We've found no fingerprints anywhere inside the vehicle. It appears that every surface has been wiped. A general examination of the vehicle shows very little wear and tear to any seats except the driver's seat. There's little evidence that anyone else, other than the driver, ever uses the car. Inside the boot we found medical supplies. Bandages, gauze and various ointments. Everything you would expect to find given her profession. We've done full fibre analysis and taken tapings, so there may be something to come from those at a later stage when we have something to compare them against. I'm sorry I can't be more positive.'

Danny gave a brief smile. 'Me too. At the end of the day, you can only find what's there. Thanks for all your hard work today. I know it's been a long day for you and your staff.' Danny looked at Tina. 'How did the formal identification go?'

'Dennis Billson formally identified his sister, Angela, this morning. He's subsequently been interviewed at length by DC Bailey, who will now take on the role of the family liaison officer. Perhaps you can let us know what he had to say, Helen?'

DC Bailey cleared her throat. 'He was extremely upset when we spoke. Dennis and his sister were obviously very close. Having said that, they didn't live in each other's pockets. They stayed in touch and spoke frequently on the telephone. He's informed me that, as far as he's aware, his sister did not have a significant other. There was no man on the scene that he knew about. His sister had been married in the past. She divorced her husband after he had an affair with his secretary and has since used her maiden name again.'

Danny asked, 'Should we be looking at this ex-husband?'

'I don't think so, sir. According to Dennis, the errant husband moved to New South Wales shortly after the divorce and has lived there ever since. We still have to confirm that this is the case though.'

'How long have they been divorced?'

'They were divorced in 1978, so almost ten years now.'

'Okay. Do the relevant checks and see if we can confirm that he's still living in Australia. Anything else?'

'Her brother describes Angela as being dedicated to her

work. She apparently loved her job as a health visitor, working in the community. Visiting people at their homes and helping them overcome their problems.'

'Tina, I'm sure you've got this in mind already,' Danny said to her. 'We'll need to establish exactly who Angela visited during her last few weeks at work.'

'That does form part of my enquiry plan for tomorrow.'

'Good.'

Danny now addressed Lynn Harris. 'Any problems with the observations team?'

'None. The council have co-operated fully. I've got the keys and the alarm codes, ready for DC Paine and DC Blake when they come on duty in an hour. I'll stay on duty and drive them in myself to make sure they get into the building okay.'

'Thanks, Lynn. What sort of view will they have of the car park?'

'From the first-floor windows, they can see the entire car park. It's very dark, so I called in at headquarters and borrowed two pairs of night-vision goggles from the Special Operations Unit. They can wear those and get any car registration numbers.'

'Good thinking. Any joy on your CCTV trawl from the Mount Hooton Road area, Jag?'

'Nothing at all. I found two cameras, but neither of them offered a view of the road. They were focussed on the doors to the premises they covered. I've made an enquiry with the local bus company, to see if their cab cameras have picked up anything relevant. They are still collating their tapes, so I'll be able to view them first thing tomorrow.'

'Good.' Danny looked at DC Jeff Williams and DC Nigel Singleton. 'Anything from your door-to-door enquiries on Cross Street?'

Jeff Williams shook his head. 'Nothing startling, boss. A

lot of people know of Angela Billson, but nobody knows anything about her. She's been described, variously to us, as very private, a woman who keeps herself to herself, etcetera. Nobody describes any comings or goings at her house. Nobody mentioned any visitors. I can confirm that neighbours have seen her driving the burgundy Mini Metro, and that they never saw anyone else in the vehicle with her. One of her neighbours thought she was a nurse at the hospital. That's it, really. It appears that Angela Billson was a quiet, reserved woman who led an ordinary life. Somebody with no enemies.'

'Except one.'

He let the comment hang heavily in the air before continuing, 'Okay, everyone. It's been a long day, but we've made significant progress. We could have been a little more fortunate as far as forensics goes, but that's life. We've another busy day tomorrow. The key for this enquiry could lie either in something we don't yet know about her personal life, or with her work in the community. Our top priority tomorrow will be to interview all her colleagues at Bestwood Park Health Centre. We need to start compiling a list of her patients within the community. I want you all back on duty tomorrow morning at eight o'clock, ready to be briefed on your individual assignments. Finish up what you've got left to do, then get off home. Thanks, everyone.'

As Danny walked back to his office, his thoughts were mixed. He had felt a sense of elation earlier when the car had been found, but his hopes of an early forensic breakthrough had been dashed this evening. What was more concerning was that he now knew the person responsible for the death of Angela Billson was cunning, and obviously no fool. He knew his quarry would be extremely difficult to find, and even more difficult to convict.

As he wrote up his notes in his investigation log, he

thought to himself that tomorrow was another day. Maybe, he hoped, the breakthrough would come when they started looking deeper into the private and work life of Angela Billson, or maybe it would come from the night-time observations being undertaken at Woodthorpe Grange Park.

10

10.00pm, 23 July 1987
Nottinghamshire Police Headquarters

Danny knocked on the office door of Detective Chief Superintendent Adrian Potter and waited.

After what seemed an age, the head of CID shouted, 'Enter!'

The arrogant, condescending way his immediate supervisor spoke to him used to aggravate and annoy Danny. Now, he simply smiled and walked in.

As usual, Potter was sitting at his desk, still wearing his suit jacket.

He looked over his glasses perched on the end of his pointed nose and said in a broad Yorkshire accent, 'Well. What was so urgent, Chief Inspector?'

Danny remained standing and said, 'I wanted to update you on the new murder enquiry the MCIU is investigating, sir.'

Flicking through the paperwork scattered on his desk, Potter said, 'You mean the woman found in the park two days ago? I had expected at least a courtesy telephone call from you before now.'

'As you can imagine, it's been a pretty hectic two days. We've now positively identified the victim. Her name's Angela Billson, and she was a resident in Arnold. The post-mortem examination reveals that she was manually strangled. We think the park where she was found is just the deposition site, so we are yet to establish a murder scene. Next of kin have now been informed. Enquiries are continuing, and I intend to put out a press appeal in the next twenty-four hours.'

'Do you have any suspects?'

'No, sir. But it's early days.'

'Very well, keep me informed of any progress. Don't let me keep you, Chief Inspector.'

Danny knew that was his cue to leave.

He walked out of Potter's office and made his way through the headquarters building to the press liaison office. He needed to thrash out a press release with the press liaison officer before he left headquarters.

11

2.30pm, 25 July 1987
2 Fairview Road, Woodthorpe, Nottingham

DC Nigel Singleton parked the car outside the detached property on Fairview Road.

'Are you sure this is it? It looks very grand.'

DC Simon Paine glanced at his enquiry sheet. This was the fourth address on their list. They were methodically visiting every patient who had appeared in Angela Billson's appointment list. According to her list, she had visited this address five days ago. The day before her body had been discovered.

'This is it, mate. It's a priority address. According to her appointment book, she should've visited here the day before she was discovered.'

Nigel yanked on the handbrake, switched the engine off. 'Right. Who's the patient?'

'A bloke by the name of Saul Peleg.'

The two detectives got out of the vehicle and made their

way down the short driveway, past the dark grey Ford Sierra, to the front door.

Nigel pressed the doorbell. There was a long delay, so he pressed it again. This time he repeatedly jabbed his index finger on and off the button.

They heard a shout from inside. 'Alright! I'm bloody coming!'

The detectives heard the lock turn, and the door swung open.

They were shocked to see a man in a wheelchair.

The man said angrily, 'Well? What's so bloody important that you've got to ring the doorbell like that? If you're Mormons or Jehovahs, you can sod off!'

Trying to defuse the anger in the man's voice, Nigel said calmly, 'Neither of the above, sir. We're from the CID. We'd like to speak with Saul Peleg.'

Both detectives held out their warrant cards for the man to inspect.

Calming down a little, the man in the wheelchair said, 'That's me. I'm Saul Peleg. Why do you want to talk to me?'

'May we come in for a moment?'

After a momentary pause, Saul Peleg said, 'Yes, of course, follow me.' As he wheeled himself down the hallway, he shouted over his shoulder, 'Close the door behind you.'

The detectives followed him into a spacious lounge. Peleg pointed at the settee and said, 'Take a seat.'

As soon as the detectives were seated, he said, 'What's the problem? Has something happened to my brother?'

'No. It's not about your brother,' Nigel replied. 'I want to ask you some questions about your health visitor, Angela Billson.'

'I've got some questions for her too! She should have been here a few days ago and never showed up. It's so bloody annoying. I'd waited in for her all day, and she just didn't show.' He grinned and continued, 'You just can't get the staff these days.'

Nigel ignored the joke and asked, 'What time was your appointment?'

'It was arranged for three o'clock.'

'Excuse my ignorance, Mr Peleg, but why did you need a visit from a health visitor?'

'Because I live here on my own now. My dad left years ago, my mum's no longer with us, and my brother has gone to live abroad. The health visitor comes to make sure I've got everything I need, and that there aren't any issues with my private health care visits.'

'This is a big place for one person, Mr Peleg.'

'Tell me about it.' He banged the wheels of the chair. 'I'm stuck in this bloody thing, so I have to pay for a cleaner and a gardener to look after everything. That's on top of my private health care bills. It costs me a fortune every month.'

'I can imagine, the price of everything these days. How do you manage it?'

'I ended up in this chair because a doctor fucked up. I got a payout from the health authority, so I don't have to worry about money.'

'I see. So the health visitor comes here just to make sure you're okay?'

'That's it. When she can be arsed, that is!'

'Has she ever missed a visit before?'

'No, never.'

'Did you call the health centre when she didn't show?'

'I didn't think there was any point. Like I said, it was just a welfare visit, and I'm fine.'

'How many times does the health visitor come and see you?'

'Once a month usually.'

'Is it always Angela Billson who visits?'

'It's always been Angela. I know I've moaned about her a bit today, but she's a lovely person, and I do enjoy her visits. Why all the questions about her? Is she okay?'

'I'm afraid not. Angela Billson has been found dead. We're just trying to piece together her movements and establish what may have happened to her.'

Saul Peleg's hand shot to his mouth. In a shocked voice, he said, 'Oh my God! That's awful, the poor woman.'

With genuine concern, Nigel said, 'I'm sorry to break the news to you like that, Mr Peleg.'

'I just can't quite believe it, that's all. It's like I said before, she was a lovely woman.'

'Can you tell us anything about her?'

'What, you mean personally?'

'Yeah.'

'No. I only ever saw her professionally. She would always make us a coffee, and we'd sit and have a quick chat. The thing with Angela was, she had a way of steering the conversation away from her, back to you. I'm sorry, I couldn't tell you a thing about her.'

'No problem. We'll leave you to it, Mr Peleg. We've still got quite a few other people to see.'

As the detectives stood to leave, Saul Peleg said, 'I'm sorry I couldn't be more help.' He followed the detectives along the hallway.

Nigel opened the front door, handed Peleg a card with his contact details on, and said, 'If you remember anything that you think could help us, please give us a ring.'

Saul took the card and nodded. He was about to close the front door when DC Paine said, 'Who owns the Sierra?'

'It's mine. It's adapted so I can drive it with hand controls.'

He grinned before continuing, 'I shouldn't really be telling you this, but it goes like shit through a goose, Detective.'

Simon smiled back. 'I bet. Take care.'

Peleg closed the door, and the two detectives walked back to their car. Simon Paine drew a line through Peleg's name and said, 'I reckon we can scratch the wheelchair-bound Saul Peleg from the list.'

12

5.30pm, 31 July 1987
City Ground, Trent Embankment, Nottingham

Five minutes before the final whistle was due to be blown, Dixie Bradder turned to the three men standing next to him on the terraces, and said, 'Come on. It's time for us to disappear. The football's shit anyway; we're not missing anything.'

Nottingham Forest was cruising to a win in the preseason friendly against Leeds United. Three quick-fire second half goals had seen to that. The game of football was only ever secondary for Dixie and his mates. What they were really interested in was the violence that went with the football. All four men were from the Halton Moor council estate in Leeds. They had been close friends since their schooldays and were all members of the notorious Leeds United Service Crew – a gang of violent football hooligans who took their name from the public service trains they used to travel to away games.

Dixie dreamed of establishing his own crew of hooligans. He and his friends were all founder members of the Halton

Moor Casuals. Dixie was a natural leader. He stood six feet tall and was very muscular, working out regularly in the boxing gym on the estate. He was instantly recognisable with his yellow-blonde hair cut in a wedge style with a centre parting.

Earning good money from his job as a welder in a local foundry, he was able to afford the casual designer-label clothes favoured by all aspiring hooligans. The days of skin-head haircuts, team scarves, Doc Martens boots and braces had long since disappeared. None of his crew sported any team colours. No scarves or hats bearing the clubs logo were to be seen. Instead, they wore Burberry, Ralph Lauren, Lacoste and Adidas casual trainers.

Dixie had spent the weeks leading up to the game talking to Dave Connors. Carefully planning the post-match confrontation. Connors was a leading light in the Nottingham Forest hooligan gang known as the Executive Crew.

The two men had planned the fight for immediately after the game, at a nearby park in West Bridgford. The arrangements had been established between the two men. Five men from each crew would meet up, ready to fight for supremacy and bragging rights. It was not only the numbers that had been agreed. Connors had insisted it would be a fight with no weapons. Dixie had felt uneasy about not carrying his favourite weapon of choice, a Stanley knife, but he didn't want to back out of the confrontation.

The four men from Leeds had travelled to Nottingham in a Vauxhall Astra car owned and driven by Sam Creedon. The other two men were Geoff Hoskins and Wes Handysides. Geoff's brother, Nick, would have been the fifth man. He had let them down at the last minute because he had been called in to do an extra shift at the warehouse where he worked.

This meant Dixie and his crew would now be a man

down for the fight. None of them were bothered; they all had faith in their own abilities. They had fought all their lives, and they all knew what it felt like to take a hard punch from a man. They also knew how to administer violence in the most effective, dispassionate way.

They were all violent men who revelled in administering pain.

Sam Creedon was the smallest of the group. He was only five feet six inches tall but was very stocky and an accomplished amateur boxer. What he lacked in size was made up for with speed and aggression. The oldest of the group was the Jamaican, Wes Handysides. He was a giant of a man. At least six inches taller than Dixie and just as muscular. Geoff Hoskins was a quiet individual who only seemed to spark into life during a fight, a vicious, calculating thug who was never happier than when he was involved in violence.

None of the four men had ever been arrested. Dixie and Wes had come close on a few occasions but had, somehow, always managed to escape the attentions of the police.

The only thing the four men enjoyed more than fighting other football hooligans was attacking the police. The Halton Moor estate was a notorious no-go area for the West Yorkshire police. It was a dark and dangerous place, and these men were all in their element living there. They had learned from an early age that to survive, you had to be bigger and stronger than the next man.

And they were all survivors who understood that violence was the key to that survival.

Dixie led his mates down the steps from the top of the Spion Kop terrace at the City Ground. At the rear of the stand, there was a row of public toilets. Like all toilets at all football grounds, these toilets were disgusting. They stank of urine, vomit and worse. He knew that nobody would bother to check the toilet after the game. His plan was to remain hidden there just long enough for the police to escort the main bulk of the Leeds United supporters away from the ground.

The group of four would then slip out of the ground and make their way to the park at West Bridgford.

They had parked their car on Hound Road – a leafy, tree-lined street that ran alongside the nearby Trent Bridge cricket ground. It was in the perfect location, less than two hundred yards away from the prearranged meeting point.

Dave Connors had been explicit in his directions. The Leeds crew were to leave the rear of the football ground and make their way along Colwick Road before crossing over Radcliffe Road and onto Fox Road. Fox Road led into Hound Road; then it would be a left turn and a short walk onto Bridgford Road and the park.

The four men had arrived in Nottingham early. After having a few beers, they had used the time to familiarise themselves with the location. There was every chance that, during the melee, they would get separated. Each man would need to know exactly how to get back to the car.

As the men slipped unseen into the toilet block, the final whistle was blown, and the match ended. Dixie could hear the police shouting instructions at the Leeds fans still on the terracing. He glanced at his watch. It was now five thirty. The fight with the opposing fans had been arranged for five fifty. He would remain hidden for five minutes before leaving the ground. They would easily make the meeting point in fifteen minutes.

He looked at his three mates. All three were now smiling broadly. The anticipation of the confrontation was building, and all of them could feel the adrenalin rising.

Not long to wait now.

13

5.30pm, 31 July 1987
9 Fairview Road, Woodthorpe, Nottingham

Deirdre Godden was starting to get really concerned.

She hadn't seen the curtains on the house across the road move for ages, and there had been mail sticking out of the letterbox for the last few days. She had watched the postman ramming more mail into the letterbox at eight o'clock that morning.

It wasn't that Deirdre was nosy, she just felt an obligation to keep an eye on the more elderly residents of Fairview Road. As the neighbourhood watch coordinator, she felt it was her duty. She would leave being nosy to the woman whose house she was looking at now.

Gladys Miller really was a curtain twitcher, and a gossip to boot. If she ever needed to know anyone's business on the street, she could always rely on Gladys to have all the information.

Deirdre didn't dislike Gladys; she could be very funny and

witty when she had time to chat. She could understand, to a certain extent, her neighbour's nosiness as well. At the grand old age of eighty-two, what else was there left for her to do other than sit and watch the world go by outside her window?

Living directly opposite, she often saw Gladys first thing in the morning, when she went for her morning walk around the front garden. The two women would always wave. Deirdre tried to recall when she had last seen her elderly neighbour. When she realised it was close on three weeks ago, she decided she must act.

Some months ago, she had persuaded Gladys to give her a duplicate key so she could get in the house if she had a tumble or anything. Her neighbour had been reluctant at first, valuing her independence, but in the end, she had seen sense and handed over the key.

After rooting through the kitchen drawer where she kept all her miscellaneous bits, Deirdre found the Yale key with the label attached. It simply read, SPARE – GLADYS.

She grabbed the key and her coat and made her way across the street. As she walked down the driveway, Deirdre tried to reassure herself, saying out loud, 'Everything will be fine; stop worrying.'

Deirdre rang the doorbell. When there was no answer, she knocked loudly on the heavy wooden door.

Still no answer.

With a rising sense of trepidation, she slipped the key inside the Yale lock and made the quarter turn.

She pushed hard against the heavy door until it slowly opened.

As she opened it, she shouted, 'Gladys! Are you okay?'

The hallway was gloomy, and there was a terrible smell. Taking a deep breath, she stepped inside and shouted again, 'Gladys! It's Deirdre! Where are you?'

A feeling of dread washed over her, and for the first time she felt afraid. As her eyes became accustomed to the gloom, she could see a bundle of old coats lying on the floor at the foot of the stairs. She thought she saw movement inside the coats, so stepped closer.

Suddenly, several dark shapes emerged from beneath the coats and scuttled towards the kitchen. She jumped in fright as a larger furry object shot out from beneath the coats and ran past her feet, through the open front door.

To her horror she realised it had been a rat, a big one.

Summoning up every ounce of courage within her, she stepped forward and moved the bundle of coats. As she moved the first coat, she saw a sight that she knew would stay with her for the rest of her life. Underneath the coats, dressed only in her dressing gown, was the decomposing body of her friend and neighbour.

The coats had been used to cover her body. Unfortunately, they hadn't prevented the vermin from feasting on her remains. Her face was barely recognisable. It was discoloured, and large chunks of flesh had been removed by the scavenging rodents.

Deirdre recoiled in horror and stumbled backwards out the front door. She ran from the house of horrors, sprinting back across the road to her own home, where she grabbed the telephone.

In a panicked, breathless voice she said, 'Police.'

The operator put her through to the police, and after a brief delay she said, 'Please help me. You need to send somebody quick. I've just found my neighbour; she's dead.'

There was a shorter delay as the police operator tried to obtain details.

'My name's Deirdre Godden,' Deirdre spluttered. 'I live at number nine Fairview Road at Woodthorpe. My neighbour's at her house, number eight. Please hurry; it's just awful.'

As she put the telephone down, her legs suddenly felt very weak. She sat down on the bottom stair and instantly recalled the horrifying image of her dead neighbour at the foot of her own stairs. Tears started to roll down her cheeks, and her entire body began to shake with the shock.

In the distance she could hear sirens; she prayed it was the police rushing to her.

14

5.45pm, 31 July 1987
City Ground, Trent Embankment, Nottingham

The four men slipped out of the football ground and made their way towards Radcliffe Road. On a normal match day, this area would still be filled with noisy Forest supporters. As the match today was only an unimportant preseason friendly, it had been poorly attended by the home fans. Consequently, the area was almost deserted.

They walked onto Hound Road, and Sam Creedon paused next to his Vauxhall Astra. He opened the boot and retrieved a garishly painted truncheon. He had bought the weapon while on holiday in Spain two weeks ago. It had a single Spanish word written on it, the literal meaning of which was devastation.

Dixie scowled. 'The arrangement was for no weapons.'

'I know,' Sam replied. 'It was also for five people, and we haven't got that either.'

Dixie shrugged. 'I suppose not. Anybody else want to get tooled up?'

The other two shook their heads.

Sam slammed the boot and slipped the heavy truncheon up the sleeve of his Stone Island jacket. The men walked along Bridgford Road and into the park. Not far from the entrance, he could see a group of eight men waiting beneath a huge tree.

Wes Handysides growled. 'Looks like these pussies can't count! I thought you said it would be five.'

Dixie was raging. He could see Dave Connors standing at the centre of the group. He had met him a couple of times before, at England games, and recognised him straight away.

He turned back to his small group. 'I know it's two to one, but I still want to have these bastards. Are you all up for a ruck?'

Geoff Hoskins was wild eyed, and his face flushed. He said quietly, 'We're the Halton Moor Casuals. We can take these wankers.'

Nothing else was said. No other words were needed. The four men made their way across the grass.

15

---

*S*olomon Peleg lay on top of the bed in his darkened bedroom. He had left the curtains open and was still fully dressed. He had been staring at the ceiling for almost four hours now, weighing up his options.

The events of the evening had pushed him to the breaking point, and he felt cornered. His day had started badly and just got worse. He had arrived at work at nine thirty and been called straight into the manager's office, where he was unceremoniously fired and told to leave. He hated working at the poxy dental technicians, but at least the job had kept his mother off his back. It had been mundane, repetitive work, and Solomon had soon become bored. His work was shoddy, and he was lazy. He didn't blame the manager for sacking him.

He had spent the day in Nottingham drinking, wandering from pub to pub. By the time he had arrived home at seven o'clock that evening, he felt quite tipsy.

He had expected some abuse from his mother when he broke

the news to her that he'd been fired and was jobless again. What he hadn't expected was her vehement condemnation of his behaviour. She had launched into a nasty, spiteful, vitriolic tirade that had culminated in her demanding that he leave the family home in the morning. She had in effect thrown Solomon out. He had looked to Saul for some support, but all he got was a smirk.

Saul had joined in the verbal assault, saying, 'I agree with Mother. If you can't pay your way, you should leave.'

After all the crap he'd taken because of his brother, Solomon felt betrayed and hurt. The vast quantity of alcohol he had consumed earlier amplified those feelings. He had stormed out of the kitchen and gone to his room. As he stomped up the stairs, he heard his mother's strident voice behind him. 'Pack your stuff. I want you out in the morning!'

Solomon had collapsed on his bed. He was distraught and panicking. He had no money, no job, and as of tomorrow, he would be homeless as well. He had lain on his back, with his hands clasped behind his head. He had thought of countless options, but he kept coming back to the same conclusion. This was all totally unfair. Saul's stupid, reckless actions on that motorcycle had caused his crippling injury and effectively ruined his own life. Solomon now realised that action had ruined his own life too. His mother was an unfeeling bitch who only cared about his brother. He would be better off out of her way. Somewhere he wouldn't have to listen to her constant sniping criticism.

The solution had come into his mind slowly.

It had slipped in greasily.

There had been no eureka moment, no massive fanfare of trumpets. Slowly the thought that it was them who needed to be out of the house, and not him, wormed its way into his brain.

Once the idea was there, he couldn't get rid of it. He needed to think of a way he could make them leave. He had spent four hours in his room, watching the light fade outside until darkness had enveloped the room. The darker his room had become, the more the thoughts inside his head mirrored that darkness.

He had heard his mother getting Saul ready for bed before going into her own room. He knew she was a creature of habit and would read until ten o'clock before going to sleep.

He glanced at his bedside clock; it was now eleven thirty. He had formulated his plan and had thought through all the implications. It would work, it had to work.

He sat up on the bed and remained there for another ten minutes, pausing as he made one more mental run-through of what he was about to do. It was a massive step, but it would mean the start of a new life for him.

He crept downstairs and opened the internal door into the garage, where he retrieved a length of blue nylon tow rope. He quickly got to work on the rope and soon fashioned the item he would need.

Carrying the rope, he walked back upstairs and made his way along the gallery landing. He looked in on Saul first. He was in the bedroom opposite his mother and was fast asleep, snoring loudly.

Solomon closed the door quietly before stepping across the landing and into his mother's bedroom.

He placed the rope on the floor and stepped over to the bed. His mother was lying on her back, her mouth wide open. Her breathing was slow and rhythmic. She was in a deep sleep, her arms tucked beneath the duvet.

Solomon knelt astride her, pinning her arms under the bedclothes. Feeling his weight on her chest, his mother stirred. He waited until her eyes opened; then he gripped her neck with both hands and started to squeeze, pressing his thumbs hard into her windpipe.

He saw her eyes bulging and could feel her arms and legs starting to thrash about under the duvet.

Trapped beneath the bedclothes, her movements made no sound.

He squeezed harder, his hands now starting to ache, until suddenly, the thrashing limbs twitched a few times before stopping altogether. His mother's eyes, which seconds before had been bulging and panicked, became dull and lifeless. He released his grip and used his index finger to feel for a pulse in her bruised neck.

It was still there – faint and sporadic – but still there.

He got off the bed and walked downstairs to the garage, where he got a stepladder. He carried the ladder back up the stairs and opened it up beneath the loft hatch cover. Climbing the stepladder, he reached above his head and tied the makeshift blue nylon noose onto one of the wooden beams in the loft space.

Leaving the noose hanging down from the rafters, he walked back into his mother's bedroom. He dragged the unconscious woman out of her bed and onto the gallery landing.

Rebecca Peleg was physically small. She was less than five feet three inches tall and weighed just under eight stone. It was an easy task for the powerful Solomon to lift his mother as he balanced halfway up the stepladder and placed her head in the noose.

He supported his mother's weight as he clung to the ladder and could hear her rasping breath as she tried to draw air into her damaged windpipe.

He whispered to her, 'It didn't have to be like this, you cold-hearted bitch. If you had for once just listened to me, everything could have been alright.'

Suddenly, her eyes opened. She was terrified and tried to speak. Startled, Solomon let go of her. As her body weight caused the noose to tighten, the nylon rope immediately bit into her neck, just below her mandible. Her hands feebly reached up for the rope, but she could do nothing. Her legs, beneath her nightie, began to kick out, hammering into the metal stepladder. The kicking didn't last very long this time.

After less than a minute, all movement stopped. She was dead.

He walked over to his brother's bedroom and quietly opened

the door so his brother would see his mother's body hanging from the loft hatch when he woke up.

Solomon closed the stepladder and carried it back downstairs to the garage. He walked back upstairs to his room and wrote out a brief suicide note. In disguised, longhand writing he wrote, 'I can't take this. My beloved husband walking out was the last straw. I can't bear to see my boy like this any longer. I feel trapped, and this is the only way out for me. My boys will be better off without me.'

He smirked as he wrote the last sentence, then put the note on his mother's vanity unit. He straightened up the bedclothes on her bed, as he didn't want there to be any revealing signs of a struggle.

Feeling reborn, Solomon walked back to his own room. He got undressed and took a long hot shower.

He needed to get some sleep before his brother's shouts woke him in the morning.

16

The fight in the park in West Bridgford was vicious and brutal. Even though they had greater numbers, the Forest fans were no match for the Halton Moor Casuals. The level of violence meted out by the four men from Leeds was on a different level to anything the Forest fans had seen. Three were soon unconscious on the ground, and three more were lying bruised and battered beside them. The last two, Dave Connors and one of his fat sidekicks, had run from the park towards Hound Road.

Wes Handysides caught up with them first. He grabbed the fat man around the neck, dragging him to the floor. Dave Connors aimed a kick at the side of the West Indian's head. He should have kept running.

No sooner had the wild kick landed than Sam Creedon arrived on the scene. Without hesitation, he smashed the heavy truncheon down onto the back of Connors's head. Dixie Bradder and Geoff Hoskins followed that up with a flurry of punches to the face and head of the Forest hooligan. With both Forest fans now on the floor, all four men began laying into them with heavy kicks and punches.

Suddenly, there was a shout behind them. The men from Leeds whirled around and saw a police officer running towards them. He was speaking into his radio as he ran, requesting urgent backup.

He was already between the Leeds fans and their car.

'Leave these fuckers!' Dixie shouted. 'We've got to get out of here before more cops arrive.'

As the four hooligans ran past him, the lone policeman made a grab for Geoff Hoskins. He held onto him and pulled the hooligan to the ground. The officer's helmet flew off as the two men wrestled on the ground. Instantly, the other three men doubled back and went back for their friend. Sam Creedon once again used the truncheon to deadly effect, repeatedly bringing it down hard onto the policeman's head. As the unconscious, defenceless officer released his grip on Hoskins, the other three men started kicking him repeatedly.

Geoff Hoskins hauled himself to his feet and aimed two particularly vicious kicks at the policeman's face before the four men ran back to their car.

They were laughing as they jumped into the car, and Sam Creedon drove off at speed.

Further along Hound Road, Dave Connors helped his dazed friend to his feet and said, 'Come on, Jacko. We need to get the fuck out of here.'

As the two Forest hooligans staggered away, PC Mark Warden, who had bravely come to their rescue, lay unmoving and bleeding on the pavement.

17

6.30pm, 31 July 1987
9 Fairview Road, Woodthorpe, Nottingham

Danny could feel himself starting to sweat under the forensic suit. It was very warm and humid, a typical late July evening. He walked across to Tina Cartwright, who was waiting by the open front door of the detached property on Fairview Road.

'Scenes of Crime are already inside,' Tina said. 'I'm just waiting for Seamus Carter to arrive. I didn't know you were coming out?'

'I'd literally just arrived home when the control room notified me. I didn't even have time to take my jacket off. What have we got?'

'Elderly female, believed to be the owner of the house, found dead at the bottom of her stairs. From the state of the body, I reckon she's been dead around a month.'

'Who found her?'

'Deirdre Godden. Neighbour who lives across the street at

number eight. Came to check on the old lady after noticing a build-up of mail and not seeing her around for a while.'

'Do we have a name for the deceased?'

'Gladys Miller.'

'Who's with Mrs Godden?'

'DC Bailey's getting her statement. Mrs Godden is still very shaken up. I've told Helen to take her time.'

'Good. First impressions?'

'When I first saw the location of the body, I wondered if it was a domestic accident. She was over eighty years old, and I thought she could have simply fallen down the stairs. The first officer who attended made a cursory check of the property before withdrawing. When I arrived, he informed me that he had found signs of forced entry at the back of the property. Tim Donnelly has just confirmed that there's a broken window at the rear, and that there are signs that the property has been searched. I haven't had a close look at the body yet; I was waiting for the pathologist.'

'So what are you thinking? Burglary gone wrong?'

'Could be.'

Just then, Seamus Carter's Volvo came to a stop on Fairview Road, and he got out, accompanied by his assistant. They both quickly donned forensic suits and overshoes and joined the two detectives on the doorstep.

'What's happened to this area?' Seamus said, shaking his head. 'Two suspicious deaths in just over a week. Woodthorpe used to be such a nice area.'

It suddenly dawned on Danny that they were less than four hundred yards away from Woodthorpe Grange Park, where the body of Angela Billson had been found.

'I think this poor woman was dead a long time before Mrs Billson,' Tina said.

'I see,' Seamus said. 'Been here a while, has she?'

'Looks that way.'

'Okay, let's get inside and have a look.'

They all gave their details to the officer manning the entry log, before stepping inside the hallway of the property. The Scenes of Crime team had already set up arc lights. The once gloomy entrance hall was now flooded in a brilliant white light. The coats that had covered the body had been removed by the Scenes of Crime team. The deceased was lying on her back, her disfigured face looking up towards the ceiling. She was dressed in an old dressing gown. One slipper was on her right foot; the other was nowhere to be seen.

Seamus stepped forward and took a closer look. 'I see what you mean. This woman's been dead for a while.'

'How long?' Danny asked.

Seamus stroked his bushy beard thoughtfully. 'Rough guess, four to six weeks. These marks on her face and neck look like bites.'

Tina said, 'The neighbour who found her told me that she had disturbed rats around the body.'

'Charming. Yeah, they would cause those sorts of marks.' He motioned to his assistant and said, 'Brigitte, can you give me a hand to turn her, please?'

She stepped forward, and between them, they rolled the dead woman over onto her front. Seamus felt the skull with his gloved hands.

He was thoughtful for a second. 'I think this is a murder. I can feel a distinct, depressed fracture at the top of the skull. It feels like the kind of indentation I would expect to find after a blow from a heavy, blunt instrument. It's not the sort of fracture I would associate with a fall.'

'I didn't tell you before, Seamus, but there are signs of forced entry at the back of the property, as well.'

'Bloody marvellous. It's all so unnecessary. Even if she had disturbed the burglars, someone this frail could easily be manhandled back into the bedroom. The force that's been used here is way over the top.' He shook his head again. 'Anyway, that's enough of my ranting. I'll be able to tell you for sure at the mortuary. Are the undertakers on their way?'

Tina said, 'I've already called them; they should be here within half an hour.'

Danny asked, 'Has Tim got everything he needs from the body?'

'Not quite. They still want more photographs and samples from directly around the site of the body.'

Seamus said, 'We can lend a hand with all that while we wait. Shall we say eight o'clock at the City Hospital for the post-mortem?'

Danny said, 'I'll see you there. Tina, can I have a word outside, please?' The two detectives stepped out into the evening light. 'Rob's back from his annual leave tomorrow, so I'll get him to head up this enquiry. You've got your hands full already with the Angela Billson enquiry. I'll attend the post-mortem tonight and brief Rob when he gets back. There's no need for you to attend as well. I'd like you to stay on here this evening and manage the scene. Delegate someone to make a start getting any house-to-house mastered. A lot of it is bound to overlap what we've already done on the Billson enquiry. I didn't realise they were so close, geographically, until Seamus made that comment.'

'I know. I seem to recall from the house-to-house team that this was one of the few outstanding houses on Fairview Road. Now we know why.'

'It's a shame the detectives who visited didn't notice the accumulation of junk mail. They wouldn't have gone to the rear of the property, not on a first visit.'

'They would have no cause to, boss. It would just be marked down to revisit.'

'Agreed. It wouldn't have made any difference. It's obvious that Gladys Miller was dead long before Angela Billson was murdered. Let the team know there'll be a full briefing tomorrow morning at nine o'clock.'

Danny walked around the side of the property until he came to the wooden gate that led into the rear garden, where a uniformed officer was standing.

'I'm Chief Inspector Flint,' he said to the officer. 'Were you one of the first officers to arrive?'

'Yes, sir. My partner and I were first to respond to the three nines call. He's manning the log on the front door while I guard the scene back here.'

'Can you show me where the forced entry is?'

'This way, sir.' The officer directed Danny to a kitchen window. The smaller transom window above it had been smashed before the offender had leaned in and opened the larger window below. There were scuff marks on the windowsill where someone had climbed through.

Danny could see the glass from the smashed window all over the worktop in the kitchen.

'When you arrived, was the back gate open or closed?' he asked.

'Definitely closed,' replied the officer. 'I had to climb over and undo the gate.'

'Thanks. Have you had a look at the bottom of the garden?'

'Yes, sir. When I first got here, I had a look round. It's quite overgrown, but someone has made a start on it. I noticed some of the shrubs and weeds have been cut back, and a start has been made to dig the garden over. All the pulled-up weeds have been thrown into one corner of the garden.'

'Is there any access from the back?'

'There's what looks like a footpath that runs behind all the houses. It's probably a service path or similar.'

'Probably. Good work today. Make sure you and your partner submit your statements as soon as you can, please.'

'Will do, sir.'

Danny looked down the rear garden, where he could see the area of the garden described by the uniformed officer, before heading back around to the front of the property and taking off the forensic suit. As he screwed the suit up and put it in the bin liner outside the front door, he was joined by Tina again.

He motioned to the back garden. 'There's an alley that runs along the back of these houses. Arrange for it to be searched while we've still got some daylight. There's every chance it was used by our burglar, or burglars, to approach the property. I'm going up to the City Hospital now. See you in the morning.'

'Will do, sir. Are you sure you don't want me at the post-mortem?'

'No, you've got enough to sort out here. I'll handle the post-mortem.'

She nodded and walked back inside the crime scene.

Danny got in his car and scribbled 'Check local burglary offenders' into his enquiry log.

He glanced at his watch; it was now almost seven thirty. He had time to get a coffee from the staff canteen at the hospital before going to the post-mortem. His throat felt parched.

18

2 Fairview Road, Woodthorpe, Nottingham

*S*olomon was woken by his brother's anguished cries.

He clambered out of bed, pulled on a pair of jogging bottoms and walked slowly from his bedroom out onto the gallery landing. He was confronted by the image of his mother hanging from the open loft hatch. The blue nylon rope had bitten deep into her neck. Her tongue was protruding out from her black-ened face. This macabre sight was accompanied by the wailing coming from his brother's bedroom.

He faked an anguished cry of his own. 'Oh my God! Mother, what have you done?'

Hearing his brother shout, Saul shouted, 'Solly, help me, please. I need the toilet, and I can't reach my catheters.'

Solomon walked into his brother's bedroom and pushed the remote-controlled hoist to within his reach.

As Saul operated the controls, Solomon pretended to break down and cried, 'What are we going to do?'

Having successfully inserted a catheter and relieved himself in the wet room, Saul manoeuvred the hoist so he could reach his wheelchair. Instinctively, Solomon tried to help, but his brother snapped, 'Get the fuck off me. I can manage. For God's sake, cut her down, and I'll call the police.'

Through fake tears, Solomon said, 'Do you think I should, before the police get here?'

'I can't stand to look at her like that; cut her down. Please, Solly.'

Solomon ran downstairs and grabbed a carving knife from the kitchen. He stood on his tiptoes and could just reach above the noose. Without supporting his dead mother, Solomon sliced the sharp kitchen knife through the thin rope. His mother dropped like a stone onto the hardwood floor, cracking her head loudly as she landed.

Saul made his way to the purpose-built lift and went downstairs to the kitchen, where he called the police. Through his sobs, he tried to explain what had happened down the phone. Eventually, he said, 'Thank you,' and replaced the handset.

Solomon sat next to his brother and said, 'What did the police say?'

'They're sending someone out; they'll be here shortly.'

'I don't want you to worry about a thing, bruv. I can look after you. We'll be alright.'

Saul nodded, tears streaming down his cheeks. 'Why do you think she did it, Solly? Am I that much of a burden?'

'Don't think like that. She's been down ever since Dad left. She always put on a brave face when you were around, but I used to hear her crying at night after she'd put you to bed. She just couldn't understand why he left us.'

'When she came up to say goodnight to me last night, she was fine. I heard you two arguing later though. What was all that about?'

'It was nothing.'

'It wasn't nothing,' Saul insisted. 'I heard her tell you to leave. She threw you out.'

'No. We had words, but everything got sorted out later, and she was fine.'

'I thought you hated her.'

'Of course I didn't hate her. She was our mum; how could I hate her? It's like last night, even though she got mad, I knew she'd be okay about things this morning. I couldn't help getting fired; the manager there is a prick.'

'I'm sorry I joined in having a go at you, Solly. It just upsets me so much when Mum gets angry.'

'Don't worry about it. I know you didn't mean those things you said.'

'Are you staying, then?'

'I was never leaving. It's just you and me against the world now. We'll be fine; you can rely on me.'

'Thanks, Solly.'

Their conversation was interrupted by a loud knocking on the front door. Solomon opened it and saw a policeman standing there. He could see that the officer was a sergeant. He was short and very fat; the buttons on his tunic were straining to keep his bulk in check.

'Saul Peleg?'

'No. That's my brother. He called about our mum; she's killed herself.'

'Can I come in?'

'Of course, sorry. Is anybody else coming?'

'No, just me, son. I'll be able to sort this out, don't worry.'

Solomon introduced the police sergeant to Saul and said, 'She's upstairs on the landing.'

The sergeant said to both brothers, 'My name's Sergeant Calderwood. Who found your mum this morning?'

'I did, but I couldn't do anything,' Saul said. 'I was in bed and couldn't get to my hoist to reach my wheelchair. I had to wait for Solomon to wake up.'

Noticing for the first time that Saul was in a wheelchair, Sergeant Calderwood turned to Solomon and said, 'Do you want to show me upstairs?'

As they walked up the stairs, Solomon said, 'I hope I haven't done the wrong thing. I cut her down already.'

On the gallery landing, the old sergeant said, 'You really shouldn't have cut her down, son.'

'My brother asked me to. He couldn't stand to see her hanging. I didn't want to.'

'Had she given any indication this was on her mind?'

'Thinking back to some of the things she said, and her mood swings, I suppose the signs were there. She was depressed about Saul's situation anyway, and when Dad moved out, she changed for the worse. Looking after Saul is hard work. He has no feeling from the waist down, and this causes a lot of problems. She used to do everything for him. Just lately, I've heard her crying at night. I don't think she could cope after Dad left.'

'Well, the house is certainly well adapted for your brother. It must have cost a fortune.'

'Yeah. Saul received a huge medical negligence payout that paid for all this. At least he'll never have to worry about money.'

'Which room's your mum's?'

Solomon showed Sergeant Calderwood into his mother's bedroom and waited by the door.

He watched as the portly sergeant found and read the suicide note. The sergeant took out an evidence bag from one of his tunic pockets and placed the note inside. 'I'll need to get a statement from you and your brother. Are you okay to do that now?'

'I am. I don't know about Saul, though. I should think so. What happens now?'

'I'll arrange for your doctor to come out and pronounce life extinct, and then we'll arrange for undertakers to come and collect your mother. Who's her doctor?'

'Dr Temple at Arnold.'

'Okay, son. You go back downstairs and be with your brother. Don't worry, I'll get things sorted for you.'

Solomon walked slowly down the stairs and sat quietly next to his brother. Upstairs, Sergeant Calderwood knelt at the side of the body; he had a cursory look at the dead woman's neck and saw how deeply the nylon rope had gone into her neckline. The whole area around the rope was discoloured. It was an angry red colour below the rope and black above it.

It was as clear a suicide by hanging as he had ever seen. In his twenty-nine years and eleven months service, he had seen plenty. There was no need for him to trouble the CID over this death. They could make a simple job very complicated. Sorting out the coroner's file for a suicide would just about see him through to his retirement in a few weeks' time.

He grabbed his radio. 'Sergeant Calderwood to control. This job on Fairview Road, it's a suicide; there's no need for the CID to attend. Can you contact the Arnold Medical Centre and request Dr Temple attend this address? Over.'

'Will do, Sarge. Over.'

He slipped the radio back in its harness and thought to himself, Just another death. Hopefully, this would be the last he would have to deal with.

19

7.00pm, 31 July 1987
Hound Road, West Bridgford, Nottingham

Detective Sergeant Pete Hazard had only been with West Bridgford CID for a month. He was on the late turn with DC Flowers. They were the entire CID cover for the evening. He had attended Hound Road after hearing the first reports of an attack on a colleague.

By the time he and DC Flowers had arrived, the ambulance was already speeding away with the critically ill constable. He had apparently sustained severe head injuries after attempting to arrest several men involved in fighting on the street. A witness in one of the nearby flats had provided sketchy details of the events but couldn't give any significant details.

Sergeant Hazard had dispatched DC Flowers to the Queen's Medical Centre, to keep track of the young officer's condition. He looked at the uniform sergeant standing next to the pool of blood. 'Any idea when Scenes of Crime are going to arrive?' he asked. 'There's blood further down the street that I need samples of before it disappears.'

'I've just been onto the control room, apparently most of the Scenes of Crime staff are all tied up at a suspicious death in Woodthorpe. The control room have requested they attend here, and they will be sending someone as soon as they can.'

'Well, can your guys find something to cover the blood? Until they get here.'

'Will do. Any news from DC Flowers at the hospital?'

'It's not looking good. PC Warden's still unconscious. They're talking about rushing him into surgery.'

'Bloody hell!'

'What's he like?'

'What do you mean?'

'PC Warden. What's he like? I don't know him.'

The old sergeant said, 'This is typical of Mark. He's a good man with more balls than brains. If he thought someone was in danger, he wouldn't hesitate or wait for backup. He'd be straight in there.'

'Let's hope he comes through this. Delegate as many of your staff as you can spare to start visiting every house on this road. We need to try to find witnesses. There must be someone who can tell us what happened. It's broad daylight on a Saturday evening, for Christ's sake! Someone will have seen something. Where's that bloody Scenes of Crime van!'

20

8.30pm, 31 July 1987
City Hospital, Nottingham

The post-mortem examination of Gladys Miller had been going on for almost half an hour. Danny felt the bile rise in his throat, maybe caused by the strong coffee he had drunk before coming to the mortuary. He had drunk it quickly, which was never a good idea.

The full extent of the damage to the old woman's body, caused by the vermin at the house, had only become apparent when the dressing gown and nightwear had been stripped from her frail body. There were extensive parts of the abdomen and chest cavity that had been gnawed away.

He swallowed hard and took shallow breaths, trying to stem the feeling of nausea overtaking him. Lately, his life seemed to be one endless round of bloodstained crime scenes and grisly post-mortems.

He knew it went with the territory, but that didn't make it any easier. He felt a tangible sense of relief when Seamus Carter began to speak.

'It's as I suspected at the scene.'

The pathologist had peeled back the skin covering the crown of the skull, to expose a long, cigar-shaped indentation in the creamy-coloured bone.

'So you don't think that injury could have been caused by a fall?' Danny asked.

'Not a chance. If I had to stake my reputation on it, I would say a heavy metal bar of some description. A length of pipe, a crowbar, something like that.'

'Is that the cause of her death?'

'It's a combination of that injury and the broken C3 in her neck.'

'She's got a broken neck?'

'Undoubtably caused by the fall down the stairs. Tina said they found the missing slipper at the top of the stairs. My guess is that she disturbed whoever struck her at the top of the stairs. The blow would have been enough to render her unconscious and make her tumble down the stairs. She would have died very quickly. All the other injuries you can see are post-mortem, caused by the rats.'

Danny felt the bile rise again. 'When can you let me have your report?'

'I'll get it to you tomorrow, probably late morning.'

'Thanks. I'd better get back and start getting things organised. DC Williams will finish up here and bring all the exhibits back.'

'Take care, Danny. Try to get some rest; you look dreadful.'

Danny waved without looking back as he walked out of the examination room. The confirmation of the cause of death meant he now had two ongoing murder enquiries to oversee.

21

9.00am, 1 August 1987
MCIU Office, Mansfield Police Station

Danny had arrived in the office just after eight
o'clock. He hadn't been surprised to find several of
his team already there. DI Rob Buxton was talking
to DC Lorimar at his desk.

Danny walked over. 'Good to see you, Rob. Good
holiday?'

'It was the Algarve in July, what's not to like? Seriously, it
was brilliant, just what the doctor ordered.'

'So you're all refreshed and raring to go, then?'

'Sounds like I'm going to have to be. Glen was just filling
me in on the Angela Billson and Gladys Miller murder
enquiries, and now there's the attack on the cop as well.'

Danny's shock must have shown on his face, because Rob
said, 'You haven't heard?'

'No. Come and tell me all about it.'

The two men walked into Danny's office. Danny closed

the door behind him. 'Don't tell me we've got a man down as well.'

'No, we haven't. PC Mark Warden's still alive, but it's touch-and-go.'

'I don't know anything about this. Why didn't the control room inform me?'

'Probably because he's still alive. For now, West Bridgford CID are dealing with it.'

'What do we know?'

'From what Glen could find out, apparently PC Warden tried to break up a fight between football hooligans. The hooligans then turned on him and gave him a right kicking.'

'How's he doing now?'

'He had emergency surgery last night and is now in the Intensive Care Unit at Queen's.'

'Bloody football hooligans! And it's only July, for Christ's sake!'

'Forest played Leeds United in a preseason friendly yesterday. There had been no trouble at all inside the ground, and everyone thought the match had passed off without a hitch. Almost an hour after the game had finished, a call was received from a member of the public, saying rival fans were fighting in Bridgford Park, near to the ground. A short time after that first call, there was another that said one of our officers was very badly injured.'

'Didn't he have a chance to call for backup?'

'West Bridgford control room have logged a radio message from the officer requesting assistance, but the location was garbled. They didn't have a clue where he was.'

'Bloody hell! Let's hope he recovers. We need to be prepared for this to come our way.'

'My thoughts exactly. I think as soon as the chief constable hears about it, he'll be demanding that we take over the enquiry.'

'It will stretch us to the limit if he does. We can cope with two major enquiries; three will be pushing it.'

'Like you said, I'm fully refreshed and raring to go.'

Danny smiled. It felt good to have his friend and colleague back alongside him. 'Right, let me bring you up to speed on the two enquiries we definitely do have.'

22

10.30am, 1 August 1987
Nottinghamshire Police Headquarters

Danny hadn't been surprised by the call from Chief Superintendent Potter. The instruction was brief and to the point. Danny was to attend a briefing at headquarters straight after the MCIU morning briefing. It had been a detailed briefing at the MCIU. Danny had outlined the priority enquiries for the Gladys Miller murder to his team of detectives. He had made good time getting from Mansfield to headquarters, so he wasn't late.

What had surprised him, however, was seeing Chief Constable Jack Renshaw sitting next to Potter in his office.

Jack Renshaw had a face like thunder as he growled, 'Sit down, Chief Inspector.'

As soon as Danny had taken a seat, the chief constable said, 'What do you know about this attack on PC Mark Warden?'

It was typical Jack Renshaw. No pleasant introductions or niceties, just straight down to business.

Danny said, 'Very little, sir. Only what we could gather from the radio message logs and the West Bridgford control room logs.'

Renshaw looked at Potter. 'That's my bloody point right there, Adrian. Every cop on this force should know, chapter and bloody verse, what's happened to their colleague, but people are still having to scratch around for information.'

Danny got the impression that he had walked straight into the middle of a heated argument between the two men.

Potter started to say something, but with a wave of his hand, Renshaw dismissed him. 'I understand your unit are already investigating two murders in the city,' he said to Danny. 'If I asked you to investigate this attack on our colleague as well, would your team be able to cope?'

Danny took a moment to think. 'If you had asked me that question last week, I would have had to say we couldn't have done it, but we now have a few staff returning from summer holidays, so we should be able to manage the increased work-load. Can I count on your support to abstract officers from divisional CID and the Special Operations Unit onto the MCIU, to bolster our numbers if needed?'

'Whatever you need. I want your team to investigate this attack with the utmost vigour. I won't have it; these bastards must be brought to book.'

'Who's running the enquiry now?'

'Detective Chief Inspector Mayweather at West Bridg-ford,' Potter replied.

'Does he know the MCIU will be taking it over?'

'He will in about ten minutes' time. I want you to arrange for a full handover from him at West Bridgford at eleven thirty this morning.'

Jack Renshaw said, 'Get cracking, Danny. I want these bastards caught.'

Danny knew that was his cue to leave. 'Yes, sir.' As soon as he closed the door, he could hear Jack Renshaw's raised voice as once again he made his point to Chief Superintendent Potter.

He walked along the corridor and picked up the telephone on the desk of Potter's secretary.

'Rob, meet me at West Bridgford nick at eleven thirty. I want you to lead the enquiry into tracking down PC Warden's attackers. Tina and I will have to manage on the other two enquiries. I'll explain better when I see you, but I've got an agreement from the chief constable that you can abstract divisional CID and SOU staff as and when you need them. See you at West Bridgford nick. Don't be late.'

Danny ended the call and said to Potter's secretary, 'Can you give me the number for Detective Chief Inspector Mayweather at West Bridgford CID, please?'

23

9.30pm, 10 June 1987
2 Fairview Road, Woodthorpe, Nottingham

I t had been ten days since he had killed his mother.

Solomon Peleg was now satisfied there would be no comeback or consequences for his actions. The old sergeant who had come to the house on the day his mother died had been in touch and advised him of the date for the coroner's inquest. It had been set for later in the year. Sergeant Calderwood had also informed him that the coroner had now released the body of his mother for burial. That confirmed there was no CID investigation for Solomon to worry about. It was now time for him to put the second part of his plan into operation.

Although he enjoyed living in the splendour and luxury of the house on Fairview Road, he didn't relish the idea of looking after his disabled brother twenty-four seven for the rest of his life. Although Saul had private health care specialists and carers, Solomon now realised that the situation was putting a huge strain on his own private life. He was having to spend all day, every day with his brother.

Saul never liked to be left on his own. His mental health was extremely fragile, so Solomon felt tied to the house. He might as well be in that bloody wheelchair himself for the amount of freedom he had.

It was that single thought that had initially formed the germ of an idea.

He had since spent days refining his outrageous plan.

After the initial thought had come to him, the more he thought it through, the more he realised he could make it work. With the right amount of planning, it could be achieved. Very soon, he would be the only person living in the house, and within certain constraints, he would be able to live a life of indolent luxury.

His plan was as simple as it was deadly.

He intended to kill his identical twin brother, then adopt his identity. He would become Saul. He would take on all the characteristics and the persona of his severely disabled brother. That way, he would have none of the onerous caring to do but would have free rein to enjoy the disability benefits from the medical negligence payout. He would need to cancel the private health care visits every other day. He would just inform the healthcare company that he had got a better price from a rival company. He would do the same to the general carers who washed and cared for Saul. He would dismiss them and tell them he had employed the services of another company. He would need to employ a housekeeper to help keep the house clean and tidy. He hated housework.

He planned to lead a double life. He would be Saul Peleg, wheelchair-bound paraplegic, by day, and Mick Heeton, successful businessman around town, by night.

He had already put in place arrangements to fake his emigration to New Zealand. As part of that process, he had spoken to the private care company who attended the house twice a day to look after Saul. The carers would get him up in the morning and assist with his personal needs. He was quite capable of looking after himself throughout the day. The carers would then return in the evening to get Saul ready for bed.

Everyone at the care company was now aware that Solomon Peleg intended to leave the UK on the sixteenth of June to begin a new life in New Zealand.

He had purchased a one-way ticket to Auckland from a local travel agent. He had deliberately discussed his plans for a new life with the agent who made the arrangements. If questions were ever asked later, it was vitally important there were people who could verify that Solomon had indeed left the country.

The final part of his plan that still needed some refinement was the actual killing and disposal of his brother's body.

And he had now stumbled across a way this could be done.

The night before, he had been outside in the back garden when he heard a noise at the very end of the property. He had walked down the garden and been surprised to find that a wooden gate formed part of the boundary fence. Though they had now lived at the house for a number of years, he had no idea that the gate was there. Intrigued, he had walked through the gate and found that it led into a narrow service path that ran behind all the other houses on the road. He had strolled along it, looking into the rear gardens of the neighbouring properties.

The large back garden at number eight was completely overgrown and uncared for. He knew the neglected property was owned by Mrs Miller. She was an elderly lady who lived alone, which explained the state of the overgrown garden. It would have been a huge undertaking for a young person to look after such a big garden; for an elderly female who lived alone, it was impossible.

The more he thought about that uncared-for, neglected space, the more it seemed like the perfect final resting place for his brother.

The service path at the rear of the houses made it a viable idea. The rear fence at number eight was only four feet high. He could easily carry Saul from his house, along the service path and drop him over the fence into the garden of number eight. It would then take no time at all to bury him in a shallow grave and cover the disturbed soil with vegetation.

He had made his mind up.

Saul would be killed on the night of the fifteenth and buried the same night. On the morning of the sixteenth, Solomon would spend his first day as Saul. He would call the care company late on the fifteenth and inform them that he had now employed a different care company and that their services would no longer be required.

He just needed to get through to the sixteenth.

He intended to inform the coroner that he was leaving for New Zealand on the fifteenth, but that he had already made provisional arrangements with an undertaker to carry out his mother's funeral. He intended to lie and say that the job offer he had received from New Zealand had been made on the understanding that he could start work on the eighteenth of June.

It would be further confirmation to the authorities that Solomon had indeed left the country.

He sipped his coffee and smiled.

His plan would succeed; nothing could stop it. He had seen how quickly Saul had sided against him when their mother wanted to kick him out. Now he would pay the same price as their mother.

He felt no remorse or guilt. None of it had been his fault. Saul had caused his own disability and had then deliberately allowed his brother to take all the blame. It was now time for Solomon to take control of his own destiny.

24

12.30pm, 1 August 1987
West Bridgford Police Station, Nottingham

The meeting between the MCIU detectives and DCI Mayweather had been cordial and concise. The truth of it was that there wasn't much information to share. Also present at the meeting had been Detective Sergeant Pete Hazard, the senior CID officer who had attended the scene on the night.

DCI Mayweather had made it abundantly clear from the outset that the handover briefing should be left to Detective Sergeant Hazard to complete, and had excused himself early from the meeting.

Pete Hazard had given precise information of his actions on the night of the assault. He had been constrained by a lack of staff but had made the best of what he had available. Danny had been impressed by the calm demeanour and efficiency of the sergeant. He asked if he would like to be seconded onto the MCIU for the duration of the enquiry. Pete Hazard had jumped at the chance and had delivered the handover with even more gusto. He outlined what house-to-house enquiries had been carried out, and what areas still needed to be completed. He explained how he had also taken on the role of unofficial family liaison officer, with the parents of the injured officer. He had kept them informed every step of the way and had provided them with regular updates from the hospital. The parents were both elderly and infirm, so were unable to get to the hospital to see their son.

Danny made a mental note to go and visit the parents at his earliest opportunity.

'What can you tell me about Mark Warden?'

'Mark Warden's forty-two years of age. From what I can gather, he has recently come through a bitter divorce where he ended up losing the family home. He's been living back with his parents in Ruddington ever since.'

'Any kids?'

'No.'

'Does the ex-wife know what's happened?'

'His mum has let her know, but she's not bothered. Sounds like she's moved her fancy man into Mark's house already.'

'Bloody hell. Do you have any ideas to drive this enquiry forward?'

'Yes, sir. I've set up a meeting with the football liaison officer based at The Meadows police station. I know PC Grainger well, and what he doesn't know about the Forest football hooligans isn't worth knowing. I know that he has links with other football liaison officers up and down the country. I was hoping he may be able to put us in touch with his counterpart at Leeds United.'

Rob said, 'When's the meeting with PC Grainger arranged for?'

'It's set up for the third of August, at nine o'clock. He's off work today and asked if I could give him a day to do some digging before the meeting to see what he can find out.'

'That's excellent,' Danny said. 'We'll both be at that meeting with you. I'll go and find DCI Mayweather and give him the good news that you're working with us for the duration.'

'Do you think he'll agree to it, sir?'

'He can either agree with me, or phone the chief constable and be told to agree. It's up to him. I think we need you on board. Come on duty at Mansfield tomorrow morning and bring all the paperwork with you. I want all the statements that have been taken, house-to-house forms, the works. Anything you have, I want to see it. I'd like you to spend the rest of the shift today chasing up on the forensics with Scenes of Crime. You can also introduce me to Mark's parents tomorrow. I want to let them know how hard we're going to work to find the people responsible for injuring their son.'

'Okay, sir. See you tomorrow.'

As Danny and Rob walked back to their car, Danny said, 'Drive down to Hound Road. I want to see for myself where this all happened.'

25

10.00am, 2 August 1987
2 Fairview Road, Woodthorpe, Nottingham

Tina Cartwright and DC Helen Bailey rang the doorbell. It was opened almost immediately by a young woman with long dark hair.

'Can I help you?'

Tina held out her warrant card. 'Good morning. We're from the CID. Do you live here?'

Before the young woman could answer, a male voice said behind her, 'God forbid! No, she doesn't. Chloe was just leaving.'

The young woman smiled and said, 'See you tomorrow morning, Saul. Detectives, eh? I wonder what you've been up to?'

She giggled as she walked past the two detectives.

Tina looked at the man in the wheelchair. 'Saul Peleg?'

'I'm Saul. What can I do for you?'

'We need to ask you a few questions about your neighbour Mrs Miller. Can we come in?'

'Of course, this way.'

He led them into the spacious lounge and gestured for them to take a seat. 'I heard about what's happened to Mrs Miller. It's dreadful. I don't mind telling you, it's made me feel very vulnerable. I live here alone now. Chloe is my house-keeper. She comes here most days to clean and occasionally prepare meals for me. I also have visits from carers and specialist medical people, but if somebody wanted to get in here and rob me at night, I wouldn't stand a chance.'

Helen said, 'I can ask our crime prevention people to come and check your security is up to scratch if you like?'

'That won't be necessary. The house is fitted with a state-of-the-art alarm system that's connected to the local police station. I also have a panic alarm that does the same thing, so I should be okay. It just makes you nervous when something like that happens so close to home.'

'How well did you know Mrs Miller?'

'I knew her, but I couldn't tell you anything about her. On the odd occasion we were outside on the street at the same time, we would always say hello and exchange pleasantries, but that's it. I can't remember the last time I spoke to her.'

'Have you noticed anything strange on the street lately? Any unwanted callers touting for work or selling door to door? Any strange vehicles hanging around outside?'

Saul Peleg looked thoughtful. 'There is something I remember. I don't know if you'll think it's relevant, as it's from a while ago.'

'Go on.'

'I remember seeing a van I hadn't seen before parked near her house.'

'When you say a while ago, how long?'

'I don't know for sure. Around three or four weeks, some-thing like that.'

'Did anything stand out to you about the vehicle?'

'Only how dirty it was. It was a small red van, like a Ford Fiesta size, but it was absolutely filthy, like they had been driving it off road or something.'

'Have you seen it again since then?'

'I'd never seen it before, and I haven't seen it since.'

'Did you see anybody with the vehicle?'

'There were two men. I watched them sitting in the van. Don't ask me what they looked like though.'

'Are you sure you can't remember anything about them? It could be important, Mr Peleg.'

'They both had long, dark hair. I thought they looked like gypsies, that's why I watched them. I didn't see them get out. When I next looked, an hour or so later, the van had gone.'

Tina said, 'That's great. Thanks very much, Mr Peleg. I'd like my colleague to get a statement from you, outlining what you've just told her. Are you okay for time?'

He smacked the wheels of the wheelchair with his open palms and said, 'Thanks to this little beauty, I've got all the time in the world. I'm not going anywhere, am I?'

26

S olomon Peleg crept from his bedroom and made his way stealthily along the gallery landing to his twin brother's room. He paused outside the bedroom; it was the point of no return. He knew if he walked through that door, there was no going back.

He muttered, 'Fuck it,' under his breath and gripped the door handle, turning it slowly. He stepped inside the room and made his way over to Saul's bed. His brother was fast asleep, lying on his back. He was slightly raised into a half-sitting position to assist his breathing. The carers positioned him in this way because he wasn't able to move during the night.

He picked up one of the spare pillows that were kept by the side of the bed and gripped it in both hands. Stepping closer, he pushed the pillow down hard onto his brother's face. After a few seconds, he could hear muffled groans from beneath the pillow.

Suddenly, Saul's hands shot out from beneath the bedclothes and gripped Solomons wrists. Solomon ignored his brother's frantic *efforts and pushed down harder. The grip on his wrists gradually lessened until Saul's hands fell away, dropping limply onto the bed. Still, Solomon pushed down. He remained in that same position until the muscles in his arms burned.*

After what seemed an age, he eased the pressure and removed the pillow. His brother's eyes were wide open, staring sightlessly at the ceiling.

Solomon hurled the pillow across the room and felt for the carotid pulse in his brother's neck.

There was nothing.

Saul was dead.

Solomon reached down and hoisted his brother off the bed, carrying him, fireman's lift style, from the bedroom and down the stairs. He dropped him on the kitchen floor, near to the door that led out into the rear garden, disabled the security lighting and slipped on a black coat.

He opened the back door and stepped outside to test that the lighting had been disabled. Nothing happened, so he walked down to the bottom of the garden and opened the wooden gate. After checking that the spade he had left by the fence was still there, he wedged open the gate, walked back to the house and hoisted Saul up onto his shoulder. He trudged down the garden, picked up the spade and made his way along the service path until he reached the overgrown garden at number eight.

After dropping his brother's body over the four-foot-high fence, he climbed over and started digging a shallow grave.

Twenty minutes of concentrated digging later and the grave was just over two feet deep. More than enough to do the job. Following his exertions, Solomon was breathing hard. He paused and looked around him. Everywhere remained dark and silent.

Having got his breath back, he grabbed Saul and lowered him face first into the shallow grave. He then began the task of shovelling the excavated soil back into the hole, onto the body of his brother. He worked slowly, trying to be careful not to make too much noise as the blade of the tool slipped into the damp earth. After another ten minutes' toil, the grisly task was complete. He stamped down on the disturbed earth, flattening it beneath his feet. Grabbing swathes of tall weeds, he piled the vegetation over the shallow grave until it was completely hidden.

A sixth sense made him suddenly stop what he was doing and look towards the house at the far end of the garden. There was now a soft light in one of the top windows. For a second, he thought he saw a fleeting shape move across the window before the light was extinguished, plunging the house back into darkness.

Was his mind playing tricks?

Had someone been watching him?

He squatted down and watched the house intently for another thirty minutes. Nothing moved or changed. No phantom lights, and no noises from inside the house. Satisfied that all was well, he grabbed the spade and clambered silently back over the fence and onto the service path. He made his way back to his own garden, closed the gate behind him and left the spade next to the fence.

Moving fast, he hurried back to the house, reset the security lighting and locked the door. His hands and clothes were covered in soil and dirt, and he quickly showered before grabbing a pair of pyjamas identical to the ones Saul had been wearing. He stripped all the bedclothes from Saul's bed and put them in the washer. He then made the bed and climbed in.

It felt strange.

From this moment on, Solomon Peleg no longer existed. He was now Saul Peleg, a wheelchair user, disabled from the waist down.

EXHAUSTED from the night's physical exertions, he quickly fell into a deep sleep.

Tomorrow would be the first day of Solomon Peleg's new life.

27

6.00pm, 2 August 1987
MCIU Office, Mansfield Police Station

Danny walked into the MCIU offices, followed by DS Pete Hazard. They had just returned from the home of PC Mark Warden, visiting Mark's elderly parents. He had promised to keep them personally informed of every development in the enquiry. They were pleased that the force was making every effort to catch the people responsible for hospitalising their only son.

Danny had contacted the Queen's Medical Centre prior to the visit and was able to tell the couple that Mark was now in a stable condition and was responding well to treatment. Although the policeman was still critical, his prognosis had improved slightly.

As he entered the office, Tina was at her desk. 'Have you got five minutes?' he asked her. 'I need to run something by you.'

Tina followed him into his office and closed the door.

Danny motioned to one of the chairs in front of his desk.

'Grab a seat. I wanted to run this idea past you before I speak to Andy. Rob's going to be fully committed on this football hooligan enquiry, and he'll be getting a lot of downward pressure from command. I'm going to be spending a lot of time fending that off and helping Rob to achieve a successful outcome. That means, with the best will in the world, I'm not going to be able to assist you as much as I'd hoped with the two outstanding murders. I don't want you to think this decision is in any way a slight against you, because it isn't, but I want Andy Wills to oversee the enquiries into the murder of Gladys Miller.'

He paused, waiting for a reaction.

When it came, he was pleasantly surprised.

Tina simply replied, 'Good idea.' She then echoed Danny's phrase and said, 'With the best will in the world, I'm not ready to oversee two murder enquiries. It's alright working in tandem with Rob, but it's a bit much doing it for two separate jobs that aren't linked in any way.'

'So if I speak to Andy and tell him what I want him to do, you're okay with that?'

Tina laughed. 'Honestly, it's fine by me. At the end of the day, we all work as one big team anyway, and it's not like we haven't worked together before.'

'It just made sense to me. With DS Hazard working alongside Rob, there was no need for another detective sergeant on that enquiry.'

'You're right, it makes perfect sense.'

'That's great. How have you got on today?'

'I was with Helen doing some of the house-to-house enquiries on Fairview Road earlier, talking to Gladys Miller's neighbours. We've got a useful lead from a guy called Saul Peleg, who lives at number two. He saw a dodgy van, with two men inside, parked outside the old lady's house around the time of the murder. It's early days, but Helen's working hard to develop that lead.'

'Okay. You'll need to pass that information, and every-thing else, on to Andy as soon as I've spoken to him. If he's out there, will you send him in, please?'

'Will do, and thanks, boss. I was starting to panic a little about running both cases.'

'As you say, Tina. We're one big team, anyway.'

28

P C Nick Grainger walked into the uniform sergeant's office at The Meadows Police Station. Already in the room, waiting for him, were Danny, Rob and Pete Hazard.

The football liaison officer wasn't at all how Danny had envisaged him to be. Nick Grainger was in his late twenties, very short and stocky. He must have only just scraped through the height regulation when he joined, thought Danny.

He had chosen to wear a short-sleeved uniform shirt and had tattoos on both his muscular forearms. It was obvious that he spent a lot of time at the gym.

Pete Hazard said, 'Sir, this is PC Grainger. Nick, this is DCI Flint and DI Buxton.'

Nick extended a hand and said, 'Good to meet you, sir.'

Danny shook hands and was taken by the strength of the young officer's grip. As he shook hands, he felt a twinge of

pain in his own forearm. A painful reminder of the recent
stab wound he'd suffered when arresting Mike Grant, the
serial arsonist.

'You too. I hope you can help us. Grab a seat, and let's
make a start.'

Nick placed a folder he was carrying on the desk and sat
down. 'In this folder,' he began, 'there are up-to-date
photographs and a brief résumé of all the main players in the
Executive Crew.'

Rob said, 'You're going to have to excuse my ignorance,
Nick. What the hell is the Executive Crew?'

'Not *what*, sir. It's *who*. The Executive Crew are an ultra-
violent group of like-minded individuals who follow football,
Nottingham Forest in particular. They regularly engage in
large-scale disorder with other football supporters. As well as
the violence, they're also involved in low-level crime, such as
car thefts and organised shoplifting. They're not averse to
using weapons and are highly organised.'

Danny had picked up the folder and was flicking through
the mugshots of the hooligans.

'How many of these thugs are we talking about?'

'I would estimate there's a hard core of between fifty and
seventy-five individuals, with another hundred on the
periphery.'

Danny let out a low whistle. 'That many?'

Nick nodded before continuing, 'The fanatical element of
supporters at most football clubs have similar set-ups.
Arsenal have the Gooners, Manchester United have the Red
Army, Chelsea have the Headhunters, and West Ham have
the Inter City Firm. They're all highly organised and regularly communicate with each other. As police tactics have
improved inside the grounds, and segregation has got much
stricter, they've adapted.'

Danny asked, 'How?'

'They regularly organise confrontations away from the grounds. These meets are set up by a main player from each group. During these discussions, numbers and certain rules are set down; then they get together and battle it out for bragging rights. Woe betide any poor sod who gets in the way.'

'Do you think that's what's happened here? Has PC Warden stumbled into one of these prearranged fights?'

Nick hesitated. 'Kind of.'

'What does that mean?' Rob asked.

'Well, if it had been a confrontation set up by the main firms, I would have expected the numbers to be higher. Possibly between twenty and thirty from each group. From what DS Hazard has told me, I understand you have a witness who's described a very small group, maybe four or five. Is that right?'

Pete Hazard nodded. 'That's right. Our witness says she saw four men attacking Mark Warden.'

'I could be wrong, but that sounds like two smaller subgroups within the main group. It sounds like somebody trying to make a name for themselves.'

Danny's simmering anger boiled over. 'Bloody hell! Who do they think they are? We're not at war. It's only a bloody football game.'

'With respect, sir. You're totally wrong. To these individuals, it's just that, a war. Kudos is everything to them. The game of football is secondary; it's just a means to an end. It provides the sense of tribal belonging these men crave. When this all started in the early seventies, most hooligans were from a deprived background. Poor social housing areas generated violent teenagers. Football gave a reason for these men to come together with a common cause. These supporters took their passion for football and morphed it into a battle for supremacy over neighbouring clubs, towns and cities. Since those early days, they've become far more sophisticated.

They've evolved and continue to do so. The ringleaders all tend to have well-paid jobs and are intelligent. Following football is an expensive hobby these days. Most, not all, are now from middle-class backgrounds. Bored men getting their kicks from violence on a Saturday afternoon.'

Danny was thoughtful. 'Thanks, Nick. You obviously know your subject.'

'I try to think like them, sir. When I travel to away games, I liaise with other football liaison officers. Part of my role is to identify the main organisers of violence within the Executive Crew. We use prior intelligence from sources when we can get it. Very often, confrontations are nipped in the bud, and nothing happens.' He paused. 'Can I ask you something, sir? When was the last time you attended a topflight football match?'

'It's been a couple of years, and it wasn't topflight football. I used to watch Mansfield Town with my father. I've seen plenty of violence at those games though. I've seen the pack mentality in action.'

'Well, it's got much worse lately. The violence is off the scale. They use double-bladed Stanley knives, coshes, knuckledusters, anything they can get their hands on.'

'I hear you, Nick. I'm glad you have such an understanding of the men we're trying to catch. Your knowledge is going to be invaluable.'

Rob said, 'You mentioned all those hooligan firms earlier. Does the fanatical element at Leeds United have such a group?'

'Oh, yes. They're known as the Service Crew. They adopted the name from the train service they use to travel to away games. They're notorious. One of the worst and most violent groups in the country.'

Rob continued, 'Do you have a counterpart in Leeds? An officer who has your level of knowledge about that crew?'

'I've worked with PC Bill Keenan from the West Yorkshire force on several occasions. He was down here at the weekend for the preseason friendly with Leeds.'

Danny asked, 'Have you spoken to him about what happened after that game?'

'Constantly. We've arranged a meeting to pool our knowledge. He's in the process of trying to glean what he can up in Leeds while I do the same down here. We're very much intelligence led. I have several sources inside the Executive Crew, and I'm sure Bill will have the same within the Service Crew. We're in the process of rattling the tree branches to see what falls out.'

'Good. Keep at it. Please have that meeting as soon as you can. We need to trace these individuals fast. There was a lot of blood left at the scene after the attack on Mark. There could well be forensic evidence on footwear and clothing if we can get to them fast enough.'

'I understand, sir.'

'How soon will you have any information?'

'Within the next couple of days.'

'I'll be straight with you; our enquiries are turning up nothing. We don't even know who we're looking for yet, so as far as CCTV at the ground is concerned it's useless, and we've only found one witness to the assault. We need your expertise, Nick.'

'I'm on it, sir. I'll contact DS Hazard as soon as I have anything.'

'Do whatever it takes, Nick. This was a deliberate and vicious attack on one of our own. We need to send a clear message that it will not be tolerated. Understood?'

'Crystal clear, sir.'

29

S ue used the tips of her fingers to gently massage the trapezium muscles across Danny's broad shoulders. He was sat at the dining table, and spread before him were photographs of hard-looking men.

As she gently massaged his taut muscles, Sue said, 'You've been staring at these men for over an hour. Who are they?'

He began to gather the photographs before sliding them back inside the manila folder. Stretching his lower back and leaning into Sue's massage, he said, 'Football hooligans. We think it's men from this group, or a similar group, who were responsible for attacking that young copper after the game at the weekend.'

'I heard about that. It sounds awful. Some of my colleagues on the neuro ward were saying he almost died.'

Danny's ears pricked up. 'Do you know the doctors who are treating him?'

'Not the actual doctors, no. But the neurosurgeons at our

hospital all know the surgeons at Queen's who operated on the officer.'

'All I can ever find out from the hospital is that he's had an emergency operation on his head injury, and that he's now stable on ICU.'

'What else do you need to know?'

'Well, whenever I ask for a prognosis, all I get is a one-word answer. Anything from good to fair. I never get told any details.'

'From what I've heard my colleagues saying, these are the details. The patient suffered a major head trauma. A heavy blow, or blows, to the side of the skull, just above his right ear. There was a depressed fracture, and a bleed on the brain was detected. It was this bleed that necessitated the emergency surgery. He also suffered multiple bruising and lacerations to his face and body. He lost a lot of blood after the attack, and this caused major problems during surgery. I've heard that despite those complications, he came through the operation very well and is steadily improving.'

'When will he regain consciousness?'

'That I can't tell you. I know the doctors will be keeping him in an induced coma. This will help him to heal and allow the swelling on his brain to lessen.'

'Will he make a full recovery?'

'I'm sorry, sweetheart. I can't answer that. Even the consultant neurosurgeons at Queen's won't know the answer to that question until he starts to come round. They'll then be able to test his cognitive abilities properly. That's still a long way off. Your colleague is by no means out of the woods yet. He could very easily deteriorate.'

'He could still die?'

'It's possible, but so far all the indications are that he will make a recovery. Let's just say he's moving in the right direction.'

'Thanks, sweetheart. I feel better now I at least understand what he's going through. It's made me even more determined to catch these thugs.'

'Good. I think that's enough work for one evening, don't you?' She leaned forward and kissed him on the neck.

Danny grinned. 'That feels so good; don't stop.'

30

2.00pm, 4 July 1987
2 Fairview Road, Woodthorpe, Nottingham

It was a beautiful sunny afternoon, and Solomon Peleg had been out for a drive. The Ford Sierra had been especially adapted to be driven by Saul, using hand controls. It had taken Solomon a little while to get used to driving the disability car. But now that he had mastered it, he enjoyed driving it.

As he manoeuvred himself out of the driver's seat and into the lightweight wheelchair, he saw his elderly neighbour from number eight. She was carrying what looked like a heavy bag of shopping and walking slowly along the street.

He waited for her to draw level, then said cheerily, 'Good afternoon, Mrs Miller. It's a beautiful day for a trip to the shops.'

Obviously in a bad mood, the old lady scowled at him and said, 'I don't know what you think you're playing at. I saw you the other night in my garden. What the hell were you doing?'

Startled by her comments, he said quickly, 'What are you talking about? You couldn't have seen me in your garden. I'm stuck in this chair.'

The old lady huffed and muttered, 'I don't think so. I know what I saw. You were up to something. I'm not as stupid as you think. I've known you two boys long enough to know who's who. I knew it was you straightaway, the way you always slouch along.' As she walked off, she shouted back, 'You can't fool me, Solomon. I know exactly what and who I saw.'

Solomon didn't respond, but he continued to watch his elderly neighbour until she walked onto her driveway. He was worried by what she had said. She'd seen him in her garden. What was even more worrying was the fact she had called him Solomon when he was sitting in the wheelchair, masquerading as Saul.

Thoughts raced through his mind. What exactly had she seen? How long had she been watching him? Had she watched him burying his brother? Had she called the police?

As he opened the front door and wheeled himself into the house, he carefully weighed up his options. He couldn't risk waiting to see if the old woman called the police or spoke of her concerns to another neighbour.

He knew the old lady talked all the time to that nosy cow across the street, at number nine. The woman who ran the neighbourhood watch scheme. If she repeated to her what she had just said to him, the police would almost certainly be called.

The more he thought about it, the more he knew he needed to act. He couldn't afford to wait and risk the police discovering Saul's body in the back garden of number eight.

He racked his brain for a solution, but after hours of deliberation, he realised he had been backed into a corner. He had no option but to pay his elderly neighbour a visit later and sort the problem out once and for all.

31

2.00am, 5 July 1987
2 Fairview Road, Woodthorpe, Nottingham

Solomon Peleg picked up the metal crowbar and tucked it in the small of his back, down his jeans. He disabled the external security lights again before stepping out into the rear garden of his house.

There was a full moon, and the sky was clear and the air cool and crisp. He breathed in deeply. He knew what he had to do but still felt uneasy. He had spent the day trying to think of an alternative. There wasn't one.

Deep down, he knew he had no choice. If he wanted to carry on living the life he had chosen, he needed to act decisively.

He didn't enjoy killing; he wasn't a monster.

It had just become a necessary evil.

He made his way along the service path until he reached the overgrown back garden of number eight. He climbed over the four-foot fence, the metal bar pressing into the small of his back reminding him of its deadly presence.

Moving stealthily, he made his way towards the rear of the

detached property. He moved slowly, not knowing if the old lady had motion-activated security lights protecting the back of her house.

He reached the back of the house, and no lights had come on. There was also no alarm box to be seen, but that didn't mean the house wasn't alarmed. He knew that once he forced entry, he would have to act fast in case there was a covert security system.

He identified the window that led into the kitchen. There was a long transom window that ran above two larger windows below. Using the crowbar, he tapped the glass in the corner of the transom window. The glass broke with a sharp crack, but the pane had fragmented and not smashed. He set to work easing out individual pieces of glass with his gloved hands and after a few minutes had cleared enough of the glass to reach through and lift the latch on the larger window.

He climbed through the now open window and climbed down from the worktop. He squatted down on his haunches and waited. The house was still and deathly quiet.

As he made his way through the house, he looked for an alarm control panel. He couldn't see one anywhere, so maybe the house wasn't protected after all, and he began to relax. Gripping the heavy crowbar, he made his way upstairs, stepping on the very edges of the treads to avoid creaks.

The house was a similar layout to his own. It had a gallery landing at the top of the stairs, with several doors leading off it. Every door was closed. He carefully opened the first door and found a family bathroom. He moved on to the next door and opened it. This door led into a small box room. As he emerged from this room, the door opposite began to open.

His elderly neighbour stood there, dressed in an old dressing gown and slippers.

They were both shocked, but it was the old lady who recovered first. She said angrily, 'What the hell are you doing, Solomon? Get out of my house!'

She pushed past the stunned Solomon and made her way along the landing, towards the stairs. 'I'm calling the police!'

The words stung Solomon into action, and just as the old lady reached the top of the stairs, he brought the heavy crowbar crashing down onto her head. There was a sickening crunch as the metal bar bit deep into her skull. She made no sound and toppled forward, falling down the stairs and landing in a crumpled heap at the bottom.

Solomon bounded down the stairs after her. Slipping off a glove, he felt her neck for a pulse. There was none. His elderly neighbour was dead.

He put his leather glove back on and let out a sigh of relief.

Problem solved.

All he had to do now was make it look like a burglary. He went back upstairs and began ransacking the bedrooms, tipping out drawers, and emptying cupboards.

He did the same downstairs, then threw old coats over the body before climbing back out of the kitchen window. The last thing he did was to smash the remaining glass of the transom window, ensuring that glass fragments were scattered inside the kitchen.

He then made his way back along the service path back to his own house. He hid the bloodstained crowbar in his wheelie bin – he would dispose of it properly in the morning. He would take a drive into the countryside and dump it a long way from here. He would have time. The old lady never had visitors, so she wouldn't be missed for a while.

He walked slowly up the stairs, got undressed and took a long, hot shower. As the hot water cascaded down his body, washing off the grime and detritus from the murder, he reflected on how his life had changed.

He made a vow to himself. That the killing tonight would be the last.

Everything was in place now; he could begin to enjoy life.

32

9.00am, 10 August 1987
MCIU Office, Mansfield Police Station

Danny leaned back in his chair and said, 'I've called you both in to go over the current state of the murder enquiries. I want to know if we're making any progress at all.'

Sitting opposite him were Tina Cartwright and Andy Wills. Neither volunteered a comment, so Danny said, 'Tina, how are you getting on?'

Shifting uncomfortably in her seat, she said, 'Progress is minimal, I'm afraid. The house-to-house enquiries are almost complete. Unless you think it's worthwhile extending the perimeter even further?'

Danny looked at the map in front of him. The house-to-house enquiries already covered a vast area; he could see no point in extending it further.

'I don't think that would be of any benefit. What about the night-shift observations at the park? Have they yielded anything?'

'Other than some embarrassment for errant wives and husbands, not a thing. We've followed up on every sighting. Nothing. Over the last week, those sightings have dried up too. Word has obviously got out that the police are taking an interest in people using the park at night.'

'Okay.' Danny sighed. 'Discontinue the observations. It was always going to be a long shot. Anything from the professional appointments made by Angela Billson?'

'My team have followed up everyone she either saw or was due to see in the days leading up to her disappearance.'

'Is there anyone who raises a concern? Who was the last person she saw?'

'Her last appointment was with a woman who lives in Bestwood. Muriel Haynes has ulcerated legs and is regularly seen by the district nurse. Because she has limited mobility, Angela Billson checked up on Mrs Haynes once a month to ensure she was coping. That was the last appointment she kept. She never made it to her next appointment.'

'And who was that with?'

'That appointment was with a man who lives alone and is confined to a wheelchair. He has carers twice daily to help him and private medical care for other issues every other day. Angela visited him once a month to make sure he was coping with his situation. He lives on Fairview Road, not far from Gladys Miller.'

'Coincidence?'

'I would think so, sir. Like I said, Angela Billson's client is wheelchair bound. It's the same man who gave us the information about the vehicle sighting. The small, red-coloured van seen hanging around outside Mrs Miller's house.'

'I remember. What's his name again?'

'Saul Peleg. I made notes after interviewing him. He was left a paraplegic after an incidence of medical negligence following a motorcycle accident.'

'Does he have access to a vehicle?'

'He has an adapted car, so he can get out and about, but it would have been impossible for him to leave the body where it was found.'

'So we can rule him out?'

'I think we have to.'

'Okay. I want you to organise another press appeal. Speak to the family and see if they want to be involved. Let's see if we can turn someone up who knows a bit more about this woman's private life. You've done a thorough job in investigating her work life, but I think we've only scratched the surface of her private life.'

'Will do, sir.'

Danny turned to Andy. 'I take it you've had enough time to get fully up to speed with the enquiry by now?'

'Yes, sir.'

'Okay. As we're already talking about him, let's start with Saul Peleg on Fairview Road. Has anything come from his reported sighting of the van?'

'We've interviewed everyone else who lives on Fairview Road and can't find anybody who can corroborate that sighting. I find it strange that Saul Peleg describes the vehicle virtually parked right outside the neighbourhood watch coordinator's house, and she never saw it.'

'What are you saying?'

'I think it's strange that nobody else has seen this vehicle. Helen has worked like a Trojan, going over hours of footage from traffic cameras, trying to spot this vehicle. She's found nothing.'

'Why would he make up a bogus sighting?'

'I'm not suggesting he has; I just think it's strange that we haven't found some corroboration somewhere.'

'Okay. Go back and talk to him again. Try to get to the bottom of it.'

'Have we found anything from the searches?'

'Special Operations Unit officers have carried out searches in the neighbouring gardens for a possible murder weapon. They've also checked all the drains. The problem is the killer could have just dropped the weapon in a dustbin. Between the time of her death and the time she was found, there have been two dustbin collections.'

'Has the house-to-house turned anything up?'

'Apart from that dodgy vehicle sighting, not a thing.'

'Anything from forensics?'

'We haven't had everything back from the lab that's been submitted, but so far nothing of any interest. Plenty of finger-prints found inside the house, but they're all from the deceased. To be honest, we're struggling to move the enquiry forward, sir.'

'Have you located any family?'

'No, sir. It seems that Gladys Miller had no surviving relatives.'

Danny was thoughtful and then said, 'Extend the house-to-house and arrange a comprehensive press appeal. I don't mind if you put the sighting of the red van in it. You'll either find some corroboration, or it will confirm your suspicions about it being a bogus sighting. Make sure you interview Saul Peleg yourself and do a bit more digging into his family back-ground. I'm intrigued as to what motive he could have for giving us a false sighting.'

'Will do, sir.'

'Both of you need to stay focussed. There will be answers out there. It's down to us to find them. Keep me informed of any developments, please.'

33

3.00pm, 17 July 1987
2 Fairview Road, Woodthorpe, Nottingham

S *olomon Peleg was relaxing on his bed in the front bedroom*
of the house, listening to the radio. The music was on loud,
but he could have sworn he'd heard the doorbell. He
reached over, turned the volume on the radio down and listened.

There it was again. Somebody was definitely at the door. But
who? He wasn't expecting any visitors. With a rising sense of
panic, he realised that the wheelchair was downstairs. He couldn't
risk going down the stairs or going down in the lift. Either way, if
someone was standing outside, looking through the glass in the
front door, he would be seen.

He ignored the doorbell and crept over to the window of the
bedroom. Looking down, he could see a woman walking down the
driveway, back to her car. She was wearing some sort of light-
weight jacket with a hood, and he couldn't see her face. Just as she
reached her car, she looked back towards the house. Solomon
instinctively ducked down and hid. He waited a few seconds and
then cautiously glanced back out of the window. He cursed

inwardly when he saw that the woman was now making her way back up the driveway, towards the house.

The hood of her jacket was now down, and he instantly recognised the woman. It was Saul's health visitor, coming to check if he was okay. Solomon racked his brains, trying to remember her name. He knew it began with the letter A.

He cursed himself for not remembering her visits and raced downstairs and jumped into the wheelchair just as the doorbell rang again.

34

3.00pm, 17 July 1987
2 Fairview Road, Woodthorpe, Nottingham

Angela Billson was puzzled. It wasn't like Saul to keep her waiting on the doorstep.

She could hear loud music blaring from inside the house, so she persisted and rang the doorbell again. The music was turned down, so she rang again. Still, nobody came to the door. After waiting a few minutes, she turned and walked down the driveway. As she reached her car, she glanced back over her shoulder and looked towards the impressive, detached house.

She was just about to take her cagoule off when she spotted movement in the main bedroom. Somebody had been standing watching her and had then ducked down. Her curiosity getting the better of her, she turned and walked back up the driveway. The car that Saul owned was still on the drive, and she had seen movement upstairs. Somebody was inside the house.

She rang the doorbell again.

This time there was a voice from within. 'Just a second.'

The door opened.

Angela looked at the man sitting in the wheelchair and said, 'Finally. What kept you, Saul? I've been ringing that doorbell for ages.'

'I'm sorry.'

As Solomon looked at her closely, he finally recalled her name. He smiled and said, 'Don't stand on the doorstep, Angela. Come in.'

She stepped inside and said, 'Is anyone else in the house?'

'No. It's just me. I don't get visitors. Why do you ask?'

'I thought you might have been upstairs; I was ringing that doorbell for ever.'

'I didn't hear you; I was in the kitchen, listening to the radio, sorry.'

Angela was puzzled. She was sure she had seen somebody standing at the upstairs window, looking down at her. There was no way Saul could have got down in the lift as quickly as that to open the front door.

Then the weight of what she had just thought hit home. Somebody had been standing at the upstairs window, not sitting.

With a concerned look on her face, she said, 'Saul, are you sure nobody's upstairs?'

'Of course I'm sure. Go and have a look round if you like. Be my guest.'

Keen to get to the bottom of the mystery, but starting to feel a little nervous, Angela said, 'I'll only be a minute.'

She made her way upstairs and checked each of the rooms. With her heart pounding in her chest, she stepped inside the room where she had seen the figure standing. It was empty, but there was a radio playing softly on the bedside cabinet. She looked at the bed and could see that somebody had been lying on top of the bed; the top covers were disturbed.

Saul was acting strangely and wasn't his normal self. Something wasn't right; she walked slowly downstairs.

Saul was in his wheelchair by the front door.

'Can I get a glass of water, please?' she asked. 'My mouth's bone dry.'

With an edge of animosity in his voice, he said, 'Of course. You know where everything is. I'll wait for you in the lounge.'

Angela walked into the kitchen and ran the cold tap for a few seconds before filling the glass with cool water. She scanned the kitchen for a radio. There wasn't one.

Carrying the glass, she walked into the lounge and sat down on the sofa opposite Saul.

She put the glass on the coffee table. 'How many radios have you got?'

'Just one. Why?'

'You told me you didn't hear me ringing the doorbell because you were listening to music on the radio in the kitchen. There's no radio in there, but there's one upstairs in the bedroom. What's going on, Saul? Who else is in the house?'

He scowled. 'What are you like? I've already told you, there's only me here.'

'Look, if you've got somebody here staying with you, that's fine. Just tell me. It's not a problem, honestly.'

He shook his head. 'And I've already said, three times now, there's nobody else here.'

'Saul, I saw somebody standing at the bedroom window. I know someone's here with you. I'm just worried why you aren't telling me. Are they threatening you in some way?'

She had emphasised the word 'standing', and Solomon knew that she had seen him standing at the window, watching her leave. Once again, he felt backed into a corner. He had vowed no more killing, but if she kept pushing, he would do whatever he needed to.

His murderous thoughts were interrupted when Angela said, 'Talk to me, Saul. If you don't, I'll have no option but to phone my boss and ask her to come out here and join us.'

'Why are you hassling me?'

'I'm worried about you, not hassling you. I can't just leave you

*here to fend for yourself when I know someone else is here. I'm
worried about you; I'm not threatening you.'*

Solomon remained silent; he didn't have an explanation that
would placate the experienced health visitor. He knew that as soon
as she made that call to her supervisor, his lie would become apparent. He was left with no choice; he needed to act to stop her.

Angela stood up. *'I'll go and make that phone call.'*

Suddenly, Solomon launched himself from the wheelchair and
jumped over the coffee table. He grabbed Angela and threw her to
the ground. She lay sprawled on her back, and Solomon sat astride
her. He could see the fear in her eyes as he slipped his strong hands
around her throat.

She gasped for air and said in a wheezy voice, *'You're not Saul.'*

He squeezed harder and growled, *'Got it in one, you nosy
bitch!'*

She began to thrash her arms and legs around as she fought for
breath, but there was no way she could dislodge Solomon; he was
too strong.

Gradually, the wild movements became spasms, and finally
they became little more than a twitch. Satisfied that she was dead,
he stood up.

His arms and hands were aching. He flopped back in the
wheelchair, exhausted.

He stared at the dead woman. His thoughts immediately
turned to exactly how he was going to get her dead body out of the
house.

35

1.30am, 18 July 1987
Forest Recreation Ground, Nottingham

As he drove the Mini Metro onto the Forest Recreation Ground, Solomon switched off the lights. He drove slowly along the top lane from Mount Hooton Road back towards Mansfield Road.

There was nobody around, so he stopped the car about a hundred yards short of the Mansfield Road entrance.

It had taken him the best part of an hour to think of a way to get rid of the car and the body. He had initially put her in the shed in his back garden. He knew it would be impossible to move either the car or the body until it got dark.

As soon as darkness fell, he had sprung into action. He had carried the body from the shed back into the house and propped it up near the front door. He stripped off her maroon-coloured cagoule and went through the pockets until he found the car key for the Mini Metro she had arrived in.

It was almost one o'clock in the morning before he opened the front door and stepped outside. Fairview Road was as quiet as the grave. Opening the boot of the Ford Sierra, he returned to the house and hoisted the dead health visitor from the floor, then carried her slight frame out to his car. He placed the body in the boot, then quietly closed and locked it.

Back inside the house, he grabbed the maroon-coloured cagoule and slipped it on. It was quite a snug fit, but it didn't look ridiculously small. He put the hood up and, carrying his own dark Harrington jacket, walked from the house, up the driveway to the Mini Metro she had parked on the street earlier. It had taken him twenty minutes to drive to the Forest Recreation Ground, keeping to the back streets.

He now took one last look around, then got out of the car and put the car keys back in the cagoule pocket before throwing it on the back seat. He then slipped on his own Harrington jacket and quietly closed the door of the Metro before setting off walking at a brisk pace towards Mansfield Road.

If he walked at a steady pace, it would take him less than an hour to get to Fairview Road at Woodthorpe. He had already decided where he was going to dispose of the health visitor's body.

36

3.00am, 18 July 1987
Woodthorpe Grange Park, Sherwood, Nottingham

By the time he had walked back to Fairview Road, it was almost three o'clock in the morning. On two occasions during the long walk home, he had been forced to duck into the shadows as patrolling police cars had driven by. He had also kept a keen eye out for police officers patrolling on foot but hadn't seen any.

Keeping to the side streets as much as possible, it had taken him much longer to get back to Fairview Road than he had thought, but the road was still deserted as he finally walked towards his house. He retrieved his car keys from the pocket of his jacket and slipped quietly into his Ford Sierra.

He turned the ignition, keeping the revs to a minimum, and drove off slowly. He didn't have far to drive, but he didn't want to disturb any of his neighbours. It would be awkward trying to explain to them where he had been driving to at that time of night.

The car park at Woodthorpe Grange Park was thankfully deserted when he drove slowly into it, and he wasted no time. He got out of the vehicle, walked to the boot, flipped it open and grabbed the body of the dead health visitor. He had forgotten she was wearing a lambswool jumper, and he quietly cursed as his black Harrington jacket was quickly covered in pink fibres.

He grunted as he hoisted the dead weight onto his shoulder before walking off towards the pitch and putt golf course. On this part of the course, there was a large overgrown area surrounded by trees and covered in long unkempt grass, weeds and brambles. It had been deliberately left in this condition by the gardeners to encourage wildlife. It also made a hazard for the golfers to avoid.

It was the perfect place to hide the body. He was satisfied that it would be a long time before anybody found her.

He walked into the middle of this wild area, his trousers constantly snagging on brambles. When he thought he was near the middle, he threw the body on the floor. She landed on her back, her eyes half open but glazed over. He leaned forward and placed her legs together before placing her arms at her sides. He quickly grabbed some tall weeds and pulled them out of the ground, roughly covering the body, before he made his way back out of the wild area, covering his tracks as he did so.

It was almost three forty-five by the time he got back to his house; it would start getting light soon. He sat quietly for a few moments, checking that the street was deserted before making his way back inside the house.

Once inside, he took off the jacket, sighing when he saw pink wool all over it. If it didn't brush off, he might need to get rid of the jacket. That would be a shame, as he had only just bought it, but he couldn't afford the police to match fibres later. For now, he hung it back in the coat cupboard next to his other coats. He suddenly felt very tired and craved sleep. All the walking had worn him out. He slowly made his way upstairs, got undressed and into bed.

He put his head on the pillow and drifted off into a deep sleep.

37

10.00am, 11 August 1987
MCIU Office, Mansfield Police Station

PC Nick Grainger walked into the MCIU offices. 'Sorry to disturb you,' he said to DC Fran Jefferies. 'I'm looking for Pete Hazard. Is he around?'

'He's in with DI Buxton and the boss,' Fran replied. 'Is he expecting you?'

'I think they're all expecting me. I'm Nick Grainger, the football liaison officer; they wanted to see me this morning.'

Fran stood up. 'Follow me.'

She knocked loudly on Danny's office door, opened it and said, 'PC Grainger's here, sir.'

'Send him in, Fran.'

Nick stepped inside the office, and Danny said, 'Good to see you, Nick; grab a seat. Do you have some news?'

'I think I've identified one of the Forest fans involved in the fighting on Bridgford Park immediately before PC Warden was assaulted.'

'That's great. What's the strength of the information? Have we got enough to nick him?'

'I'll let you decide on how you want to proceed, sir. I've had information from two separate sources that the man responsible for organising the fight with the Leeds fans is a well-known player within the Executive Crew. His name's Dave Connors. He's nowhere near the leadership level, but he has ambitions, if you know what I mean.'

Pete Hazard asked, 'Do you have anything other than your sources? Anything that can confirm this?'

Nick grimaced. He felt like he was being told how to suck eggs. 'It would be a bit of a waste of time me coming here if that was all I had, Sarge,' he said quietly.

Realising the condescending nature of his previous question, Pete held up his hands in a gesture of apology. 'Sorry, Nick. Just tell us what else you've got.'

'After getting the initial information, I did some digging into Dave Connors. I checked with local hospitals and discovered that on the night PC Warden was assaulted, Connors went to the Queen's Medical Centre, Accident and Emergency department. He had five stitches put into a head wound. He claimed he had fallen from a chair at home, reaching up into a cupboard. No doubt a bullshit story. I went back to my sources, and apparently Connors has been bad-mouthing the Leeds fans, saying that the wound to his head had been caused by a cosh, even though the agreement had been no weapons.'

Danny said, 'That's brilliant work, Nick. I want everything you've got on Dave Connors. Current addresses, known associates, the works. He's going to be our starter for ten. I want him arrested as soon as possible.' Directing his next words to Rob, he continued, 'I want you and Pete to sit down with Nick and get everything organised for a dawn raid on

Connors's last known address. I want him in custody by the thirteenth.'

'We're on it, boss.'

38

10.00am, 11 August 1987
2 Fairview Road, Woodthorpe, Nottingham

His housekeeper, Chloe, had just left.
She was very pretty with a bubbly personality, and the tight tracksuit bottoms she wore when cleaning fitted her well.

Solomon always looked forward to her visits, but she had just told him that she wouldn't be around for just over a week, as she was going on holiday. But, apart from not having Chloe to look forward to for the next week or so, life was pretty good for Solomon.

It had been almost three weeks since he'd been forced to kill the nosy health visitor. He had since managed to get into an easy routine, leading his double life. Chloe always did whatever he asked her to do. He could arrange for her to get his weekly shopping and even cook meals for him to put in the freezer. She did all the laundry and cleaning and kept the house spotless.

After practicing for hours, scribbling in an old notebook,

he had finally perfected Saul's signature. He now had no trouble accessing funds, as and when he needed them, from Saul's account. The bank knew of his circumstances, so unless it was an exceedingly large amount, there was never a request for him to go into the local branch. All transactions with the bank were done over the telephone.

He had started venturing out after Chloe's morning visit. He had day trips out to the east coast, where he could abandon the wheelchair and have a stroll along the seafront, safe in the knowledge that nobody would recognise him there. At night he would drive out to neighbouring towns and cities, where he would go clubbing. Whenever he was chatting to women, he always gave the name Mick Heeton.

The one rule he had to live by was to always be back in the house by eight thirty in the morning, before Chloe arrived at nine o'clock.

After a difficult start putting everything into place, life was now very sweet for Solomon Peleg.

39

6.00am, 13 August 1987
52 Eugene Gardens, Meadows, Nottingham

Rob Buxton and Pete Hazard sat in a plain car two streets away from Eugene Gardens. They were listening to the radio traffic of the Special Operations Unit officers as they prepared to raid the home address of Dave Connors.

PC Nick Grainger was working alongside the SOU men. He would be one of the first through the door so he could be on hand to identify the renowned football hooligan.

Connors was a violent individual, with several previous convictions for serious assault. He was also known to carry weapons, so the SOU men would take no chances when making the arrest.

Their orders at the briefing from the man leading the raid, Sergeant Graham Turner, had been simple. Enter the property hard and fast and secure all rooms as quickly as possible. Any resistance from Connors was to be met with the appropriate force.

Sergeant Turner's voice came over the radio. 'Are all units in position?'

One by one, the various call signs acknowledged that they were indeed in position.

The next order was a single word. Turner shouted into the radio, 'Strike!'

The men tasked with forcing entry into the property smashed their way through the UPVC front door. As soon as the door was off the hinges, other black-clad officers, shouting 'police' at the tops of their voices, steamed into the two-bedroomed, semi-detached house. Each team of two had been designated a room to enter and search for the suspect.

PC Nick Grainger and PC Tom Naylor entered the front bedroom of the house, both shouting 'police' as they made entry. Connors was already out of bed. He was wearing a pair of boxer shorts and had grabbed a baseball bat from the side of the bed. Swinging the bat from side to side, he advanced towards the two officers.

Connors swung the baseball bat towards the helmeted head of Tom Naylor, who ducked to avoid the blow. The force of the missing swing caused Connors to lose balance, and he toppled forward.

In an instant, Nick Grainger grabbed the bat and began to wrest it from the grip of Connors. Tom Naylor then launched himself at him. Between them, the two officers quickly had Connors disarmed and under control. Nick hauled Connors to his feet. 'David Connors, I'm arresting you on suspicion of the attempted murder of Mark Warden.'

Connors just growled an unintelligible response.

Nick Grainger spoke on the radio. 'Target identified and arrested.'

It was the radio message Rob Buxton and Pete Hazard had been waiting for. Pete turned the ignition on, gunned the engine and drove towards Eugene Gardens.

The Meadows estate was a hostile environment, and in the few minutes it took the two detectives to reach Eugene Gardens, groups of youths were already beginning to gather on the street. Members of the Special Operations Unit not engaged in searching the target premises were actively engaged in keeping the gathering youths at a respectful distance so they couldn't interfere with the police operation.

As the CID car came to a stop outside number fifty-two, the two detectives were met by Sergeant Turner.

He stooped and spoke through the window to Rob. 'Target's been detained, sir. As soon as PC Grainger brings the prisoner out to the car, can I suggest you get out of here and transport him straight back to the Meadows nick. We can complete the search; the mob will soon lose interest when they know Connors has been carted away. It will make my life easier here.'

Rob nodded. 'Okay, Sarge. Any problems arresting Connors?'

The tough sergeant grinned. 'He tried to take Tom Naylor's head off with a baseball bat but missed. There are no injuries to my men or to your prisoner. So it's all good, sir.'

'Great stuff. Tell Nick to fetch Connors out, and we'll get him out of here.'

Graham Turner spoke into his radio. 'Sergeant Turner to PC Grainger, your chariot awaits. You can fetch Connors out now.'

A crescendo of loud boos and catcalls from the gathered youths went up as a now fully clothed but handcuffed Dave Connors was led out of the house towards the CID car.

Nick Grainger gripped the man's right arm tightly as he led him out. 'Don't even think about causing me any problems, Connors,' he growled.

Dave Connors smiled. 'I haven't done anything. I grabbed

the bat because I thought you were burglars. You've got nothing on me, copper.'

Nick opened the car door, pushed Connors inside and got in beside him. 'Save your lies for when you're being interviewed.'

Pete Hazard drove steadily away; the gathered youths parted as the car drove through them. A couple of them made half-hearted attempts to bang on the roof. Two turns in the road away from Eugene Gardens, the car was once again being driven along deserted early morning streets, heading for Meadows Police Station.

On the back seat of the car, a now worried-looking Dave Connors sat quietly next to Nick Grainger. The mask of bravado had fully slipped from the hooligan's face. He had made his mind up. There was no way he was going to be sent down for attempted murder. He would do and say whatever he had to, to stay out of prison.

40

10.00am, 13 August 1987
Meadows Police Station, Nottingham

Rob Buxton and Pete Hazard sat in the CID office at the Meadows Police Station. They were discussing the forthcoming interview with Dave Connors while they waited for Nick Grainger and Sergeant Turner to tell them the result of the search of Connors's home address at Eugene Gardens.

'I think you and Nick should do the interview. Nick already knows Connors well and will already have a level of rapport with him, and you know the details surrounding the assault on PC Warden. It makes sense. I can observe the interview through the one-way glass they have here.'

'Fine by me, boss. Did you see Connors's face when he was being booked in? He's already shitting himself. He's only done one prison stretch before, and that was only for three months when he was still a juvenile, four years ago. I think the thought of a long sentence has got him spooked.'

'Good. Use that, Pete. At every opportunity, tell him he's

going away for a long time. We need the names of the individuals who carried out the assault.'

Hazard agreed just as Nick Grainger and Sergeant Turner
came in.

Rob said, 'Have you recovered anything significant?'

'We've recovered various weapons,' Graham Turner
replied. 'Obviously, the baseball bat he used to resist arrest, as
well as two Rambo knives and a knuckleduster. There's some
paraphernalia to do with the Forest Executive Crew. And as a
bonus, we've also found a half-kilo bag of what looks like
cocaine under his mattress.'

'That's great. Any bloodstained clothing or footwear?'

'We've seized two pairs of Adidas Samba trainers that
have stains on them. I'm not sure if it's blood, but the lab will
tell us one way or the other. No clothing, I'm afraid.'

'Great work, Graham. Has PC Naylor completed his statement corroborating the arrest of Connors?'

'He's finishing off his statement now, sir. As are the men
who recovered the seized property. All the exhibits have been
booked into the property store. I'll bring all the exhibits and
the statements up to you as soon as they're completed.'

'Thanks. Good work again, today.'

'No problem, sir.'

The burly SOU sergeant left the room, and Rob said to
Nick, 'I'd like you to lead the interview, Nick. Are you okay
with that?'

'It's not something I've done much of, sir. But I don't mind
giving it a go. I'm pretty sure Connors will talk to me.'

Pete Hazard said, 'I'll do all the introductions and
preamble; then you can step in and talk to him about the
Executive Crew. Let's see how it goes. If he starts talking, we'll
just run with it. Don't worry about drying up in the interview.
If you do, I'll just step in and take over. You'll be fine.'

'Well, the good news is he doesn't want a solicitor for his

interview. He told the custody sergeant that he didn't need one, as he hadn't done anything wrong.'

Rob said, 'Right. Get down there, and let's get a first account from him before he changes his mind about having a brief.'

41

10.30am, 13 August 1987
2 Fairview Road, Woodthorpe, Nottingham

Andy Wills rang the doorbell for the fourth time. With more than a little impatience, he left his finger on the buzzer longer than was necessary.

The constant buzzing elicited an angry response from inside the house. A man's voice shouted, 'Alright, alright. I'm coming!'

Andy was already holding his warrant card out as the door opened. The man in the wheelchair said, 'Yes, what is it?'

Andy said, 'Hello, Mr Peleg. My name's Detective Sergeant Andy Wills. Have you got a few minutes? I'd like to go over the details of this van you told my colleagues about.'

'Of course, come in.'

Andy followed him through into the lounge and sat down opposite him.

'Have you found it?'

'No. That's the problem. We can't find any trace of it.'

'That's so weird. It was outside the house for quite a while.'

'Let me check the details with you, just to make sure my colleagues didn't get something wrong when they spoke to you last time.'

'Okay.'

'You said it was a scruffy-looking, red Ford Escort van containing two men with long dark hair?'

'I said it was Ford Escort size. I wasn't sure if it was a Ford or not. Yes, definitely two men inside it. They looked very similar. Long, dark hair, swarthy looking. I thought they were gypsies.'

'Could you show me where you saw it?'

'Parked up on the street.'

'No, sorry. I meant, where were you when you saw it?'

'I was looking out of that window.'

He indicated the large bay window of the lounge, which overlooked the street.

Andy stood up and walked over to the window. There was only one place where the wheelchair could have been to enable Peleg to look out of the window. It gave a very limited view of the street.

Andy had deliberately parked the CID car outside the house where Gladys Miller had been murdered. From his position in the bay window, he could just about make out the bonnet of his car.

'Is this where you were,' he asked Peleg, 'when you saw the van?'

'There or thereabouts.'

'Can you come over and show me exactly?'

Peleg wheeled his chair across the lounge and into the space by the bay window. 'I was about here, I think.'

Andy said, 'What sort of car is that? The one parked outside Mrs Miller's house now?'

Peleg coloured up a little and became a little testy. 'I don't know. Some sort of Ford, I think.'

'It's a Vauxhall Astra. Is that where the van was parked?'

'Yes. In that exact spot. That's why I said it was Ford Escort size, because I couldn't see the make.'

'I get that. What I don't understand is how you could see the occupants from here?'

The anger that had been bubbling just below the surface began to rise, and Peleg said moodily, 'What are you implying? I'm trying to help you, and you come back here questioning me about what I saw. I think you should leave.'

'I'm just trying to make sure we have all the facts, that's all. Nobody's questioning what you saw.'

'That's not what it sounds like to me.'

'How did you see the occupants?'

'I'm sure I said this to your colleagues when they were here, as well. They kept getting in and out of the van and going towards Mrs Miller's house. That's why I watched them.'

'And this was definitely a few days before she was found in the house.'

'I said this last time too. I can't be sure when I saw the van, exactly. I just know it was before she was found. Surely somebody else must have seen it?'

'Nobody else saw it.'

'Not even that nosy cow from number nine? Dreary Deirdre, whatever her name is. She doesn't normally miss a trick.'

'Nobody.'

'Well, that's a mystery to me, because it was definitely here. Or do you think I'm making all of this up?'

'Like I said before, I'm just here to confirm all the details. What reason could you possibly have to make something like this up?' Andy left the last part of his sentence hanging.

Peleg scowled. 'Exactly! No reason at all. Is that everything, Detective?'

'That's everything. Thanks for your time.'

Andy walked into the hallway and paused by the open door. 'How often do you look out of that window, Mr Peleg?'

'I spend hours every day looking out of that bloody window. That's what prisoners do, Detective. I'm a prisoner in this chair. I may have got the time or the day wrong, but there was a red van, with two men inside it, parked on the street. That's the God's honest truth.'

'Okay, Mr Peleg. Take care.'

As he walked back to his car, Andy was troubled. He couldn't shake off the feeling that Saul Peleg was lying to him.

42

10.30am, 13 August 1987
Meadows Police Station, Nottingham

The interview had pretty much gone to plan so far. Connors had insisted at the start of the interview that he still didn't want a solicitor. Pete Hazard had quickly made all the introductions and then allowed Nick Grainger to start questioning Dave Connors.

Grainger had spoken in general terms about the football club and how long Connors had been following them, before targeting the questions towards his involvement with the Forest Executive Crew. Although a little more reticent to talk about the hooligan firm, Connors had carried on talking.

With an almost imperceptible nod of his head, Pete Hazard signalled Nick to start asking questions about the attack on PC Warden.

Nick said, 'You've been arrested for taking part in the attack on PC Warden after the match against Leeds United. What part in that assault did you take?'

Connors said, 'You see, that's the bullshit part of all of this. I wasn't involved at all.'

'Tell me about the wound on the top of your head. How did you get that?'

'I fell off a chair at home.'

'I've spoken at length to the doctor who stitched you up at the Queen's Medical Centre on the day that happened. He told me there's no way that injury could have been caused by a fall. The position of the wound is all wrong. The doctor's opinion is that it was caused by a downward blow onto the top of your head. Did PC Warden cause it with his truncheon?'

Connors was quiet for a few seconds; then he blurted out, 'It wasn't the copper who belted me, it was one of them.'

'Who?'

'One of the Leeds fans. The agreement was no weapons, and this dickhead had some sort of flash cosh. I thought he'd caved my skull in when he hit me.'

'Where did this happen?'

'About fifty yards away from where they attacked your mate.'

'My mate?'

'Yeah. That copper. I was getting a right shoeing when he just appeared around the corner and shouted at them to stop. They left me alone and ran towards the copper. He tried to grab one of them, but they all turned on him. He got clobbered with the same cosh they had used on me.'

'How many?'

'There were four of them.'

'Did you see who hit the police officer?'

'I was dazed myself after getting whacked, but I could see they were all laying into him. He was completely out of it, and they were still all putting the boot into him. I fucked off before they came back for me. Look, I had nothing to do with attacking that copper.'

'Where did all this happen?'

'On Hound Street.'

'Why were the Leeds United fans there?'

'There was a fight organised for after the game, at Bridgford Park.'

'You said earlier, there was supposed to be no weapons. I take it you'd been instrumental in organising this meetup?'

'Yeah, but it was just supposed to be the two firms involved. Not members of the public or the cops.'

'Who did you organise it with?'

'It's a group calling themselves the Halton Moor Casuals. I never had a name, just a telephone number to ring.'

'What were the arrangements?'

'The arrangement was five of them and five of us, no weapons. We agreed to meet on Bridgford Park for a ruck. It was meant to be a bit of added excitement after the game.'

'If it was arranged for Bridgford Park, how did you all end up on Hound Road?'

'They were fucking nutters! They came at us with weapons, and in no time, we were fucked. I legged it to get away, and they chased us.'

'You said us. Who else was with you?'

'Look. I'm only talking to you because I didn't attack that copper. I'm not a fucking grass.'

'How many Forest fans were on Hound Road?'

'Me and one other. Don't ask me who, like I just said, I'm not a grass.'

'Did this other Forest fan witness the attack on the officer?'

'I don't think so. He was even more out of it than I was. He'd already taken a right battering.'

Nick stared at the hooligan. 'How do I know all this isn't a load of crap?'

'Get hold of the Leeds lads who did attack him, that's how. I'm not bullshitting. What I've told you is the truth. You know me, and you know I've got no love for coppers, but I swear I never attacked him. Truth is, that copper probably saved me from getting put in the hospital.'

Pete Hazard said, 'You said you had a contact telephone number for this group calling themselves the Halton Moor Casuals. I take it you've still got it?'

Connors nodded.

Pete said, 'The tape machine can't record you nodding your head. Do you still have that contact number?'

'Yes.'

'Where is it?'

'It's at home. I wrote it down on the back of an old *Shoot* magazine. It will be in my bedroom, on the drawers at the side of my bed.'

'Okay. When you used that number, who did you speak to?'

'I never got a name. It was weird though, because it was like someone else answered the phone and then put their main man on to do all the talking.'

'We now need to talk to you about weapons and drugs that were found at your house this morning.'

'Oh, fuck off. You're kidding me, right. I think I might need that brief now.'

'Okay. If you want a solicitor, we'll stop the interview and arrange for you to have one. Do you want a solicitor?'

'Yeah. I'm fucked if you've found the drugs.'

43

11.30am, 13 August 1987
Meadows Police Station, Nottingham

'I've just sent two detectives back to Eugene Gardens,' Rob said, 'to recover the *Shoot* magazine with the telephone number on. Do you believe his account?'

'I think I do. It tallies in with what I've already been told about it being a prearranged confrontation between rival groups. He doesn't normally give us the time of day, so for him to sit there and give us chapter and verse about what happened was quite surprising. I think it probably was the Leeds fans who assaulted Mark Warden. I never expected Connors to tell us the names of his mates who were also there. If he did that, he would be finished as part of the Executive Crew.'

Pete said, 'Have you heard of this Leeds group he was on about, the Halton Moor Casuals?'

'No, I haven't. After we've finished the interviews, I'll get onto Bill Keenan in Leeds and see if he's heard of them. My guess is that they'll be some sort of subgroup of the Leeds Service Crew, wanting to make a name for themselves.'

'Finish off here, then make your way back to Mansfield,' Rob said to Pete. 'I'm going to update the boss on how things have gone this morning. I'll see you at Mansfield later.' He turned to Nick. 'Good work today, Nick. Good interview. What's the betting he goes "no comment" to everything you ask him from now on?'

'With a brief pulling his strings, I wouldn't expect anything else, sir.'

'Keep me posted when you get anything back from Bill Keenan in West Yorkshire.'

'Will do, sir.'

44

10.30am, 17 August 1987
Nottinghamshire Police Headquarters

The meeting with Chief Superintendent Potter was routine. It was an unwelcome duty that Danny had to perform every week or so, to keep his immediate line supervisor updated on all cases currently being investigated by the MCIU.

It was a task that Danny loathed. Especially when there was very little progress to report on those cases. It always left him feeling ineffective and undervalued.

Potter was immediately into the only case that really interested him – the assault on the constable that had roused the anger of the chief constable. Danny knew that pressure for a result was being applied from above onto Potter.

The diminutive Yorkshireman said, 'I understand you've made an arrest on the Mark Warden enquiry?'

'Yes, sir. We arrested David Connors, a well-known Nottingham Forest hooligan, and we are following up on intelligence gained from that arrest.'

'Will Connors be charged for the assault?'

'No, sir, but he does face other charges.'

There was an audible tutting sound from Potter before he said, 'Are we any closer to identifying those responsible for the attack?'

Danny was cautious. He didn't want to sound too optimistic, only for it all to fall flat later. He thought for a moment and then said, 'We're actively seeking a group of men from the West Yorkshire area who we think could help us significantly with our enquiries.'

Potter glared over the top of his glasses and said, 'And that's what I'm supposed to take to the chief constable, is it? Come on, Danny. What do you know?'

'It seems likely that a group of football hooligans, known as the Halton Moor Casuals from Leeds, were responsible for the attack on PC Warden. We're working alongside our West Yorkshire colleagues to try to identify the individuals within that group. As soon as we make any progress, I'll inform you, sir.'

'Very well. This is a top priority. We need those men arrested and put before the courts. Have you any update on PC Warden's medical condition?'

'He's still in a coma but is improving slightly. He's no longer on the critical list. Thank God.'

'Well, at least that's some good news. Even better news would be that we've made arrests. Understood?'

'Yes, sir.'

'How are you faring with the two outstanding murder enquiries? Any progress to report?'

'No, sir. There are still active leads we're following on both cases, and the two press appeals have been quite fruitful, but there are no immediate breakthroughs to report.'

'Okay, Chief Inspector. Well, don't let me detain you any

longer. I want to know the moment you have identified these suspects in Leeds, understood.'

Danny stood up. 'Understood, sir.'

45

11.30am, 20 August 1987
2 Fairview Road, Woodthorpe, Nottingham

Solomon had treated himself to a lie-in that morning, as he knew his housekeeper Chloe wasn't back until this evening. He had arranged for her to come in for a couple of hours at six o'clock to catch up on the housework, as she had been away for ten days. He had been up and about for thirty minutes and had just finished the bowl of porridge he had made, when he heard the doorbell ring. He stood up from the armchair and sat in his wheelchair before making his way through the house. He wasn't expecting a visit from anyone.

When he opened the front door, he was surprised to see a fat, middle-aged woman, whom he vaguely recognised, standing on the doorstep.

The woman smiled, revealing two rows of tobacco-stained teeth, and said, 'Well, aren't you going to invite me in?'

The nonplussed look on Solomon's face must have been extremely evident because the woman blustered, 'Don't you recognise me, Saul? It's your aunt Lillian. I've come for a visit.'

Solomon did recall that his mother had a sister called Lillian, who lived on the Isle of Man. He had been twelve or thirteen years old when he had last seen her. He also remembered how his mother had always referred to her own sister in a derogatory manner. He had often heard her calling his aunt an interfering old cow. She was well known in the family for her meddlesome nature and unwanted visits.

This was not a visit Solomon welcomed at all, but he maintained a modicum of calm and said politely, 'Aunt Lillian, it's been such a long time. You'd better come in.'

Carrying a large carpet bag, she brushed past him into the hallway and exclaimed loudly, 'This is such a lovely house. Last time I visited, you were all living in that dingy little place in Calverton. This is so beautiful. Did you win the football pools or something, dear?'

Solomon said patiently, 'No. The house was bought using the money I got from my accident. Didn't Mum tell you about the accident that put me in this bloody wheelchair? It wasn't a bloody football pools win.'

'I was only joking, my sweet. The last time I spoke to your mum, she told me all about your terrible accident. Talking of my wonderful sister, where is she?'

Solomon said, 'You'd better come through to the lounge. I've got some bad news for you.'

Aunt Lillian took off her coat, hurled it over the banister rail, and put her carpet bag down before following Solomon into the lounge. She sat down, and with a concerned expression on her face, she asked again, 'Where is everyone? Where's your mum?'

'I'm afraid Mum's dead. I'm sorry to have to tell you like this, Aunt Lillian. I thought you knew. Solomon was supposed to contact everyone.'

The shock of the news was evident on her face. After a brief silence, she said, 'What happened?'

'It's a long story. Things were very tough after my accident. The strain on both my parents was enormous. In the end my dad couldn't cope, and he walked out. After he left us, Mum found it hard to manage. I think it broke her heart when he left. Anyway, she left a note saying she couldn't cope anymore.'

'A note? You mean she killed herself?'

Solomon nodded sadly.

'Oh my God! That's awful. You poor thing. So it's just you and Solomon living here now?'

'No. It's just me. Solomon emigrated to New Zealand. I live here alone, now.'

'That's terrible. You must be so lonely. How do you cope, being stuck in that thing?' As she spoke, she gestured towards his wheelchair.

'I cope very well. The house has been especially adapted to suit my needs, and I have carers who come in twice a day, and specialist private nurses who look after me medically. Between them, they do for me whatever I can't manage myself.'

'That must cost you a fortune.'

'It's not cheap, but I have money left over from the damages settlement.'

Aunt Lillian sat back in the settee and surveyed the plush surroundings. It was all so much more opulent and luxurious than her scruffy, one-bedroom flat in Douglas on the Isle of Man. She very quickly came to a decision.

'This won't do, Saul. I can't have my own flesh and blood being looked after by complete strangers. You must sack your carers. It will save you an absolute fortune. I'll move in and look after you myself. It's what Rebecca would have wanted.'

It may have been what his mother would have wanted; it

wasn't what Solomon wanted at all. He could see all his plans and his comfortable life going up in smoke before his very eyes.

Taken aback by the suddenness and finality of the proposition from his aunt, he spluttered, 'I couldn't possibly ask you to do that for me, Aunt Lillian. I know how much you enjoy your home on the Isle of Man. I manage perfectly well, thank you. Honestly, everything is fine.'

Lillian Rhodes wasn't going to be put off so easily from the new comfortable lifestyle she could see for herself. She said firmly, 'I won't hear of any arguments, nephew. I'll telephone my landlord tomorrow and quit the tenancy of my flat. There's no time like the present. I can move in here straight away and go back for my personal belongings later.'

She grinned that tobacco-stained smile again and said, 'Shall I make us both a nice cup of tea, to celebrate?'

In a worried voice he said, 'The kitchen's through there.'

He watched his fat aunt as she waddled from the lounge towards the kitchen. He studied her appearance. She looked dishevelled; her clothes were scruffy and unwashed. She made little attempt to look after her personal hygiene, and a strong smell of body odour followed her wherever she went. Her shoes were plain and unpolished. This was a woman on her uppers. No wonder she wanted to move into his palatial home.

He couldn't and wouldn't allow that to happen.

After killing the health visitor, he had vowed no more killing. Right now, he felt backed into another corner. He couldn't see any other way out of this new predicament. He needed to get rid of this obnoxious woman before Chloe arrived tonight.

Before he did anything drastic, there were a few things he needed to check first. He waited for her to come back into the room, carrying a tray with two mugs of tea on.

As she set the tray down on the coffee table, Solomon said, 'Did you find everything okay?'

She grabbed her tea from the tray and said, 'No problem.'

He said, 'How was your journey?'

'Very long and very tiring. The ferry was awful, and then the train down to Nottingham was late. At least the taxi from the station to here was cheap. Even if the bloody driver could hardly speak a word of English.'

'What made you visit now, Auntie?'

'I hadn't heard anything from Rebecca for so long, I wanted to check everything was okay. It's a good job I did.'

'Isn't it. I'm so sorry Solomon never got in touch with you to tell you what had happened. He was too preoccupied sorting out his move abroad. What about your job, won't you have to give any notice?'

'Don't worry about any of that. I was made redundant last year. I'm between jobs right now, so there's no notice to give. It's perfect timing. My new job will be to look after and care for my favourite nephew.'

Solomon smiled at her, but he thought to himself, no job and a crappy one-bedroom flat to live in. No wonder she wants to move in here.

One last thing to check before he decided what to do.

He said, 'What about all your friends? Won't they miss you?'

'Hmph! What friends? My so-called friends don't want to know me now. After I lost my job, my neighbours at the flats don't speak to me anymore. We can be company for each other here, Saul.'

He stared at her, a strange calm descending over him. 'You can't stay here with me. I want you to leave.'

Shocked at his statement, but disregarding it, she blustered, 'Don't be silly. I won't hear of it. I'm staying. I know what's best for both of us.'

His voice became more insistent. 'I'm not asking you; I'm telling you. I want you to leave right now.'

The old woman sat back on the settee and took another sip of her tea. 'At least let me stay today, I'm exhausted from my journey. If you're on your own here now, you must have a spare room. Let me stay one night. You might think differently in the morning. I still think it would be great if I stayed; we could be company for each other.'

He knew she wasn't going to shift her fat, scruffy arse off the settee, whatever he said. He glanced at the clock; it was now almost one o'clock; she had already been there for over an hour. He had to do something before Chloe arrived later. He needed to act, but he knew he would also need time to clear up the mess.

Once again, he felt like the walls were closing in around him. He knew he had no option but to deal with the problem in the same way as before.

He tried one more time. 'I can't let you stay, Aunt Lillian; you must go.'

She grinned at him, exposing her dirty, rotten teeth. 'I know you don't mean that. My tea's gone cold. I'll just nip and put the kettle on and make us both a fresh pot.'

Solomon slowly stood up, stepped away from his wheel-chair, and walked towards his aunt.

She sat open mouthed, not quite believing what she was seeing. 'What is this?' she spluttered. 'How can you walk? I don't understand; aren't you supposed to be stuck in that chair?'

'Dear Aunt Lillian, you never could tell us apart, could you? I'm Solomon, not Saul. The last thing I need right now is for you to be here meddling in my life, so you've left me no choice.'

'What do you mean, no choice? Where's Saul?'

'Saul's dead. Your precious sister's dead. They're all fucking dead, and now you've got to join them.'

He lunged at her and pulled her from the settee onto the floor. The cold cup of tea she was holding flew from her hands and smashed on the hardwood floor. She tried to scream as he straddled her and put his strong hands around her throat. The terrified scream was stifled as he squeezed her windpipe. She began to struggle violently, and he was surprised at her strength, but the more he squeezed, the less violent the struggles became. Eventually, they became little more than spasmodic twitches until finally his aunt was totally still.

He crawled off her and sat on the settee.

He put his head in his hands, squeezing his eyes tightly shut.

When would this nightmare stop?

Every time he thought he was free and clear, something else happened that tipped him down into this murderous abyss.

He felt like he was losing his mind.

When would the killing end?

He now had another problem. He only had until six o'clock that evening to hide every trace of his aunt Lillian before Chloe arrived to start work. He would then have to think of somewhere to dispose of the odious woman's body that night after Chloe had left. He breathed deeply, trying to calm his heightened heart rate. He felt like he was enduring a living hell.

46

2.00am, 21 August 1987
Strelley Village, Nottingham

It had been wonderful to see a tanned and happy Chloe earlier the previous evening. The young housekeeper had been her usual bubbly self and had spoken enthusiastically about her recent holiday to Butlins at Skegness with a load of girlfriends.

As much as he had enjoyed her company and listening to her holiday exploits, for once he was pleased to see her leave.

As soon as she left, he retrieved his aunt's body from the garden shed. He had struggled to manhandle her – his aunt had been an idle, unambitious woman, and her body reflected her sloth-like existence. She weighed a ton.

By the time he had manoeuvred her through the house, Solomon was sweating profusely and breathing hard. He took a few minutes to get his breath back before dragging the body and her belongings out to his car on the driveway. He had reversed the car until it was right outside the front door and had already opened the boot. After checking there was nobody around, he unceremoniously tipped his aunt's body inside.

He had waited until one o'clock that morning before he went back to his car and drove slowly off the drive. He kept to every speed limit and tried, as much as possible, to stick to the side roads.

He had formulated a plan to dispose of his aunt's body earlier in the day as he waited for Chloe to arrive. The first idea he had was to drive out to the Peak District and abandon her body on the moors. The plan he had finally settled upon had come to him as he thought about what route to take out to Derbyshire. He had remembered a farmer's bridge that spanned the M1 motorway just outside Strelley village. It had been built to enable the farmer to get his herd of cattle from one side of the motorway to the other.

His parents had often visited the nearby Strelley Hall when he and Saul had been young children. Now, as he drove past the Georgian manor house, happy childhood memories came flooding back. Having passed the hall, he turned left at the sign for Robinetts Lane and saw the bridge was less than a hundred yards away. He knew there was a padlocked gate at each end to keep out unwanted visitors. It meant he had to carry the dead weight of his aunt for the last part of the journey.

He stopped and turned the car around on the narrow lane so the boot was facing the five-bar gate. He was grateful that the recent weather had been dry and the ground was firm. Taking one last look around him, he got out and reached into the boot to grab his dead aunt. Grunting and straining with the effort, he dragged her body up to the gate before lifting her over.

The body landed with a heavy thud over the other side of the gate, and he leapt over to join it before dragging the dead woman out to the centre of the pitch-black bridge. The traffic whizzed by beneath him, heading south.

He propped his aunt against the side of the bridge. Summoning all his strength, he lifted the dead weight up and onto the bridge railing. Looking out along the almost deserted motorway, he could see a huge articulated truck thundering its way along the slow lane.

He waited, the muscles in his arms burning under the strain of supporting the bulky woman. Finally, when the truck was no more than seventy-five yards from the bridge, he released his grip and let her fall.

47

2.00am, 21 August 1987
Strelley Village, Nottingham

The body of Lillian Rhodes dropped like a stone, landing in the slow lane seconds before the articulated truck arrived at the bridge.

The startled driver had seen something drop from the bridge right in front of him, the falling object picked out by the vehicle's powerful headlights.

He had slammed on his air brakes at the same time as he felt his wheels collide with the object. The massive truck came to a shuddering halt some two hundred yards beyond the bridge.

The driver manoeuvred the truck onto the hard shoulder and switched on the vehicle's hazard warning lights. With rising trepidation, he got out of the cab and walked slowly back along the hard shoulder.

Fifty yards behind his truck, he saw what appeared to be a bundle of rags lying half in the slow lane and half in the hard shoulder. There was a slick of dark liquid smeared from the bridge in the distance right up to the pile of rags.

A passing car illuminated the bundle as he approached it, and to his horror he saw it was a body. He waited for the road to empty of traffic before stepping out onto the slow lane and looking closer.

The only way he could tell he was looking at a body was by the ripped and damaged clothing. The injuries were extensive and horrific. He had no idea if he was looking at the remains of a man or a woman. Looking back along the motorway towards the bridge, he could see various objects scattered along the tarmac.

He walked towards one such object lying in the hard shoulder just as another car sped past. The lights from another passing vehicle lit up the remains of a severed foot still inside a black leather lace-up shoe.

Unable to contain his rising nausea, the driver turned away and staggered into the grass verge, where he vomited.

After a couple of minutes of dry retching, he made his way back along the hard shoulder. He sat on the grass verge next to his truck and waited. He knew the hazard warning lights would be seen, and it was only a matter of time before the motorway police would come and investigate what had happened to the abandoned heavy goods vehicle.

It was another ten minutes before he saw the flashing blue lights speeding southbound along the motorway towards him. He had sat on the damp grass, waiting in the darkness and listening in horror as passing vehicles had smacked into the scattered body parts at high speed as they hurtled by.

Their drivers totally unaware of what they had just hit.

48

1.00pm, 21 August 1987
City Hospital Mortuary, Nottingham

Danny walked into the mortuary, followed by DC Rachel Moore. Waiting in the corridor just outside the examination room was a uniform sergeant. Danny saw the white cap under the officer's arm. 'Sergeant Banner?' he asked.

The traffic patrol sergeant looked up. 'Chief Inspector Flint?

Danny inclined his head. 'Your phone call, requesting the MCIU attend this post-mortem, was a bit of a surprise. What's the problem?'

'The pathologist was halfway through the examination when she called a halt and asked me to contact the CID, as she suspected foul play.'

'Where's the pathologist now?'

'She nipped upstairs to make a telephone call while we waited for you to arrive.'

'Okay. Well, while we're waiting for her to come back, why don't you tell me the backstory.'

'I was asked to attend the post-mortem this morning by the night shift at the motorway post. They attended the report of a suicide last night. A woman had jumped from one of the bridges over the motorway, straight in front of an articulated vehicle. As you can imagine, it wasn't pretty. They asked me to attend today so I could provide the evidence for the coroner's file once we've identified the woman.'

'So you don't know who she is yet?'

'Not yet. There was no identification found with the body last night.'

'What was it that made the pathologist stop the examination?'

'I saw evidence of manual strangulation on the victim's neck.'

The woman's voice behind him made Danny wheel around in surprise. He hadn't seen or heard the pathologist approaching.

'Excuse me,' Danny said to her. 'I didn't see you. I'm Detective Chief Inspector Flint. I don't think we've met.'

The woman extended her hand. 'Professor Natalie Santos. No, we haven't met. I'm standing in for the pathologist who usually works here, for the next week or so, while he recovers from minor heart surgery.'

'This is a new scenario for me, Professor. Do I need to call out a Home Office pathologist to continue the examination?'

'There's no need. I am one. I usually cover the area around Leicester city, but nobody else was available at short notice to take on Dr Matthews workload. Now that you're here, I'll continue the examination and point out the areas that raised my concerns. Do you and your colleague want to gown up?'

Danny and Rachel quickly slipped on bottle-green scrubs and followed the professor into the examination room.

In the centre of the room, on a stainless-steel bench, lay the remains of a white female. The injuries to her body were extensive. One arm and one leg had been severed completely, and the foot of the other leg was also unattached. All severed limbs were also on the bench, adjacent to where they should have been anatomically. The injuries to the torso were massive: the trunk seemed to have split along one edge, and Danny could see intestine and bone protruding through flesh.

The pathologist stood at the side of the body. 'Fortunately, the head and the neck escaped most of the impact from the vehicle; otherwise I probably wouldn't have spotted this.'

She indicated two marks at the front of the trachea. Deep purple bruises, the size of plums, covered the hard edge of the windpipe.

She moved the head to the right and said, 'Now if you look here, these marks confirmed my fears. Can you see the bruising running from her clavicle up towards her ears?'

Danny nodded.

The pathologist turned the head the other way, and he could see identical marks on the other side of the woman's neck.

Danny said, 'Manual strangulation?'

'Yes. The classic, black banana fingermarks around the throat.'

'When do you think she died?'

'Best guess would be sometime yesterday.'

'Obviously, I'll need to get a Scenes of Crime team here to take photographs and samples. Are you okay for time?'

'I have other work I can be getting on with in the office upstairs. If you want to come and get me when your enquiry team gets here, that's fine.'

'Thank you. We should be ready to continue within the hour.'

'The mortuary attendant will tell you where to find me. See you shortly, Detective.'

Danny stepped back outside the examination room. 'Rachel, get onto the office. I want a team from Scenes of Crime here immediately. Are you okay to take on the role of exhibits officer?'

Rachel agreed and said to the mortuary attendant, 'Where's the nearest phone I can use?'

The attendant indicated a small office just off the corridor. 'There's a phone in there. Just dial nine to get an outside line.'

As Rachel disappeared into the office, Danny said to Sergeant Banner, 'Do you know if anybody searched the bridge this woman fell from last night?'

'I don't know.'

'It's a murder enquiry now, and there's every likelihood that this woman was deliberately dropped from that bridge. I need it secured as soon as possible.'

'It is secure.'

'Excuse me?'

'It is secure. It's the bridge at the top of Robinetts Lane, in Strelley. It has a padlocked gate at each end. It was built in the sixties so the farmer could get his livestock from one side of the motorway to the other. The farm was sold off for housing years ago, so the bridge is no longer used.'

'That's the first good news I've heard since I got here. Make a call to the motorway post and get an officer up to that bridge straightaway. I want it taped off at each end, fifty yards back from those padlocked gates. We need to ensure nothing on that bridge is disturbed. I'll get someone from my office to relieve them as soon as possible.'

'Yes, sir.'

Sergeant Banner ducked into the same room Rachel had gone in, and waited patiently to use the telephone.

Danny was left alone in the corridor with his thoughts. This was the third ongoing murder enquiry his team were investigating, as well as the unsolved serious assault on PC Warden.

He shook his head. It was turning into an extremely busy summer.

49

5.00pm, 21 August 1987
Robinetts Lane, Strelley Village, Nottingham

Sergeant Banner drove the powerful traffic patrol car onto Robinetts Lane. From the passenger seat, Danny could immediately see a white Scenes of Crime van and a couple of CID cars parked on the lane.

'Thanks for dropping me off, Chris. I bet you never expected this circus when you agreed to go to the post-mortem this morning.'

Banner chuckled darkly. 'You can say that again, boss. Just a thought going forward – people committing suicide by jumping off motorway bridges is, thankfully, a rarity. However, I was thinking maybe we should agree on some protocols for the next time it happens. Who initially attends? Who investigates? That sort of thing. If Professor Santos hadn't been so on the ball this morning, we could have allowed a murder to be written off as a suicide.'

'Totally agree. I'll put you in touch with Detective

Sergeant Lynn Harris. If the two of you can put some ideas down on paper, I'll take it from there.'

Danny got out of the car and said, 'Thanks for the ride.'

The sergeant raised a hand and accelerated away.

Danny could see Andy Wills up ahead, next to Tim Donnelly. Blue and white police tape had been erected fifty feet in front of the five-bar gate, and Andy held it up so Danny could duck beneath it.

'Rachel not with you?' Andy said.

'She's taken the car we were in back to Mansfield to get all the exhibits from the post-mortem into the property store. I got a lift here with the traffic sergeant who initially called us in. Have you found anything?'

'Not yet. Tim has found evidence that a car was driven up to the gate recently. There are scuff marks in the dirt consistent with a vehicle being turned around. The ground's too hard and dry for any meaningful tyre tracks, but you can see distinct tracks in the grass verges. Tim has measured the distance between the tyres and should have some idea of the size of vehicle used from the axle length.'

'Any cameras on the bridge?'

'Nothing on the bridge. I've got DC Singleton out scouting the area to try to find any cameras.'

Tim Donnelly approached. 'Hello, sir. We've drawn a blank so far, but I think I can pinpoint the area on the bridge where the body was dropped from. There are fresh scuff marks on the top rail, possibly where the killer has hauled the body over. It looks like she was held in place until a suitable vehicle was approaching the bridge. I've got my technicians working that area, looking for any stray prints or fibres. We may just get lucky.'

Danny wasn't convinced. 'And we might not. Has a fingertip search been done across the entire length of the bridge?'

'Not yet, but it will be.'

'Okay.' He glanced around, assessing the scene. 'The body was fully clothed but carried no identification. We may be missing a dropped handbag or purse somewhere in this area. I want a thorough search done while we still have the light.' He looked at Andy. 'I need to get back to Mansfield to start pulling things together. If I take your car, can you get a lift back with either Tim or Nigel? I want you to stay here and work the scene. Top priority, we need to identify this woman. I'll arrange a briefing for all available officers at nine o'clock tonight.'

Andy fished his keys from his pocket and handed them over. 'Okay, boss. Hopefully, we'll be back in time for that.'

Danny looked grim. 'Preferably with some evidence.'

50

9.00pm, 21 August 1987
MCIU Office, Mansfield Police Station

Danny stood at the front of the briefing room. 'Right, team. Let's get cracking. It's been a long day, and it's late, so Tim, let's start with you. What did you find at the bridge?'

'Forensically, not very much, I'm afraid. The only significant find was a bunch of fibres embedded under a sliver of flaking metal on the railing. They could be important, as they were at the point where the scuff marks are. To me, it looks like the offender had propped his forearms against the metal while he supported the victim, waiting for a truck to pass below. The fibres could be from the sleeves of whatever he was wearing.'

'That's good work. Anything else?'

'There are tyre marks on the grass verges of the bridge. It's far too dry for tread impressions, but what we were able to do was measure the distance between the front wheels. This will give us a ballpark idea of what vehicle was used. Preliminary enquiries suggest we're looking for a saloon-size vehicle. I know that's vague, but it could help to rule out a lot of vehicles later.'

'You can only find what's there, Tim. Good work on the fibres. Let me know how that develops, please. Rachel, can you brief everyone on what was found at the post-mortem, please?'

'Yes, sir. The deceased was a middle-aged female, possibly late fifties, early sixties. At the time of her death, she was wearing a tweed twin set. Photographs have been taken of the clothing and will be forming part of the Scenes of Crime bundle. Hopefully, we'll have them by tomorrow.'

Tim Donnelly interrupted, 'I can confirm the photographs will be ready for viewing tomorrow morning.'

Rachel acknowledged his words with a nod and continued, 'The cause of death was manual strangulation. Obviously, there are multiple injuries caused by her collision with the articulated vehicle on the motorway, but these are all post-mortem. The pathologist informed me that the deceased has never borne children. She has no operation scars that could aid identification. Dental impressions and fingerprints have been taken. Having said that, the left hand was too badly crushed to take any meaningful impressions, so we only really have prints from the right.'

'When her clothing was removed, did you find anything that could aid identification?' Danny asked.

'No, sir. The clothes all looked very worn, almost scruffy. There were no labels inside the clothing that could have helped us.'

'When will Professor Santos be sending her full written report?'

'She assured me you'll have it by tomorrow afternoon, sir.'

'Okay. Good work, Rachel.' Danny turned to DC Singleton and said, 'Nigel, how did you get on with CCTV?'

'Nothing so far, boss,' Nigel replied. 'I do have an appointment tomorrow morning to see the curator at Strelley Hall. The hall is now a business centre. There are numerous small businesses all renting office space inside the main hall. There are cameras at the main gates, but there was nobody there yesterday evening to access the recordings. I'll be on that first thing in the morning.'

'Okay. Keep me informed on that tomorrow.' Danny paused as he wrote a few notes into his enquiry log, and then said, 'Right. Finish up what you've got left to do, and then get off home. I want everyone back on duty at eight o'clock tomorrow morning. We now have three ongoing murder enquiries, so it's going to be all hands to the pump. You all need to keep abreast of every development in every case because we will need you to carry out enquiries on all three cases. We're going to be stretched to the limit, but if we can maintain our professionalism and drive, we'll get results. One last thing, as of this moment all rest days and annual leave days are cancelled. I'm sorry, but there's no alternative. If you've got leave booked in the next couple of weeks, come and see me tomorrow, and I'll try to work something out. See you in the morning.'

51

10.30am, 24 August 1987
2 Fairview Road, Woodthorpe, Nottingham

I t was a beautiful morning. The sun was shining, and it already felt incredibly warm. Solomon was relaxing with a cup of coffee and hot buttered crumpets, sitting outside on the patio at the back of the house.

The wonderful Chloe had brought the crumpets and coffee out to him. As he breathed in deeply, he could still faintly smell her delightful perfume.

He finished the last of the crumpets and took a sip of the hot strong coffee. This was how life should be. He reflected on the last couple of days of drama and hoped that things would settle down again now. All he wanted was to live his best life. He didn't need all the stress and anxiety of the last few weeks. He stared out at the back garden. The lawn was just beginning to look like it needed cutting.

He shouted towards the house, 'Chloe!'

The young carer came outside, with her usual beaming smile, and said, 'Did you call?'

'When's the gardener due? The lawn's just starting to look a bit shabby.'

'I'll have a look on the calendar, just a sec.'

She ducked back inside the house, returning seconds later.

'According to the calendar, they'll be here tomorrow morning. I'll be getting off in a minute; can I get you anything else before I go?'

'Another coffee would be great, thanks.'

She picked up the mug and plate and scooted off, saying, 'No problem.'

As he waited for his coffee, his mind wandered back to his hideous aunt Lillian. For a second, he imagined her handing him a lukewarm mug of tepid tea for breakfast every day. He shuddered at the thought of it.

His thoughts were broken by Chloe returning. She was holding a fresh mug of coffee in one hand and a letter in the other.

She grinned her sexy grin and said, 'Looks like somebody loves you, Saul. There's perfume on this letter.'

He blushed a little. 'Don't be daft. I never get letters, never mind love letters.'

She winked. 'They told me the quiet ones were the worst.'

Laughing as she walked away, she said, 'I'm back this evening. I'll cook you a lasagne for your tea. See you later.'

That was something he could look forward to. He smiled and waved at her back as she walked inside the house.

He waited until he heard the front door slam before picking up the strange letter. He held it to his nose and sniffed. It did indeed smell of perfume. Cheap and harsh, nothing like the classy scent Chloe wore. He looked at the handwriting on the envelope. It was written in biro by a weak, childlike hand. The lettering was spidery and disjointed.

Intrigued, he ripped the envelope open and began to read the letter.

He was stunned by the first line.

To my beautiful boyfriend, Saul

It was indeed a love letter.

The writer of the letter was annoyed because Saul hadn't been in touch. She demanded to know what was going on, and hoped that everything was okay between them. She hoped she hadn't scared him off by talking openly about marriage the last time they met.

Every line held yet another startling revelation. Solomon had no idea that his twin brother had been romantically involved with anyone, let alone discussed marriage. It was all very worrying.

He raced to the bottom of the letter. It was signed.

Your darling forever, Laura

Solomon's mind was in a spin.

He grabbed the letter, threw the remainder of his coffee on the grass and wheeled himself back inside the house. Once inside and away from any possible prying eyes, he jumped out of the chair and raced upstairs into his bedroom.

At the foot of the bed was a carved ottoman. It had spare bedding inside, but he knew Saul had always kept his most personal belongings in there as well. He had deliberately kept them after he had killed Saul, so he could keep up the pretence of being his twin.

He threw out the bedding and began to sift through the paperwork at the bottom of the ornate chest. After a minute of frantic searching, he found a bundle of letters tied together with string. He undid the knot. Inside the first envelope, he found several photographs of a blonde-haired girl sitting in a wheelchair and smiling towards the camera. He flipped over the first photo. Written on the back were four words, *Laura Higgins – Portland College*

He started to read the letters.

An hour later, he had finished reading the last letter. He stared open mouthed at the pile before him. Part of him felt angry that he had known so little about his brother's life.

How come he had never heard of Laura Higgins? Did his mother know about Saul's intention to marry this girl?

The main question at the forefront of his mind was, how was he going to resolve the problem of Laura? He realised that he needed to formally end the relationship. He also knew that before he did anything, he would need to make some discreet enquiries and look closer at Laura Higgins. He knew nothing about her. Until he did, he wouldn't know how she would react to him ending their love story.

He replaced the letters and the bedding in the ottoman and walked slowly downstairs.

Picking up the telephone, he dialled the number for Portland College. It was time to find out what he could about Laura Higgins.

52

11.30am, 24 August 1987
MCIU Office, Mansfield Police Station

The meeting had been called at short notice by Danny after Rob had received a telephone call that morning from PC Grainger. The football liaison officer had informed Rob about vital information he'd received from his counterpart in Leeds, PC Keenan.

Sitting in Danny's office, waiting for Nick Grainger to arrive, were Danny, Rob and Pete Hazard. There was an urgent knock on the door, and a breathless Nick Grainger walked in.

Danny greeted him. 'Grab a seat, Nick. Rob told me about the information you've had from Leeds. We need to discuss the best way to act upon that information. Perhaps you should start by telling us all exactly what PC Keenan told you.'

'Hi, everyone. My colleague Bill Keenan has been working hard, trying to establish credible intelligence about a group calling themselves the Halton Moor Casuals. The first time anyone had heard of them was when Dave Connors was interviewed. It's taken Bill a while, but he's finally got some good information on this group. The Halton Moor Casuals unsurprisingly all come from the Halton Moor estate in Leeds. They are a very tight, small group that are ultra-violent and like to use weapons as standard. One of the more interesting things he has turned up is that there seems to be a major conflict brewing between the hierarchy of the Leeds United Service Crew and the leadership of the Halton Moor Casuals. Bill is pursuing this, trying to find out more. From what he's told me so far, it seems like the person running the Casuals sees himself as the long-term leader of the Leeds United Service Crew.'

Nick took a sip of the coffee the team had left out for him before continuing. 'As you can imagine, that hasn't gone down too well with the current leadership. The other thing about the Casuals is that their violence is off the scale. They've made it clear that injuring rival fans isn't enough; they want bodies. Bill has found names hard to come by, but by systematically working through his informants, he's managed to find out that the leader of the Casuals is known as Dix or Dixie. The only other name he's been given so far is a lad who goes by "Creedo". After trawling through old intelligence reports submitted about the Leeds United Service Crew, he now thinks that "Creedo" is most likely a man named Sam Creedon.'

'Creedon rings a bell,' Pete Hazard interrupted. 'Do you remember the contact number Connors gave us that we dismissed as being a bullshit number because of who it belonged to? I'm sure the old woman's name was Creedon. Give me a second, boss.'

Pete rushed from the office and returned a minute later clutching an intelligence report. 'It's here,' he said excitedly.

'The telephone number found written on the *Shoot* magazine came back to an elderly woman called Mavis Creedon. Her address was 16 Chapel Street, Gravelythorpe. I wonder if that's anywhere near Halton Moor?'

Danny said, 'It won't take long to find out. Nick, fire a call into Bill Keenan and find out where Gravelythorpe is. Let's see if it's close to Halton Moor. Also, ask him to establish if there's any connection between Sam and Mavis Creedon.'

Ten minutes later, Nick returned. He was grinning from ear to ear.

'Come on, don't keep us in suspense,' Danny urged him. 'What did Bill tell you?'

Nick said, 'Firstly, Gravelythorpe is an estate right next to the Halton Moor estate. Secondly, the last known address for Sam Creedon was 16 Chapel Street in Gravelythorpe. I've just done a quick Voters Register check, and it confirms Mavis Creedon and Sam Creedon live at that address.'

Danny took a moment to think before clapping his hands together. 'Right, you three. I want you to get up to Leeds and liaise with Bill Keenan. I want you to find out everything you can about Sam Creedon and the Halton Moor Casuals. Let's establish who Creedon's associates are and then formulate a plan to start making arrests. One other thing that hasn't ever been established is how these shits got from Leeds to Nottingham on the day of the assault. Before you travel up to Leeds, let's find out if any vehicles were seen in the area around the cricket ground on the day of the assault.'

Pete Hazard spoke up. 'That enquiry has been done, boss.'

'And?'

'We only have one witness who states she saw what she thought was a Vauxhall Astra being driven at speed away from Hound Road. She couldn't give any details of the vehicle other than the make. She wasn't even sure if it was grey or blue in colour. She just remembered that the exhaust was blowing, and it made an awful racket.'

'Okay. Bear that in mind when you start digging in Leeds. I want to be kept informed of all developments. Don't forget.' He sighed. 'I've got Potter breathing down my neck this end.'

53

4.30pm, 24 August 1987
MCIU Office, Mansfield Police Station

Danny switched his computer terminal off and slipped his jacket on. It would be the first time in days that he would arrive home at a reasonable hour. He had been at work since six o'clock that morning, and his eyes felt tired and heavy.

He was looking forward to being able to spend a couple of hours with his baby daughter, Hayley, before she was put down for the night. It seemed like days had passed since he had last seen her or been able to cuddle her.

An abrupt knock on his office door snapped him away from all thoughts of home.

'Come in.'

Andy Wills walked in. 'Thought you'd want to know, boss. We've just identified the woman from the motorway.'

Danny sat back down. 'Go on.'

'We've got a positive identification from the fingerprints we took at the post-mortem. The dead woman had numerous convictions for shoplifting. Her name's Lillian Rhodes, date of birth is 16 March 1935.'

'Is she local?'

'No. Her last known address is Flat Three, Crispin Court, Douglas, on the Isle of Man.'

'How the hell does somebody from the Isle of Man end up being thrown from a motorway bridge in Nottinghamshire?' Danny pondered his own rhetorical question. Finally, he said, 'Andy, have you ever been to the Isle of Man?'

'No, sir.'

'I want you and Rachel on the next plane or ferry. I want you to make enquiries in Douglas and find out whatever you can about Lillian Rhodes. Once we establish who she was, and what she was doing here in Nottinghamshire, I think we'll be closer to catching her killer.'

'Okay, boss. I'll look into the travel arrangements and get over there as soon as possible.'

Danny smiled. 'You might need a couple of days over there, so find a cheap bed and breakfast, not the bloody Hilton hotel, okay?'

Andy held an innocent expression on his face and said, 'As if I would?' He grinned. 'I'll keep you informed, boss.'

'Thanks.'

As Danny left the police station, his mind was whirling. Things were progressing well on the football assault enquiry, and now they had a positive identification for the motorway bridge victim.

For the first time in days, he felt optimistic.

54

8.30pm, 24 August 1987
Mansfield, Nottinghamshire

The telephone call ringing in the hallway was both persistent and strident. Danny raced from the lounge and snatched the receiver off the hook just as Hayley started to cry upstairs.

He cursed under his breath as Sue stepped past him to go upstairs and settle their daughter back down again.

Danny, keeping his temper in check, murmured, 'Hello.'

'Sorry to call you at home, sir,' a familiar voice said. 'It's Inspector Henson in the control room. I've been asked to contact you by Staff Nurse Richards on the Intensive Care Unit at the Queen's Medical Centre. Apparently, there's a note for them to contact you if there are any changes in the condition of Mark Warden.'

With a feeling of dread rising within him, Danny asked, 'What's the message?'

The inspector said, 'I'll read it verbatim, sir. The condition of Mark Warden deteriorated this afternoon. Tests revealed that he had suffered a second bleed on the brain. He was taken to the operating theatre for emergency surgery at two thirty and has just returned. The operation went well, but the next forty-eight hours will be critical. That's the entire message, sir.'

'Have we been in touch with Mark's parents? They're going to need our support.'

'I'm sure the hospital will have updated them, but I'll arrange for officers to visit their address now and offer them our help.'

'Thanks. His parents are elderly, so they may need help with transportation to the hospital if they want to go in.'

'Leave it with me, sir. I'll get everything sorted. Fingers crossed our man can come through this.'

'Amen to that. Thanks for letting me know, and don't hesitate to call again if anything changes.'

'Will do, sir.'

Sue was just coming back down the stairs as Danny hung up. She whispered, 'Is everything okay? You look terrible.'

'It's that policeman who was beaten up by the football thugs, he's had a relapse.'

'A relapse?'

'He deteriorated this afternoon. His doctors have found a further bleed on his brain.'

'Is he in surgery?'

'No, he's out of surgery. Apparently, the surgery went well, but the hospital says the next forty-eight hours will be critical.'

Sue put her arms around her husband. 'I know you're going to anyway, but try not to worry, sweetheart. It's not uncommon for this to happen. Severe head trauma can result in two, or in some cases three or more, separate bleeds. The good news is it sounds like they found it quickly, and he's in the best place to deal with it.'

Danny sighed. 'Let's hope so. Has Hayley settled down okay?'

'Yeah, she's fine. She's like her dad, lying flat on her back and snoring her head off in seconds.'

Danny gave a weak smile. 'I suddenly feel exhausted. Do you fancy an early night?'

'Sounds good to me.'

55

The Feathers, Brayton, Selby, North Yorkshire

The drive along the A19 from Leeds to Selby into neighbouring North Yorkshire had been as expected. The road at that time of night was deathly quiet after the early evening commute.

What hadn't been expected was the telephone call he had received just as he was about to leave work for the day.

The call had been put through to his office by the switch-board. The operator had cautioned PC Bill Keenan that the caller refused to give his name. Bill Keenan had taken the call anyway. He instantly recognised the gravelly voice of Craig Jackson.

He had been in conversation with the self-styled leader of the Leeds United Service Crew on many occasions. Theirs was a precarious relationship. Although they regularly engaged in conversation, both men despised each other.

Jackson had been blunt on the telephone, saying, 'We need to talk. I'm told you've asked the club to start imposing life bans on some of my friends and associates. Which will prevent them attending home games.'

Bill had been surprised at just how well informed Jackson was. It was an idea he had mooted in what he had thought was a private conversation with the club secretary just two days ago.

Bill had bluffed with his reply. 'That's one of the many measures we're going to start imposing on you and your associates. You need to understand that football hooligans are yesterday's news. Football's big business now. Your violent behaviour is starting to interrupt the revenue stream for that business. By attacking that copper in Nottingham, your associates overstepped the mark.'

There had been silence on the telephone, so Bill had pressed on, 'I don't even know if I'm talking to the right person anymore. The word I'm hearing is that you're no longer the main man.'

That comment had the desired response. Jackson had reacted angrily. 'You heard wrong. Like I said, it's in both our interests to have a conversation, sooner rather than later. I'm not going to discuss it over the phone, so meet me at the Feathers pub in Brayton tonight at ten o'clock. Come alone. I have something you want.'

Bill Keenan had been intrigued, but he wasn't stupid.

These were violent men.

There was no way he was going to a pub, in an area he didn't know, on his own.

He had arranged for backup before driving to Brayton. Bill had also checked the pub on the intelligence systems and found nothing.

Now as he drove into the car park of the pub, he was on high alert.

The Feathers was an old coaching inn. It was in the centre of the small village and looked like the last place on earth you would find a football hooligan. He locked his car and looked around the car park. There were five or six other vehicles already parked. In the far corner sat a nondescript Ford Transit van. He could just make out the shapes of two men sitting in the front of the vehicle. He felt reassured; his backup was there if this was all a trap.

He walked into the lounge bar, scanning the room carefully. There were two couples obviously enjoying a romantic night out. At the far end of the room, sitting alone in a booth, he could see the hulking figure of Craig Jackson. He was staring into the pint of beer on the table in front of him and hadn't seen Bill Keenan walk in.

Bill walked to the bar and ordered a pint of bitter. Grabbing the frothing drink, he walked over to the booth and sat down opposite Jackson, who looked up at him for the first time.

Taking a sip of his beer, he said, 'I'm here, Craig. What have you got for me?'

A sly smile formed on the scarred face of Jackson. 'Not so fast, copper. I want some reassurances first.'

'Like that's ever going to happen. Say what you've got to say so I can go home.'

'I don't blame you for wanting to get home. You've got a lovely house. It's a bit isolated though, stuck in between those golf courses outside Shadwell. Do you play golf, Mr Keenan? Must be lonely in that cottage for your wife and your two daughters, what with you being out at work all the time.'

Bill Keenan could hear the barely veiled threats and growled, 'Don't fucking threaten me, Jackson.'

The sly smile was replaced with a deadly serious face, and Jackson said, 'But it's okay for you to threaten me and mine, Keenan. So what's the fucking difference?'

The tough policeman looked the hooligan in the eye and

said with real menace, 'The difference is, I'll take you down. Are we done?'

Jackson adopted a more conciliatory tone and said, 'Look. I'm not making any threats. I was just making a point, that's all. I still think what you suggested was bang out of order. There was never any need to ban my boys from home games before. So why now?'

'You know why. Your "boys" went too far in Nottingham.'

'Not my boys, Keenan.'

'I had heard that some of your boys are now beyond your control. I've also been told that your power is slipping.'

'Wrong on both counts. I can give you what you want tonight. I'll tell you exactly who attacked that copper, but I want something in return.'

'What's that?'

'I want all this nonsense about banning orders to disappear. Believe it or not, the football comes first for us. It always has and always will.'

The banning orders he had proposed had already been rejected out of hand by the club secretary anyway. Craig Jackson's informant had obviously been unaware of this fact.

Keenan said, 'I'll see what I can do. But it will be my bosses who make the final decision. Obviously, if I can say that the people responsible for the attack in Nottingham had no links to the Leeds United Service Crew, it would go a long way in helping them come to the right decision.'

'Is that the best you can do?'

'If you give me the people responsible for attacking that cop, I'll make sure the proposed banning orders never materialise. How's that?'

Jackson was silent; then he said quietly, 'You mentioned other measures you would be taking against us. What other measures?'

'Come off it, Craig. I'm not going to tell you that. Let me

just say this, if you go to football matches and don't cause violence and mayhem, there won't be a need for any other measures. I can't be straighter than that.'

'Fair enough. One more thing. Somebody told me that you were going to bug our houses and phones.'

'Fuck me!' Keenan almost laughed. 'Do I look like James Bond to you? Of course we're not.'

'Okay.'

'So, can we start talking names?'

'Fine.' He lowered his voice. 'It's a group calling themselves the Halton Moor Casuals. The four who caused the havoc in Nottingham were Dixie Bradder, Sam Creedon, Wes Handysides and Geoff Hoskins. Obviously, none of this came from me, right?'

'Okay. Fair enough. But don't you go giving them a heads-up now you've told me. If you do, I'll make sure things come back down on you. Understood?'

'Listen, Keenan. Dixie Bradder's an arrogant shit. I won't be telling him fuck all. He deserves exactly what's coming to him.'

Bill Keenan took another sip of his beer, then leaned forward and said quietly, 'There's one last thing, Jackson. If you ever make threats towards my family again, I'll fucking bury you. There'll be no arrest, no court case. I'll just take you for a drive up onto the moors, and you won't be coming back. Got it?'

Craig Jackson gave a malevolent grin as he stood up. 'Got it.'

56

9.00am, 25 August 1987
Leeds Central Police Station, Leeds, West Yorkshire

Bill Keenan smiled broadly as he opened the door to his office, allowing Rob Buxton, Pete Slater and Nick Grainger to enter.

Nick said, 'You look pleased with yourself, Bill. What's going on?'

'Let's just say I had a bit of a breakthrough last night. I had a clandestine meeting with Craig Jackson.'

'The main man from the Service Crew?'

'The very same. It seems that power struggle between the Service Crew and the Halton Moor Casuals is very real. Jackson has given them up.'

'What?'

'He gave me the names of the four men who attacked your colleague.'

'That's great news!' Rob said. 'Have you managed to confirm what he told you yet?'

'I only got the information late last night. I thought if we spend today researching the four men, finding out everything we can about them, we'll be able to carry out raids on their addresses at first light tomorrow. We can arrest them, get them in for questioning, and search their homes. I know from the preliminary digging I've done this morning that one of the men owns and drives a Vauxhall Astra. If we act quickly, forensic evidence may still be available.'

Rob asked, 'Who are these men?'

'The four names I've been given are Dixie Bradder, Sam Creedon, Wes Handysides and Geoff Hoskins. Bradder's the leader of the Halton Moor Casuals.'

57

3.00pm, 25 August 1987
Ballasalla Airport, Douglas, Isle of Man

Andy Wills and Rachel Moore walked out of the
arrivals hall at Ballasalla Airport on the Isle of
Man. The short flight from East Midlands airport
had taken less than an hour. Andy scanned the empty hall for
their contact. Prior to setting off that morning, he had telephoned Pulrose Police Station and arranged to be met on
arrival by Detective Sergeant Jenny Hays.

When Andy had explained the reason for their visit and
given the name of the murdered woman, Detective Sergeant
Hays had told him that Lillian Rhodes was well known to
many officers at Pulrose Police Station. She was a prolific
shop thief and, in Jenny's words, a royal pain in the arse.

The door from the car park into the arrivals hall burst
open. Andy and Rachel saw a tall, slender woman in her mid-
thirties rush inside. She was wearing a charcoal grey business
suit, and her dark hair was cut in a neat bob style. Her face
was flushed, and she looked harassed.

The woman looked urgently around the hall and quickly locked onto Andy and Rachel. She hurried over and said, 'Andy and Rachel?'

Andy raised his hand in greeting. 'Sergeant Hays? Thanks for meeting us here. I hope it wasn't any bother.'

Jenny Hays said, 'Call me Jenny. And it's no bother at all. I just got stuck in the afternoon school run traffic. The car's out the front, this way.'

As they walked outside to the car, which had been abandoned in the 'Police Only' parking bay directly outside the front doors, Jenny said, 'How long are you going to be here?'

Rachel said, 'Just a couple of days. I don't think our enquiries will take any longer than that.'

'Where are you staying?'

'Andy's got us booked into some dingy, backstreet hotel. He's tight like that.'

The two women laughed as they all got in the vehicle.

As they drove from the airport, along the main A5 road back to Douglas, Jenny said, 'It's like I said to you on the phone this morning, Andy. Loads of us at Pulrose nick have had dealings with Lillian Rhodes. I know she's got no family here on the island, but I think she did have relatives on the mainland.

'I'll get you settled in at your digs first; then we can go for a couple of beers and something to eat. I'll arrange for you to visit her address in the morning. I know the landlord of the flats where she was living. He'll have a duplicate key and will let us in.'

'That sounds like a plan to me, thanks,' Andy said.

'So where exactly have you booked to stay?'

'Contrary to what my colleague has told you, we're booked in for two nights at Cubbon House, on the seafront.'

Jenny wrinkled her nose in disgust and said, 'Seriously?'

A concerned Andy said, 'Why? What's wrong with Cubbon House?'

She laughed loudly. 'Nothing. It's a lovely little place. Your face was a picture though.'

Still chuckling, Jenny continued, 'Come on, let's get you two booked in. There's a great pub on the seafront that does nice food. We can have a drink, and I'll tell you all about our kleptomaniac friend Lillian Rhodes.'

58

6.15.am, 26 August 1987
Leeds, West Yorkshire

The briefing at Leeds Central had been detailed and had taken well over thirty minutes.

After a lengthy telephone conversation about the intended raids, Rob had taken Danny's advice and called in the services of the Special Operations Unit and Scenes of Crime teams led by Tim Donnelly from Nottinghamshire to undertake the raids that morning in the West Yorkshire police area.

Six SOU officers, alongside one of their counterparts from West Yorkshire, would visit each of the properties identified for the suspects. The arrest teams would set off in convoy. That convoy would comprise a Transit van containing the SOU officers, a CID car to convey the prisoner back to Leeds Central after arrest, and a smaller Ford Escort van containing Scenes of Crime personnel.

The initial arrests of the four violent offenders would be carried out by the Special Operations Unit officers. As soon as the prisoners were detained and compliant, they would be escorted away by CID personnel. A thorough search of the premises would then be carried out by SOU and Scenes of Crime staff.

Interviews with the suspects would be undertaken at Leeds Central by Rob Buxton, Pete Slater, Nick Grainger and Bill Keenan.

The four men had spent the entirety of the previous day researching their targets and carrying out the planning required to mount the operation effectively and safely.

One of the four men would accompany an arrest team to each of the target premises to identify and arrest the offenders.

It was going to be a long day.

Rob brought the briefing to a close, saying, 'I want to hit every address simultaneously at six forty-five. There are to be no phone calls. You know who we expect to find at each address. However, that intelligence doesn't consider any possible overnight visitors. We know these men are violent and are willing to use weapons. Make your entries hard and fast and secure the premises quickly. Expect resistance. If you don't get any, it will be a bonus. Good luck and stay safe.'

59

6.45.am, 26 August 1987
Ingleton Drive, Halton Moor, West Yorkshire

R ob sat in the front seat of the CID car; he was
feeling apprehensive. Ahead of him, he could see
the shadowy outlines of the men from the Special
Operations Unit. They were moving with purpose, silently
making their way down the side of the semi-detached house
at the centre of the Halton Moor estate.

This was the home address of Dixie Bradder. According
to intelligence reports, Bradder lived at the house with his
partner and five-year-old son. The council had provided
plans of the house, so the raid party knew exactly where the
main bedroom of the property would be.

Rob got out of the CID car and made his way to the property. He waited near the back door behind the line of SOU
officers.

He heard a single loud crash as the rear door of the property was smashed down. He could then hear shouts of
'Police!' as officers stormed into the house. The first two men

made their way straight up the stairs and into the master bedroom. Rob followed behind them.

Bradder was pulling on a pair of tracksuit bottoms as the officers burst into the bedroom. He stood up and raised his hands above his head. 'There's a young boy in the room next door!'

'Just do as you're told and no harm will come to you or your family.'

Bradder smiled. 'You'll get no problem from me, Officer. I just hope you're going to pay for all that damage.'

His girlfriend was sitting up in bed, with the duvet pulled around her. Bradder snarled at her, 'Get dressed and look after the boy.'

Ignoring any embarrassment she may have felt, the woman immediately jumped out of bed even though she was completely naked. She grabbed a dressing gown from the back of the bedroom door, slipped it on and started to walk out of the bedroom.

One officer said, 'Wait!'

Once his colleague had finished putting handcuffs on Bradder, the officer said, 'Now you can get the boy.'

She pushed past the officer, snarling, 'Fuck you, filth! Telling me what I can and can't do in my own home. Who the fuck do you think you are?'

Rob walked back down the stairs, followed by an officer gripping Bradder's arm.

As soon as they were downstairs, the officer in charge of the raid said to Rob, 'Premises secure; target arrested.'

Rob Buxton walked inside the living room and saw a bare-chested Dixie Bradder sitting in handcuffs on the settee. 'Get him a top to wear,' he said to one of the officers, 'and something to put on his feet.'

He turned to Bradder. 'Dixie Bradder, my name's Detective Inspector Buxton from Nottinghamshire CID. I'm arresting you on suspicion of the attempted murder of Mark Warden.'

Bradder chuckled. 'You've come a long way for fuck all. I haven't got a clue what you're talking about.'

Rob then led Bradder out to the CID car. As they walked out, Scenes of Crime officers moved in, ready to commence a thorough search of the house.

60

6.45.am, 26 August 1987
16 Chapel Street, Gravelythorpe, West Yorkshire

Sam Creedon sat at the breakfast table in the kitchen of his grandmother's house. As usual, his elderly grandmother was fussing around him, preparing his bacon and eggs and mug of sweet tea.

She always cooked the fried eggs just as he liked them, so the yolk was runny enough to dip the crispy bacon in. His tea would always be made in his Leeds United mug and the tea bag left in. The mug was one Sam's father had been given when he was a small boy.

Mavis Creedon doted on her only grandson, and he looked after her in return. Both of Sam's parents had died in a road accident, when the motorcycle ridden by his father had inexplicably left the road on the way to Whitby. His mother had been a pillion passenger, and both had died instantly as the motorcycle hit a dry-stone wall. Sam had been just three years old.

Under such tragic circumstances, his grandmother had

gladly taken the young child under her wing. Losing her only son so soon after losing her husband had been a heavy burden for Mavis to bear. Looking after young Sam had been a lifesaver for her. She had devoted her life to her grandson.

Times had become even harder eighteen months ago when she had been diagnosed with early onset dementia. Now, she had good days and bad days. Today was a good day. It meant she could fuss around Sam as though everything were normal. On the bad days, the roles would be reversed, and Sam did everything for his ailing grandparent.

Just lately, it seemed to Sam as though Mavis had more bad days than good ones.

As Sam greedily tucked into the last of his bacon and eggs, he had no idea that his life was about to be turned upside down. Just as he took a last mouthful of tea, there was an almighty bang as the front door came crashing in. He could hear shouts of 'Police' and the thunder of boots racing through the house.

He was startled and, in his shock, dropped his mug of tea. His favourite Leeds United mug shattered into a dozen pieces as it hit the hard tiles on the kitchen floor.

Within seconds, black-clad police officers had burst into the kitchen and grabbed him. He looked at his grandmother. All the colour had drained from her face.

'Alright, alright!' he shouted. 'I'm not going to cause any bother. Be careful around my grandma. She's not well, you bastards.'

As the handcuffs were tightened around his wrists, he was almost relieved to see one of the police officers helping his ageing grandmother to a chair. He looked over towards her and said, 'I'm sorry, Grandma. I didn't know this was going to happen.'

As she looked back at him, he expected a response, but

none came. He could see her eyes had already glassed over, and she stared into the middle distance.

What had been a good day had instantly become a bad day.

Inside, Sam was raging. He didn't want to make the situation worse by resisting arrest, so he just complied. As he was led from the kitchen, he growled, 'If anything happens to her, I'll kill the fucking lot of you.'

A voice behind him said, 'We'll look after her, Sam. Don't worry about your grandmother. Do you know why we're here?'

Sam wheeled around and could see a man wearing a smart, dark grey suit standing in the hallway.

'Who the fuck are you?' Sam snarled. 'I haven't got a clue why you're here. Why did you have to nick me here in front of my grandma?'

The man in the suit said, 'My name's Detective Sergeant Pete Hazard. I'm from Nottingham CID. Sam Creedon, you're under arrest for the attempted murder of Mark Warden.'

'That's bullshit.'

'Where are the keys for the Vauxhall Astra parked on the street outside?'

'I've no idea. It's not my car.'

'It's registered in your name and has been taxed and insured by you. I think we both know it's your car, Sam.'

'Fuck off! Do what you want. I'm not saying another word until I get a brief.'

SOU officers were already starting the detailed search of the premises.

Pete Hazard addressed the sergeant in charge: 'Any news from the other addresses?'

'All targets arrested.'

'That's great. Can you arrange for a full lift to transport the Vauxhall Astra back to the forensic examination bay at

Nottinghamshire HQ? I'm taking the prisoner to Leeds Central for questioning now. You know what we're looking for, so please do a thorough job of the search.'

The disgruntled sergeant replied, 'We always do a thorough search. I'll tell the Scenes of Crime staff to arrange for the full lift, and I'll get in touch with the local police and ask them to send a policewoman out to look after Mrs Creedon.'

'I tell you what, let's err on the side of caution, shall we. Instead of the local police, call an ambulance out, and make sure Mrs Creedon is checked over at the hospital. This must have all been a massive shock for her this morning. The last thing we want is for anything to happen to the old lady.'

'Will do.'

As they walked to the waiting CID car, Sam Creedon said, 'There's no need for the hospital; she'll be okay. My gran has dementia; shocks and sudden surprises don't do her any good.'

'Well, let's just be on the safe side, eh?'

'I appreciate that, thanks. Where are you taking the car?'

'Nottingham.'

'Fuck me. Will I get it back? I need it for work.'

'If there's nothing in your car, you'll get it back. Now it's best if you don't say anything else until we get back to Leeds Central.'

'Okay. This is all bullshit though.'

'Yeah.' Pete smiled grimly. 'You already said that.'

61

9.15am, 26 August 1987
Flat 3, Crispin Court, Douglas, Isle of Man

Detective Sergeant Jenny Hays had arrived at Cubbon House at exactly nine o'clock. There were no outward signs of the copious amounts of alcohol she had consumed at the lovely little pub on the seafront the previous evening.

It had been an informative discussion between Jenny, Andy Wills and Rachel Moore. The time had been spent over a nice meal and a few drinks, looking out over the sea. The detectives from Nottingham had learned a great deal about Lillian Rhodes from the experienced Isle of Man detective.

As the evening had drawn to a close, DS Hays had promised to pick up Andy and Rachel at nine o'clock sharp so they could search the home address of Lillian Rhodes.

True to her word, she had arrived on time, and together they had made the short drive across town to the imposing grand residence that was Crispin Court.

Well, seventy-five years ago, it would have been grand,

and it would have been imposing. It had been built at the turn of the century by a wealthy sea captain. The four-storey house looked out across the rooftops of Douglas, down towards the harbour. However, the once striking building now looked dilapidated, in a very poor state of repair, and was now a house of multi-occupancy. Each of its many rooms had been turned into a bedsit.

Jenny brought the CID car to a gentle stop. 'I've arranged to meet the landlord here so he can let us into Lillian's flat without causing any damage.'

Andy said, 'What's the landlord like?'

'Jeff Barber's sound. He owns a lot of the properties in Douglas that are rented by people on social benefit. His properties are also rented by a lot of our clientele, if you know what I mean. I try to maintain a good relationship with Jeff. He always keeps me informed where people are staying. I work with him as opposed to just smashing his flat doors down and arresting people. It works well. I get a lot of good intelligence from him, and he never asks for anything back.'

'I wish some of our landlords were as cooperative.'

'When I spoke to him last night about meeting us here this morning, he told me that he was planning to evict Lillian on her return. Apparently, she owes him six months' rent. He told me that he had given her plenty of opportunities to pay the arrears, but she never had. He had no idea she'd gone to England.'

'Did you tell him she was dead?'

'No. I'll let you make that call when you meet him. Personally, I don't see any harm in telling him. I don't think he would bump someone off over six months' unpaid rent, but it's your call, Andy. Here he is now.'

Jenny indicated a black Range Rover sport parked across the road.

Jeff Barber was in his sixties; a self-made millionaire, he

still enjoyed remaining hands-on with his property empire. It made life worthwhile for him. It was his reason for getting out of bed. He had tried retirement but had quickly got bored.

He smiled as he walked over the road to meet Jenny and her companions.

The detectives got out of their car, and Jenny made the introductions.

Jeff Barber said, 'So, Ms Rhodes is on the mainland now. Will she be coming back soon? She still owes me quite a chunk of outstanding rent.'

Andy said, 'We'll have a chat about Ms Rhodes shortly. Would you mind letting us in the flat first? So we can have a look around.'

'Of course. No problem. I don't know what state it will be in. I last came over here to collect the rent about six weeks ago. I was disgusted by her flat, and I told her so. It was filthy. I was shocked because previously she's always kept it so clean and tidy.'

As they walked into the flats and made their way upstairs, Rachel asked, 'How long has Ms Rhodes been your tenant?'

'I'd have to check, but it's got to be almost eight years.'

'Is she a good tenant?'

'Up until six months ago, yes. She's always been the perfect tenant. She always paid her rent on time and always looked after the place.'

'So what changed?'

'I don't know. I heard a rumour that she'd been made redundant, but she's never said anything to me about her work situation. I'm going to serve an eviction notice on her when she does get back from England. I hate doing that, but I've got no choice.'

Andy had made his decision.

'She won't be coming back, Mr Barber. Lillian Rhodes died in Nottingham.'

There was genuine shock on the landlord's face, and he said, 'Oh my God! That's awful. How?'

'She died in a road accident.'

'That's terrible. What was she doing in Nottingham?'

'That's what we're hoping to find out in her flat. Have you any idea why she would go to Nottingham?'

The landlord used a duplicate key to unlock the door and said, 'I haven't got a clue. She never said anything to me about Nottingham. I know she talked quite a bit with Patricia Wilson, the lady who lives upstairs at flat number six. She may know something. Do you need me to stay while you have a look around?'

'No, not at all,' Jenny said. 'We can close the door on the latch when we leave. I'll call you later and let you know if we take anything from the flat.'

'Thanks, Detective. Hopefully, you'll find six months' rent under the mattress.'

'If we do, you'll be the first to know.'

The landlord left, and the three detectives were left alone in the scruffy bedsit. The air was fetid and musty.

'Does anybody mind if I open a window?' Rachel asked.

When there were no objections, she pushed up the sash window and allowed a waft of fresh air to fill the flat.

The bedsit was one large room with a bay window. There was a kitchenette at one end with a sink, a cooker and a fridge. A single bed was tucked into one corner of the room, and a single armchair was stuck in front of the small television. There was a bookcase, a chest of drawers and a wardrobe. Everything in the space had seen better days.

Andy opened the fridge. Apart from an out-of-date cherry-flavoured yoghurt and a miniscule block of cheddar cheese, it was empty. He opened the only cupboard in the kitchenette and found a tin of Heinz baked beans and an almost empty bottle of tomato ketchup.

'She wasn't exactly living the high life, was she?'

Rachel and Jenny concentrated their search on the wardrobe and the chest of drawers. The wardrobe was almost empty, and the clothes that were inside were tatty and well worn. There were two pairs of flat shoes in the bottom of the wardrobe. The heels on both were worn down, and there were holes in the soles.

Jenny was rooting through paperwork in the top drawer. She held up a piece of paper. 'Well, this explains the lack of money. It's a notice of redundancy.'

'Was there any redundancy payment?' Andy asked.

Jenny shook her head. 'It says here that she didn't have enough time in to qualify for redundancy pay. That would also explain why she's been nicked for shoplifting so often recently. She was having to steal food.'

'Is there anything in there that would give us a clue what she was doing in Nottingham?'

'Nothing.'

Jenny then lifted the cushion from the single armchair and found an old address book that had been stuffed underneath. She flicked through the pages. 'There's a couple of Nottingham addresses in here.'

'Go on.'

'There was an address in Calverton, Nottingham, but that's been lined through. It's been replaced with 2 Fairview Road, Woodthorpe, Nottingham.'

With a note of astonishment in his voice, Andy said, 'I visited that address on Fairview Road recently.'

Rachel said, 'What for?'

'I went to check on some intelligence the occupant had given about a vehicle he'd seen around the time his neighbour was murdered. Gladys Miller lived on Fairview Road.'

Rachel said, 'Of course.' She looked at Jenny. 'Is there a name with that address?'

'Rebecca. That's it. There's no surname.'

'We're going to need to take that address book, Jenny.'

An exhibit label was completed, and the address book was slipped inside an evidence bag. The only other item taken from the bedsit was a small, wooden frame that contained a recent photograph of Lillian Rhodes. That too was bagged up, and the exhibit label signed.

'I think we're done here,' Andy said. 'Before we go, let's go and have a chat with Patricia Wilson who lives upstairs.'

As they left the sad, dog-eared bedsit, Jenny closed the door behind them, ensuring it closed securely on the Yale latch. All three detectives then made their way upstairs.

Jenny knocked on the door.

The door was opened on a security chain. The detectives could see the face of an old lady peering nervously through the two-inch gap.

Jenny smiled and held up her police identification so the old lady could see it through the gap.

'Mrs Wilson, we're from the CID. My colleagues here have travelled over from England to make enquiries about your neighbour Lillian Rhodes. I understand you were good friends with her. Would it be okay if we came in and asked you a few questions?'

The old lady sounded nervous when she said, 'I can't see your identification from there. Pass it to me so I can have a proper look with my glasses on.'

It was never a good idea for a police officer to physically part with their warrant card, but Jenny decided to make an exception. She handed the warrant card through the small gap.

The door was instantly slammed shut.

The detectives exchanged nervous glances as a worrying

couple of minutes passed before the door was opened again. This time there was no security chain, and Mrs Wilson handed the warrant card back to Jenny, saying, 'You'd better come in.'

The detectives entered the bedsit, which was similar in proportion to the one they had just searched. The similarity ended there. Mrs Wilson kept her room fastidiously clean and tidy. There was a small settee and an armchair, and two wooden chairs at a small table in the kitchenette.

As she sat down in the armchair, she said, 'Please take a seat.'

Jenny and Rachel sat on the settee opposite the old lady, and Andy sat on one of the wooden chairs.

Mrs Wilson said, 'Is Lillian alright?'

Jenny said gently, 'I'm really sorry, but Lillian is dead. She died in Nottingham.'

The old lady looked shocked. 'Oh, that's terrible. What on earth happened?'

'She had an accident, I'm afraid. Do you have any idea why Lillian was in Nottingham?'

'Yes, dear. She was going to visit her sister, who lives there.'

'Would that be Rebecca?'

'Yes. She only had one sister. I know she hadn't heard from her in ages. She was worried and wondered if everything was okay. Have you spoken to Rebecca yet?'

'No, we haven't. Not yet. What's Rebecca's surname?'

'I'm not sure. Lillian told me once that her sister had married a Jewish man. He had a strange surname. I think it was Beleg or Begel, something like that.'

'We've just come from Lillian's flat,' Andy said. 'It's pretty obvious that she was short of money. How could she afford to travel to England to see her sister?'

'I lent her the money to go. She was so worried and so

desperate to see her sister. She came here in tears one evening and begged me to lend her the money. I didn't have the heart to refuse her. I lost my own sister many years ago and would give anything to see her again, so I understood her need.'

'How much did you give her?'

'Two hundred pounds.'

'I'm really sorry, Mrs Wilson, but I don't think you'll ever get that money back.'

'Do you know if Lillian saw her sister before she died?'

'I'm sure she did, why?'

'Well then, if she did, it's money well spent. I don't care that I won't get it back.'

'That's extremely generous of you. How well did you know Lillian?'

'Not that well. She was always lovely to me, such a friendly person. She changed recently though. I noticed she looked sad all the time and was beginning to look a bit shabby. Do you know what I mean? She was always such a smart woman, very sharp and clever. In the last few months, she had been very unhappy, I think.'

'Did she ever talk to you about her family?'

'Not really. I knew her only family lived in England, and that they weren't that close.'

'Did her family ever visit her here?'

'No, never.'

'Is there anything else you can tell us about Lillian? Do you know if she had any enemies here on the island?'

'I don't know for certain, but I doubt it. Lillian was a harmless woman. She didn't have many friends, but she didn't have enemies either.'

'Okay. Thanks, Mrs Wilson. You've been a huge help to us, and I'm sorry about your money.'

'I'm glad I could help. Don't be sorry. It's only money.'

The detectives left the flat and made their way back to the car. Andy said, 'Are you okay for time, Jenny?'

'Sure.'

'I think we've done all we can do here. Would you be able to take us back to Cubbon House so we can collect our things? If you could take us to the airport straight after, I think we might as well catch the next flight to East Midlands. I know there's one scheduled to leave at two o'clock today.'

'Of course. It's no problem at all. If you need anything else from me, Andy, you've got my number.'

62

6.00pm, 26 August 1987
Leeds Central Police Station, Leeds, West Yorkshire

As soon as he had received word that all four suspects had been arrested as planned, Danny had made the decision to drive up to Leeds that morning.

It wasn't something he had planned to do. It just felt like the right thing to do. There was nothing breaking in Nottinghamshire that needed his attention, and if anything did crop up unexpectedly, he trusted Tina to deal with it until he returned the next day. So he had instructed DC Jefferies to field all his calls, and had driven north along the M1 to Leeds.

He now sat patiently waiting for Rob Buxton and Bill Keenan to finish the last of the interviews with Sam Creedon. Waiting in the CID office with him at Leeds Central police station were Pete Hazard, Nick Grainger and Tim Donnelly.

The interviews with the suspects had been ongoing throughout the day. Rob had teamed up with Bill Keenan to interview Dixie Bradder and Sam Creedon, while Pete

Hazard and Nick Grainger had concentrated their efforts on interviewing Wes Handysides and Geoff Hoskins.

There had been the usual delays, waiting for the solicitors requested by the suspects to arrive. Then further delays after disclosure had been given, and the solicitors spoke with their clients.

Interviewing was always a painfully slow process.

The suspects had all followed their legal advice to the letter and had answered every question with a well-rehearsed 'no comment' reply.

Undeterred by the 'no comment' responses, the detectives had patiently and painstakingly gone through the allegation and the circumstances leading up to the serious assault on the police officer in Nottingham.

Further interviews had concentrated on the items of clothing and weapons seized from the various addresses. Once again, these questions were met with either stony silence or the verbalised 'no comment' response.

It had been a frustrating day. After the euphoria of the planned arrests all going like clockwork, the interviews had been a disappointing, if not somewhat expected, anticlimax.

The final interview with Sam Creedon had been planned to concentrate on his Vauxhall Astra, the vehicle that had been seized for forensic examination. It would be important to establish certain points: Who had access to the car? Where had it been recently? Had it ever been driven to Nottingham?

This final interview with Creedon had started almost an hour ago, so the waiting group knew the interviewing detectives wouldn't be much longer.

Growing impatient, Nick said, 'Does anybody else want a coffee?'

The silence was deafening.

As Nick stood up to make himself a drink, the door opened. A stony-faced Rob walked in, followed by Bill.

Rob slammed the folder he was carrying down on the desk and said, 'Bloody "no comment" to every sodding question.'

Danny waited for Rob to calm down and then said quietly, 'It might not be a bad thing.'

Still seething below the surface, Rob snapped back, 'How on earth can a "no comment" interview ever be a good thing?'

Danny said, 'I know it's frustrating. I always hated "no comment" interviews too. But let's look at this dispassionately and concentrate on the evidence we have, or more correctly what we might have.'

Rob held his hands up and said, 'I'm listening, boss.'

Danny turned to Tim Donnelly and said, 'As I understand it, you've seized a lot of exhibits from each of the addresses. Let's start by going through that.'

Tim looked at his notepad. 'Right. From Bradder's address we've seized four pairs of training shoes, numerous pairs of trousers and jeans as well as weapons.'

'What were the weapons?'

'Three Stanley knives, found in his bedside drawers, not a toolbox. A baseball bat and a flick knife.'

'Okay. What about Handysides?'

'No weapons. Numerous training shoes, heavy boots and several pairs of jeans and trousers. It was very similar at Geoff Hoskins's house. We recovered two sets of knuckledusters and a Rambo knife from beneath his bed. As well as the usual training shoes and clothing.'

'And Sam Creedon?'

'The main item recovered from Creedon's address was obviously the Vauxhall Astra. That's been seized on a full lift and will be in the forensic bay at our headquarters now, ready for a full forensic examination. As well as the car, we've also seized similar clothing and footwear as the others. There was also a garishly coloured truncheon. It has some Spanish writing on it. I'd say it was probably purchased from a trip abroad, one of the Costas in Spain or similar. You see them for sale over there all the time.'

'Where was the truncheon found?'

'Beneath his bed. Interestingly, there are marks on it that can still be seen with the naked eye.'

'Blood?'

'Could be. I wanted to do the tests under lab conditions rather than risk losing samples using a field examination kit.'

'So all in all, we have a wealth of possible evidence seized from our offenders. We know there was a hell of a lot of blood at the scene of the assault on Mark Warden. There's every likelihood that some of that blood may have been transferred onto our suspects during the attack.

'I know your interviews will have been thorough and covered every reason possible for contact between the offenders and Mark Warden. If they chose to go "no comment" to those questions, they won't be able to come up with an excuse later. That's how "no comment" could suit us. We just need to get lucky and find that forensic evidence.'

Danny paused before turning to Tim. 'If you fast-track all these exhibits through the Forensic Science Service, how soon could we get answers?'

'Even fast-tracked, I'd say a month, to be on the safe side. That will also give me time to go over the Astra with a fine-tooth comb. I can then get any samples and swabs recovered from that sent off to the lab as well.'

'Right. Let's bail these muppets for four weeks. Make sure you insist on bail with strict conditions. They're not to have any contact or association with each other. They must have a permanent residence, which shouldn't be an issue. I also want them all to sign on at Leeds Central at different times every day. I want it made clear to them that when they eventually do answer their bail, it will be at Mansfield Police Station. I want them down on our turf.'

Rob and Pete stood up. Rob said, 'We'll go down to the custody office now and start sorting out their bail conditions with the sergeant.'

63

8.00am, 27 August 1987
MCIU Office, Mansfield Police Station

The telephone call he had just received from the control room inspector was just the tonic Danny had needed after a disappointing day in Leeds.

It was good news from the Queen's Medical Centre. PC Mark Warden had come through his most recent neurosurgery and continued to improve. He was to be taken off the critical list later that morning.

Danny sat back in his chair, a broad smile on his face. He had been praying the officer would get through his ordeal and make a full recovery. It had been a sustained and savage attack on him, and he was still fighting hard.

A small part of Danny was also pleased because he wanted the officer to be able to identify his assailants.

His thoughts were pushed to one side by a loud knock on his office door. 'Come in!'

Andy Wills and Rachel Moore walked in.

Andy said, 'Is now a good time to give you an update on the Lillian Rhodes enquiry?'

'Ah, yes. How was the Isle of Man?'

'It's a lovely place, and our visit was worthwhile. Our enquiries over there have uncovered a very strange coincidence.'

Danny frowned. 'I don't do coincidences. What did you find out that's so strange?'

'There's a possible link between Lillian Rhodes and a couple of our ongoing murder enquiries.'

Danny was now intrigued, 'Okay. Now, I'm all ears. Please explain.'

Rachel said, 'Lillian Rhodes was in Nottingham to visit her sister, Rebecca. Rebecca lived at 2 Fairview Road in Woodthorpe.'

'The same Fairview Road where Gladys Miller was murdered?'

'Yes, sir. Unbeknown to Lillian, her sister, Rebecca, took her own life some time ago. Only one of her sons lives at the address now.'

'You said there was a connection to two of our ongoing enquiries?'

'That address was also visited as part of the enquiry into the murder of Angela Billson. The son who still lives there was one of the last scheduled visits on Angela Billson's patient list before she was murdered.'

'I remember now. The man who lives there is wheelchair bound?'

'That's right, sir. Saul Peleg is a wheelchair user.'

'Andy, you revisited this Saul Peleg recently about the sighting of the van. How did you get on?'

'He's a very strange individual. Obviously, he has his problems, being confined to that wheelchair, but there was just something about him that set alarm bells ringing with me.'

'What do you mean?'

'After I'd spoken to him, I just couldn't shake off the feeling that he was lying to me. I've got nothing to back this up, and I don't really know if it takes us anywhere. After all, he's confined to a wheelchair, so he couldn't be involved in what we're investigating.'

Danny was silent for a moment. 'Andy, I want you to dig deeper into Saul Peleg. Start by going to see him again. This time ask him about Lillian Rhodes. I want you to gauge his reaction when he knows that we've linked her death to his address. I want you both to look closer into Angela Billson's involvement with Saul Peleg. We know she visited him as part of his welfare, but was she involved with him in any other way? Reinterview her colleagues at the health centre, her fellow health visitors. Let's see if there are any other possible links between them.'

Andy paused. 'I'm already leading on the enquiry into Lillian Rhodes's death, boss. Would it be okay if I allocate another detective to work alongside Rachel to do some of the legwork at the health centre?'

Danny nodded his assent. 'That's fine, but I do want you to go and interview Saul Peleg personally about Lillian Rhodes's visit.'

'Thanks. Will do.'

'Andy, also as part of your main enquiry, I want you to start backtracking Lillian Rhodes's journey from the Isle of Man to Nottingham. Was it by air or by ferry? Did she arrive in Nottingham by coach or by train? Most importantly, how did she travel from Nottingham city centre to Fairview Road? There could be a taxi firm out there that has the answer. It's going to be a lot of work, but we need to show Lillian Rhodes arriving at Fairview Road.'

Andy said, 'Will do.'

'Come and see me after you've spoken to Saul Peleg. Like I said, I don't believe in coincidences. There's something about all of this that just doesn't add up.'

64

2.00pm, 27 August 1987
2 Fairview Road, Woodthorpe, Nottingham

The sun was high in the sky, and the temperature was soaring. Solomon Peleg was lying on a sun lounger, soaking up the rays. He was sipping a cold beer and reading the latest James Herbert horror novel. Just lately, he felt like his own life had resembled a plotline from one of the esteemed writer's books.

He was wearing a pair of swim shorts, making the most of the warm sunshine, and the lounger was strategically placed so it couldn't be seen by any of the neighbours. The wheelchair was nearby, should he need it, and there was a pair of grey, loose-fitting jogging bottoms and a white T shirt draped over the back of the wheelchair.

The patio doors that led from the garden into the house were wide open so he could hear the doorbell. Even on a lovely day like this, he could never truly relax. As he sipped the cold beer, his mind was in turmoil.

Yesterday morning, after Chloe had left, he had typed a

letter out. It was in response to the one he had received from Laura Higgins. He had sat staring at the envelope for over an hour before finally posting it.

The fact that his brother, Saul, had been in a romantic relationship with this young woman, who was a resident at the nearby Portland Training College, had come as a complete shock to him.

He had only managed to establish a few facts about Laura Higgins. He had ascertained that she was originally from Gloucester but was now a residential student at the nearby college as she undertook rehabilitation for life-altering injuries.

Having done some digging, he could understand the attraction between her and his brother, Saul. There were similarities in their circumstances that would have drawn them together. He had injured his spine following a motor-cycle accident, and she had damaged her spine after a fall from a horse while taking part in a cross-country event.

Solomon still had no idea how they had met in the first place, and where they had continued to meet after their friendship blossomed into something more. Saul had certainly never brought her to the house. From the letters he had found and read, it appeared that most of their courting was done at Portland College.

The letter he had typed had been short and to the point. He had made some feeble excuses for not seeing her recently and had then simply ended the relationship. He had coldly informed Laura Higgins that he was no longer interested in her or their relationship, that it was over and she shouldn't bother contacting him again.

He had been deliberately blunt and unfeeling, in the hope that it had the desired effect and she wouldn't bother to contact him again.

A complication like Laura Higgins was the last thing he

needed. All he wanted now was to have some time without any more dramas.

He drained the last of the beer from his glass and stood up. He stretched his long back before walking into the kitchen and retrieving another cold can of Foster's from the fridge.

After sitting in the hot sun, the kitchen felt very cool, and he felt an involuntary shiver pass over his body. As he stepped back out into the sunshine, he popped the ring pull of the can. The beer was a little lively, and he hastily tipped the foaming liquid into his glass before it spilled all over the patio.

He was just about to take his first mouthful of the refreshing liquid when the doorbell rang.

'Shit!' he exclaimed aloud.

He put the glass on the small table near the lounger, slipped on the pair of jogging bottoms and the T shirt, then sat in the chair and wheeled himself into the house. Just as he reached the hallway, the doorbell rang again.

'Just a minute!' he shouted. 'I'll be there shortly.'

He opened the front door and saw a smartly dressed man he instantly recognised standing on the doorstep.

It was the detective sergeant who had been to the house recently, making enquiries about his elderly neighbour's death. He remembered him because he had pushed him about how he had seen the occupants of the vehicle. He had been like a dog with a bone.

As if to confirm his thoughts, the man thrust out his identification card and said, 'Mr Peleg, I don't know if you remember me. My name's Detective Sergeant Wills. I'm making enquiries into the recent death of a woman, and I'd like to ask you a few questions. Do you mind if I come inside for a moment?'

Solomon looked at the man and said, 'I thought I recognised you. I've already told you everything I could remember about the van I saw.'

Andy said, 'I haven't come about your neighbour Mrs Miller. This is something else I need to ask you about. May I come in?'

'Sorry. Of course, come in. I was out on the patio, enjoying the sunshine. Let's go out there, it's far too nice a day to be stuck inside.'

The detective walked behind Solomon as he wheeled his chair through the beautiful house. As they entered the kitchen, he said, 'I've already got a drink outside; can I get you anything?'

Andy shook his head and said, 'No, thanks, Mr Peleg. I'm fine.'

As they emerged into the bright sunshine, Solomon positioned the chair next to the small table where his beer sat. He gestured for the detective to take a seat on the garden furniture.

Andy glanced around the garden and noticed the crumpled towel on the lounger nearby.

Solomon applied the brake on his wheelchair and said, 'Please call me Saul. Mr Peleg's my dad, and I haven't seen him in donkey's years.' He let out a nervous chuckle at his own small joke and continued, 'You said this visit isn't about my neighbour?'

'Have you had any visitors to the house recently, Saul?'

'No.'

'Nobody at all?'

'No one. Why do you ask?'

'Do you know Lillian Rhodes?'

Solomon allowed a puzzled expression to pass over his face. 'I have an aunt whose name is Lillian something, but she lives on the Isle of Man.'

With a note of incredulity in his voice, Andy said, 'Don't you know your aunt's last name?'

'To be perfectly honest, I'm not sure. I haven't seen my aunt Lillian in years. She's estranged from the family, if that's the right expression.'

'When did you last see her?'

'Years ago. I would only have been a small boy of about eight or nine. My mum and dad never got on with her. We were still living at Calverton the last time I saw her.'

'Did your aunt know that your mother passed away recently?'

'I think Solomon let her know what had happened before he left for New Zealand. I couldn't tell you for certain if he did or not.'

Andy took out a small photograph from the folder he was carrying. It was the photo of Lillian Rhodes that he'd recovered from her flat in Douglas. He passed it across. 'Is this your aunt Lillian?'

'Yes, that's her. Look, when you asked to come in, you said you were making enquiries into the death of a woman. Now you're asking questions about my aunt. What's going on?'

'I'm afraid the dead woman I was referring to is, I believe, your aunt Lillian. She was found dead on the M1 motorway, below a bridge. She had been struck by a heavy goods vehicle.'

There wasn't a flicker of emotion on Solomon Peleg's face as he took in what he had just been told. He picked up his beer and took a long drink before saying, 'So she killed herself, too, just like her sister. It must run in the bloody family.'

Andy was a little taken aback by the coldness of the comment, but he said, 'Lillian Rhodes didn't take her own life.'

Suddenly, there was real interest shown by the man in the

wheelchair. He carefully put down his glass and said, 'What are you saying? That she was deliberately killed by somebody?'

'We believe your aunt was murdered before being dropped from the motorway bridge.'

Solomon tried to feign indifference, but it was impossible. He had been convinced that the articulated lorry ploughing into the body of his aunt would have mangled her body to such an extent that it would have covered his tracks.

He suddenly felt extremely hot and flustered. 'I just don't believe it,' he spluttered. 'Why would this happen on the motorway? What was she even doing over here? She lives on the Isle of Man.'

'Are you sure she hasn't contacted you?' Andy persisted. 'Maybe a letter? A telephone call, perhaps?'

'No. I haven't heard from her or seen her in years. Do you think she was on her way here to visit me?'

'It's possible. I've recently been to the Isle of Man and made enquiries in Douglas. It seems that your brother never got round to telling Lillian that her sister had died. I believe she was coming here to visit her sister.'

'That's impossible. The last time she came to visit, we were still living at Calverton. Have you made any enquiries in Calverton? It's possible she went to the old address. She certainly hasn't been here, Detective.'

'I will be visiting the Calverton address later today. But you're adamant your aunt has never been to this address?'

'She hasn't. I haven't seen her since I was a child. Do you know why she was coming here now? After all these years?'

'I know you said that the family were estranged, but I believe Lillian kept in touch with Rebecca. When she hadn't heard from your mother for a while, she was desperate to find out if everything was okay. She had no idea that her sister, your mother, was already dead.'

'I see. This is all so bizarre. This is all because my bloody brother couldn't do the one job he had to do. He was far too interested in swanning off and leaving me to it. It makes me so mad.'

'You haven't asked me where your aunt is now,' Andy said carefully. 'Don't you want to know?'

Peleg was silent for a long time; then he said, 'I don't know. I never knew the woman. What will happen to her now?'

Andy shrugged. 'Does she have any other family anywhere who could meet the cost of a funeral?'

He shook his head. 'I don't think so. Even if I knew where to contact him, which I don't, my father wouldn't be interested. I wouldn't be able to contact my brother either, not that he'd be bothered. I suppose it's going to be down to me to pay for her burial.'

Again, there was that coldness in his voice. Estranged or not, he was talking about his family, and it was obvious he couldn't care less.

Andy cleared his throat. 'That's everything for now, Saul. Thanks for your help.'

'No problem. Could you find out if I'll need to pay for her burial? And if I do, how much it will all cost?'

'Yes, I'll do that. I'll ask the coroner's officer to give you a call. He'll be able to apprise you of the situation better than I can. Do you want me to see myself out? It will save you coming back through the house.'

'Would you mind? This has all come as a bit of a shock to me.'

65

10.00am, 29 August 1987
Intensive Care Unit, Queen's Medical Centre, Nottingham

The small side room on Level E at the Queen's Medical Centre was bathed in a subdued blue light. The soft beeping sounds made by the machines in use had been turned down to the minimum. Everything had been done to reduce any kind of stimulation within the Intensive Care side room.

Ever since he had been brought here straight from the operating theatre, this room had been home for PC Mark Warden. He had initially undergone emergency surgery to stop the bleed on his brain caused by the head injuries he had sustained during the vicious assault at the end of July.

The only time he had left the intensive care unit was when he had been rushed back to theatre for a second emergency operation. This surgery had been required to stem a further, smaller bleed on his brain.

That was five days ago.

Staff Nurse Brenda Cookson had nursed Mark Warden

for much of the time since his first admission and subsequent return from theatre. Along with two other colleagues, she had been the person mainly responsible for his care.

Throughout his hospitalisation, Mark had been constantly monitored and never left alone. There was always an intensive care unit nurse with him. He had been intubated and ventilated, to aid his respiratory function, and was heavily sedated.

Brenda had just finished updating his medical notes. She had carefully written down the latest set of figures for his blood pressure, respiratory rate and heart rate. She had just replaced the notes on the end of the bed when the door opened. Consultant Neurosurgeon Heather McStay and Intensive Care Unit Sister Leigh Grant came quietly into the room.

Heather picked up the notes that Brenda had just placed at the foot of the bed, scanned them quickly and whispered, 'Good. He's been stable for over seventy-two hours now. Have you noticed any abnormal posturing or myoclonus? Any signs of a seizure at all?'

Brenda shook her head. 'Nothing. The only movement I've seen, and it's recorded in the notes, are two separate occasions when the patient has reached for the ET tube.'

The consultant reached forward and gently lifted each of Mark Warden's eyelids in turn. Using a penlight, she examined the pupils. 'Wonderful. His pupils are normal. They look equal, and there's no evidence of either of them being blown.'

Once again, she studied the medical records, this time paying greater attention to the blood pressure, heart rate and respiratory rate. She was checking for any signs of Cushing's triad. There was no indication in the notes of any high blood pressure or low respiratory or heart rate that could have indicated raised intercranial pressure. The danger signs of raised pressure around the brain would suggest a further cerebral oedema, another bleed.

Satisfied that there was no evidence to suggest this, Heather said to Sister Grant, 'I think we're ready to wake this patient, Leigh. Let's start reducing the levels of sedation this morning. I'm in theatre all morning, but I'll be at the hospital until seven o'clock tonight. Please contact me straight away if there are any issues.'

Leigh Grant nodded. 'Of course.'

Heather McStay smiled as she left the room. The operation to stem the smaller, secondary bleed had gone without a hitch. The policeman was recovering well.

'Isn't that fantastic news,' Leigh whispered to Brenda. 'Let's make a start and bring this man back to the land of the living, shall we?'

Brenda was grinning broadly as she updated the medical records with the consultant's recommendations. It had been touch-and-go whether her patient would survive at all, and now he was about to be taken off sedation and intubation. She just hoped that it wasn't too soon.

66

Danny was sitting in the canteen at headquarters, nursing a half-full cup of lukewarm coffee. He was spinning the cup in its saucer as he thought about the meeting he had just had with Detective Chief Superintendent Potter.

He hated these regular meetings with his line manager at the best of times, but when he had no real positive updates to give him, they became a total nightmare.

Unfortunately, the enquiries into the murders of Angela Billson, Gladys Miller and now Lillian Rhodes were all grinding slowly to a halt. Any meaningful leads had long since dried up. Danny had found himself working hard just trying to maintain his detectives' individual work ethic and enthusiasm.

As an experienced detective himself, he understood how difficult it was to maintain the same energy levels when all leads had been exhausted.

There wasn't any better news on the enquiry into the assault on PC Mark Warden. Yes, four Leeds United supporters had been arrested and questioned about the vicious assault, but they had all been subsequently bailed, pending forensic test results.

The voice of Tim Donnelly dragged him away from his troublesome thoughts.

'Mind if I join you?'

Before Danny could answer, Tim put his coffee on the table and sat down in the chair opposite him.

'What brings you to headquarters?'

Danny remained staring at his half-empty cup and said, 'What always brings me to headquarters. I had a meeting with Adrian Potter.'

'You looked miles away just now; did it go badly?'

'Not really. I just didn't have much to tell him.'

'That might change this afternoon.'

Danny finally looked up from his cup and saw that the Scenes of Crime man was smiling broadly.

'How come?'

'We've found traces of blood in all the passenger footwells of the Vauxhall Astra we seized in Leeds. The blood is a match for PC Mark Warden. As soon as I've finished this coffee, I'm joining the technicians in the forensic bay where we have the Vauxhall Astra. We're going to carry out a luminol procedure to see what else can be seen in those footwells.'

Danny grinned grimly. 'Excellent. Remind me, I know what luminol does, but never really understood how it works.'

'The science of it is this: a solution of luminol and an oxidant is sprayed over the area where you believe the blood has been. The iron in blood catalyses the luminescence, allowing detection of even trace elements of blood.'

'And if it's there, how can we produce it as evidence?'

'In a darkened room it creates a blue glow that lasts about thirty seconds per application. That glow can then be documented by a long-exposure photograph.'

'So you can photograph whatever's in those footwells?'

With a smug smile, Tim said, 'Yep.'

'And you're doing that now?'

'As soon as I've finished my coffee.'

'Forget your coffee! Come on, I want to see this for myself.'

Tim laughed and got to his feet.

Ten minutes later they were both standing in the vehicle bay, next to the Vauxhall Astra.

'Is everything ready?' Tim asked the technicians.

The female technician replied, 'We're ready, but you'll both need to put masks on. This stuff isn't good for your health.'

Danny and Tim quickly donned masks as the lights in the examination bay were dimmed.

As one of the technicians sprayed the solution, the other began taking photographs. Without getting in the way of the technicians, Danny leaned forward and was amazed at what he saw.

A blue glow shining from the front passenger footwell had illuminated the perfect impression of two prints from the soles of training shoes.

Danny exclaimed, 'Bloody hell!'

The process was repeated in the two passenger-seat footwells in the rear of the Astra. Impressions of footwear soles were also found in each of those footwells.

'Did you get those?' Danny asked the technician taking the photos.

The technician nodded. 'Yes, sir. The images are fantastic, very clear.'

'So what I'm seeing,' Danny said to Tim, 'is an impression of a training shoe sole that has at some time stood in the blood of PC Warden.'

'Exactly that.'

'And we've seized a lot of footwear from the raids in Leeds?'

'Yes, we did. These photographs will now be developed and magnified, and hopefully we'll be able to match the impressions of the soles to the shoes we've seized.'

'Have all those trainers already been tested for blood traces?'

'We'll do everything in order. First and foremost, we'll swab all the trainers to see if we can find any trace of Mark Warden's blood on them. Then we'll do comparison tests on the soles to see if we can match them to the impressions found in the car.'

Danny was ecstatic. 'And if you find blood and match the soles, we can put the owner of that shoe at the scene of PC Warden's assault.'

'Depending on where we find blood on the shoes, we may even be able to prove that not only were they there, but that they were also involved in the actual assault.'

'This is brilliant work, Tim. I won't keep you. Crack on as quickly as you can and keep me informed on how the tests on the seized trainers pan out.'

'Will do. The only downside so far is that we haven't found any traces of blood shown by the luminol solution on the driver's side.'

'For now, I'll gladly take what we've got. Great work.'

67

3.00pm, 29 August 1987
Bestwood Park Health Centre, Bestwood, Nottingham

'Are you sure I can't get you a tea or a coffee?'

The voice belonged to Louise Rogers, the practice manager at the Bestwood Park Health Centre.

DC Jagvir Singh shook his head, and Rachel Moore said, 'No, thanks, Mrs Rogers. We're fine.'

'I can't tell you what a shock this has been. When I came to work yesterday and was told the news, I was devastated. Angela was such a lovely woman and a fabulous health visitor. She's going to be sorely missed by an awful lot of people.'

Rachel said, 'So you haven't been spoken to by the police about her death yet?'

'No. I only came back to work yesterday. I've been off work for quite a while, recovering from an operation.'

Jagvir said, 'Didn't any of your work colleagues let you know what had happened?'

'No. You know what it's like, out of sight, out of mind. The first I heard about it was this morning when I was chatting to the other health visitors. I couldn't believe it.'

'How long had you known Angela Billson?'

'We've both worked here for the last eight years. I started a month after she did.'

'What was she like?'

'Wonderful. A lovely woman. She was one of those people who could never do enough for you. She was the same with her patients. She always went the extra mile.'

Rachel said, 'One of her patients was a man called Saul Peleg. He's a wheelchair user who lives in Woodthorpe. Do you know if there was a specific reason why Angela had Saul as a patient?'

'Saul Peleg is a paraplegic. One of the major difficulties people with that disability experience is effective bowel and bladder control. This can lead to major self-esteem problems, as well as clinical ones.'

'Would Angela deal with those incontinence issues?'

'No. That wasn't her role. She would visit Saul to see if he was coping well mentally. She would also ensure that he had supplies of catheters, bags and any other medical supplies he may need.'

'And if Angela didn't do that for Saul, who would?'

'Saul Peleg was able to catheterise himself. His mother was very patient with him in the early days of his disability. She instructed him how to do it for himself. As a result, he was able to manage his bladder issues very well indeed. As for his bowel movements, he paid for a private health care company to visit him every other day to manage his bowel issues.'

Rachel said, 'Do you know which private health care company?'

'No. I'm sorry. We don't keep that information.'

'Did Angela ever mention Saul Peleg to you?'

'Oh, yes. We talked about him a lot. I think she had a real soft spot for Saul, what with everything he had been through. She told me all about Saul and the great love story.'

'Excuse me? What love story? Angela wasn't involved romantically with Saul Peleg, was she?'

Louise Rogers laughed. 'Don't be silly. Angela was far too professional for that. No, she played the role of cupid in his love story.'

Rachel looked bemused and said, 'Now you've really lost me, Mrs Rogers.'

'Let me explain. Angela persuaded Saul to start attending the social nights they hold at the Portland Training College. They're nothing much, just small discos and quiz nights put on by the staff and volunteers. It helps their disabled residents to mix with each other.'

'Go on.'

'Saul took a lot of persuading, but eventually he started going to these social nights. And it was at one of these events that he first met Laura.'

'Who's Laura?'

'Laura Higgins is a resident student at Portland Training College. Angela told me that Laura was lonely, as she was away from home. This is where the cupid bit comes in. She introduced the two of them when she was working at the social club one evening.'

'Angela Billson used to run the social nights at Portland College, as well?'

'Yes. She used to volunteer. She said it was a good bridge between the community health visitor work she did and her care of the disabled. Like I said before, she was a lovely woman, devoted to her job.'

'And she played cupid by introducing Saul Peleg and Laura Higgins to each other?' Jagvir asked.

'That's it. The last time I spoke to Angela, she was really

excited because Laura and Saul were talking about getting married and had invited her to their wedding.'

'How can we get in touch with Laura?'

'Laura's still a resident at Portland College. Just go to the college and ask at reception.'

'Thanks, Louise, this has been a huge help to us. I'm really sorry for the loss of your friend.'

Louise Rogers sniffed. 'I still can't quite believe it.'

As they walked from the health centre to their car, Jagvir said, 'Portland Training College?'

'And don't spare the horses. Our Mr Peleg's a very dark horse. I've already spoken to him a couple of times, and he never mentioned Laura Higgins at all. Makes you wonder why? Most people planning a wedding are usually boring everyone else to death by constantly talking about the details of their impending marriage. Let's see if Laura Higgins is any more forthcoming about this great love story.'

68

3.30pm, 29 August 1987
Portland Training College, Nottingham

Rachel and Jag waited patiently in the reception area at Portland Training College. She looked at her watch. Fifteen minutes had passed since she had explained to the receptionist that she needed to speak to Laura Higgins about Angela Billson and Saul Peleg. Fifteen minutes was plenty of time for the student to have made her way from the classroom to reception.

She stood up and walked back over to the reception desk. 'Is there a problem? Surely Laura would have got here by now.'

The young receptionist also glanced at her watch, then said, 'It does only take five minutes to get from the classrooms to here. Just a minute, I'll ring through again.'

Rachel waited at the desk, listening to half a conversation. Eventually, the receptionist said, 'The tutor said Laura doesn't want to speak to you; she's too upset.'

Rachel said patiently, 'It's upsetting for everyone. That's

why we need to speak to the people who knew Angela Billson.'

'It's not Angela she's upset about, it's Saul Peleg.'

'Even so, we still need to talk to her today. Is she still in the classroom? We can walk down and see her there.'

'She's not there now. She's gone back to her bungalow.'

Rachel was determined. 'Look, it's imperative that we speak to Laura today. Can you direct us to the bungalows, please?'

The receptionist realised that the detective wasn't going to be easily dissuaded. 'Just a minute. I'll get her tutor to come and see you here first. If she thinks it's appropriate, she'll take you to see Laura.'

'Thank you. I appreciate your help.'

'No problem, take a seat.'

Five minutes later, a harassed-looking woman walked into reception. She made a beeline straight for Rachel and Jag.

Not wasting any time on pleasantries, the woman said abruptly, 'Detectives, I'm Ms Carmichael, Laura's tutor. What's so urgent that you've got to speak to her today?'

Rachel stood up. 'I'm DC Moore; this is DC Singh. The urgency is we're trying to solve the murder of a woman who did an awful lot of work for this college. We need to speak to everyone who may be able to help us. We're not unfeeling, and we'll be very careful and considerate in the way we question Laura. I appreciate how upsetting it is to lose someone in this fashion.'

What happened next surprised Rachel.

Ms Carmichael softened instantly. 'Please sit down, Detective,' she said. 'I need to explain to you why Laura's so upset. It has nothing to do with the tragic death of Angela Billson.'

Rachel sat down. 'Go on?'

'I take it that you're already aware of the romantic involvement between Saul and Laura, which was initiated by Angela?'

'We've only just been made aware of it by the staff at Bestwood Health Centre, but yes, I'm aware of it. Why would us being here upset Laura so much?'

'It's all to do with her relationship with Saul. For some inexplicable reason, he's broken off the engagement between the two of them. Understandably, this has upset her greatly, as she can't understand his sudden change of heart.'

Rachel was deep in thought. None of this made any sense. It was now even more important that she speak to Laura. 'We really do need to speak to Laura about Saul Peleg. I can't say too much to you, but something just isn't right here. Do you think she'll talk to us if you're there as well?'

'If you really think it's that important, I'll come with you to her bungalow. Obviously, I can't make her talk to you, but I suppose if I'm there, she might. Follow me.'

The two detectives walked behind Ms Carmichael through the beautiful, landscaped gardens of the college to the residential bungalows.

She stopped outside number seven and knocked quietly on the door.

The door was opened by a young woman in a wheelchair. She had long blonde hair tied back in a ponytail and soulful brown eyes. On closer inspection, Rachel could see that her eyes were bloodshot and red rimmed. It was obvious the young woman had been crying.

'Hello, Laura,' Rachel said gently. 'My name's Rachel. I can see that you're upset, and that you probably don't want to talk to anyone, let alone detectives, about Saul. I'm sorry if this upsets you, but I really think it's vitally important we have a chat with you today. Would that be okay?'

Laura retrieved a tissue from the sleeve of her navy-blue

tracksuit and wiped her eyes. After a few seconds she said, 'You'd better come in.'

Ms Carmichael said, 'Would you like me to stay, Laura? If you want me to, I will.'

Laura shook her head and said, 'I'll be fine, thanks.'

The two detectives followed Laura inside the bungalow and into the open-plan living space. At one end of the room, there was a sideboard and a three-seater settee in front of a television set.

'Take a seat, please. Can I get you a drink?'

'I'll make the drinks,' Jagvir said, 'while you have a chat. What does everyone want?'

Rachel was impressed by Jag's thoughtful actions. She realised that he knew there was more chance of Laura talking openly to Rachel, so he had made himself scarce.

Rachel said, 'Coffee would be great, Jag, thanks.'

Laura said, 'Coffee for me too. The kitchen's just through that door. Everything's in the cupboard below the kettle. Everything's down low so I can reach it.'

Jagvir said cheerily, 'Two coffees coming right up.'

'I know he's the last person you want to talk about right now,' Rachel said, looking at Laura, 'but I'd like you to tell me about Saul.'

'I take it Ms Carmichael told you that me and Saul aren't together now?'

'Yes, she did. So I understand how difficult this is for you. What happened?'

'That's just it, Detective. I don't know what happened. One minute, we were fine. Making plans, having fun. The next thing, there's no contact for weeks, and then this arrived.'

She pushed herself over towards a set of drawers, opened the top drawer and retrieved an envelope, which she then handed to Rachel.

'Go on, read it.'

Rachel took the typed letter from the envelope and began to read. The language used in the short letter was cold and unfeeling. It was devoid of all emotion and very matter of fact. It was a letter instructing Laura that the relationship was over, and that she wasn't to contact him again.

The detective now understood completely why Laura was so upset. It was never easy when a relationship ended, but for one to be ended in this way was particularly cold and heartless.

Rachel placed the letter back inside the envelope and handed it to Laura, who put it back in the drawer and said, 'I've kept it so when I start to miss Saul, I can read his uncaring words again. It helps me realise that I'm better off without him.'

'You said, one minute you were fine, then the next thing, no contact at all. What did you mean by that expression, no contact?'

'Saul used to telephone me every day. We would sit and chat for hours, mostly about rubbish stuff. We just enjoyed hearing each other's voices, I suppose. When I first came here from Gloucester, I was very lonely. Saul changed all that. Then one day, for no reason, the telephone calls stopped, and Saul never came to visit anymore.'

'Did you try to call him?'

'No, I didn't. I was angry and hurt that he'd stopped visiting or calling me. I know this might sound stupid, but I didn't want to sound like I was begging.'

'I totally get that, Laura. When did the telephone calls stop?'

'Let me get my diary, just a minute.'

She wheeled herself into the bedroom next door, returning a minute later with a pink diary on her lap.

Jag walked back into the lounge area and put the coffee

mugs on the small coffee table in front of the settee. 'I'm just popping outside for a cigarette.'

Rachel said, 'Thanks, Jag.'

Laura flicked through the pages of the diary. 'Here it is.' She handed the diary to Rachel. There was a one-line entry. It read, 'Saul didn't call!'

Rachel noted the date; it was the sixteenth of June.

She handed the diary back and said, 'Did he phone you on the fifteenth?'

'Yeah. He was his usual funny self. We had a laugh. We were chatting until about eight o'clock that night. I remember it because we were talking about the food we were going to choose for our wedding reception.'

She started to choke up, and Rachel said quickly, 'So there was nothing said that night that gave you any hint of what was to come next?'

'Nothing. Everything seemed fine.'

'What do you make of the letter he sent you?'

'I don't understand. What do you mean?'

'You've described to me, on a couple of occasions now, how you and Saul liked a laugh. Was he always good fun to be with?'

'Always.'

'That letter is so cold. Does it sound like Saul to you?'

'Not the Saul I fell in love with, that's for sure.'

'I know his mother died sometime around that date. Do you think that could have changed him?'

'We talked a lot about his mum taking her own life. That was a massive shock to him. On the night before his mother did that awful thing, we talked about our future living together at Fairview Road. He told me that night that it would just be the three of us, as his brother, Solomon, was leaving. He said something about there being a huge row between his mum and Solomon, and that she had told him to leave the family home.'

There was a pause as an emotional Laura swallowed hard and dabbed her eyes.

Having composed herself, she said, 'After a couple of weeks, I think Saul was starting to come to terms with his mum's death. Then there was another shock shortly afterwards, when Solomon decided he wanted to leave the country. It was after his brother moved out that Saul stopped calling me. I think he must have felt that everything was changing too quickly. Perhaps it all became too much for him, and that's why he called the engagement off? One minute, we were busy planning our future life together, then nothing.'

Laura dabbed more tears from her eyes as she began to get upset again.

Rachel said quickly, 'Did Saul's mother know about your plans?'

'Oh, yes. She was all for it. She was so happy for Saul. He told me that his mother was really looking forward to the two of us moving into Fairview Road as man and wife. Which makes what she did even harder to understand.'

'What about his brother, Solomon?'

'Don't talk to me about that idiot.'

'Why?'

'Saul and his brother never got on. Saul once confided in me that the accident that had caused his spinal injury was all Solomon's fault. He really despised his brother, and from what Saul told me, I think Solomon felt the same way.'

'Did you ever meet Solomon?'

'No. I never went to Saul's house. I can't drive, so he always came here in his Motability car. We had made plans to go and see his mum and brother at Fairview Road. That never happened because Rebecca took her own life, and then Solomon moved abroad.'

'I've spoken to Saul a couple of times about Angela Billson. He never mentioned to me that he'd recently been engaged to be married. Do you find that odd?'

'Not really. At one time, it was all either of us spoke about. You've read the letter; he obviously doesn't feel the same way about me now. I just don't understand how a person can change so much in such a short space of time. It's as though he's turned into a different person.'

'Me neither, Laura. That's men for you, I suppose. I'm sorry to have to drag all this up, and I appreciate you talking to me. If you think of anything else, can you give me a call, please? I'll leave you my number.'

'Here, just write your number in the back of my diary.'

As Rachel wrote the number down, she said, 'When had you planned to get married?'

'At the end of next month, the thirtieth of September. I'm starting to think that I've had a narrow escape.'

'It certainly sounds like it. You wouldn't want to spend the rest of your life with someone who can change that much overnight, would you?'

'Definitely not. I'm glad I've spoken to you, Rachel. I feel a bit better about things now.'

Rachel left the bungalow and found Jagvir loitering near the front door. 'How did it go?'

'It was very informative. Thanks for making yourself scarce, Jag. I don't think she would have opened up to me like that if we'd both been there.'

'That's what I thought. I do think sometimes, you know.'

'Yeah, right. I know you do. I think we need to get back to Mansfield. Before we go off duty, I need to talk to Andy.'

69

5.00pm, 29 August 1987
MCIU Office, Mansfield Police Station

When Danny walked into the main office, he could see Andy and Rachel with their heads together. They were talking in excited tones. Even though he was on his way home, curiosity got the better of him.

'You two look very pleased with yourselves; have you had a productive day?'

Andy looked up at Danny and, with a note of seriousness in his voice, said, 'Actually, have you got a minute, boss. There's something we need to discuss with you.'

'Of course, let's go into my office.'

As the three of them walked into Danny's office, Andy said, 'I warn you now. This is going to sound a bit crazy.'

Danny took his jacket off and sat down. He gestured for Andy and Rachel to take a seat and said, 'Okay. What's going to sound crazy?'

Rachel started the discussion. 'It's about Saul Peleg.'

'The guy in the wheelchair who lives on Fairview Road? The one you have your suspicions about?'

'That's him. Well, those suspicions have just been ramped up even higher. Today, I found another link between him and our victim Angela Billson. As well as visiting his home as a health visitor, Angela was also instrumental in introducing Saul to the social events at Portland Training College.'

'Okay?'

'After finding out that Angela worked as a volunteer at Portland, we also made enquiries there. We've now ascertained that not only did she introduce Saul Peleg to the social nights, but she was also responsible for introducing him to his fiancée.'

'Who's the fiancée?'

'A woman named Laura Higgins. She's a resident student at the college and is also a wheelchair user. I interviewed Laura this afternoon, and she told me that up until very recently, she and Saul were engaged to be married. They planned on getting married next month, but Saul ended their relationship suddenly and without any reason.'

'There's always a reason. Just because Laura Higgins didn't tell you about it doesn't mean there isn't one there. Didn't you know about this already? Surely Saul would have mentioned this to us when he was spoken to before?'

'He's been seen on three occasions, and he's never even mentioned Portland Training College, never mind having a fiancée and planning to get married.'

'Okay. This is all very interesting. But does it really help us to move forward the Angela Billson enquiry?'

'Well, this is the crazy part, sir. It was something that Laura said to me today that started me thinking.'

Danny was intrigued. 'Go on?'

'The way he broke off the relationship was by letter and very cold. No, it was more than cold, it was heartless and uncaring. Laura told me that it wasn't like Saul at all. He was always very caring and loving towards her. She told me that it was as if Saul had turned into a different person.'

Danny stared at her, nonplussed. 'What are you saying?'

Andy took over. 'Saul Peleg now features prominently in all three of our recent murders. Angela Billson because of his connections with her just prior to her disappearance. He may have been one of the last people to see her alive, and now we've found this second connection with her, at Portland Training College. His neighbour Gladys Miller, where he provided what DI Cartwright is convinced is a false lead. Finally, his estranged aunt, Lillian Rhodes, travels from the Isle of Man to visit Saul Peleg's home and is found dead on the M1 motorway. Although he's closely tied to all these enquiries, we've always discounted his involvement for the same reason.'

'The fact that he's a paraplegic and is wheelchair bound.'

'Exactly. But what if Saul Peleg isn't a paraplegic?'

Andy paused for a moment. 'When I informed him of the horrific circumstances of his aunt Lillian's death, he didn't show a single flicker of emotion. The man has expressionless, dead-fish eyes.'

Danny tried to take it all in. 'It's all very interesting as a theory. Do you have anything else to back up this idea of yours?'

Andy said, 'I've spent the day researching the entire Peleg family. There's one loose end that I can't bottom out.'

'Which is?'

'The current whereabouts of Saul Peleg's brother.'

'I thought he'd moved abroad following the death of their mother?'

'That's what Saul said. He's the one who told us that Solomon had gone to New Zealand to start a new life. I've spent hours today researching all the flights from the UK to New Zealand. I've concentrated on the time Saul told us that Solomon had left the country. I've made enquiries at every airport and can find no trace of Solomon Peleg on any flight manifest.'

'Could he have travelled under a false name?'

'For what reason? He isn't a criminal trying to evade capture, he was just a man emigrating to start a new life. I've even made enquiries with New Zealand customs and excise to see if they have any record of Solomon Peleg entering the country from any country other than the UK. They could find nothing.'

'So are you thinking Solomon never left the UK?'

'If he did, we don't know how. I'm pretty certain he hasn't gone to New Zealand, as Saul suggested.'

'There's one other thing,' Rachel said. 'Don't forget Saul and Solomon Peleg are identical twins.'

'Do we have photographs of them both?'

'I've seen photographs of them both at Fairview Road,' Andy confirmed. 'They're truly identical. Other than the fact that one was sitting in a wheelchair and the other standing, I couldn't tell them apart.'

'Have you seen Saul Peleg's medical history and spoken to his doctors?'

'I've spoken to his doctor. He wouldn't go into any detail, for obvious reasons. He did confirm that Saul Peleg is a paraplegic and will be confined to a wheelchair for the rest of his life. There was no doubt about the severity of the injury. That's why he was awarded such a high sum in damages at the high court.'

'Damages?'

'Yes, sir. The spinal injury he suffered was caused by

medical negligence following a motorcycle accident. Saul Peleg was awarded a seven-figure sum.'

'Which makes him, financially, a very rich man.'

Danny sat back in his chair as the reality of what his detectives were suggesting began to sink in. 'We know that Saul's a genuine paraplegic. So there's no way he could be involved in the crimes we're investigating. Your theory relies on the fact that, somehow, he isn't confined to that wheelchair. That's the only way he could be involved in these deaths.'

Rachel said aloud what they were all starting to think. 'What if Saul isn't Saul? What if it's his twin brother, Solomon, sitting in the wheelchair when we visit Fairview Road? What if it was Solomon who wrote the crushing letter to Laura Higgins?'

'Two questions though,' Danny said. 'Why would Solomon want to spend his life living as a paraplegic? And if that is what's happening here, where is Saul Peleg?'

Andy said, 'The answer to the first question could be something as simple as money. I've researched Solomon, and he's flitted from dead-end job to dead-end job. He's only survived because of his family's generosity. Even when he couldn't contribute financially in any way, they've always allowed him to remain at the family home. Maybe he's decided he didn't want to rely on their charity anymore? Perhaps he's come up with a plan that would enable him to have it all?'

Danny was silent. The two detectives sitting opposite remained quiet, allowing him time to think.

Finally, he said, 'Thanks for bringing this to me. It's great work, both of you. I need time to process what you've told me. Andy, can you let me have all the paperwork detailing your research into the Peleg family. I want to know exactly what other enquiries you've completed. I need to have a serious think about how to move forward with this. I think I need to keep this within the department for now. I don't see any way that Potter will allow us to act on this sort of tenuous information. Leave it with me; I'll give it some thought and speak to you both in the morning.'

70

10.00am, 30 August 1987
MCIU Office, Mansfield Police Station

After carefully considering his options to move the enquiry forward after speaking to Andy and Rachel the night before, Danny had decided on a course of action and had called a briefing.

The last person to arrive for that briefing was Chief Inspector Jim Chambers from the Special Operations Unit. Already waiting in the briefing room were DI Cartwright, DS Wills and DC Moore.

Danny said, 'Thanks for coming over so promptly, Jim. I'm going to need the help of your department for this operation.'

'I'm always happy to help if I can. What's the job?'

'I want to set up observations on an individual. I'll need staff to maintain a static observation point on the target's home address.'

'I see. Would this be a twenty-four-hour commitment?'

'It would be twenty-four hours a day,' Danny confirmed,

'and open ended. I want to run it until I can show, one way or another, that our suspect's either involved or not.'

'A twenty-four-hour commitment such as that will take a lot of staff. I could probably provide that level of manpower for two weeks, at a push. Do you think that will be long enough?'

'I would hope so, but the truth is, I just don't know. However, I would rather run the operation for just two weeks than not at all.'

'Our diary is pretty clear at the moment. The football commitments don't start in earnest until next month, and we have no visiting royals or politicians whom we need to provide security for. So I will be able to provide you with a full section for your operation.

'I'll speak with Sergeant Turner, who supervises C Section, and get him to liaise with you. That way the two of you can thrash out all the details of the operation and when exactly you want it to start. He can organise his ten men to provide the twenty-four-hour-a-day cover you require. Rather than us using our observations vehicles, do you have any premises that could provide us with an observation post? The vans we use are okay, and we can easily do the job from them. The problem with them is they tend to stick out after a few days being parked in the same place, on a road. Premises are infinitely better.'

'Can you leave that with me? I've got some premises in mind, but I haven't approached the householder yet.'

'Okay. Where are the observations? Who are you watching? And more importantly, why?'

'The suspect is an individual named Saul Peleg. The target premises are at number 2 Fairview Road, Woodthorpe, Nottingham. The suspect is confined to a wheelchair and is registered disabled. He does have access to a Motability vehicle, which is a converted Ford Sierra. The vehicle's dark grey in colour and is always parked on the driveway of the target's premises.'

'Obviously, my men will be in place to give you the off, as and when the suspect leaves his house. What arrangements are you putting in place for a vehicle surveillance? At some stage he's likely to drive away from the house.'

'I intend to keep the surveillance in-house. All the detectives on the MCIU are insured to drive their own private vehicles on police business. We're going to maintain a capability for three vehicles to be available at all times. It will be down to my staff to carry out any surveillance.'

Jim Chambers was thoughtful for a minute, then said, 'Does the command corridor know about this operation?'

'No. Not yet. I can't risk them turning the operation down over the cost. As far as I'm concerned, it needs to be done. But I also know how bizarre it sounds. I just don't think Chief Superintendent Potter would sanction the cost of an operation like this. I'm intending to watch someone for twenty-four hours a day who appears incapable of carrying out the offences we're investigating. Can you honestly see him approving that?'

Jim Chambers ignored the question and instead said, 'Are you convinced this is the only way to determine what you need to know?'

'One hundred per cent. I've known you a long time, Jim. If you want me to go to Potter and ask him to sanction the operation before you commit your staff, I'll understand.'

'No, don't do that, Danny. Personally, I think you're right. There's no way he would sign off on an operation as costly as this. Especially if he knew we were intending to maintain observations on a person confined to a wheelchair. Why don't you just tell me how your enquiries so far have brought you to this point?'

Danny asked Andy, Rachel and Tina to brief Chief

Inspector Chambers of their suspicions. The three detectives painstakingly briefed him on all the enquiries they had carried out that had raised those suspicions.

After listening carefully for twenty minutes, Jim Chambers said, 'So, in a nutshell, you think the man using the wheelchair is actually able-bodied, and that he's the identical twin brother of the man who should be in the chair?'

Andy said, 'That's it.'

Chambers grinned from ear to ear. 'It certainly sounds crazy, but there's only one way to find out. Let's watch him and see for ourselves.'

Danny breathed a sigh of relief and said, 'Thanks, Jim.'

'No problem. As far as me and my department are concerned, this operation was always sanctioned. I hope it comes off for you, Danny. If it doesn't, you could be in a mountain of shit.'

'I know that, but it's a risk I've got to take. If I'm right, we could be in a position to solve three murders.'

Andy said, 'Make that four or possibly even five.'

Danny said, 'How so?'

'If it is Solomon masquerading as Saul in that wheelchair, the big question then becomes where's his twin brother? What's happened to Saul? The other thing I'm not happy about is the suicide of the mother, Rebecca Peleg. I want to have a closer look at that today.'

'There's something else Laura said that relates to Mrs Peleg,' Rachel added. 'Saul had told Laura that his mother and Solomon had a massive row the night before she killed herself. She had apparently ordered Solomon to move out of the Fairview Road address.'

Danny said, 'That's an interesting development. Find out what you can about the suicide, Andy. Let me know how you get on.'

'How soon do you want to start the observations?' Jim asked.

'I want to speak to Deirdre Godden later today,' Danny replied. 'She owns a house that's virtually opposite the target premises. She's the neighbourhood watch co-ordinator for the area, so I'm hoping I can persuade her to let us use her house as a permanent observations post. As soon as I've done that, I'll need to brief Sergeant Turner and C Section. I've also got to organise the vehicle surveillance with my own staff. Can we pencil in the start date for the second of September in three days' time?'

'Sounds good to me. I think you should take Sergeant Turner with you when you go to speak with Mrs Godden. He'll know if the premises are suitable for the job. He'll also be able to inform the householder exactly what having an observations team in her house would entail. Are you intending to use the premises to gather evidence for court? Or just to give your surveillance team the heads-up when the suspect leaves the target premises?'

'The latter, why?'

'If you intend to gather evidence from this woman's private dwelling that could be disclosed in open court later, she needs to appreciate that there may be risks involved.'

'I just want to know when the suspect leaves the house in his vehicle, that's all. I'm sure he'll be extremely careful to maintain his paraplegic act until he's well away from home.'

'Okay, Danny. One final thought, do any of your detectives ride motorcycles?'

'I do,' Andy said. 'Phil Baxter and Glen Lorimar also have motorbikes.'

Jim said, 'It would be a good idea if you made motorcycle availability a top priority. It's always so much easier to carry out surveillance on a vehicle if you have a motorcycle at your disposal.'

'Very true,' Danny agreed. 'I'll bear that in mind. Is Sergeant Turner on duty today?'

'He's on at four o'clock this afternoon. C Section are doing a public order patrol in the city centre tonight, mopping up the drunks and the brawlers.'

'I'll make sure I'm at headquarters for four o'clock today so we can go and speak to Mrs Godden together.'

'I'll phone Graham when I get back to headquarters, then, and instruct him to come on duty at two o'clock this afternoon. That way, when you go and see Mrs Godden, you can take your time and get everything sorted properly. It will be better than him rushing back to get his section briefed for their city centre duty. Is that okay with you?'

'That's fine by me. I'll be at headquarters for two o'clock.'

71

2.00pm, 30 August 1987
9 Fairview Road, Woodthorpe, Nottingham

Danny stood on the doorstep and rang the doorbell again. Standing immediately behind him was the imposing figure of Sergeant Graham Turner.

'Looks like she's out, sir.'

Danny pressed the bell again.

A gate at the side of the house suddenly opened, and a woman stood there with a face like thunder.

'Whatever it is you're selling, I don't want any,' she said angrily. 'Can't you read the bloody sign?'

Danny glanced back at the front door and noticed the sign that said, 'No Hawkers & No Peddlers'.

He reached into his jacket pocket and took out his identification. 'I'm sorry to disturb you. My name's Detective Chief Inspector Flint, and this is Sergeant Turner. I was hoping to speak to Mrs Deirdre Godden.'

The woman's demeanour changed instantly. The anger dissipated , and she said, 'I'm sorry. I was in the back garden; I didn't hear the doorbell. It's such a lovely day. I was enjoying a coffee outside. Please follow me, gentlemen?'

She led the way back through the gate and into the garden at the rear of the house. It was a very private garden, not overlooked by any of the neighbouring houses. Danny felt comfortable talking to the woman there.

Deidre sat down on one of the four cast-iron seats that surrounded an ornate table, and gestured for the police officers to take a seat opposite. She noticed her own coffee cup and said, 'I'm sorry. Where are my manners? Can I get either of you a drink? A coffee? Or something cold perhaps?'

Danny said, 'No, thanks. We're fine.'

'Well, what can I do for you, Chief Inspector?'

'I understand you're the neighbourhood watch coordinator for this area?'

Deidre drew herself up. 'Yes, I am.'

'I wondered if I could ask a huge favour of you. I must warn you that this favour will involve some disruption to your everyday life.'

Her curiosity aroused, she said, 'Of course, what is it?'

'This must be in the strictest confidence. What I'm about to tell you mustn't go any further.'

She shook her head and whispered conspiratorially, 'I won't tell a soul. I never speak to anyone about police business.'

'Okay. I have some suspicions about one of your neighbours. I'm concerned that they may be involved in criminality.'

'Who is it? Which neighbour?'

'It would probably be better for all concerned if I didn't divulge who it is at this stage. It could all turn out to be nothing, and if that's the case, I don't want you to feel awkward around your neighbours.'

'I understand, and thank you for being so considerate. How can I help?'

'It would help us enormously if we could use one of the rooms at the front of your house to carry out some round-the-clock observations.'

'That should be okay. I have a small box room at the front of the house. It's a junk room now that I never use. It's a little bit cluttered, I'm afraid. Do you want to have a look and see if it's suitable?'

'Yes, please. Then if it isn't what we're looking for, we needn't trouble you any further.'

'Okay. This way, please.'

Deirdre Godden led the two police officers through the house and upstairs into the box room. Graham Turner stepped forward to the window. It was covered with a fine mesh net curtain. Looking out of the window, he could clearly see the driveway at number two. There was also clear line of sight to the front door and a good view of the Ford Sierra parked on the driveway. 'It's perfect, sir.'

Danny said, 'Mrs Godden, this would be fantastic. But before you agree, I need to fully explain what the observations would entail.'

'I'm pleased it's suitable, Chief Inspector. Shall we discuss it further outside? It's a little stuffy in here.'

'Okay.'

Back outside, sat around the garden table, Danny said, 'I want to run these observations for two weeks, starting on the second of September. It will mean you'll have plain-clothes police officers in your house twenty-four hours a day and seven days a week. There will always be a minimum of two officers here. They will be self-sufficient, so you won't see them. They'll remain in the box room at all times.'

She said, 'There's a toilet right next to the box room. Your men would be welcome to use that.'

'Are you okay with the fact they'll be in your home constantly?'

'Yes, of course. You have a job to do. How will it work?'

Graham said, 'The officers will work twelve-hour shifts. The first team will work from six o'clock in the morning until six o'clock at night. They will then be relieved by the second team, who will work from six o'clock at night until six o'clock in the morning. There will be an overlap of an hour, where there will be four officers in the house, but they will always stay out of your way. They will enter the property via the same side gate we came in today. Would you feel comfortable trusting us with a house key? That way, we can let ourselves in and out. It will keep disruption down to the minimum.'

'Of course, I trust you. I think that would be best. It will save me constantly being on hand to let your men in and out.'

'The men will always arrive and leave the house separately. They'll ensure they are not seen doing so. Do you have any questions?'

'Can I ask what kind of criminality it is you're investigating?'

Danny said, 'Again, it's probably better at this stage if you don't know.'

'That's fine. I shouldn't pry. I'm just interested, that's all.'

'I don't think you're prying. I think it's great that you're prepared to help us out like this.'

'It's the least I can do. If there's a criminal on the street, I want to help you catch him or her, whoever it is.'

'Then we won't keep you any longer, Mrs Godden. Sergeant Turner will be in touch nearer the day to make the final arrangements. Thanks again.'

Danny and Graham stood up and left the garden. As they walked back to the car, Danny said, 'What was the view like from the box room?'

'When I said it's perfect, I meant it. We can see everything we need to see from that room. It's also warm, dry and comfortable. My blokes will think they've won the lottery. To top it all off, the window is already covered with net curtain. Seriously, if you made a wish list for an observation post, that would be it.'

72

8.00pm, 30 August 1987
The Kings Head, Grant Street, Leeds, West Yorkshire

Sam Creedon walked into the dingy public bar of the
backstreet pub. It was a dark and uninviting room
that reeked of spilled ale and cigarettes.

In an area of the city earmarked for redevelopment by the
council, the ancient pub was the last building standing. All
the rows of uninhabited, dilapidated terraced houses that
used to surround the pub had been demolished. With its
lifeblood of customers gone, the pub was dying a slow,
lingering death.

The pub was now surrounded by vast open spaces that
resembled the rubble-strewn townscapes reminiscent of post-
war London after the Blitz. Its isolated location was one of
the main reasons Dixie Bradder had chosen to meet Wes
Handysides, Geoff Hoskins and Sam Creedon there.

He knew that the four of them could arrive at the location
separately and not be seen by prying eyes. The last thing he

needed was to be arrested for breaching the non-association with co-accused part of his bail conditions.

The other reason he had chosen the Kings Head was because he knew the scruffy pub would have few, if any, customers inside. This meant they would be able to talk openly.

Sam Creedon was the last to arrive. He scanned the dimly lit room and saw his three friends tucked away in the far corner. They were sitting in the booth furthest away from the bar and the overweight landlord, who was perched precariously on a stool behind the bar. The landlord was obviously counting down the days until he could shout last orders for the last time. He looked as downbeat and scruffy as his pub, wearing a food-stained vest and jogging bottoms. There were the remains of a roll-up cigarette dangling from his mouth. It had long since gone out, but it was obvious that he couldn't be arsed to take it from his lips.

Sam said, 'Pint of bitter, mate, ta.'

With an audible grunt, the landlord eased himself off the stool and, without speaking, pulled the pint of beer.

He put the filled pint glass down on the sticky bar and said, 'Seventy-five pence, mate.'

Sam handed over the exact amount, then picked up the pint glass, took a huge gulp of the strong beer, and walked over to join the others.

When he sat down in the booth, Dixie Bradder growled, 'What fucking kept you? We've already been in this shithole for half an hour.'

'I haven't got the motor, have I?' Sam protested. 'I've had to catch two buses to get here.'

'Well, you're here now, so let's crack on and then get out of here.'

Wes said, 'What's so important that we had to meet up

anyway? It's way too risky. If we get caught breaching our bail, we could all get sent down.'

'That's why I suggested this place. Nobody's going to see us arriving, and as you can see, no fucker drinks in here anymore. It's important that we all stick together. I need to know that we're all solid, and that nobody's going to talk when we answer bail.'

Geoff Hoskins said, 'They'll already know that we went to the Forest match. Why don't we just say that we travelled to Nottingham together. That way, we can provide an alibi for each other. My brief says the cops have got no eyewitnesses to the assault. He reckons they're on a massive fishing expedition, and that they've got fuck all.'

Wes and Sam both nodded eagerly. They agreed with Geoff's suggestion. Sam had found it extremely challenging to keep saying 'no comment' when he was questioned.

Dixie said, 'I don't agree. My brief reckons that if we all just say "no comment" to everything the cops ask, we'll all be free and clear. I think that's what we should do. Whatever bullshit the cops come up with, we just keep saying "no comment". They're bound to try some snide tricks to trip us up because they've got fuck all. That's why they bailed us in the first place, coz they've got nowt.'

Sam said, 'Is that really what your solicitor said, Dix?'

'Yeah. She was adamant that's what we should do. Provided we all do the same thing, we'll be cool. Without any evidence, they won't even be able to charge us.'

Sam breathed a loud sigh of relief. 'Thank Christ for that. I can't afford to get sent to prison; I've got my gran to look after. If I get sent down, she'll end up in a fucking home. I'm not having that.'

'Don't worry, Sam. They've got nowt.'

'They've still got my bloody car. They won't let me have it back, and they know I need it to get to work.'

'That's just the cops being bastards. There's nothing in the car for us to worry about, is there? You did empty the boot when we got back from Nottingham, didn't you?'

Sam took a long swig of the warm, flat beer and said, 'Of course I did. I'm not bloody stupid.'

'That's all good, then. You'll probably get your car back when we answer bail in Mansfield. What else did the cops take from your house when you were nicked?'

'Just some clothes and trainers. They found that cosh I brought back from Benidorm last year. I wiped it down before I hid it. So there'll be nothing on that.'

'I hope you wiped it down really well, Sammy boy. Didn't you use that fancy cosh to batter that Forest fan and the copper?'

'Yeah. That's what split the cop's head open.'

'I know it was. You proper creamed the interfering arse-hole. His head was pouring with blood after you'd finished with him.'

Sam laughed and said, 'Well, you three didn't hold back either. I saw you all sticking the boot in.'

The four of them laughed at the memory.

Wes said, 'All they took from me was clothes and trainers. The twats took all my good trainers, that's why I'm having to wear this Dunlop Green Flash shit on my feet now.' He lifted his right foot high above the table, pointed at the crappy trainers he was wearing, and laughed out loud.

The others joined in with the laughter before Geoff sniggered and said, 'That's all they took from my house, jeans and trainers. They never found my collection of knuckledusters that I'd stashed up the chimney breast. Twats.'

'So we're all agreed,' Dixie said. 'We stick to saying "no comment". When they try to pull their bullshit tricks, we just stick to it. We don't let them browbeat us into admitting anything. Just remember, they've got fuck all.'

They all agreed.

'Right. Wes, you go first, then Geoff in five minutes. I'll leave next after another five minutes, and because you kept us all waiting, you can be the last man out, Sammy boy. It will give you time to finish drinking that shit beer.'

They all laughed before Wes stood up and left.

After ten minutes, Sam was on his own. He finished his beer and left the scruffy pub. As he walked away across the wide-open, rubble-strewn development land, he was worried.

He kept thinking about Dixie's comment about the cosh he'd brought back from Benidorm. He knew he'd only given it a cursory wipe-down with a damp cloth. He also knew that there had been a lot of blood on it after he'd used it on the copper. Maybe he hadn't done enough to remove all traces of the cop's blood.

73

8.00pm, 30 August 1987
Intensive Care Unit, Queen's Medical Centre, Nottingham

Danny hated hospitals with a passion. Whenever he walked into one, he was confronted with painful memories of the past. Visiting his sick parents before they passed away, or seeing his friend and colleague Rachel Moore critically ill after being attacked and left for dead by Jimmy Wade.

He swallowed hard and made his way through the long corridors of the Queen's Medical Centre. Eventually, he found the lift that would take him to E Floor.

Danny had wanted to check on his injured colleague Mark in person ever since the assault had happened. Instructions from the medical team caring for Mark had prevented it until now. He had received a message earlier from the control room, informing him that Mark was now conscious and breathing unaided.

As soon as he had been notified by the control room of

the update in his injured colleague's condition, Danny had telephoned the Intensive Care Unit and had been given permission by the sister in charge of the unit to visit. She had cautioned him not to expect too much.

There was a loud pinging sound as the lift stopped, and the doors opened. Danny stepped out into another corridor. He could see the glass doors at the end of the corridor that led onto the ICU ward. He started to walk towards them, and as he passed the open door of an office on his right, he heard a woman's voice say, 'Can I help you?'

Danny stopped and walked back to the office. A nurse in a navy-blue uniform sat behind the desk. 'My name's Chief Inspector Flint. I'm here to see PC Mark Warden. I think I spoke to you earlier.'

The woman smiled. 'Yes, you did, Chief Inspector. I'm Sister Grant. I think you may have had a wasted trip though; Mark's sleeping now.'

'If sleeping is good for his recovery, I don't mind a wasted trip. How's he doing?'

'Take a seat, Chief Inspector.'

Danny didn't like the sound of that. Was she preparing him for more bad news?

As he sat down, he said, 'Now you're making me worried. Is everything okay?'

'Everything is as well as can be expected. It's still very early days for Mark. When we took him off the propofol sedative, he responded well and woke up fairly quickly. Staff Nurse Cookson remained with him throughout the process, and after an hour or so, he was able to obey simple commands. The ventilatory support was at a minimum, and he was able to cough effectively.'

'Cough effectively? Why is that important?'

'It's one of the criteria we need to see before we attempt to extubate his breathing tube.'

'The message I got from our control room is that Mark is now breathing unaided. Is that still the case?'

'Yes, that's still the case. Mark continues to improve, but he'll remain with us for at least another forty-eight hours, as we have him under enhanced monitoring. He's undergone two very serious procedures. He may still require further medical support that couldn't be managed on a ward.'

'You said he continues to improve. When do you think we'll be able to ask him about what happened?'

'That really is the million-dollar question, Chief Inspector. The short answer is, I don't know. What I do know is that Staff Nurse Cookson has been talking to him about the reasons why he's in hospital. Unfortunately, he has no recollection of the events that led to him being hospitalised. He could remember his name but had no clue about what he does for a living, or where he currently was.'

'Do you think that will change?'

'His cognitive function will be judged by a process of ongoing assessment. It will be determined by his behaviour, his ability to speak and articulate his thoughts, as well as his memory recall of certain events. There are other determining factors that I won't go into. The bottom line is, it's far too early to say what sort of recovery Mark will make. He could recover completely and lead a perfectly normal life, or there may be a certain level of cognitive dysfunction that never changes.'

'Are you telling me that he may not recover well enough to ever return to work?'

'From what we've seen so far, that's a very distinct possibility. Like I said, it's still very early days, and his condition could improve greatly over time. Do I think he'll ever be well enough to carry out the role of a police officer? All the signs right now aren't good, but I've been wrong before. I'm just trying to give you the worst-case scenario, Chief Inspector.'

Danny was devastated. He'd only ever thought about his

colleague's survival. To be confronted now with the brutal truth that he may never recover fully was a hard pill to swallow.

'Have you spoken to Mark's parents about this prognosis?'

'Not yet. That's a conversation his consultant neurosurgeon will have with them in another seventy-two hours, when we can be a little more certain. I'm sorry it's bad news.'

'He's alive and breathing, that's what matters, and I can't thank you all enough for that. The police force will help him, and his parents, in his recovery. However long that may take.'

'Are you any closer to catching the people who did this to him?'

'I've got a team of people working flat out to try to bring them before the courts. I think we both know that, even if we're successful, the punishment administered by the courts won't ever fit the crime.'

'He could still improve, Chief Inspector. Don't give up on him just yet. My staff here have all commented on what a brave fighter Mark is.'

'Don't worry. Nobody is giving up on him. Can I see him before I go?'

'Of course. I'll take you to him.'

Danny followed Sister Grant into the ward and to the bedside of the sleeping Mark Warden. There were no tubes in his mouth and nose, but there continued to be the constant soft beeping sounds of the machines that monitored his heart rate and other vital signs. Mark looked at peace and pain-free as he slept. Danny could clearly see the vivid red scars of recent surgery on the right side and top of his shaven head. His face still looked discoloured and swollen from the heavy bruising sustained during the assault.

Danny bit his lip as he felt a sudden surge of anger and emotion race through him. 'Get well soon, Mark,' he said quietly. 'Don't worry, I'll get the bastards who did this to you.'

He walked quickly away as he felt tears start to sting his eyes.

74

9.30am, 1 September 1987
Willow Cottage, Main Street, Gonalston, Nottingham

Andy Wills parked his car directly outside the stone cottage on Main Street, Gonalston. The tiny hamlet had no pub, and the nearest shop was a farm shop in nearby Caythorpe. It really was off the beaten track. The perfect place for a peaceful retirement, thought Andy.

The cottage was owned by retired police sergeant Anthony Calderwood. It had been Sergeant Calderwood who had attended the sudden death of Rebecca Peleg. He had been responsible for preparing the file on the woman's apparent suicide for the coroner.

Andy had spent the previous evening examining that coroner's file. It was obvious to his experienced investigative eyes that many corners had been cut by the police sergeant, as he rapidly approached retirement.

Sergeant Calderwood had failed to call out a detective from the CID to attend the scene of the suicide, which was blatantly against standing orders. He had also somehow managed to get the local detective sergeant to sign off the coroner's file as completed.

The thing that really concerned Andy was the photographs of the scene taken by Scenes of Crime officers. Unfortunately, the body of the deceased had already been cut down prior to the arrival of the police. This wasn't an unusual occurrence, but it was normally done in order to attempt to save the person's life. This was not the case with this death. Mrs Peleg had already been dead for hours prior to being cut down by her son Solomon.

The photographs showed just how high the loft hatch was above the gallery landing. The rope used as the makeshift noose had been tied to one of the beams in the loft space.

Andy had noticed from the file that Mrs Peleg was only five feet three inches tall. There was no way she could have climbed into the loft without the use of a ladder. Even more worrying was the fact that the rope had been tied to a beam that was at least six or seven feet above the open hatch. There was no way Mrs Peleg could have physically reached up high enough to make the rope secure.

Then there was the handwritten note, apparently left by the deceased. The file didn't specify what tests had been carried out on the handwriting to establish if it was indeed the dead woman's writing. Andy was sceptical that those handwriting enquiries had been made. He also doubted that the sergeant had carried out any general enquiries with friends and relatives as to the dead woman's state of mind prior to her supposed suicide.

Andy felt convinced that Sergeant Calderwood had adopted the line of least resistance throughout the investigation. He had carried out a very lazy enquiry, probably with a view to doing as little work as possible prior to his retirement date.

He hoped he was wrong, but he was about to find out.

He had phoned the retired sergeant late last night and arranged to meet him this morning at his home address. As Andy walked up the garden path, the front door to the cottage opened.

The detective realised that Anthony Calderwood had been watching him approach the cottage from his lounge window. He gave a friendly smile and said, 'Mr Calderwood?'

Calderwood said, 'That's me. You must be Detective Sergeant Wills.'

Andy could see by the expression on Calderwood's face that it grated on him to be referred to as plain old Mr Calderwood.

That's tough, Andy thought to himself, *get used to it.*

Andy waited on the doorstep for Calderwood to invite him inside. Eventually, he was asked into the cottage.

Calderwood gestured for him to take a seat in the lounge. 'Can I get you a drink?'

Andy replied, 'No, I'm fine, thanks. I've just had a coffee.'

'It's just us in the house, Sergeant. My wife's nipped into Nottingham for the day. So if you want a proper drink, that's fine with me.'

'It's a bit early for me. Feel free if you want one.'

Anthony Calderwood looked worried. Andy watched the retired sergeant as he poured himself a large whiskey and sat down.

Calderwood said, 'You said on the phone that you wanted to talk to me about Rebecca Peleg's suicide?'

Andy placed the coroner's file on his lap. 'That's right. I have a few concerns over this death. Some aspects of it don't sit too well with me.'

Anthony Calderwood took another sip of the whiskey and said bluntly, 'What aspects in particular?'

'Why didn't you feel it necessary to call out the CID to what was a possible suicide?'

'Because there was nothing possible about it. I've been to countless hangings in my time, and there was nothing unusual about this one.'

'Didn't it bother you that the deceased had been cut down prior to your arrival?'

'In my experience, I've found that's often the case. The son was distraught. He didn't like seeing his mother that way.'

'Which son?'

'The one in the wheelchair was the most upset, the other one not so much.'

'Obviously, it was the able-bodied son who had cut his mother down?'

Starting to feel emboldened as the strong liquor took effect, Calderwood replied, 'Well, it wasn't going to be the one in the wheelchair, was it?'

'Did you measure the height of the loft hatch from the floor of the gallery landing?'

'Of course I did. It's all in the file you've got.'

Andy opened the file and flicked to the relevant page. 'It says here it was seven feet three inches from the floor to the loft hatch.'

'If that's what it says, that's what it was.'

'Didn't it worry you that the deceased was only five feet three inches tall?'

'No.'

'How do you think she got into the loft hatch?'

'Using a stepladder, I suppose.'

'Was there a stepladder still in situ when you arrived?'

'No. But there was a set of ladders in the garage.'

'So you think Mrs Peleg, in her suicidal state of mind, bothered to replace the ladder back in the garage after securing the makeshift noose?'

'I've seen stranger things.'

'Did you measure how high the noose would have been from the floor?'

'How could I? She'd already been cut down.'

'Did you measure the entire length of the rope used?'

'No.'

'I've retrieved the exhibits taken at the scene from our property store yesterday. The length of rope from the knot on the beam to the cut was seven feet ten inches. The post-mortem report shows that the length of rope removed from the neck of the deceased to the knot in the noose was eight inches. That means the total length of the rope used would have been eight feet six inches. If we say the total height from the top of the beam, where the rope was secured, to the floor of the gallery landing was fifteen feet and one inch, that means the distance between the noose and the floor of the gallery landing would still have been six feet seven inches. How do you think five-foot-three Rebecca Peleg managed to hang herself from a rope that she couldn't physically reach?'

Andy could see the colour rising in the face of Anthony Calderwood. He knew it had nothing to do with the amount of whiskey the retired sergeant had consumed.

He pressed on, 'This stepladder you've mentioned. The one you think she could have used. Did you have it examined by Scenes of Crime to see if Mrs Peleg's fingerprints were on it?'

'No, I didn't. I didn't think it was necessary. It was a straightforward suicide. The woman had left a note, for Christ's sake.'

'Let's talk about that note. What enquiries did you make to compare the handwriting on the note with samples of the deceased's handwriting?'

'Now you're just being bloody ridiculous. I've never gone to those lengths.'

'If you had bothered to take the measurements that cast

doubt on her ability to take her own life in that particular way, would you have gone to those lengths then?'

'I don't think I like your tone, Detective. I think you should leave.'

'At the moment, all I'm trying to establish is whether this apparent suicide is something I need to investigate further. If you don't want to cooperate with me, that's your choice, and I'll leave. But I'll then be duty bound to inform the professional standards department of my suspicions. Your retirement won't stop them carrying out a full investigation into your shoddy police work. We both know what implications that could have on your pension. The choice is yours, Mr Calderwood.'

'Alright, alright,' Calderwood snapped. 'Let's not be too hasty. Maybe I did cut a few corners, but there was nothing glaringly obvious. It looked like every other death by hanging I've ever been to.'

'So I'll ask you again, what handwriting enquiries were carried out?'

'None.'

'Who did you speak to about the deceased's state of mind prior to her death?'

'Her two sons.'

'Anybody else?'

'No.'

'What did the sons say?'

'The one in the wheelchair was totally shocked. He couldn't believe what had happened. The other one said he wasn't surprised, because she had been depressed and crying a lot recently.'

'So two totally different accounts?'

'I suppose so.'

'Which one was right?'

'I don't know.'

'Did you attend the post-mortem?'

'No. I sent a young probationer to attend, as she hadn't been to one before.'

'Had she been to the scene of the hanging?'

'No.'

'So she wouldn't have been able to answer any questions the pathologist may have had in relation to any unexplained bruising to the deceased's neck?'

'I suppose not. I spoke to her when she came back from the hospital. She told me that the pathologist had said it was death by hanging and that there were no other injuries of concern.'

'Do you still think Rebecca Peleg took her own life?'

'After everything you've said, I honestly don't know anymore. At the time, I was a hundred percent certain she had.'

Andy stood to leave and said, 'I'm going to report all this to my DCI. I'll be informing him that, in my opinion, we need to reinvestigate this death, as there is a distinct possibility of foul play. It will be his decision to involve the Professional Standards Department or not. Personally, I hope he does. Your lazy investigation could have allowed a murderer to avoid justice.'

Andy walked out of the cottage and back to his car. He got inside and slammed his fist on the steering wheel and said aloud, 'God save us from bone-idle cops!'

75

6.00pm, 1 September 1987
MCIU Office, Mansfield Police Station

D anny had asked Sergeant Graham Turner and Detective Inspector Tina Cartwright to brief him on the final arrangements for Operation Sentinel.

Sentinel was the code word designated for the operational order prepared by Graham Turner. It covered every aspect of the implementation of round-the-clock observations on Fairview Road. The operation was due to commence at six o'clock tomorrow morning.

Danny started the meeting by saying, 'Good job on the operational order, Graham; it's first rate.'

'Thank you, sir. All my lads are keen to get started. It's been a while since we did a lengthy surveillance task, and when I described the observation post, they were all ecstatic. They usually end up out in the freezing cold, lying beneath hedgerows, or worse.'

'Have you already allocated your two-man teams?'

'Yes, sir. They all know when they're due to be in the

observation point, and they've all rehearsed insertion and extraction. They'll approach the observation post from the end of the road furthest away from the target premises. This will eliminate any chance of them being seen by the suspect. They'll extract in the same direction. We've allocated different vehicles for the insertion and extraction every day. This will help to alleviate any suspicions from neighbours.'

'Good work. Will your teams be keeping a log?'

'It's standard practice, sir. I don't suppose there'll be that many entries on this job. I don't anticipate too many visitors to the target premises, and I don't expect our suspect will be going out and about much. If there are any new vehicles sighted, we'll obviously run the registration numbers through the Police National Computer and will alert you if we have any concerns.'

'Thanks.'

Danny then turned to Tina. 'I take it we're prepared to carry out any vehicle surveillance should our suspect decide to leave the house?'

'Yes, sir. I've arranged a rota that enables us to always have a three-vehicle capability. The nearest vehicle to the target premises will be regularly rotated to avoid suspicion.'

'Motorcycles?'

'I've arranged for a motorcycle to be available as part of the three-vehicle group at all times. I've also put in contingencies where, depending on the time of day, we may also be able to supplement the three planned vehicles with other mobiles. In any event, there will always be a minimum of three vehicles in position, ready to pick up the target vehicle as soon as it moves from the target premises.'

'That's good work, Tina. Are your teams fully briefed on what's required? This is purely an observational task. Unless somebody's life is in danger, I don't want our suspect to know what we're doing. Has that been made clear to the teams?'

'Yes, boss.'

'Good. What about communications between yourselves and the SOU observations teams?'

'We'll all be using the Cougar radio sets. This will enable us to be in constant touch with the obs teams. It also means our operational needs won't interfere with normal police radio traffic.'

'I'd like to be provided with a Cougar set if possible. I'd like to monitor what's happening while I'm on duty.'

Graham said, 'I can arrange that, sir. I'll also provide you with the relevant battery charger, so you can keep it charged up and working.'

'Excellent, thanks. Who's first up from our side, Tina?'

'Phil Baxter will be using his Kawasaki 500cc motorcycle, supplemented by me in my Astra and DC Williams in his Mazda.'

'All sorted then. Good luck tomorrow, and let's hope Peleg shows his hand sooner rather than later.'

As soon as Graham and Tina had left the office, there was a knock on the door. Danny shouted, 'Come in!'

Andy Wills stepped inside and closed the door behind him. 'I know you're busy,' he said, 'but there's something I need to discuss with you that's quite delicate.'

Danny could see the worried expression on the detective sergeant's face.

He said, 'Of course, grab a seat. What's the problem?'

'I've got real concerns over the death of Rebecca Peleg.'

'You don't think it's suicide, do you?'

'Not a chance. I checked over the coroner's file that was prepared by Sergeant Calderwood, ready for the inquest scheduled for the end of November. You could drive a bloody stagecoach through some of the holes in it.'

'Okay. What is it exactly that's causing your concern?'

'I've checked all the exhibits. The rope would have been

too far from the floor for her to reach without stepping onto something. There was nothing found at the scene that she could have used to do this. Add the fact that Rebecca Peleg was only five feet three inches tall and couldn't reach the loft hatch without a stepladder. You can start to see we have a problem. The final clincher for me was the rope in the loft was secured to a beam that was over seven feet from the loft hatch. It would have been impossible for her to have reached up and tied the knot to make the rope secure.'

Danny was aghast. 'Why wasn't any of this picked up before?'

'This is why it's delicate, boss. The hanging was attended by recently retired Sergeant Anthony Calderwood. It's obvious he's just paid lip service to the investigation, as he counted down the days to his retirement. He never involved the CID. By the time he arrived at the scene, the body had already been cut down by Solomon Peleg. Because no suspicions were flagged up, the pathologist did the bare minimum post-mortem necessary to determine the cause of death. When nothing suspicious was found, the pathologist subsequently informed the coroner, who released the body for burial. It's been a fuck-up from start to finish.'

'If you think her death was staged by somebody else to look like suicide, how do you think she died?'

'The post-mortem report says death was caused by cardiac arrest after oxygen was starved to the brain. Nothing else showed up as a possible cause of death. If it was foul play, I'm guessing she must have been strangled.'

Danny grabbed the telephone on his desk and dialled the number for Seamus Carter.

After a brief delay, he said, 'Good evening, Seamus. It's Danny, I've got a problem, and I need your advice.'

Seamus Carter said, 'You sound worried, my friend; what's the problem?'

'I'm concerned that a woman we first thought took her own life by hanging may actually have been strangled, and her suicide staged. There are two things I need to know. Firstly, would a run-of-the-mill post-mortem be able to establish the difference between death by hanging or strangulation?'

'If the pathologist was on their game and was aware of the possibility of foul play, they may find evidence of a manual strangulation. If they weren't aware, then probably not. Quite simply, they wouldn't be looking for it, so they wouldn't find it. What's the second thing?'

'If I went through all the procedures with the coroner to have this woman's body exhumed, do you think you would be able to find evidence of foul play at a new post-mortem examination?'

'When was she buried?'

Danny flicked through the inquest file that Andy had brought with him. 'The death was on the second of June, and the post-mortem was carried out later that day. The body was released to the family on the eighth of June. The subsequent funeral and burial took place on the fourteenth of June.'

'So she's been interred for just over eleven weeks now?'

Danny knew it was rhetorical question. He waited patiently, allowing the pathologist time to think.

After a couple of minutes, Seamus said, 'Start making the preparations for the exhumation. It will take you the best part of a week to complete all the necessary paperwork required and for the coroner to agree to take ownership of the body again. It's quite a complicated procedure, with lots of archaic practice involved. It would be a good idea to seek out the coroner's officer who initially worked on the suicide. He'll be able to advise you and will also be present on the day of the exhumation. Let me know as soon as you've got a date for the exhumation. I'll make sure I'm free to carry out the post-mortem. If there's anything amiss, I'm sure I'll be able to find it.'

'Even after three months?'

'I was just thinking back to my university days when I was training under Professor McBride. I observed him work on a body that had been exhumed six months after burial. He was still able to establish that the victim had been strangled. It's not a pleasant task, but I'm sure if there's anything to suggest foul play, I'll find it.'

'Thanks, Seamus. I'll be in touch.'

Danny hung up and said to Andy, 'Could you hear what he was saying?'

Seamus Carter had a booming voice, so Andy had been able to hear him clearly. 'I could. I'll get in touch with Bernard Wragg, the coroner's officer who worked on the suicide, and start things moving. Have you ever done this before, boss?'

'Exhumed a body?'

'Yeah.'

'No, never. There's a first time for everything, I suppose. I want you to keep me informed on how things are progressing. As soon as you establish a date for the exhumation, I'll need to let Seamus know. He'll need plenty of notice to carry out the new post-mortem.'

'Will do.'

'One last question, Andy. Where's Rebecca Peleg buried?'

'The big cemetery at Redhill, in Arnold.'

'In that case, you'll need to contact Gedling Borough Council. You'll need to establish a point of contact with whoever oversees the administration of the cemetery. The council will need to provide the gravediggers on the day of the exhumation.'

'Okay, boss.'

'When are you scheduled to work on Operation Sentinel?'

'Not for a few days. I'm using my motorcycle, so I can't really miss that.'

'No, you can't. I know Fran isn't involved in Operation Sentinel. Brief her about the exhumation. She'll be able to help you chase the council and the coroner's officer. She can prepare and submit all the paperwork involved.'

'That's great. Thanks for that. This job just keeps getting more and more complicated.'

Danny shook his head. 'It's certainly a strange one.'

76

9.00am, 9 September 1987
MCIU Office, Mansfield Police Station

Danny took another sip of hot coffee and glanced at his watch. He and Tina Cartwright were waiting for Sergeant Graham Turner to arrive. At exactly nine o'clock, there was a polite knock on the door, and Sergeant Turner walked in.

'Spot on time,' Danny said. 'Thanks for coming over. This shouldn't take long. I wanted to have a quick debrief now that the first week of Operation Sentinel has finished.'

Graham placed the observations logs on Danny's desk and said, 'There's nothing much to report. The only visitor to the premises all week has been the suspect's carer. We've noted down her vehicle registration number, if you need it.'

'That can't be right. Have you only seen one carer?'

'Just the one. White female, mid-twenties, dark hair.'

'There should be a team of carers who visit twice a day and other medical professionals who visit every other day.'

'Nope. Just the same young woman every day.'

'What about the suspect?'

'Haven't seen Peleg at all. He hasn't left the house. The Ford Sierra hasn't moved off the driveway all week.'

'So nothing out of the ordinary, then?'

'There's one entry in the logs that I thought you should be aware of. Two mornings ago, after the carer had left the target premises, the obs team reported seeing a figure walk past an upstairs window.'

'Go on.'

'I've spoken to the officer who made the entry. He's adamant that he saw something. He described how the shape was walking very slowly. It was the window of Saul Peleg's bedroom where he saw this figure. He can't give any meaningful description. He described what he saw to me as being "just a fleeting shadow". He entered it in the log because he knew the only person in the house at that time was the suspect, who's supposedly confined to a wheelchair.'

'That's very interesting. Does your section still have the capability of staffing the observation post for another week?'

'We're okay until the eighteenth of this month. After that, we've got too many commitments already pencilled in. I couldn't commit further staff to Operation Sentinel after that date.'

'If nothing's happened by then, I'll have to pull the operation anyway. If nothing happens this week, I'll have a decision to make.'

'I'm sorry we can't commit to the operation for any longer than that, sir.'

'No problem. Fingers crossed, there'll be some movement this week.'

'Okay if I get straight back to headquarters now, sir? I've got a strategy meeting at ten o'clock with Special Branch. We're formulating the operational order for the royal visit next month.'

'Not at all, I appreciate you coming over this morning. We'll run Operation Sentinel until the eighteenth. If nothing happens by then, we'll have another debrief on the nineteenth, then cancel the operation.'

'Okay, sir.'

Sergeant Turner left the office, and Danny said to Tina, 'What do you make of the lack of carers?'

'I don't really know what to think. It could be very significant.'

'Do we know who the care providers are?'

'No. The health centre at Bestwood couldn't help us with that query.'

'I think it's something we need to bottom out. Start making enquiries with all the care providers that cover the Nottingham area. Let's see if we can establish who looks after Saul Peleg.'

'Will do, boss.'

'How are we fixed for next week? Have we got cover for our side of the operation?'

Tina looked at her operational order. 'We're okay except for the night shift on the sixteenth. Right now, I've only got two vehicles and a motorcycle that night. So far, I've always managed to have three vehicles and a motorcycle. I think it's stretching it a bit too fine to run a full vehicle surveillance with just two cars and a motorcycle.'

'I agree. Put me down to work that night shift. I'll make your third vehicle.' He smiled ruefully. 'Bloody hell, what have I just done? I haven't worked a full night shift for years.'

Tina laughed before saying, 'Well, you're going to love this, because we've been working from six o'clock at night to six o'clock in the morning. Pulling twelve-hour shifts.'

'Great. I'd better bring a huge flask of coffee to keep me awake.' Danny sat down at his desk. 'Thanks, Tina. Keep me updated on any developments this week.'

Tina smiled briefly and left the office.

A couple of minutes later, Andy Wills walked in. He was followed by a tall, thin man in his late fifties with a full head of steel grey hair. Danny recognised him as Bernard Wragg, the coroner's officer who had been assisting Andy with preparations for the planned exhumation of Rebecca Peleg. The exhumation had been planned for tomorrow morning, at four thirty. Danny had already given notice to Seamus Carter that tomorrow was the day.

The pathologist had not only committed himself to undertaking the subsequent post-mortem, but had also volunteered to be at the graveside to help supervise the exhumation process.

Danny gestured for both men to sit down. 'Is everything in place for tomorrow morning?'

'Everything's ready,' Andy replied. 'Gedling Council have arranged to have two of their grave-digging staff at the grave-side for four thirty. They have already been briefed and will carry out the actual excavation. I've arranged for a firm of undertakers to convey the deceased to the City Hospital once the coffin has been removed from the grave. Bernard will be present throughout, to make sure everything runs smoothly at the graveside.'

'Excellent.' He addressed the coroner's officer: 'Has all the paperwork that commits the body of Rebecca Peleg back to the control of the coroner been completed?'

Bernard coughed once and said, 'I've spoken to the coroner personally this morning, and that's all taken care of. Dr Melrose is fully aware of what's happening and the reason for it. He's more than happy to accept custody and control over Rebecca Peleg's body once again.'

'Thanks, Bernard. You've been a massive help to us. As you can imagine, this isn't something either Andy or myself have ever been involved with before. I really appreciate all your time and help, both with the coroner and with Gedling Borough Council.' Looking at Andy, he asked, 'Is everything else in place for the graveside? Do we have the correct forensic tent and lighting arranged for privacy?'

'We do. Scenes of Crime will also be attending to make a full video recording and to photograph the exhumation as it progresses. They'll be providing the tent and lighting. They'll also be providing the correct protective clothing for everyone involved.'

'Sounds like we're good to go. Do we know what the weather forecast is?'

'The forecast is for a bright morning. There's no rain forecast until tomorrow evening.'

'That's good news. Heavy rain would have made the process a whole lot trickier. What time's the briefing?'

'The briefing will be at headquarters at three thirty tomorrow morning, an hour before we need to be at the graveside.'

'Good. Thanks, both of you. I'll see you both at the briefing tomorrow morning.'

The two men left the office, leaving Danny alone with his thoughts.

His head was spinning. This was like no case he'd ever worked before. He was faced with investigating four murders that he suspected had all been committed by a man who physically couldn't have carried out the act.

He knew he needed something from Operation Sentinel to stand any chance of making a case against Peleg.

77

4.30am, 10 September 1987
Arnold Cemetery, Redhill, Nottingham

Danny pulled his parka coat tighter around him. It was a chilly cold morning, and the wind whipping across the open cemetery made it feel ten degrees colder than it was.

At least it was dry.

Danny stood next to Tina Cartwright. Next to her was Seamus Carter and his assistant, Brigitte O'Hara. They were all a respectful ten yards away from the graveside. Andy Wills and Bernard Wragg were giving instructions to the two council gravediggers. The council employees looked anxious as they prepared for the grisly task of exhuming the body of Rebecca Peleg.

The plan that had been agreed was for the gravediggers to dig down until they reached the casket. As soon as they connected with the coffin, they would stop digging and allow Scenes of Crime personnel to erect a tent for privacy. The sun wasn't due to rise until six thirty that morning, and the cemetery was still in total darkness.

There was a loud humming sound as a generator was started up. Suddenly, the graveyard was bathed in an eerie white light from the portable floodlights. Danny was pleased that the grave of Rebecca Peleg couldn't be seen from the busy Mansfield Road. Even at this ungodly hour, the white lights in the cemetery would have quickly aroused a lot of interest.

With the lights on and the grave illuminated, Danny shouted over to Andy, 'Let's get cracking, Sergeant.'

Andy spoke to the two gravediggers, and they both began digging in earnest. Soon there was a large mound of freshly dug earth next to the grave.

After twenty minutes of digging, there was a loud clunking sound from within the open grave.

One of the gravediggers shouted, 'We've hit the casket, sir.'

Andy called over the Scenes of Crime personnel who weren't already engaged in taking photographs or video recording the event. He instructed them to quickly erect the tent over the open grave.

Within a matter of minutes, the privacy tent had been erected. Taking much more care now, the gravediggers continued their macabre task.

Andy walked over to Seamus Carter. 'We're almost ready to lift the casket out of the grave now. There's quite a lot of historical damage to the top of the casket, probably from the weight of the clay soil. Do you want to see the body in situ before I call the undertakers in?'

Seamus Carter was surprised. With a note of concern in his voice, he said, 'Is it damaged so badly that you can see the corpse?'

'I'm afraid so. The end where the head and chest are has

remained intact, but the bottom half of the coffin has been completely smashed in. The legs of the body are exposed, and there's a lot of soil and debris inside that part of the casket.'

'I'll have a quick look, for what it's worth. Let's get the casket out of the ground as quickly as possible. The sooner I get cracking on the post-mortem, the better.'

As Seamus and his assistant moved forward to inspect the damaged casket, Andy called the undertakers' van forward. The vehicle was reversed into position until it was directly adjacent to the opening of the privacy tent.

The damaged casket was carefully raised by the gravediggers and undertakers, then placed straight into the back of the funeral director's transit van.

'City Hospital mortuary, please, gentlemen,' Seamus said. 'I'll see you there and supervise the body being lifted from the casket. Please don't attempt to do it before I arrive. The body will be in a very fragile state, and we'll need to be extremely careful how we do this.'

The undertakers nodded that they had understood the instruction.

'It's almost five thirty now,' Seamus said to Danny. 'I'll need at least three hours to remove the body from the casket, and then another hour to prepare the body for examination. Shall we say ten o'clock, to be on the safe side. I should be ready to start the post-mortem by then.'

Danny said, 'We'll see you at the mortuary at ten o'clock. Will the damage to the casket have any bearing on what you might still find?'

'Fortunately for us, the head end of the coffin is still intact. That part isn't filled with soil, so if there's anything to find, we should still be able to find it.' He headed to the door. 'I'll see you at ten o'clock.'

78

10.00am, 10 September 1987
City Hospital Mortuary, Nottingham

The examination room at the City Hospital was much more crowded than normal. Seamus Carter and his assistant, Brigitte, stood on one side of the stainless-steel table where the putrefied remains of Rebecca Peleg now lay.

The two pathologists were fully gowned and masked. They looked more like surgeons preparing to operate. The personal protective equipment was a very necessary precaution – working on an exhumed body that had suffered months of decay posed a very real threat to their health.

Immediately opposite the pathologists were Danny, Tina and Andy.

Tim Donnelly and four of his Scenes of Crime staff were also present in the room. One was filming the post-mortem examination on a video recorder. Another was taking photographs. These images would eventually be placed in a booklet and used as an evidential document. The other staff were there to act as exhibits officers and to generally assist the pathologist.

Standing in the far corner of the room, well out of the way, stood Bernard Wragg. The coroner's officer would observe the proceedings, then report directly back to the coroner.

Everyone in the room wore the same protective garments as the pathologist. In the harsh, white light of the examination room, the blue-clad figures took on an eerie, surreal appearance. Though the small room contained a lot of people, it was strangely silent. An air of reverence hung heavily in the air, creating an almost oppressive atmosphere.

Danny stared at the remains of Rebecca Peleg.

He had seen a lot of dead bodies and had attended countless post-mortems, but this was different to anything he had previously witnessed. He knew the sights and smells he was experiencing now would remain with him for the rest of his life.

The body on the bench looked very small, almost childlike. The flesh around the legs, up to the hips, had all but disappeared, and the bones were visible. The upper half of the body appeared to consist of a yellow, waxlike substance. The woman's hair was still long, but her eyes had completely disappeared. The sockets were now just large holes in the front of her face.

Seamus broke the heavy silence. 'If everybody's ready, I'll start. I will begin on the neck area and then move on to a general examination. I don't intend to make a verbal recording, as the examination is already being video recorded with sound. Please don't interrupt me, and save any questions until after the examination.'

With that, the pathologist stepped forward and began to closely examine the neck. Danny also took a step closer to watch the skilled pathologist work. He could see the livid, purple bruising still evident around the neck of the cadaver. Bruising that had been caused, in the main, by the makeshift noose – and God knows what else.

Seamus made an incision into the waxy flesh, across the front of the neck, exposing the trachea. He bent forward and looked closer. 'Brigitte, have a look at this and tell me what you see.'

His eager assistant stepped forward and examined the exposed trachea.

'It looks like it's been fractured in two places. The first break is high up, just below the chin. The other one is lower down, above the clavicle bones. I can see two specific indentations in the area of the lower fracture that shouldn't be present if the injury were caused by hanging.'

The furrowed lines at the corners of his eyes betrayed the fact that Seamus was smiling broadly beneath his mask. His assistant had correctly identified exactly what he'd found. 'This woman was manually strangled,' he said to Danny. 'The two indentations in the trachea, which Brigitte has just confirmed for me, would be made by the thumbs of an offender pressing hard into the windpipe. It's an injury we often see with victims of strangulation.'

'Could they have been caused by the rope if she did hang herself?'

Seamus shook his head and pointed higher up the exposed trachea. 'Do you see that linear indentation that runs directly across the windpipe, just below the jawline?'

Danny nodded.

'That's caused by a rope. This woman was manually strangled. Then her neck was placed in a noose, and she was hanged. The only thing I can't say after all this time is whether she was alive or dead when the hanging took place. It could have been either. The manual strangulation could have killed her, or it could have rendered her unconscious. If it was the latter, then death would have occurred when the noose did its job and cut off her airway.'

'So we're looking at murder as opposed to suicide?'

'Definitely. I'm going to make a full examination now just to ensure no other underlying causes of death were missed on the previous post-mortem.'

Danny nodded and took a couple of steps back, away from the stainless-steel bench. The photographer was busy getting close-up shots of the exposed trachea that had provided the, previously overlooked, damning evidence.

Forty-five minutes passed slowly by until finally Seamus said, 'Okay. We're finished. There's nothing else of any consequence. This woman was killed by either strangulation or by hanging. Either way, she didn't take her own life. She was murdered.'

'When can I have your full written report?' Danny asked.

'I'll get it to you by tomorrow afternoon. A full toxicology exam was carried out at the original post-mortem, which was negative. So I haven't taken samples for another.'

'Thanks. What happens now?'

'I'll stay here with Brigitte and supervise the morticians moving the body into storage. The body will remain here in the mortuary until the coroner decides to release her for reinterment.'

'Okay, thanks for everything today, Seamus.'

'No problem. Good luck finding the person responsible.'

79

2.00pm, 10 September 1987
MCIU Office, Mansfield Police Station

Danny sat in his office with Tina and Andy, discussing the significance of the morning's events. Andy came straight to the point. 'Do we arrest Peleg now?'

Danny pondered this. After a pause he said, 'I don't think we've got enough to arrest whoever it is in that house for murder.'

'But you heard Seamus Carter,' Andy persisted, 'the woman was strangled, and her death made to look like suicide.'

'I heard that,' Danny said calmly, 'but I didn't hear him say who had strangled her. That's what we'll need to prove beyond any doubt. And we're nowhere near being able to do that yet.'

'Well, the handwriting comparison enquiry I carried out on the supposed suicide note has come back as a negative for Rebecca Peleg. Whoever did scribble that note, it wasn't her.'

'Excellent work. That will be good evidence, at the right time.'

'If we're not going to arrest the person in that house,' Tina said, 'what do you suggest as the next course of action?'

With a hint of frustration and anger in his voice, Andy said, 'We all know it's Solomon Peleg in that house, pretending to be his crippled brother. And he's continuing to get away with murder.'

'Nobody's getting away with murder!' Danny said sharply. He allowed himself a moment before saying in a softer tone, 'Andy, I know you're tired, so I'll ignore the note of disrespect in your voice, this time. We all need to take a step back and think this through clearly. Yes, we all have our suspicions, but they're not enough. Never forget, we need to be able to prove it. It's down to us to enable others to see who's responsible.'

'You're right, and I apologise.' Andy shook his head in frustration. 'But how are we going to do that?'

'I think we continue with Operation Sentinel. We let Solomon Peleg do the job for us. I'm convinced that sooner or later, he'll make a mistake, and his deception will be exposed. We just need to make sure that we're right behind him when that happens.'

'Isn't that strategy just a bit too risky, boss?' Tina asked. 'I mean, if Peleg is our killer, isn't there a real chance he could kill again?'

'At the moment, he's under twenty-four-hour observation, so that's not going to happen. If nothing happens prior to the conclusion of Operation Sentinel, then I'll have to review my decision. I may then have to show my hand and make an arrest. My decision for now is that we maintain the observations and the surveillance and wait for him to slip up.'

80

7.00pm, 15 September 1987
2 Fairview Road, Woodthorpe, Nottingham

Chloe had left an hour ago, and as usual, Solomon had gone straight to the secret stash of canned lager that he kept in a locked refrigerator in the integral garage. He poured himself a beer, walked into the lounge and switched the television on.

This was his routine now. It was boring, and he was beginning to feel stir-crazy.

As he took another long drink of cool beer, the telephone began to ring. It startled him. It never rang. He snatched up the phone and said, 'Hello?'

There was a pause. Then a soft, sultry voice said, 'Hello. Is that Mick?'

Solomon was taken aback. Whenever he went out at night, he always used the name Mick Heeton. He racked his brains, trying to recognise the woman's voice.

'Are you there, Mick? It's Vicki. You told me if I was ever down here on business again, to give you a call.'

In an instant, everything came flooding back to him. He had met Vicki on a night out in Derby city centre. She had been in the city on business and was enjoying a night out after a day of meetings.

'Hello, Vicki,' Solomon finally replied. 'This is a very welcome surprise.'

In her soft, north-west accent, the glamorous divorcee said, 'I'm down this way on business again. I'm trying to push through a deal in Sheffield, but I'm heading back to Liverpool in a couple of days. I thought it might be nice if we could catch up before I have to drive back.'

He didn't respond, so she repeated, 'You did say if I was ever down this way again, I should call you. Is everything okay?'

Solomon thought back to that champagne-fuelled night in Derby. He had driven to the neighbouring city to have a night out. He thought it would be far enough away from Nottingham for him not to be recognised.

He had only been in the upmarket champagne bar for fifteen minutes when he saw Vicki standing alone at the bar. She was in her early forties with blonde hair and a voluptuous figure. She wore a clinging black dress that accentuated her curves. She oozed class and sex appeal. He'd been shocked when she had flashed him a radiant smile across the bar, and even more shocked when she walked over and engaged him in friendly conversation.

Solomon had always been shy around women. He couldn't quite believe how interested in him this gorgeous, sexy woman was.

He had splashed the cash, and after drinking a couple of bottles of expensive champagne, Vicki had invited him back to her hotel in the centre of Derby.

They had spent an amazing night together, but it had to end prematurely, as he'd needed to get back to Nottingham before Chloe arrived for work. He had made an excuse about needing an early start for work, and hurriedly left the hotel.

That had been at the beginning of July, just after he had killed his elderly neighbour.

Vicki's voice interrupted his thoughts. With a note of impatience she said, 'Well, do you want to meet up?'

'That would be wonderful. Where are you staying?'

'I'm booked in at the Cavendish Hotel in Baslow. Do you know it?'

'I know Baslow, so I'm sure I could find it.'

'Look, I've got to be back home on the seventeenth. Why don't you come over to the hotel tomorrow night? We could have a nice meal and then spend another gorgeous night together.'

'That sounds perfect. I can be there between seven thirty and eight o'clock tomorrow night; that's not too late to eat, is it?'

'Of course not. We can have a few drinks and who knows what else.' She giggled at her last comment before adding, 'I'll see you tomorrow night. I'll be waiting in reception for you. Don't be late.'

He couldn't quite believe his luck. Smiling broadly, he said, 'See you tomorrow.'

He put the telephone down and took another long drink.

Ever since he'd been forced to kill his aunt Lillian, he had stayed in the house. The whole episode had rattled him. The only people he had seen during that time had been Chloe and that pain-in-the-arse detective. Prior to his aunt arriving on the scene and spoiling everything, he'd been going out at night a couple of times a week. He would drive to neighbouring towns and cities where nobody knew who he was, then park the car up some distance away and spend the night drinking.

He always used the name Mick Heeton on his nights out

and masqueraded as a businessman. In fact, business had been the main topic of conversation with Vicki Allison when they had first met. As far as she was concerned, Mick Heeton was very successful.

It was time for him to start going out again.

He had spent too long cooped up in the house. Everything he'd done, every horrendous act he'd been forced to carry out, was so he could go out and enjoy his life. He refused to spend it locked in the house like some political prisoner.

Tomorrow night he would go out. He would meet the gorgeous Vicki and start living his life again.

81

4.30pm 16 September 1987
Mansfield, Nottinghamshire

I t had been a wonderful day.

Danny had spent the morning asleep. Waking refreshed, he had taken Sue and his baby daughter, Hayley, for a walk around the beautiful lake at Rufford Abbey.

It had been weeks since he'd been able to take an entire day off, and it had been lovely being able to spend some quality time with his wife and child. Though technically today wasn't really an entire day off – he was due to work a twelve-hour night shift later, carrying out surveillance on Operation Sentinel.

Volunteering for the night shift had seemed like a good idea at the time. It showed the junior detectives on the Major Crime Investigation Unit that he was still willing to muck in and do his bit, that he wasn't content to just sit in his office, dishing out orders.

Now, as he prepared a flask of strong, black coffee and

sandwiches for the night shift, he was seriously doubting the wisdom of his decision. As if reading his mind, Sue said, 'It won't be that bad, sweetheart. You're only working one night. Christ, I used to have to do seven night shifts straight when I was at the hospital.'

Danny was acutely aware of the long hours his wife used to put in as a doctor working at the accident and emergency unit of King's Mill hospital but said nothing and just poured the scalding hot water into his thermos flask. He tucked the flask under his arm and picked up his lunch box.

He kissed his wife on the lips. 'I'll see you in the morning. All being well, I should be home by seven.'

Walking into the lounge, he bent down and kissed his sleeping baby daughter gently on her forehead. Before leaving, he kissed Sue again and said, 'Don't worry tonight. If this shift pans out the same as all the others on this operation, I'll be spending the night sitting in my car, trying to stay awake.'

'I know. You told me that already, sweetheart. Please be careful anyway. I'll see you in the morning. Will you want any breakfast when you get home?'

He grinned. 'I think I'll just want my bed. See you tomorrow.'

82

7.00pm, 16 September 1987
Fairview Road, Woodthorpe, Nottingham

D anny had finished his turn parked on Fairview
Road. He had driven his dark blue BMW away as
he saw Rachel Moore pull in and park her Mini
behind him. He had been positioned seventy-five yards from
the suspect's home address. He'd watched the carer leave the
property at six fifteen. There had been no movement since,
and nothing reported from the observations team inside
number nine Fairview Road.

He drove the short distance to the car park at
Woodthorpe Grange Park, where he joined Tina Cartwright
in her Astra and DC Phil Baxter sitting astride his Kawasaki
500cc motorcycle. The car park had been used as a standby
point throughout the operation.

Danny got out of his car and was just about to speak to
Tina when the Cougar radio set in her vehicle burst into life.

'PC Naylor to surveillance team. We have movement at
the front door. Stand by.'

Danny jumped back in his vehicle and started the engine. He heard Rachel Moore acknowledge the Special Operations Unit officer's message. She gave the two-clicks response on her Cougar handset.

'From PC Naylor. The front door is now open, and the suspect has emerged in his wheelchair. He's out of the premises and has closed the front door behind him. He's approaching the target vehicle now. Stand by.'

The surveillance officers all waited for the next signal.

'From PC Naylor. Suspect has got himself in the vehicle. Wheelchair is now folded and placed in the vehicle, behind the passenger seat. Stand by.'

There was another pause. 'From PC Naylor. Target vehicle now reversing off the driveway. Direction of travel to follow. Stand by.'

Again, Danny heard the two-clicks signal from Rachel.

'From PC Naylor. Target vehicle is now off off and is heading towards Woodthorpe Drive. Repeat. Target vehicle is off off and heading for Woodthorpe Drive.'

The next voice on the Cougar radio was Rachel Moore.

'From Charlie Three, I have the eyeball. Vehicle is now held at the junction of Fairview Road and Woodthorpe Drive. It's now a right right, towards the A38 Mansfield Road. Convoy check?'

Danny had been first out of the car park. 'Charlie One. I'll be right behind you in five seconds.'

Tina quickly followed. 'Charlie Two. In convoy.'

Finally, Phil Baxter, on his powerful motorcycle, said, 'Mike One. In position.'

Rachel said, 'Convoy check complete. I still have the eyeball. Target vehicle is right right on the A38, towards Mansfield. Over.'

The MCIU detectives carried out a fluid surveillance,

regularly changing position. A healthy distance was always maintained between themselves and the target vehicle.

Phil Baxter was behind the target vehicle as it approached the roundabout at the junction of the A38 with the M1 motorway.

'From Mike One, at the roundabout. It's not the first, not the second. It's the third exit. Northbound on the M1. Repeat northbound on the M1. Convoy check?'

The other detectives all updated their positions as they drove onto the M1 motorway, heading north.

Danny accelerated his vehicle and overtook the Kawasaki motorcycle before slipping into the nearside lane, seventy yards behind the target vehicle. 'Charlie One. I have the eyeball. Speed is seven zero mph. I have no vehicles for cover and will continue to hang back. Charlie Two, be in position to take the eyeball when I give the word, for a change of direction.'

The surveillance continued along the motorway. As the convoy approached the turn-off for the A617, Danny saw a nearside indication on the target vehicle.

Danny said, 'Charlie One. Charlie Two, can you take the eyeball? There's a nearside indication for the next junction.'

Tina said, 'Charlie Two. In position.'

Danny followed the target vehicle off the motorway. 'Charlie One. Target vehicle is still showing a nearside indication. Charlie Two take the eyeball, I'm turning right.'

Tina said, 'Charlie Two. I have the eyeball. It's a left left onto the A617, towards Chesterfield. Repeat it's a left left onto the A617, towards Chesterfield. Convoy check?'

Once again, the detectives gave their positions. There was a brief delay from Danny as he drove completely around the roundabout before driving onto the A617 towards Chesterfield.

With constant changes in their positions, the detectives

maintained the surveillance through Chesterfield. The powerful motorcycle ridden by Phil Baxter maintained the surveillance as they negotiated the busy town centre. Finally, the target vehicle headed out of the town centre, travelling along the A619 road.

As the convoy approached the village of Baslow, Danny was sixty-five yards behind the target vehicle.

'Charlie One,' he said urgently. 'Nearside indication on target vehicle. It's a left left into the car park of the Cavendish Hotel. Repeat vehicle is into the car park of the Cavendish Hotel. To Charlie Three, I'm going straight on. Are you in a position to follow the target vehicle into the car park? To Charlie Two and Mike One, find a place to stop and wait out. Over.'

Danny drove his BMW straight past the entrance to the car park. He glanced over and saw the suspect's Ford Sierra coming to a halt. As he drove on, he looked in the rear-view mirror and saw Rachel's Mini enter the car park.

Rachel said, 'Target vehicle now stopped. I've parked at the other end of the car park. Stand by.'

Rachel reached across and grabbed the Nikon camera from the front seat. She quickly adjusted the focus and pointed the camera at the Ford Sierra.

She was stunned by what happened next.

The suspect got out of his Ford Sierra and walked nonchalantly towards the main entrance of the hotel.

The shutter on the camera clicked furiously as Rachel began taking photographs. As soon as the suspect had skipped up the stone steps and entered the building, she grabbed the Cougar handset and said, 'Suspect has just got out of the target vehicle and walked into the hotel.'

Danny was equally shocked by her message. 'Repeat your last.'

Rachel said, 'You heard me correctly. Suspect has got out of his vehicle and walked into the hotel.'

'Get yourself inside and wait in the bar,' he replied. 'Order me a bitter shandy. I'll join you inside shortly. We need to see what he's doing.'

Rachel slipped the Cougar radio handset under the passenger seat and the compact Nikon into her handbag. She grabbed her jacket off the back seat, locked the car, then made her way up the stone steps and into the main entrance of the hotel.

83

7.45pm, 16 September 1987
Cavendish Hotel, Baslow, Derbyshire

Once through the main doors of the hotel, Rachel
found herself in the reception area. There was a
door immediately to her right that led into the
hotel bar.

She walked into a room that was dominated by a large
stone fireplace at one end, and an elaborately carved, wooden
bar stretched the length of the airy space. Opposite the bar,
on the other side of the room, there was a series of French
doors that led onto a stone patio, with rows of ornate garden
furniture and spectacular views across the Derbyshire countryside.

She quickly glanced around the bar and could see no sign
of the suspect. Just as she was about to leave the room, she
saw movement on the patio. The suspect was outside, talking
to a blonde woman who was sitting at one of the tables,
enjoying the late evening sunshine. Rachel made her way to

the bar and spoke to the barmaid. 'Could I have a bitter lemon, with ice and a slice, please?'

'Sure. Anything else?'

'Yes, a pint of bitter shandy, please.'

As she fished inside her handbag for her purse, she heard the French doors open behind her. She glanced over her shoulder and saw Peleg approaching the bar. She turned her back on him and sat on one of the bar stools as she waited for her drinks.

As soon as Rachel had paid for her drinks, she heard Peleg say to the barmaid, 'Two gin and tonics with ice, please. And could I also order a bottle of Moet champagne to be sent to room forty-three. We've got a table reservation at eight o'clock in the Poachers Restaurant, and it would be lovely to have chilled champagne waiting when we get back to the room. Thanks.'

The barmaid said, 'Of course, sir. I'll make sure that's all arranged for you.'

Peleg paid for his drinks and took the two gin and tonics outside onto the patio. Rachel moved from the bar stool to a table flanked by two comfortable armchairs, near the stone fireplace. From her new position, she could still see Peleg and his mysterious blonde companion.

Just as she took her first sip of bitter lemon, Danny walked into the bar. 'Did you get the drinks in, darling?'

'Don't worry, boss. No acting required; there's only you and me in here. Peleg's sat outside on the patio with a very glamourous-looking date. He's obviously intending to make a night of it. They've got a meal booked in the Poachers Restaurant next door, and he's just splashed the cash and ordered champagne for the room.'

'I'll go to reception and see if I can book us a table at the restaurant. Any idea who the blonde is?'

Rachel shook her head. 'No idea, but the champagne is

being sent up to room forty-three. My guess is that's her room, as he didn't have time to book in at reception before he came in here to meet her.'

'Good work, Rachel. I take it our man is still walking around freely?'

'He's just walked from the patio to the bar and back. There's bugger all wrong with him, boss.'

Danny drank a mouthful of the bitter shandy. 'I'll go and see if we can get a table. We need to keep an eye on him. Did you get any photos of him walking in?'

'I did. I've got a couple of him bounding up those stone steps outside, as well.'

'Did you bring the camera with you?'

'It's in my handbag.'

'Good. We may be able to get more shots later. I won't be long.'

He returned five minutes later. 'Table for two, booked at eight fifteen.'

'That's great. What name did you use?'

He winked. 'Mr and Mrs Smith.'

Rachel laughed. 'Very original.'

She was still giggling when the French doors opened and Peleg and his companion walked back inside, arm in arm. Danny concentrated on the woman as they walked through the bar towards the restaurant next door. She was very glamorous and looked much younger than she probably was. Her make-up had been applied with a light touch, and her hair was immaculately styled. She had perfectly manicured nails and wore expensive gold jewellery. The only piece of jewellery missing was a wedding band. Her jade green cocktail dress was tight fitting and accentuated her curves. She had obviously made a lot of effort for her date with Peleg. It was also obvious that this wasn't the first time the two of them had met. They giggled in an intimate fashion as they walked through the bar and were oblivious to Danny and Rachel sitting by the fireplace.

Danny waited for the two of them to pass them, then said, 'I wonder who the hell she is? They're obviously very close.'

'My thoughts exactly. They're behaving like love's young dream.'

'Let's give it ten minutes before we go into the restaurant. I'll nip back outside and update Tina and Phil on what's happening. Phil might as well park up next to Tina's motor and stay warm in the car. I think we're going to be here all night.'

84

10.15pm, 16 September 1987
Cavendish Hotel, Baslow, Derbyshire

Danny and Rachel were back in the bar of the hotel, having just finished their evening meal at the Poachers Restaurant. Throughout the meal, they had deliberately stayed a course behind Peleg. When the suspect had finally finished his meal and left the restaurant to go back to the woman's room, Danny and Rachel had told the waiter they would take their coffees in the bar.

Danny had watched the suspect and his companion walk up the sweeping staircase. 'It's time for me to find out who our mystery blonde is,' he said. 'I won't be long.' Danny walked back to reception and spoke to the night porter. 'Is the hotel manager around?'

The porter glanced at the clock. 'Right now, he should be in the kitchens. He'll be making sure everything has been closed down correctly. Is everything okay, sir?'

'Everything's fine, but I do need to speak to him, urgently.'

'Give me a minute, sir.'

The night porter picked up the telephone and rang through to the kitchens. There was a very brief conversation before the night porter hung up and said, 'Mr Tremaine will be with you shortly, sir.'

'Thank you.'

Danny moved away from the desk to avoid any further conversation with the porter while he waited for the hotel manager.

Less than two minutes later, a red-faced man in his late fifties wearing a dark suit bustled into reception. He made eye contact with the night porter, who gestured towards Danny.

He made straight for Danny and said, 'I'm Mr Tremaine, the hotel manager. I understand there's a problem?'

Danny discreetly showed him his warrant card, ensuring it was unseen by the porter. 'My name's Detective Chief Inspector Flint,' he said in a low voice. 'I need to talk to you, in private, about one of your guests.'

The manager's eyes widened, but he kept his cool. 'Very well. You'd better come to my office. It's just behind reception.' The manager picked up the hotel register from the front desk and said, 'This way, please.'

Danny followed the manager into the office. The manager gestured to a seat in front of his desk.

'Take a seat, Detective. What can I help you with?'

'I need to know the name of the woman who's booked into room forty-three.'

'May I ask why you need this information?'

'You may have noticed that she's entertaining a male friend in her room tonight. I believe this man may be responsible for a series of serious crimes in Nottingham. He's currently the subject of a police surveillance operation. Obviously, I'm relying on your discretion in this matter. I have no intention of causing a scene in front of your other guests. I want to resume the surveillance on this man whenever he leaves your hotel. I would like to know as much as I can about the woman he's met here this evening. It could be very important to our enquiry.'

A look of shock appeared on the manager's face, and he asked, 'What sort of crimes is this man suspected of committing?'

'Other than they are serious matters, I can't divulge anything to you at this moment. Your cooperation could be vital though.'

'I just don't see how this woman could be connected to criminal behaviour – I know her well; she's a regular guest here.'

'She may not be involved at all, but it's obvious to me that they're very good... friends. The way they've been behaving towards each other all evening makes me think they know each other well.' Danny paused. 'I'm also aware that he's ordered a bottle of champagne to be sent up to room forty-three. So, read into that what you will. Now, can you tell me who she is, please?'

The manager flicked through the register and said, 'Her name's Victoria Allison. Her home address is Costock House, Nantwich in Cheshire. As I said before, she's stayed with us on several occasions. Ms Allison is an extremely successful businesswoman.'

'Anything else you can tell me?'

'Her vehicle's parked in our secure garage at the side of the hotel. It's a Bentley, and understandably, she likes to keep it secure.'

'It sounds like she's a very wealthy businesswoman.'

The manager nodded and said, 'I've spoken to her in the past, when she has been our guest before. She's the director of a company that specialises in the distribution of delicate, specialist surgical instruments. She travels all over the country, selling her products to hospitals and health trusts.'

'Thanks, Mr Tremaine. This is all very useful.'

'There's one other thing, Detective.'

'Go on?'

'She's leaving tomorrow morning. She has requested breakfast on the terrace at eight thirty and has asked for an alarm call at seven thirty.'

85

7.15am, 17 September 1987
Cavendish Hotel, Baslow, Derbyshire

It had been a very long night.

Danny could see the tiredness etched on the faces of his colleagues. They had spent the night in the car park of the hotel, taking it in turns to nap in their cars, and they were now all sitting in one car together. They were positioned so they had clear line of sight to the main entrance of the hotel and to Peleg's parked car.

Danny said, 'I'll keep this short, because we need to be ready. We know that Victoria Allison has requested an early morning call at seven thirty. I imagine our suspect will make his excuses and leave quickly; he'll want to be back home in plenty of time before any carers arrive at Fairview Road. The last thing he'll want is to raise any suspicions with the care company. Rachel, I want you to be ready with the camera. I want photographs of him leaving the hotel and walking, unaided, back to his car. I'll be inside and will give you the heads-up as he's leaving. I'll give two clicks on the Cougar so you know he's about to emerge through the main door.'

'Okay,' Rachel agreed and took the Nikon from her handbag.

Danny turned to Tina and Phil. 'I think you're going to have it all on keeping up with our suspect this morning. He'll be hotfooting it home. I don't expect him to be sticking to many speed limits.'

Phil Baxter said, 'He won't lose me on the bike. The Kawasaki will keep up, no problem.'

Danny said, 'I don't think he's going to be very surveillance conscious; he'll just be concentrating on getting home. Whatever you do, don't lose him. I don't want there to be a time when we're not behind him, watching his every move.'

Phil nodded.

'Tina,' Danny continued, 'contact the Special Ops lads on Fairview Road as soon as you can. Tell them I want photographs of our suspect as he arrives home. I want evidence of him walking to his car unaided this end and then using the wheelchair at the other end. That's going to be important. I also want you to arrange a meeting in my office at midday today. I want to see you and Andy, along with Sergeant Turner from Special Ops, and Inspector Julius from the Dog Section. Ask Tim Donnelly to be there as well. We're going to need to thrash out a plan to arrest Peleg and search his address tomorrow morning. In the meantime, stress to the Special Operations Unit that they must maintain the observations on Fairview Road until Peleg has been arrested. I know that technically today is the last day of the operation, but they must stay on it until Peleg is arrested.'

'Understood, boss.'

'Right, it's almost seven thirty. Let's get in position and get this done.'

Danny walked back inside the hotel and sat in the bar. He ordered a coffee and sat down in the armchair nearest the door to reception. From his position, he had a clear line of sight to the stairs that Peleg would have to walk down to leave the hotel.

As expected, at seven thirty-five, Danny saw the suspect hurriedly walking down the stairs. He looked pleased with himself and wore the smile of a man who'd just had a wonderful night.

Danny depressed the transmitter on the Cougar handset twice.

Outside the hotel, Rachel was waiting in her car at the far end of the car park. Hearing the double click, she raised the Nikon camera and focussed on the front door of the hotel.

The door opened and the suspect emerged into the sunlight, and she began taking photographs as he walked down the stone steps. She continued pressing the shutter as he strode quickly across the car park and got into his Ford Sierra. She quickly loaded another film and continued taking photographs as the vehicle was driven out of the car park.

Rachel watched as Tina immediately drove out of the car park, following the Sierra. She then heard the roar of Phil's powerful Kawasaki motorcycle as it sped along the A619 towards Chesterfield, closing in on the target vehicle. As soon as the vehicles were all out of sight, Rachel got out of her car and walked inside the hotel. The last part of Danny's plan was for the two of them to question Victoria Allison before she checked out of the hotel.

They knew the businesswoman had ordered breakfast on the terrace at eight thirty. They planned to speak to her as soon as she had finished her morning meal.

It was now almost eight o'clock.

86

8.45am, 17 September 1987
The Terrace, Cavendish Hotel, Baslow, Derbyshire

Victoria Allison looked as glamorous at eight thirty in the morning as she had done the night before. The only difference was her attire. This morning, instead of a jade green cocktail dress, she was wearing a navy-blue jacket and pencil skirt with a high-necked, cream blouse.

Today, she looked every inch the successful businesswoman.

Apart from the couple sipping coffee at the far end of the terrace, she was alone. She had ordered a light breakfast of coffee and croissants with jam.

It was a beautifully sunny and warm morning, and she was enjoying the spectacular views across the Derbyshire countryside. She was just contemplating ordering another cafetiere of coffee when she became aware of somebody standing beside her table. She looked up and saw it was the couple who had been drinking coffee on the terrace.

The man held out an identification card and said quietly, 'My name's Detective Chief Inspector Flint, and this is Detective Constable Moore. I need to ask you a few questions. Do you mind if we sit down?'

Victoria was shocked. Her facial expression must have given that feeling away, because the man said quickly, 'It's nothing for you to worry about, but it is important we talk. I need to ask you some questions about the man you met here last night.'

Regaining some of her composure, Victoria said, 'Please, sit down.'

Danny and Rachel sat opposite her. 'I'm sorry we've had to approach you like this,' Danny said. 'We're currently investigating the man you met last night. He's the subject of an ongoing surveillance operation.'

Victoria said, 'Investigating him? What on earth for? Is he dangerous?'

'If you're asking me if I thought you were in any danger from him personally, then the answer is an emphatic no. Having said that, I do believe he's a dangerous individual. We're currently investigating three suspicious deaths where he's heavily implicated.'

Again, she couldn't hide the shock from her face.

Danny said gently, 'When did you two first meet?'

'I first met Mick in Derby, at the beginning of July.'

'Mick?'

'Mick Heeton. That's who I was with last night.'

'Okay. Why Derby?'

'I run my own company, manufacturing specialist surgical instruments. I do a lot of travelling across the UK to gain orders. I had been in Derby for two days of meetings with surgical registrars from Derby Royal hospital. Whenever I'm working away, I always stay an extra night in the hotel after the last meeting. It allows me to drive home feeling refreshed the next morning. It's just my own quirky thing. Wherever I am, I always have that last night out on the town to unwind. These meetings can be very stressful at times. That night, I was celebrating landing a huge order, so I was in a champagne bar on Friary Street in the city.'

'Is that where you two met?'

'Yeah. I was having a nice night, but I was on my own. Anyway, I saw this tall, slim guy giving me the eye, so I went over and started chatting to him. We had a lot in common. He was in business, like me. He told me he had his own building company. He was a widower, with a young daughter. I'm a divorcee, with a young daughter.'

'So you got on well?'

'We got on very well. We had a great night. I was really enjoying his company, so I invited him back to the hotel. We had a lovely time.'

'Have you seen him since July?'

'Not until last night. Look, Chief Inspector. This isn't a great love story I'm talking about here. We're just two consenting adults who find each other attractive. That's not against the law, is it?'

'Of course not. Do you plan to meet him again?'

'Before this conversation, if I had meetings in the East Midlands, I would probably have given him a call. Now, I'm not so sure. All these questions are frightening me a little.'

'What if I told you that Mick Heeton isn't the man's real name?'

There was a pause; then she said, 'In all honesty, I wouldn't be too surprised. Men lie all the time to get what they want. Is he married?'

'No, he isn't married. His real name is Solomon Peleg. It sounds like everything else he told you about himself was a lie.'

'I see.'

Rachel said, 'I'm sorry, but this next question is extremely delicate. Please don't think I'm prying. What I need to ask you is very important. You obviously spent the night together here and when you first met this man in Derby. How was he physically?'

'Do you mean in bed?'

Rachel nodded her assent.

'Do you really need me to answer that question?'

'I wouldn't ask if it wasn't important. I'm not asking for the sake of it.'

Again, there was a long pause as Victoria weighed up what to say. In a voice quivering with more than a little embarrassment, she eventually said, 'There was a kind of naivety about his lovemaking that I found quite attractive. He was gentle and unselfish. Most of all, he was very enthusiastic and energetic.'

Danny said, 'Would it shock you to know that the man you met last night spends his life confined to a wheelchair? He lives in a specially adapted house, and the car he drives is a Motability vehicle. His folded-down wheelchair was in the back of his car parked outside this hotel last night.'

Victoria was shocked. 'That's impossible. There's nothing physically wrong with him at all. He's extremely fit and supple. Trust me, I know. I really don't understand any of this. Will you please tell me what's going on?'

'I told you earlier that we were investigating three suspicious deaths, where this man has been heavily implicated. We've always had our suspicions, but we've always had to discount this man as a suspect purely because he was confined to a wheelchair. Now can you see why we needed to ask you those very personal questions?'

'Yes, I can see that. What do you want from me now?'

'I would like you to make a written statement that puts on record what you've just told us.'

'And if I don't?'

'I can't force you to make a statement. I hope you will, because this man could be a danger to others in the future. I'm not going to lie to you. If we charge this man, you will very likely have to give evidence at Crown Court. It could prove embarrassing to you and may have an impact on your business.'

'I'm not worried about my business. I employ a brilliant publicity team that would minimise any fallout. I'm more concerned what my eight-year-old daughter would make of it all.'

'At that age, she will make of it whatever you tell her to. It's extremely important that we can use your evidence. We have our suspicions, but that's all they are. We need solid evidence to bring this man to justice.'

Victoria thought for a couple of minutes. Finally, she said, 'Okay. I'll make a statement.'

Danny said, 'Thank you. It's really important.'

She said, 'I do need to be back in the north-west by two o'clock this afternoon for a directors' meeting. How long will all this take?'

Rachel said, 'The nearest police station is in Chesterfield, which is only a ten-minute drive from here. I'll take you there and bring you back. The statement won't take long. I'll have you back here by eleven o'clock at the latest. Is that okay?'

'That's fine,' Victoria said quietly.

87

12.10pm, 17 September 1987
MCIU Office, Mansfield Police Station

The entire Major Crime Investigation Unit had gathered in the main briefing room. Danny was deliberately delaying what he hoped would be the final briefing in relation to the planned arrest of Solomon Peleg.

As he glanced at his watch for the umpteenth time, a breathless Rachel arrived. She was holding the crucial witness statement obtained from Victoria Allison earlier that morning.

Danny said, 'Do we have enough in the statement?'

'More than enough, sir,' Rachel confirmed. 'The man who Victoria Allison knows as Mick Heeton has no physical disability and is extremely fit.'

Danny smiled and then addressed the assembled detectives, 'I've asked you all here so we can plan the arrest of the man giving his name as Saul Peleg. We now have evidence to suggest that this man is Saul's identical twin brother,

Solomon. We will also need to plan the subsequent search of his address at Fairview Road. I want to briefly go through each of our current investigations prior to formulating the planned arrest. If you've anything relevant to add at any time, shout out.'

He directed his gaze to Tim Donnelly. 'Tim, make sure you fast-track development of the photographs Rachel took last night. This is a priority. I want those photographs ready for when we decide to challenge the identity of Saul Peleg. I'll also need you to provide staff in the morning for the search. The main search will be carried out by members of the Special Operations Unit, but depending on what we find, it could be that the Fairview Road address turns into one big crime scene. I need you to be able to cater for that possibility. Can you do that?'

'I'll get onto the photographs straight away,' Tim replied. 'You'll have them this evening. I'll also arrange enough staff and suitable equipment for the search of the home address.'

'Good. Thanks.' Danny paused and then said, 'Andy, can we start with what we now know about the death of Rebecca Peleg?'

'Certainly.' Andy Wills stood up to better address the room. 'Following the exhumation and post-mortem, we now know that Rebecca Peleg didn't take her own life. She was manually strangled, and then her death was staged to look like a suicide by hanging. On the night she died, the only other people in the house were Saul and Solomon Peleg. Saul Peleg is a genuine paraplegic with a severe spinal injury that prevents him from walking unaided. So the only person, other than an intruder, who could have killed Rebecca was her son Solomon.'

'Have you found any motive? Any reason why he'd kill his own mother?' Danny asked.

'My research indicates that Solomon only remained at the

family home under sufferance. We do know he had lost his job immediately prior to his mother's death. So it's possible there had been a family dispute over finance.'

'Okay. Thanks, Andy. We've got enough for our suspect to be arrested on suspicion of his mother's death. Which leads us to Saul Peleg. The question is this, if Solomon Peleg has assumed the identity of his disabled brother, what is his reasoning? Rachel, what do we know?'

'The enquiries we've completed show that Saul is very wealthy and financially secure,' Rachel said. 'The house on Fairview Road is fully paid for; there's no mortgage. He controls a seven-figure fortune. This huge amount of money was awarded to him following a medical negligence claim at the high court. The money has come from the health trust responsible for causing his spinal injury.'

'So if Solomon can successfully deceive people into believing he's Saul, he would effectively control his brother's fortune.'

'Yes, sir.'

'Which leads us neatly on to the next question. If this is what Solomon has done, where is Saul? Is his brother now dead too? Or is he still alive and hidden away somewhere?' Danny paused to let his last comment sink in, then he said, 'After we've detained Solomon, I want the house and garden of the Fairview Road address searched thoroughly. We need to find Saul.'

He then spoke directly to Sergeant Turner from the Special Operations Unit. 'I know the capabilities of the SOU search teams are second to none, Graham, and I cannot emphasise enough the importance of this search. It's vital that if there's any trace of Saul or of his current whereabouts, your teams find it.'

'Corinne,' he said to the inspector from the Dog Section, 'thanks for coming over at such short notice. Will you be able to support the search teams with a cadaver dog?'

'We do have a working cadaver dog, a springer spaniel called Tikka. She's only just finished her training, but PC Davis is a very experienced handler.'

'That's great. Will they be available tomorrow morning, from eight o'clock onwards? I would like the dog to go over the house and garden before the search teams go in and possibly confuse the issue.'

'I'll make sure they're available early doors. As you say, it wouldn't be ideal to follow a rummage team. Are there any specific areas you have in mind?'

'Definitely the garden and outdoor space. There's also a vehicle involved, a Ford Sierra. Then it will be a case of a general search of the house. Checking for any hidden recesses and cupboards.'

'Because Tikka's still a young dog, it may be better for the handler to work her in stages. Perhaps do the house first, then have a break before doing the car, and finally the garden and grounds. That will allow the search teams to get stuck into searching the house quickly.'

'That sounds like a good plan; anything to add to that, Graham?'

Sergeant Turner shook his head. 'That sounds good to me. My lads have all worked alongside PC Davis on searches before. I'm sure if there's anything to find with his dog, he'll find it.'

Danny then said to Andy, 'Can you tell everyone what we know about the suspicious death of Lillian Rhodes on the M1 motorway?'

Andy said, 'Lillian Rhodes is the sister of Rebecca Peleg, and the aunt of Saul and Solomon. She lived in Douglas on the Isle of Man. We've made enquiries in Douglas and now know that Lillian Rhodes left the island on the nineteenth of

August to visit her sister in Nottingham. Two days later, she was found dead on the M1 motorway near Strelley. The responding officers thought at first that they were dealing with a suicide. That the woman had deliberately jumped from the bridge in front of an onrushing heavy goods vehicle.'

He paused before continuing, 'However, the post-mortem revealed that Lillian Rhodes had been strangled to death before being thrown from the motorway bridge. We're currently speaking to all taxi firms in the city, trying to establish if Lillian Rhodes was taken by taxi to Fairview Road. The person we believe to be Solomon Peleg has been spoken to about his aunt. He's categorically denied that she ever arrived at the house. There is CCTV footage showing a woman answering the description of the deceased arriving at Nottingham railway station on the morning of August the twentieth. She is last seen carrying an old-fashioned carpet bag, making her way towards the taxi rank. Unfortunately, there are no images showing if she got into a taxi. To the search teams, check the photographs taken from the CCTV and acquaint yourselves with what the distinctive carpet bag looks like. It has never been recovered and is still outstanding.'

'Thanks, Andy.' Danny took a deep breath. 'Final point. Tina, can you tell us all what links Solomon Peleg to the murder of Angela Billson, please?'

'Following enquiries made at the Bestwood Medical Centre, where Angela Billson worked,' Tina began, 'we now know that one of the last people to see her on the day she disappeared should have been Saul Peleg. When officers interviewed the person they believed to be Saul, they were told that the health visitor never kept that appointment. We now believe it's likely that those officers were speaking to Solomon, and not Saul, that day. We've since found further evidence that Angela Billson had a very close working relationship with Saul. My suspicions are that Angela did make that appointment to see Saul. I believe she may have recognised that it was Solomon masquerading as Saul. It's possible that she was killed to prevent the truth getting out.

'The post-mortem of Angela Billson found an identical cause of death to that of Rebecca Peleg and Lillian Rhodes. For now, this is all just supposition. So anything the search teams can find that links Angela Billson to the house on Fairview Road would be brilliant.'

'Thanks, Tina.' Danny turned to look at his team. 'As we are all acutely aware, there has recently been another suspicious death on Fairview Road that we are treating as murder. This is the death of Gladys Miller. Peleg is linked to this because of the proximity to his home address and the fact that we believe he provided us with a false lead. This was possibly a crude attempt to deflect our enquiries, trying to make us believe that the murderer couldn't be somebody local. Until now, the man in the wheelchair at Fairview Road has always been ruled out of all these enquiries purely because of his disability. After the surveillance operation last night, we now know that this disability is all an elaborate deception. I believe that Solomon Peleg is the man in the wheelchair, not his disabled brother, Saul.'

He looked around the room. 'Does anyone have any questions before we discuss the tactics of tomorrow morning's operation to arrest Solomon Peleg?'

The room remained silent.

Danny said, 'Good. Okay, immediately after the property has been entered, and the suspect secured by the Special Operations Unit, the arrest of Peleg will be made by Detective Inspector Cartwright and Detective Sergeant Wills. The suspect will initially be arrested for the murder of Rebecca Peleg. Any questions so far?'

Once again, there were no questions, so Danny continued, 'Tina, I want you to arrest him as Saul Peleg and treat
him as such. I want him in his wheelchair, thinking that we
still believe his deception. I want to give him enough rope to
hang himself, for want of a better expression, by continuing
his charade. Any thoughts on that tactic?'

Andy said, 'How do we justify his arrest for murder if we
believe he's confined to a wheelchair?'

'We'll arrest him for conspiracy to murder initially.'

Andy agreed. 'At what stage do we treat him as Solomon?'

'As soon as we can categorically prove we're not talking to
Saul.' When Andy still looked unsure, Danny said, 'Look,
Andy, I understand your concerns, as I've been wrestling with
this issue myself. I know this isn't an everyday or ideal
scenario, but you've got to trust me on this. Very early in the
questioning, I'll want the photographs from the Cavendish
Hotel put to him. I anticipate that after that, he'll no longer
be able to maintain his lies.'

Danny continued, 'I want the suspect brought to Mansfield Police Station for questioning. We'll need him here. It's
important that we have access to all the material stored in the
various incident rooms for the different enquiries. The
searches of the property at Fairview Road and the Ford Sierra
will be undertaken as we've already discussed.'

He paused, waiting for any questions.

Tina said, 'Do you have any preference for the interview
team?'

'Glen Lorimar is our best interviewer. I would like Glen,
working alongside Rachel, to carry out the interviews. Tina,
you and I will debrief each interview immediately after they
have concluded. That way we'll be able to discuss any
changes in tactics we may need to employ. It's going to be
vital to push Solomon into reacting and get him talking. A lot
of our evidence is still only circumstantial.'

Tina nodded. 'Okay, boss.'

Danny said, 'All that's left to finalise is the timing of the operation. The final briefing will be here at five o'clock tomorrow morning. We'll be on Fairview Road, ready to make entry into the target premises, at six o'clock. Any questions?'

Graham Turner said, 'I take it you want the observations on the property at Fairview Road to continue until we actually have Peleg detained?'

'Yes. It's important those obs are maintained for one more night.' He gave a final glance around the room at his assembled colleagues, grim faced yet determined. 'If that's everything, I'll see everyone back here at five o'clock tomorrow morning for the final briefing.'

The room erupted into a cacophony of sound as people began to discuss the operation and their different roles in it.

Danny approached Corrinne Julius as everyone had started to move. 'Corrine, there's no need for PC Davis to attend tomorrow morning's briefing with Tikka. Ask him to go directly to the property on Fairview Road for seven o'clock. I'll see him there and brief him personally.'

'Will do, sir.'

'Thanks.' Danny walked into his office and closed the door. It was now almost one o'clock in the afternoon, and he realised that he, and several of his colleagues, had been awake for almost twenty-four hours.

Sticking his head back out of the door, he called, 'Rachel, Tina, have you got a second?'

As the two women entered the office, he said, 'You two must be shattered. It's going to be another very busy day tomorrow. You both need to go home now and get some rest so you're ready for it. I'm going home myself shortly.'

He turned to Rachel and said, 'Glen will do the prep for the first interview with Peleg in the morning. That will give you time to catch up when you come on duty tomorrow, okay?'

'Okay, sir.'

'Tina, tell Andy to oversee anything else that needs organising today. Then go home and get some rest. It's been a long shift. See you tomorrow.'

88

9.15pm, 17 September 1987
Meadows Police Station, Nottingham

Manjeet Ayyar was feeling worried. He had been standing outside the police station opposite the taxi rank near the Midland Railway station for ten minutes. He always felt nervous about any interaction with the police, and he wondered if he was doing the right thing. His English wasn't the best, and people sometimes struggled to understand him properly.

He had been in India for a family wedding since the twenty-second of August, only returning two days ago. When he had reported for work earlier that night at the taxi firm on Castle Street in the Meadows, he'd seen the poster in the drivers' rest room.

It was a grainy photograph of an elderly woman leaving the railway station. She was carrying a tatty old carpet bag, like the one his own grandmother used to have. The poster on the wall had been left by the police. It was asking if any drivers recalled taking this woman as a fare on the morning of August the twentieth.

He remembered the old woman, partly because of the carpet bag, but mainly because he had been forced to spray the cab with an air freshener after she had got out. She had a disgusting body odour problem. He was certain that the woman on the poster was the same woman he'd picked up from the railway station that morning.

Finally, he plucked up enough courage to walk across the street and enter the police station. He held out the poster to the constable standing behind the desk. 'Please. I need to talk to somebody about this.'

The young officer looked at the poster and then at the worried face of the man standing in front of him. 'Okay, sir. What can you tell me about this woman?'

'I pick her up in cab after she got off train.'

The officer made a note on the pad in front of him. 'I see. Can you remember where you took her?'

'She went to a very nice place in Woodthorpe. First house on Fairview Road. I think it was number two.'

'Are you sure about this?'

'Oh yes, very sure, Officer. I've only just seen the poster. I've been back to Jaipur for a wedding. If I'd seen it, I would have been in before.'

'Very well, sir.' The officer gestured to the waiting room. 'Take a seat. One of our detectives will be down to see you shortly.'

Worried, Manjeet said, 'A detective? Am I in trouble?'

'Not at all, sir. I know the CID have been trying to find the taxi driver who may have picked this woman up for quite a while. So I'm sure whoever comes to talk to you will be very pleased to hear what you've got to say. Grab a seat; they'll be down shortly.'

Manjeet still felt nervous. He could feel the butterflies in his stomach, but he had made his choice, and now he would have to see it through. The officer had said he wasn't in any trouble. He would just tell the detective what he knew; then he could get back to work and start earning some money.

89

6.00am, 18 September 1987
2 Fairview Road, Woodthorpe, Nottingham

Solomon Peleg had been in that half-awake, half-asleep state where dreams slowly blur into reality, warm and comfortable in bed, when suddenly he heard a loud crash downstairs. He was instantly wide awake. He clambered out of bed to go and investigate but stopped short when he heard heavy boots racing up the stairs. Shouts of 'Police!' rang through the house.

He made a conscious decision to get back into bed. A voice inside his head told him he needed to maintain the identity of Saul. His heart rate was racing and his breathing shallow as the first police officers burst into his bedroom.

Remaining perfectly still under the bedclothes, he shouted, 'What the hell's going on!'

The first officer said, 'Police! Don't move.'

With an air of indignant anger he shouted, 'I can't fucking move, you idiot! What the fuck do you think you're doing?'

A man and a woman wearing suits entered the room

behind the officers. He instantly recognised the man as the detective who had visited him before about the vehicle he had reported seeing outside of his neighbour's house. It had been a false report. Surely all this wasn't just about that?

He said to the detective, 'What's this all about? You can't just smash your way into my home like this. I'm going to complain; this is disgusting.'

'Saul Peleg, I'm Detective Inspector Cartwright. I'm arresting you on suspicion of conspiracy to murder Rebecca Peleg.'

Solomon felt suddenly cold, but he tried to stay calm and maintain his act. After she had cautioned him, Solomon managed to reply, 'Murder? That's my mother you're talking about. This is madness. What the fuck's going on?'

Detective Sergeant Wills then said, 'You're going to be taken to Mansfield Police Station for questioning. Do you understand what's happening?'

'How the hell do you expect me to get to Mansfield? In case you don't remember, Detective, I can't go anywhere without that wheelchair.'

'We'll help you get dressed and then take you and your wheelchair to Mansfield.'

Growing angrier by the second, Peleg shouted, 'For God's sake! I'm naked under this duvet. You're not helping me get dressed while she's still here.'

Detective Inspector Cartwright said, 'I'm leaving, Mr Peleg.' Then, to Andy: 'Get him dressed and bring him to Mansfield as quick as you can.'

She walked out of the bedroom, and Andy Wills said, 'Are you going to cooperate with us, Mr Peleg? The sooner we get you up and dressed and across to Mansfield, the sooner you can answer our questions and get this all sorted out.'

'It looks like I don't have much choice. My clothes are in the wardrobe. When can I talk to my solicitor?'

'I'll make sure you have access to a solicitor. Do you have one in mind?'

'Yes, I do. I want Richard Jacobson from Golding and Hurt, in the city. He deals with all my legal issues.'

'Okay. I'll make sure he's contacted and attending Mansfield Police Station. Don't worry, you'll be able to talk to him before we question you. Now is there anything in particular you want to wear?'

Peleg was now raging. 'I don't fucking care! Just grab the first pair of trousers and shirt you find. I want to get this shit sorted out. I'll make sure that Richard sues the police force for every penny they've fucking got! This is outrageous.'

90

9.00am, 18 September 1987
Custody Block, Mansfield Police Station, Nottinghamshire

Danny was in the custody area, talking to the on-call police surgeon. The custody sergeant had wanted Saul Peleg to be medically examined prior to being interviewed to ensure that he was fit to interview.

That examination was about to take place, and Danny needed to clear a few things up with the police surgeon first.

He said, 'I understand that a person suffering the alleged disabilities of this prisoner would have certain needs when it comes to going to the toilet.'

'That's correct, Chief Inspector,' the doctor replied. 'Everyone with this level of disability is different. Some can manage their own needs by inserting a catheter themselves every four to six hours. Others need to have that procedure done for them. As far as bowel movements go, that is generally an assisted procedure and is set to a pattern or regime. It's usually every other day. I won't know what his personal requirements are until I've spoken to him.'

'Will going to the toilet affect his ability to answer our questions?'

'Of course not. What it will affect greatly is his comfort while he's detained at the police station.'

'Yes, I understand that. The problem I have is this. I have genuine reasons to believe that this prisoner is lying about his disability, and that he doesn't suffer from paralysis or any of its associated issues. I would like you to allow the prisoner to lead the conversation on his toilet requirements. If he's genuinely disabled, I would think that would be at the fore-front of his mind.'

'It's one of the biggest problems paraplegics face daily, so I would think so too. Very well, I'm prepared to wait and see what he volunteers on the subject. Any other things I should know about Mr Peleg?'

'That's it, Doctor.'

'Okay. Let's see what he's got to say.'

The police surgeon then walked to Peleg's cell to speak with the prisoner and undertake the physical examination.

The doctor returned twenty minutes later, and as the police surgeon approached him, Danny saw he looked worried and said, 'Is everything okay?'

'Your prisoner's fit to interview. Can you tell me why you believe this man is faking his injuries?'

'I'd rather not go into detail about that, Doctor. Suffice to say, we do have evidence that leads us to think that, why?'

'Because I could find none of the severe muscle wastage of the legs that I would normally associate with someone who's been confined to a wheelchair for the length of time Mr Peleg has. Yes, his legs are thin, but the muscle tone is good. I also got the impression that he was fighting against the reflex tests I carried out.'

'That's very interesting. Did he raise any concerns about the toilet with you?'

'He never said a word about it. Which I also found very strange.'

'Thanks, Doctor. Can you enter your general observations on the custody record, please? They could be quite telling later.'

'No problem. If he does raise the toilet issue at any time, you'll have to call me back out. I'll be putting that on the record as well.'

'Of course. Thanks, Doctor.' Danny then said to Glen and Rachel, 'Before you start the interview, ask Peleg to sign a medical consent form. Tell his solicitor that it's so we can better understand his client's needs while he's in custody.'

'Okay, boss.'

'Have you given disclosure to his solicitor yet?'

'Yes. We've just been waiting for the police surgeon to do his stuff. We should be good to go now.'

'Okay. Keep your questions for this first interview limited to the death of his mother.'

'Yes, sir.'

'Good luck.'

91

9.30am, 18 September 1987
Custody Block, Mansfield Police Station, Nottinghamshire

Prior to starting the interview, Rachel had offered Saul Peleg the medical consent document to sign. He eventually signed it but only after persuasion from his solicitor that it would be in his own best interests to do so.

Ever since arriving in the custody area, he had been reluctant to sign anything.

Rachel switched on the tape machine, recording the interview.

After the preliminary introductions, Glen Lorimar said, 'Saul, you've been arrested earlier today on suspicion of conspiracy to commit the murder of Rebecca Peleg. Do you have any involvement in the death of your mother?'

'Of course not. She was my mother, and I loved her.'

'Tell me what you remember about your mother's death?'

'It was awful. I was in bed, and when I woke up, I could see my mother's body hanging from the loft hatch.'

'You could see her from your bed?'

'Yes. The bedroom door was open, so I could see out onto the gallery landing. I saw her legs just dangling there.' He looked down at the table.

Glen paused and then said, 'Did you see anything else on the landing that was unusual?'

'No.'

'What happened next?'

'I shouted for my brother.'

'And where was Solomon?'

'I think he was still asleep in bed. I had to shout for quite a while before he answered me.'

'Then what happened?'

'I couldn't stand to see my mother hanging like that, so I asked my brother to cut her down.'

'Why didn't you wait for the police to arrive?'

He shrugged. 'I don't know. I didn't know what to do for the best. I just knew I didn't want to see my mother like that. It was grotesque.'

'What do you think happened to your mum?'

'She killed herself.'

'Had she given you any indication that she was considering taking her own life?'

Again, there was the nonchalant shrug of the shoulders before he said sarcastically, 'Do many suicidal people give written notice of their intentions?'

Glen ignored the sarcasm and said, 'There can be signs of depression, leading up to the act.'

'Well, I never saw anything. I thought it was because she was fed up with taking care of me.'

'Who else was in the house on the night it happened?'

'Just me and my brother.'

'No one else?'

'No.'

'Where's your brother now?'

'He went to New Zealand for a job.'

'Long way to go for a job. Have you kept in touch?'

Again, there was the shrug; then he shook his head.

'The tape can't see you shaking your head, Saul. Have you kept in touch?'

'No. I haven't heard from him. I don't suppose I will now he's got an exciting new life. He doesn't need me to drag him down.'

'Don't you two get on?'

Saul appeared to get irritable and said, 'I don't want to talk about my brother.'

'Okay. Let's talk about your mother instead. How did you and your mum get on?'

'I loved my mum; she did everything for me.'

'Did she get on with Solomon?'

'They had a lot of arguments. Family disagreements mainly, but nothing too bad.'

'Your mum was only a small lady, wasn't she?'

'I suppose so.'

'Since your mother's death, we've carried out a further, more detailed investigation into the circumstances surrounding it. We've found some very strange anomalies that I hope you can help me with.'

Glen paused, waiting for a reaction. Saul remained silent.

'Your mother wasn't tall enough to get into the loft at your home without using a stepladder,' Glen continued. 'When the police arrived, the only ladders in the house were found in the garage. How did she manage to get into the loft and hang herself without using a ladder?'

'Somebody must have moved it?'

'Who?'

'I don't know.'

'You described earlier that Solomon was still asleep in bed when you first saw your mother hanging from the loft space. You didn't describe seeing any ladders on the landing then.'

There was a long silence.

Glen noticed a furtive look exchanged between Saul and his solicitor. The solicitor gave an almost imperceptible shake of his head.

Saul then said, 'No comment.'

'Is there any reason why you've answered that question with no comment?'

'No comment.'

'Are you suggesting to me that Solomon moved the ladder prior to you waking up?'

'No comment.'

'If that's the case, are you also suggesting that Solomon had something to do with your mother's death?'

'No comment.'

'The reason I'm asking that question is this, there's no way a woman of your mother's short stature could have reached up and secured the rope that was used to hang her to the beam in the loft.'

'No comment.'

'Somebody else tied that rope to the beam, Saul.'

'No comment.'

'You told me earlier that you thought your mother had committed suicide. That's not true, is it? Your mother was strangled; she was murdered, wasn't she?'

'No comment.'

'Did you have any involvement in the murder of your mother?'

'No comment.'

'Okay, Saul. We'll take a break there. Is there anything else you want to tell me?'

'No comment.'

Glen stated the time and date, and Rachel switched off

the tape machine. The tape labels were signed, then Saul's solicitor said, 'Before you put him back in the cell, I'd like a quick word with my client, please.'

Glen said, 'No problem. Just hit the alarm strip when you've finished.'

92

11.00am, 18 September 1987
MCIU Office, Mansfield Police Station

Danny asked, 'How did it go?'

Glen Lorimar sat down heavily. 'It was a "no comment" interview. Pretty much as I'd expected it would be. Although, he did answer a few questions to start with, which I hadn't expected.'

Rachel said, 'Did you see the look that slimeball Jacobson gave him?'

Glen agreed, frowning. 'I did.'

Danny said, 'Did he sign the medical consent form?'

Rachel removed the signed document from her folder and said, 'Eventually. He was very reluctant to sign it at first, but his brief talked him into it.'

Tina said, 'So Jacobson's not always a slimeball, then?'

'Point taken. It's just so frustrating when solicitors shut down their clients like that.'

Danny sighed. 'It's the system we all have to work to. So

when he was answering questions, did he say anything interesting?'

'There was one significant thing,' Glen said. 'He said that when he woke up, he could see his mother straight away. He then shouted for Solomon, who took an age to come, as he was still asleep. He also told us that only he and his brother were in the house and that there was no stepladder on the landing when he first saw his mother.'

'Did you question him about family dynamics?'

'I touched on it. According to him, everyone loved everyone else. He did say he often heard Solomon arguing with his mother. At one point, he totally refused to answer any questions about his brother.'

'I find it a little bizarre that he's offering up any information. Do you think he's trying to push us towards the brother, who he would have us believe is in New Zealand?'

'I get the impression that whoever it is sitting in that wheelchair, they are extremely cold and calculating. I saw the look that Rachel mentioned, but I felt that it was Saul's decision to stop talking and not the solicitor's. I could be wrong, but it seemed to me that he wanted us to hear those first answers, but that was all.'

'Okay, that's interesting. So what next?'

Before Glen could outline the content of the next planned interview, Andy Wills knocked once and walked in. 'Sorry to interrupt, boss. We've just had a breakthrough. The taxi driver who picked up Lillian Rhodes from the train station has been traced.'

'How?'

'One of the posters we left at all the taxi companies has paid off. A driver, employed by Castle Cars in the Meadows, saw the poster and remembered picking her up.'

'That's fantastic. Could he also remember where he took her?'

'He dropped her at number two on Fairview Road.'

'Peleg's house?'

'Yes, sir.'

'Has he made a written statement?'

'The statement was taken by a detective at Meadows Police Station last night. A copy of it has been faxed to this office. The original statement is with a police motorcyclist and will be delivered here within the hour.'

'Good. Two questions. Who's the taxi driver, and why hasn't he come forward before now?'

'His name's Manjeet Ayyar. He's been in India for a family wedding. Lillian Rhodes was his last fare before he went away.'

Danny turned to Glen and said, 'In light of this development, you might need to rethink your interview strategy. I want you and Rachel to sit down with Andy and Tina. Between you, work out the best strategy to question Peleg about his aunt Lillian. It will be the first time we can challenge him over a statement he's made to us before. He was adamant that his aunt never made it to the house. Let's see what he's got to say about that now.'

Glen nodded.

'I'm going to Fairview Road. I want to see for myself how the searches are progressing. Take a break when you've planned the next interview. It won't hurt to let Peleg stew for a while. Don't leave it for too long though; don't forget the custody clock's ticking. I'll be gone for a couple of hours, so don't wait for me to get back before you start the next interview.'

93

12.15pm, 18 September 1987
2 Fairview Road, Woodthorpe, Nottingham

Danny parked his car outside the Peleg house and walked up the driveway. The first person he saw, standing near the front door, was Tim Donnelly.

'Hello, Tim. How's the search going?'

'To put it bluntly, boss, we've got fuck all so far. The biggest find we've had is an old writing pad that's covered in Saul Peleg's signature.'

'You mean the type of thing we used to do as teenagers? Practicing our signatures for when we became famous?'

Tim laughed. 'Yeah, something like that. It's just page after page of Saul Peleg's signature.'

'Could it be somebody practicing forging that signature?'

'It's possible.'

'And that's all we've got?'

'That's it. It's still early days though.'

'Okay. Is Sergeant Turner around?'

'I think he's in the back garden, with the dog handler.'

The harassed Scenes of Crime supervisor led Danny through the house, out of the patio doors and into the rear garden.

He could see Graham Turner speaking to the dog handler at the top of the garden while he worked his dog. The small spaniel traversed backwards and forwards across the garden, working on a long leash.

Graham Turner saw Danny approaching and raised his hand to stop his progress, before walking down to meet him.

'Sorry, sir. I had to stop you; the dog's still working the garden. There's nothing here so far, but there was a strong indication earlier when she was sniffing around the boot of the Ford Sierra. That little dog went crazy. Davo reckons it's one of the strongest indications he's ever seen.'

'That's good news. Have you arranged for a full lift for the vehicle yet? I want it taken to the forensic bay at headquarters for a full forensic examination.'

'That's all in hand, boss.'

PC Davis put the springer spaniel on a short lead and walked down the garden towards Danny.

Danny greeted him and said, 'You've had a result in the boot of the car, then?'

Davis grinned. 'Tikka went nuts. I'd stake my pension that there's been a dead body in the boot of that car at some point.'

'Good work. Anything in the house?'

'There was a lesser indication in the lounge and another in the garden shed. Neither was strong enough to convince me of the presence of a corpse.'

'How much of the garden is there still to do?'

'I'm about done, sir. In all honesty I don't think there's much chance of finding anything here. It's all too neat and manicured. Far too pretty and well cared for, if you know what I mean. There's no recently disturbed soil or rough areas where rubbish has been thrown.'

Trying not to show his disappointment, Danny said, 'Well, you can only find what's there. Keep at it.'

He started to walk back towards the house when he had a thought. He remembered there had been an area of the murdered neighbour's garden that was just as PC Davis had described.

'How long will it take you to finish searching here?' he asked the dog handler.

'About another ten minutes, that's all.'

'When you've finished here, don't go anywhere.' He turned to Graham Turner and said, 'Come with me, Graham.'

Danny walked back out onto Fairview Road, followed by Sergeant Turner.

'What's on your mind, sir?'

As Danny walked onto the driveway of Gladys Miller's house, he said, 'I was here on the day the old lady was found murdered. She'd been dead for about a month before she was found. I just remembered that after inspecting the scene inside the house, I walked out into the back garden to get some fresh air. At the bottom of that garden is an area of ground that looks exactly like PC Davis has just described to me – where he might expect his dog to find traces of a cadaver. I might just be clutching at straws. It could be nothing.'

The burly sergeant said, 'And it could also be something. Let's check it out.'

The two men walked through the unlocked gate and made their way into the rear garden of number eight.

Danny pointed to an area of ground that showed signs of being recently dug over. It had also been crudely covered back over by the bushes and shrubs that had been there prior to being cut down.

'What do you think?'

'It could be that the old lady paid somebody to make a start on tidying the garden for her. It's a bit of a shit tip.'

'There's an alleyway that runs right along the rear of these houses. It can be accessed via a gate in Peleg's back garden. The fence is lower here, so anyone could get in.' Danny moved closer and inspected the disturbed earth. 'Do you want to know what I think? I reckon that's a grave. Or am I just seeing what I want to see?'

Graham Turner shrugged. 'It's certainly the right dimensions, sir. There's only one way to find out. I'll nip back to number two and tell PC Davis to bring his dog. We might as well let Tikka have a go here; then we'll know one way or the other.'

Graham Turner jogged back to the Peleg house and returned a few minutes later with the dog handler and his dog.

Danny pointed at the area of disturbed garden. 'Is that a bit more like what you'd be expecting to see?'

PC Davis said, 'Let's find out, sir.'

The dog handler slipped Tikka onto a long leash. Instantly, the little dog began to traverse the overgrown garden, getting ever closer to the disturbed soil. When the dog finally reached the freshly dug area, the reaction was instantaneous and massive. Barking furiously and wagging its tail, the springer spaniel began to frantically paw at the soil.

The handler went forward, praising the small dog, 'Good girl, Tikka! Good girl! What have you found, eh?'

The dog began to bark and once again began pawing at the ground. The dog handler replaced the long leash with a short one and gave his dog a small plastic toy. The dog began gnawing happily at the toy, a reward for doing the job.

An excited Danny said, 'That was a pretty emphatic response.'

'What you saw there was the textbook indication for a cadaver dog. You need to look under that soil, sir. I believe there could be something there. It might not be human, of course, but something recently dead is buried under there.'

'Graham,' Danny said to his colleague, 'would you mind fetching Tim Donnelly?'

Without answering, the sergeant sprinted away. Two minutes later he returned with the Scenes of Crime supervisor.

'Tim, the cadaver dog has just given a massive indication that something is buried under this garden. How soon can you arrange for a tent, lights and everything else you'll need for a dig?'

'I could have everything we'll need here within the hour. Sergeant Turner, will your men be available to do the digging?'

Graham Turner said, 'Of course. We're booked off to carry out this search all day. I'll go and brief my staff on what's happening.'

Danny said, 'Start making the phone calls, Tim. The sooner we find out what's buried under there, the better.'

94

3.00pm, 18 September 1987
8 Fairview Road, Woodthorpe, Nottingham

The white tent had been erected above the recently disturbed soil in the rear garden of number eight Fairview Road. Danny watched intently as the Special Operations Unit officers removed bucket after bucket of earth. They were now dressed in full protective clothing for their grisly task. They were being supervised by Tim Donnelly, and it was a painstakingly slow process that couldn't be rushed.

Danny, Detective Inspector Cartwright and Sergeant Turner observed the scene, and as soon as the decision to commence the dig had been taken, Danny had contacted the control room. He had requested they contact the Home Office pathologist, Seamus Carter, to inform him of the situation and ask him to remain on standby should a body be discovered. He had also requested that Tina Cartwright suspend any further interviews with Peleg and join him at Fairview Road.

'How were the interviews with Peleg progressing?' Danny asked Tina.

'He's gone totally "no comment" now, boss. As soon as they started the second interview, he turned his wheelchair around and faced the wall.'

'There's no need to interview him any further until we know what's happening here. If I'm right, and Saul Peleg's buried under here, it will change everything.'

He continued, 'Another thing we need to consider is how much longer we can hold Peleg in custody. Tim has outlined to me what a slow process this can be. If a body is discovered, retrieval is going to take a long time. Time that we haven't got. If we do discover human remains here, I'll need you to get a superintendent's authority to extend Peleg's detention for a further twelve hours. If we do find a body, that request will be a formality.'

'I'll start preparing the paperwork. Do you think it's wise, suspending the interviews? What if we find nothing here?'

'You know me, Tina. As a rule, I never make decisions on hunches. But after seeing for myself the way that cadaver dog reacted, I'm prepared to make an exception in this case. I'm convinced there's something buried under there.'

'It's a big call, sir.'

'I know it is. But sometimes you've just got to go with your gut instincts.'

'I'll make a start on sorting out the paperwork for the twelve-hour extension.'

As Tina walked away, Danny said, 'Thanks.'

As another bucket of earth was brought out of the tent to be riddled through the large, coarse sieve, Danny looked at Graham Turner. 'Have you and your staff done this before, Graham?'

'Once,' he replied, his gaze fixed on the sieve. 'It was a few years ago, just prior to the MCIU being set up. We recovered the skeletal remains of a young woman who'd been buried under a basement floor in a house on Forest Fields.'

'How long did that take?'

'From when we first discovered the body to completing the recovery took the best part of six hours.'

'Bloody hell.'

'If it's who you suspect it is that's buried here, he'll have been underground for at least two months. The level of decomposition will be such that the body will be in a very fragile state. We'll be guided by the pathologist on how to proceed. With the woman in the basement, we ended up having to bag her legs up separately. We were working in such a confined space that we just couldn't get her out in one piece. At least we've got room to move here.'

The tent flap opened again, and a grim-faced Tim Donnelly strode over. 'You'd better get Seamus Carter travelling; we've just found a body.'

'Find DI Cartwright,' Danny said. 'Inform her what's just happened and tell her, from me, to get Seamus Carter travelling and to make the detention extension request with the station superintendent as soon as possible.'

'Will do, sir.'

As Graham hurried off to find Tina, Danny met Tim's gaze and took a deep breath. 'Come on then, Tim. Show me what you've found.'

'Not before you get kitted up properly. The level of decomposition is very high. There's a genuine risk of contracting disease from the body. Nobody goes inside that tent without proper protection.'

'Okay. While I do, can you tell me anything about the body?'

'From the partial bit of the body I could see, it does look like a young male. As soon as we made contact with it, I instructed the SOU lads to stop digging. We need the pathologist to guide us now, to prevent any possible loss of evidence. Do you know how long it's going to take him to get here?'

'I understand he's at the City Hospital, so hopefully he shouldn't be that long. He knows what's happening here, so he'll have been waiting for our call.'

95

9.00pm, 18 September 1987
8 Fairview Road, Woodthorpe, Nottingham

The tent that had been erected earlier was now brightly illuminated from the inside by two arc lights. The white light cast an ethereal glow around the garden as dusk fell. Danny looked towards the heavens. The sky had clouded over earlier, and a rainstorm had threatened. Fortunately, the rain never came, and a fresh wind had blown through the stormy-looking clouds.

Wet and windy conditions would have made an already difficult task much more onerous.

Seamus Carter had arrived at Fairview Road less than half an hour after the body had been discovered. The body had been buried beneath a couple of feet of topsoil. As more of it had been revealed, it quickly became apparent just how badly decomposed it was. The body of a young male, dressed in striped pyjamas, was badly infested with insects and beetles. Seamus Carter was also a renowned entomologist who had made a study of determining the time of death by recording the level of infestation by insects and their larvae within the body.

He had instructed the SOU team that the best way to recover the body intact, so that it could be removed for a post-mortem examination, would be to dig two trenches parallel to the body. These trenches would be much deeper than the depth the body was buried. A thin metal sheet would then be slid through the soil, underneath the body, so there was a firm base below it.

Once this was done and the metal sheet was in position, the entire body could be lifted out of the ground. Once out of the ground, it could be slid from the metal sheet into a PVC body bag, along with all the surrounding soil. This would prevent the loss of any smaller bones, teeth or other body parts that could become detached during transit from the scene to the hospital mortuary.

Danny stared, trancelike, towards the white tent. Impatiently waiting for that moment when the body would be ready to be moved. He glanced from the tent to his watch. The clock was ticking. When it had become obvious how long the recovery of the body would take, Peleg's detention had been extended by the station superintendent for another twelve hours.

The tent flaps opened, and Seamus Carter stepped outside, his light blue protective clothing making him appear even larger than his formidable nineteen stone. He raised his arm and waved Danny over. 'We're about to make the lift. It's been a bit of a struggle manoeuvring the metal plate under the body. I've gone in two inches below, so there's going to be quite a lot of soil to lift, as well as the weight of the body.'

'Do you need any more staff?'

'No, I've got four big guys in here already. It's a bit tight for room. With one man on each corner, we'll be able to manage. The difficult part will be sliding the body off the metal sheet and into the PVC body bag. I've asked Tim to get the biggest bag there is, to make life a little easier.'

'Is there room inside the tent for me to observe?'

'Of course. For continuity you should observe any movement of the body. I've labelled both the body itself and the body bag so there's no confusion. Come on in.'

The two men stepped back inside the tent. The stench of putrefying flesh was almost overpowering. Danny was glad of the thick mask that covered his nose and mouth. Two SOU men were standing in the trenches that had been dug to each side of the body. They were gripping the metal sheet in their gloved hands, waiting for Seamus to give the order to lift.

Seamus took one last look and said, 'Very slowly, lads. Lift.'

The four men raised the metal sheet, which sagged alarmingly under the weight of the body and the soil.

'Don't delay, gents. Get it across to the body bag, quick as you can.'

The effort required to move the body was enormous. Danny could hear the four men grunting under the strain as they manoeuvred themselves out of the trenches. In a matter of minutes, the metal sheet holding the remains was lying half in and half out of the body bag.

'Very slowly, raise the left side,' Seamus instructed. As the metal sheet was slowly raised, the body and the soil began to slide slowly into the black PVC bag. Eventually, the body and soil had all slid into the bag, and the metal sheet was removed.

Seamus grinned broadly. 'Well done, lads. Great job.'

Danny said, 'Is that it? Can we move the body to the mortuary now?'

'I'm afraid I'll need another hour here, at least. I want to make sure there's nothing left around the burial site that we've missed. I also want to take insect samples from the body and the surrounding area before he's moved.' He noticed Danny's frustration. 'One hour, Danny. That's all I need.'

'Okay. I'll arrange for the undertakers to be travelling.'

'Thanks. I'll need these four guys to travel to the mortuary with me to help remove the body from the body bag and onto the examination table. This is not an easy task and needs to be done with great care and patience.'

'Understood. What time do you think you'll be in a position to start the post-mortem?'

The pathologist looked at his watch. 'It's almost nine thirty now. If we say eleven thirty at the City Hospital mortuary, we won't be far out.'

'Okay. Eleven thirty. See you there.'

96

12.30am, 19 September 1987
City Hospital, Nottingham

The post-mortem examination of the decomposed body recovered from the garden of eight Fairview Road was nearing its grisly conclusion.

The pathologist had carried out all the routine procedures associated with a post-mortem examination and was now starting the additional procedure requested by Danny.

Very carefully, the decomposed body was turned over, exposing the putrefying flesh on the dead man's back.

Carter stretched his own back before once again bending over the body. He used a scalpel to pare away the waxy skin along the spine before slowly easing the rotting flesh away from the individual vertebrae. He worked methodically, starting at the top and slowly working his way down the spine.

When he reached the lumbar area, he suddenly stopped. 'Danny, you need to come and have a close look at this.'

Danny stepped forward until he was standing alongside

the pathologist. Under the bright lights, he could see that the exposed vertebrae were a creamy, grey colour.

Using the scalpel as a pointer, Seamus indicated the vertebrae near the base of the spine. 'Just here, between the L2 and L3 vertebrae.'

'What exactly am I looking for?'

'Do you see how large the gap is between those two vertebrae compared to the rest of his spine? It's over an inch at least.'

Danny nodded slowly. 'I see it, but why is that significant?'

'That tells me this poor soul suffered a badly broken spine some years ago. As the years progress, this gap widens. Because the usual sinews and muscles that hold the vertebrae in place are so severely damaged, they no longer do their job.'

The pathologist delved deeper with the scalpel, opening the individual vertebrae and exposing what was left of the spinal cord. Again, he gestured for Danny to look, 'The spinal cord has been severed right here, between the L2 and L3 vertebrae.'

'An identical injury as the one suffered by Saul Peleg as a youngster. Will you be able to determine a formal identification?'

The pathologist looked up at the skull of the body. 'The teeth are all still intact, so we should be able to make a formal identification using dental records. Especially so, as you already have an idea of who you think this is. You'll just need to obtain Saul Peleg's dental records so I can make a comparison.'

'You'll have them first thing tomorrow morning.'

'You mean first thing this morning.' Seamus gave a tired smile. 'It's already past midnight.'

When Danny realised he'd been awake for almost twenty-four hours, a wave of exhaustion suddenly engulfed him.

Noticing this, Seamus said, 'Go home, Danny. There's nothing else you can do here. I'll finish everything off and make a start on the report. I'll make sure you have the report and all the photos from the post-mortem on your desk in the morning. I know you. You'll be back in your office at stupid o'clock this morning. You need to rest as well, man.'

'Okay, okay. You're starting to sound like my wife. I'll talk to you at eight o'clock this morning. Thanks for all you've done today.'

Seamus grinned. 'No problem. Make sure you let the phone ring until I answer it. I'll probably still be asleep when you call.'

97

6.30am, 19 September 1987
MCIU Office, Mansfield Police Station

Danny was surprised to see Rob Buxton waiting for him when he walked into the office.

'Bloody hell, Rob. I thought I was early; what brings you in at this time?'

'I heard what happened yesterday. I know you're going to have another busy day today, so I wanted to catch you early and give you some good news.'

Danny hadn't seen much of Rob over the last week or so. His close friend and colleague had been working tirelessly on the PC Warden assault case, investigating football hooligans.

Danny sat down and said, 'I'm ready for some good news, mate. Fire away.'

'We finally had all the forensic test results for the Warden case returned yesterday.'

'Just refresh my memory. I do remember about the luminol testing inside the Vauxhall Astra. That all came back positive. Photographs of bloody training shoe prints were taken from the passenger footwells?'

'That's right. When we arrested the four members of the Halton Moor Casuals, we seized a lot of clothing and footwear from their home addresses. We sent it all off for testing, and it's those tests we got back from the Forensic Science Service yesterday.'

Danny smiled. 'And I can tell by the look on your face that this is going to be good news, mate.'

'It's better than that. We can positively match a pair of training shoes to every photograph highlighted by the luminol test. We are now able to show who sat where in the car immediately after the assault on PC Warden. Subsequent tests on those training shoes have found traces of blood on the soles in between the tread patterns and inside the lace eyelets. The blood that's been found on these trainers is an identical match to PC Warden's.'

'So you can pin down three out of the four individuals? If I remember rightly, there was nothing found in the driver's footwell.'

'That's correct. The driver of the car was Sam Creedon. When we searched his home address, we recovered a decorative truncheon with a leather strap. That weapon has also been forensically examined. It was found to have traces of blood on the wood directly beneath the leather strap. It had obviously been wiped down to get rid of any blood. Unfortunately for him, he missed the minute traces of blood beneath the strap. The blood that was found on the truncheon is also an exact match for PC Warden's.'

'That's brilliant work. That's all four connected to the assault, then?'

'It certainly is. As you remember, all four of them maintained "no comment" answers to every question when they were interviewed in Leeds. I fully expect them to do the same thing when they answer bail here in a week's time.'

Danny shrugged. 'I hope they do. With all that forensic evidence stacked against them, there isn't a court in the land that won't convict. All we'll have to do is ask them once if they were at the scene of the attack. If they deny being there or make a "no comment" answer, they're fucked. Just run through the evidence that connects them to the scene, and if they choose not to offer an explanation, so be it. I'm sure the custody sergeant on the day will approve all charges. You never know, Rob. When they hear all the evidence we've got, they may try to squirm their way out of it. By coming up with some bullshit reason how the police officer's blood got on their shoes and weapons.'

'But if they've already denied being there, that's going to be a tad difficult.'

'Exactly.'

'For once in my life, I'm really hoping these shits stick to "no comment" answers.'

'It's good work by all of your team.'

'It's been bloody hard work and long hours. If we get them locked up, it will have all been worth it. I'm at a bit of a loose end today. Is there anything I can do to help on this enquiry?'

'Yes. As a matter of urgency, can you track down what dentist Saul Peleg went to? We need to fax a copy of his dental records across to Seamus Carter as near to eight o'clock as you can.'

'I'll do my best, but most dentists don't open until nine o'clock. I'll have a look at the dental surgeries that are closest to his home address and visit them personally at eight. There may be staff on the premises, even though the doors don't open to patients until nine. As soon as I locate his dentist and obtain the records, I'll get them faxed to Seamus.'

'Thanks, Rob. It's vital that we get a positive identification as soon as possible. Once we know for definite that it's Solomon we've got locked up in our cells, we'll be able to push him harder.'

'Are you hanging back from having any more interviews until you know for certain it's Saul's body you've recovered?'

'That was my plan originally, but I've been thinking about it this morning, and I'm going to change tack.'

Rob raised an eyebrow, intrigued. 'In what way?'

'I'm going to tell Glen and Rachel to have an interview with him this morning. I want them to show him the photographs from the Cavendish Hotel. It might rattle him enough to give us an account, but I expect he'll stick to "no comment" answers. The real reason I want them to have the interview is so that, just before they switch off the tapes, they can drop out that we've found the body of a young male in the garden at number eight Fairview Road. They can tell him that we're trying hard to identify it this morning.'

'I want that to sit in his brain and fester for a little while. If he knows that the deception he's trying to pull is unravelling piece by piece, he just might start talking.'

'It's a good idea, and it could work. This is a case like no other; there's all sorts of ramifications. At what stage do you identify him as being Solomon and not Saul? Will we need to re-arrest Solomon for the offence you've already arrested him for when he was posing as Saul? Will you be able to start the detention clock again? Or keep the original one running?'

Danny sighed. 'They're all good questions, mate. I've got a telephone call booked with the force lawyer at nine o'clock this morning. Hopefully, he'll be able to answer them. That's what he gets paid the big money for. The only thing I'm confident about is that there's no chance of starting the twenty-four-hour detention time all over again. There's some smart-arse lawyer out there who would drive a cart and horse through that argument and allege that we knew it was Solomon all the time and only detained him initially as Saul so we could extend his detention. That's why I got the twelve-hour extension last night. If needs be, I'll go to the Magistrates Court later today and ask for a warrant of further detention, as well.'

Rob stood up. 'What a job. I've never known anything like it. Looking at it from the outside and not working on it personally, I just can't get my head around it. I'll get cracking on the dentists and let you know when I've faxed the records to Seamus.'

'Brilliant. Quick as you can, mate, thanks.'

As Rob closed the door, Danny reflected on what Rob had said. It really had been a unique and very strange case. He expected there would be more twists to come yet.

98

9.00am, 18 September 1987
Custody Block, Mansfield Police Station, Nottinghamshire

The heavy steel door was slammed shut, leaving Solomon alone in the tiny cell. He remained seated in the wheelchair he didn't need, staring blankly at the walls. The walls that now felt as if they were closing in around him. He could have sworn that the detective who had escorted him back to the cell had been smirking.

The last interview had been full of surprises.

He had anticipated the questioning would again concentrate on the relationship dynamics within his family. What had transpired came as a total shock to him. He had managed to maintain his 'no comment' mantra to every question, but it had become increasingly more difficult. There were so many times he wanted to blurt out an answer, to give an account and make them understand.

So it had come as a complete surprise when the detective had shown the photographs of him walking into the Cavendish Hotel for his overnight stay with Victoria. He had almost answered her question, but just managed to check himself.

If the photographs had been unexpected, the comment by the other detective as he ended the interview had really thrown him into a panic.

When the detective casually announced that the police had found a body in his neighbour's garden, he had felt physically sick. He had felt his temperature rise and realised his face was reddening. But even under such pressure, he had managed to maintain a stony silence.

The detective had stared unblinking into his eyes as he told him the body was that of a white male, a similar age to himself.

Eventually, he had felt compelled to look away from the detective's accusing stare. The detective had then announced that they were confident a formal identification would be made later that morning. The tape recording had then been abruptly switched off, and the interview closed.

At that moment, Solomon had desperately wanted to tell the two detectives exactly what had happened. The reasons why he had acted in the way he had. The rationale behind his decisions.

This whole thing had turned into a never-ending nightmare. When he had taken the first step on this insane journey, this was not how he had expected things to turn out.

He had always intended to live a lie.

He had never envisaged that to simply maintain that deception, he would be forced to undertake ever-increasing malevolent acts. Each subsequent evil deed he had been forced to commit became more heinous. That simple, initial deception had quickly become one deadly lie after another.

He felt no remorse about killing his mother or his brother – that was personal. To him, it was justifiable retribution for how he had been disrespected and blamed for everything by them both.

When he had started the chain of events that would eventually see him adopt his brother's identity and seize his monetary assets, the plan had been a simple one.

The fact he had been forced to deal with every threat to that overriding deception, in such a cold-blooded and unfeeling way, meant he now felt as though he was losing a grip on his own sanity.

As he stared at the four walls, Solomon made his decision. He wouldn't wait for the inevitable.

He knew the police would soon discover that the body was his brother, Saul. He decided to abandon any thoughts of saying nothing. He needed to explain everything. He knew his solicitor would advise him against talking, but it was too late for that.

Everything had now come to a head, and he felt he needed to set the record straight while he still had the opportunity.

He needed the detectives to understand that he was not an evil man.

99

10.30am, 19 September 1987
MCIU Office, Mansfield Police Station

The atmosphere in Danny's office was tense. Rachel and Glen had returned from the cell block. They had just informed Danny that Peleg had maintained 'no comment' answers throughout the latest interview.

Even when confronted with the photographs showing him walking unaided into the Cavendish Hotel, Peleg had said nothing.

'What was his body language like when you told him we'd found the body?' Danny asked.

Rachel said, 'He coloured up a little and his neck got blotchy, but that was all.'

Tina and Andy, also in Danny's office, listened to the debrief from the two interviewers thoughtfully.

Andy said, 'You need to change direction. There must be something you can do to provoke a reaction from Peleg. A way to get him responding to your questions.'

Glen Lorimar, the most experienced interviewer in the

room, said, 'Unfortunately, it's not that simple. If we go in too heavy, his brief will cry foul. And if we keep treating him with kid gloves, it makes it easy for him to just sit there and say "no comment".'

Tina said, 'What if you tried a more personal approach?'

'The first two interviews we had with him were just that. We concentrated on his family and relationships within that unit. Apart from that initial conversation, it's been "no comment" ever since.'

There was an urgent knocking on the office door, and Rob Buxton stepped inside. 'Seamus Carter's just phoned. He's been able to make a positive identification using the dental records I faxed over earlier. The body buried in the back garden at number eight Fairfield Road is Saul Peleg. Which means we've got Solomon Peleg locked up downstairs.'

Danny said, 'Great work, Rob. Well done for tracking the dentist down so quickly this morning. This is what we've been waiting for. Glen, Rachel, I want you back downstairs. Let's get Peleg straight back in the interview room. Just hit him with it straight away. Tell him that we've positively identified the body in the neighbour's garden. That we know it's Saul, and that there's no more room for him to manoeuvre. Tell him we know who he is, and let's see what his reaction to that is.'

'Will do, boss,' Glen said. 'If he says anything at all in response to that, I'll need to arrest him as Solomon Peleg and take him back before the custody sergeant. The sergeant will need to give him his rights all over again. It's going to be a pain because it will mean shutting him down again. I'm concerned that if we don't, some barrister will call foul on procedure later at court.'

'Do what you've got to do, Glen. You know what you're doing. I think you should arrest him on suspicion of everything. The murders of his mother, brother, Angela Billson, Gladys Miller and Lillian Rhodes.'

'If I do that, it could make him close down altogether. I think it would be a much stronger tactic to question him on each murder separately. As and when he admits any involvement, I'll arrest him for that offence and move on to the next. He's much more likely to keep talking if we do it that way.'

'Okay. I can see how that would work. Try it your way.'

'Just while we're talking about procedure,' Andy said. 'Will the solicitor down there still be able to represent Solomon? When he was initially representing someone he believed was Saul?'

'Well, there definitely isn't any conflict of interest, as Saul is dead,' Danny replied. 'Glen, am I right in thinking that when you're booking Solomon in with the custody sergeant, he'll be asked about legal representation again?'

'Yes, sir, he will. It will depend on what Solomon says at that point that will determine what we do.'

'Okay. You'll just have to play it by ear.'

'Will do, sir.' He shook his head in disbelief. 'This enquiry just keeps getting crazier.'

'Rachel,' Danny said, 'I know she isn't technically the next of kin, but we should contact Laura Higgins and inform her of what's happened to her fiancé, Saul. I'd like you to go and see her once the interviews are completed. From what you told me, it sounds like you built a good rapport with her, and no doubt this will come as a huge shock to her.'

Rachel nodded. 'Okay, boss. I'll go and see her.'

100

11.30am, 19 September 1987
Custody Block, Mansfield Police Station, Nottinghamshire

Glen had briefed the custody sergeant on what was about to happen. He left Rachel at the booking-in desk while he walked down to the cell that housed Solomon Peleg.

He slipped the large key into the lock and swung open the heavy steel door. He was surprised to see Peleg sitting on the hard bench. The wheelchair had been tipped over and was now lying on its side.

Peleg didn't look at the detective. He just stared down at the floor.

'You're not Saul,' Glen said, 'are you?'

Solomon Peleg slowly looked up and made eye contact. He then stood and said quietly, 'My name's Solomon. I need to talk to you.'

'And I want to hear what you've got to say. But before we can have a conversation, I need you to see the custody sergeant so he can book you into custody as Solomon. He needs to give you your rights again. Do you understand?'

Solomon nodded.

Glen escorted Solomon back to the booking-in desk. Both the sergeant and Rachel were surprised, but not shocked, to see Peleg strolling up to the desk.

The sergeant quickly went through the booking-in procedures with Solomon. As the sergeant reached the section on legal representation, Solomon shook his head, saying, 'I don't want a solicitor. There are things I need to say, and a solicitor will want me to say nothing. It's too late for that. I need to explain my reasons for doing the terrible things I've had to do.'

Ten minutes later, and with the custody documentation all signed, Glen and Rachel took Solomon Peleg into an interview room.

Rachel switched on the tape recorder and carried out the preliminary introductions.

Glen said, 'Solomon Peleg, you're under arrest on suspicion of the murder of your mother, Rebecca Peleg. What can you tell me about your mother's death?'

'Before I answer your questions and talk to you about what I did, I need you to understand something. My mother always blamed me for everything. After the accident that was Saul's own stupid fault, I was always made to feel responsible for his devastating, life-changing injury. That was so wrong, as none of it was my fault.'

'I understand what you're saying, Solomon. How did that make you feel?'

'Angry and unloved.'

'Is that why you hurt your mother?'

'It wasn't a single thing; it was an accumulation of years of mental torture and blame. I was always made to feel worthless. At times she made me feel like dogshit on her shoe.'

'After feeling like that for years, what was it that made you finally snap?'

'They were going to throw me out onto the street. I'd lost my job again. As usual, my mother blamed me. She didn't want to know that I'd been dismissed for something beyond my control. She was going to force me to live on the streets while they both enjoyed living in the lap of luxury. That wasn't right.'

'So what did you do?'

'I waited until she was asleep that night. Then I strangled her and hanged her from the rafters in the loft.'

'Was your mother already dead when you hanged her?'

'No. I thought she was, but when the noose tightened, she started to thrash around again. It didn't take long for her to die though.'

'And what did you do then?'

'I propped open Saul's bedroom door so he would see her hanging when he woke up. Then I went back to bed.'

'What happened when Saul woke up?'

'He started shouting. I waited for ten minutes, then went into him. I cut my mother's body down, and he called the police. The sergeant who came out wasn't that interested. It was easy to convince him that she'd killed herself.'

'There was a suicide note found.'

'I wrote that.'

'Do you have any remorse at all for your actions?'

Solomon made eye contact with Glen and said coldly, 'None. She was quite prepared to put me out on the streets. She must have known I wouldn't have survived that lifestyle. She was happy for me to die, so why shouldn't I feel the same way about her? At the time, I thought killing her was my only course of action, and I still don't regret it. After her precious Saul was crippled, my mother hated every fibre of my being.'

'Let's talk about Saul.'

'I killed him too.'

Glen cautioned Solomon and said, 'You're now under arrest on suspicion of the murder of Saul Peleg.'

Solomon shrugged. 'After I killed my mother, I was forced to adopt the role of carer for my brother. I hated it. All I could think about was how Saul had also been happy to go along with my mother and throw me out. I thought about everything, and eventually I decided to steal my brother's identity and live in luxury, spending his compensation money.'

'What was the plan?'

'It was simple. We were identical twins. I mean totally identical in every way. Strangers could never tell us apart. I knew I could carry off the deception easily. It was something we always did as kids, pretending to be the other brother. I would masquerade as Saul, spending time in the wheelchair whenever I was around people who knew us. Even with that sacrifice, I knew I'd still have plenty of opportunities to lead a separate life, away from here. I would never have to worry about money again, as I'd be able to access all of Saul's damages.'

'How could you do that?'

'I quickly learned how to forge his signature. Eventually, the bank manager was happy to release funds to me over the telephone because he recognised my voice. The plan worked brilliantly at first.'

'So, if you became Saul, how did you plan to explain the sudden disappearance of Solomon?'

'I planned it so everyone thought that Solomon had left the country, to start a new life. That left everything clear for me to become Saul.'

'Not quite. Saul was still here.'

'As soon as everything was in place, I got rid of Saul.'

'How?'

'I waited until his carers had been and put him to bed for

the night. Once they had left and Saul had gone to sleep, I smothered him with a pillow.'

'Then what did you do?'

'What I did next was my biggest mistake.'

'What was that?'

'That night, I buried my brother's body in my elderly neighbour's garden.'

'Why was that a mistake?'

'Because the old woman saw me. I should have put Saul in the boot of his car and driven him miles away from here. It was a mistake that was to have devastating consequences.'

'Before we move on to those consequences. I need to ask you a couple more questions about Saul. Do you have any remorse for what you did to your brother?'

'Not really. He allowed me to take all the blame for his injuries. At any time, he could have said that it was his fault I crashed the motorcycle. But no, he was quite happy to let me take the blame for all those years. That accident not only ruined my brother's life, but he allowed it to ruin mine as well. I didn't shed any tears when I killed Saul. I just looked forward to finally being able to start living my own life.'

'You said burying your brother's body in your neighbour's garden had consequences. What were they?'

'I had to deal with the old lady, as well.'

Glen cautioned Solomon and said, 'I have to tell you, you're now under arrest on suspicion of the murder of Gladys Miller.'

Solomon said, 'I genuinely regret what I did to her, but I felt I had no choice. To continue the life I was living, I couldn't risk the old lady saying something to someone else.'

'Had she said something to you?'

'Yeah. One day, I saw her on the street, and she told me she'd seen me in her garden.'

'Couldn't you have denied it was you?'

'I tried to. Then as she walked away, she called me Solomon. Even though I was sitting in Saul's wheelchair, somehow she still knew who I was. I couldn't risk it. I had to get rid of her.'

'And how did you do that?'

'I broke into her house and staged a burglary. She heard me moving things around and confronted me on the landing. She was going to call the police, so I hit her with the crowbar I had used to break in.'

'Where did you hit her?'

'On the back of the head. I heard her head crack, and then she fell down the stairs. When I checked on her at the bottom of the stairs, she was dead.'

'When you broke into her house, had you intended to kill her?'

'Yeah. I was always going to strangle her, but when she fell down the stairs, I didn't have to.'

'How do you feel about that now?'

'It was a terrible thing to do. I just panicked when she said my name. I couldn't see any other way out. You have to under-stand I was living a lie, and I had to do whatever it took to protect that deception.'

'Was Mrs Miller the only victim of that deadly deception?'

Solomon shook his head. 'No. There are others.'

'Others?'

'Two more.'

'Tell me about the first one.'

'That was Saul's health visitor.'

Glen immediately cautioned Solomon and said, 'You're now under arrest on suspicion of the murder of Angela Bill-son. What happened?'

'It was all so unfortunate. She'd only come to the house to check up on Saul, but I didn't know she was coming. When she arrived, I was upstairs, but the wheelchair was downstairs in the hallway. I couldn't risk answering the door in case she saw me.'

'So why not just let her leave and come back another day?'

'That's what I wanted to do, but I think she saw me standing at the upstairs window. Anyway, for whatever reason, she turned around and walked back to the house.'

'What happened when she came back?'

'By the time she got back to the front door, I'd managed to get downstairs. So I let her in, and we talked.'

'And?'

'She kept asking me who was upstairs. She caught me out in a lie about a radio and realised something was wrong.'

'I still don't understand why you felt you had to kill her?'

'She was going to call her supervisor, and I knew that as soon as she did that, it would have exposed my lies. I'm telling you, I had no choice. I had to stop her.'

'What did you do?'

'I surprised her. I jumped up out of the wheelchair and pushed her onto the floor. Then I strangled her.'

'Then what did you do?'

'I left her car on the Forest Recreation Ground, then dumped her body later that night at Woodthorpe Grange Park.'

'Don't you feel any remorse about killing her?'

'Don't get me wrong, Detective. I deeply regret what happened to this woman and to my neighbour. I'm not an evil man. I was deeply troubled by their deaths, but I felt I had no choice. I felt at the time that it was either them or me. All I ever wanted was to have a life. I'm sorry for both of those women, but I had to do it.'

'You mentioned another victim. Who was that?'

'My aunt.'

Glen cautioned Solomon and said, 'You're now under arrest on suspicion of the murder of Lillian Rhodes. How did your aunt become a victim?'

'She just turned up unannounced.'

'Why was that such a problem? You could have let her visit and then leave?'

'It was a problem because as soon as I said that my mother was dead, and that Solomon had left the country, she decided she would move in with me. She was a scavenging freeloader who saw my disability as an opportunity to live in the lap of luxury. She told me I should sack my carers and that she would move in to look after me.'

'I see. And that would have a major impact on your life, wouldn't it?'

'Exactly. How could I do my own thing with that big fat cuckoo in the nest. She wasn't interested in caring for her disabled nephew, she just wanted an easy life.'

'And you couldn't let that happen?'

'Definitely not.'

'So what did you do?'

'I strangled her.'

'What did you do with her body?'

'I drove her out to the motorway and threw her off a bridge in front of an articulated truck. I couldn't believe it when detectives showed up later, telling me they had found her body and that she'd been murdered. I thought that truck would have spread her all over the motorway, destroying any evidence.'

'Don't you have any remorse about what happened to her? She was your aunt, after all.'

'For my ugly, mean-spirited, meddlesome aunt? Not a bit. It's like I said, she was motivated by greed. She saw herself living an easy life here. She wouldn't take no for an answer, so she left me with no option. I had to kill her.'

'And what was your motivation for causing all this misery and death, Solomon?'

'My motivation?'

'Yes. You said you wanted me to understand the reasons why you have committed all these killings?'

'Haven't you been listening? I've already told you. I felt justified in killing my mother and brother because of the way they had treated me. They had it coming.'

'What about the other three people?'

Solomon shrugged coldly. 'Wrong place, wrong time. The life I was living was a lie. They had to die for me to continue living that life. It's as simple as that.'

'So you don't really care about those three women. When you said earlier that you deeply regretted their deaths, that was all bullshit, wasn't it?'

'Listen, Detective. I want you to understand me, not judge me. My life ended when Saul caused me to crash that motorcycle. The accident broke his back, but it was my life it ruined too. Once I had taken the first step down that murderous road, I just had to keep walking. That's all I'm going to say.'

Glen asked a few more questions, but Solomon had stopped talking. He sat in stony silence, staring into the middle distance.

He never uttered another word.

He had said all he was going to say.

101

Danny had a broad smile on his face as he walked into Chief Superintendent Potter's office. Normally, he despised these visits to headquarters. Today was different.

Today he had very good news.

'Sit down, Chief Inspector,' Potter said. 'I understand there's been significant progress made on some of your outstanding cases.'

Danny sat down and crossed his legs. 'Last night, we charged Solomon Peleg with five murders. These charges included the murder of his mother, Rebecca, and his brother, Saul.'

'And the other three charges?'

'He's also been charged with the murders of Angela Billson, Gladys Miller and Lillian Rhodes.'

'Is the evidence strong enough to convict him?'

'He's made significant admissions to each of the deaths that corroborates the forensic evidence we already had. I'm sure he'll be convicted on all counts, sir. The evidence is overwhelming.'

'Excellent.' He clapped his hands together. 'The chief constable will be pleased. He'll also ask me what progress, if any, has been made on PC Warden's assault case. How is that enquiry progressing?'

'There are four suspects, all from Leeds. They are due to answer bail at Mansfield Police Station in a week's time.'

'I understand you were struggling for evidence when you interviewed these men after they were arrested in Leeds. Is that still the case?'

'No, sir. We now have extremely good forensic evidence linking all four suspects to the assault on PC Warden.'

'That's excellent news. And do you think that forensic evidence on its own will be enough to support charges when they answer bail? I only ask because I know these men refused to answer any questions when they were interviewed last time.'

'That's correct, sir. All four suspects maintained "no comment" answers to all questions when they were interviewed. Quite frankly, if they adopt the same tactics when they answer bail, it will play right into our hands. We'll put all the evidence to them and ask them to give an account. If they refuse to answer or to give us an account, then I'm sure they'll be charged.'

'That's encouraging. It's important that you don't allow their solicitors to know exactly how strong your forensic evidence is prior to your team interviewing their clients.'

Danny thought to himself, *Thanks, sir. Have you got any more eggs I can suck?* but he just smiled and said, 'Yes, sir. We'll make a disclosure to the solicitors that we have forensic evidence linking their clients to the crime. But as we're not obliged to give details of that forensic evidence, we won't.'

'Good. Well, keep me updated. And please pass on my congratulations to your team on the excellent work they've all done with Solomon Peleg.'

Danny stood to leave. 'Will do, sir.'

102

11.00am, 26 September 1987
Custody Block, Mansfield Police Station, Nottinghamshire

The four football hooligans had all answered their police bail. One at a time, they had been taken to the cells, given their rights and booked into custody, ready for further questioning by detectives.

Part of that process had been for the two interview teams of Detective Inspector Rob Buxton and PC Bill Keenan, and Detective Sergeant Pete Hazard and PC Nick Grainger, to give disclosure of all evidence secured to the individual solicitors who had accompanied their clients to Mansfield Police Station.

Rob Buxton and Bill Keenan were now in an interview room with Dixie Bradder and his solicitor.

Rob carried out the introductions of everyone present and said, 'We're conducting enquiries into the assault of an on-duty police officer at West Bridgford in Nottingham on 31 July. This assault occurred following the football match between Nottingham Forest and Leeds United. Were you in Nottingham on that day?'

'No comment.'

'Had you travelled down to Nottingham to attend that football match?'

'No comment.'

'Did you travel to Nottingham with Sam Creedon, Wes Handysides and Geoff Hoskins?'

'No comment.'

'Did you travel to Nottingham in a Vauxhall Astra car owned by Sam Creedon?'

'No comment.'

'After the match, where did you go?'

'No comment.'

'Did you engage with others in public disorder in the West Bridgford area after that football match?'

'No comment.'

'Did you, or any of the friends you travelled with, suffer any injuries in that disorder?'

'No comment.'

'Did you, or any of the three men you were with, have contact with any police officers after that football match?'

'No comment.'

'Did you, or any of the three men you were with, have any contact with PC Mark Warden?'

'No comment.'

Rob knew it was important to maintain a slow pace during the questioning. All too often, the no-comment answers caused interviewing officers to rush, but Rob was far too experienced to allow that to happen.

He allowed an even longer pause before sliding a photograph of a training shoe across the table until it was in front of Dixie Bradder.

'This training shoe was seized from your home address when you were arrested. Is it yours?'

'No comment.'

'Are you the only male living at that address?'

'No comment.'

'If this training shoe belongs to somebody else, you need to tell me now.'

There was a brief glance between Bradder and his solicitor. She shook her head slightly, and Bradder said, 'No comment.'

'Did you engage in an attack on a uniformed constable in Nottingham on 31 July?'

'No comment.'

'Can you give an explanation as to how traces of PC Warden's blood have been found on your training shoes?'

Again, the furtive glance was exchanged between the solicitor and her client before Bradder continued, 'No comment.'

'Was PC Warden's blood found on your training shoes because you were wearing them when you assaulted him, causing him serious head injuries?'

A sly smile passed over the lips of Bradder, and he said sarcastically, 'No comment.'

Rob then slid a photograph across the table to Bradder. This photograph showed the training shoe sole beside the luminol impression of the same training shoe sole. Even to the naked eye they looked a perfect match. Forensics had proved them to be just that.

Rob said, 'Look at this comparison photograph. Can you explain how the sole print of this training shoe was found in the front passenger seat footwell of the Vauxhall Astra owned by Sam Creedon?'

'No comment.'

'That sole print we found was made in the blood of PC Warden. Can you explain that?'

A fleeting look of concern passed across the face of Bradder, but he still replied, 'No comment.'

'Is it your intention to say "no comment" to all questions asked during this interview?'

Bradder leaned forward, put his elbows on the desk, smiled and said, 'No comment.'

'In that case, I'm now terminating the interview.'

Rob switched off the tape recorder and signed the labels for the tapes.

'Will you be having any further interviews with my client?' Bradder's solicitor asked.

Rob said, 'As you're aware, we do have other suspects to interview. Once that task has been completed, we'll decide whether a further interview with your client is necessary.'

The solicitor made an indignant, huffing sound before closing her folder.

'Your client will be placed in a cell until we need to speak to him again. You're more than welcome to wait in the foyer upstairs.'

103

2.30pm, 26 September 1987
MCIU Office, Mansfield Police Station

The interview conducted by Detective Sergeant Pete Hazard and PC Nick Grainger, with Wes Handysides, had just finished.

The two officers had returned to the MCIU office to compare notes with Rob Buxton and Bill Keenan.

'How did it go?' Rob asked Pete.

'Exactly the same as Bradder and Hoskins,' he replied. 'He answered "no comment" to everything.'

'Did you spell out all the forensic evidence we've got that ties him to the assault?'

'To the letter. We went through everything as planned. None of them are budging an inch. I'm surprised the solicitors haven't intervened; they must know by now that we're not bluffing.'

'I know what you mean. I expected at least one of them to request a further consultation with their client.'

'I wonder if Sam Creedon will be any different. Do you think he'll talk to us?'

'In all honesty,' Rob said, 'I doubt it. There is something you could try though that's slightly different.'

'What's that?'

'Well, I'm sure we're not the only ones getting our heads together. I've no doubt the solicitors will also be talking and comparing notes. They're all aware by now of the training shoe evidence and the evidence from the Vauxhall Astra. Why don't you start this interview with Creedon by concentrating on what the others have been involved in? Talk to Creedon as though we believe he was only there as the driver. Let him think we don't have anything to connect him to the actual assault. Let's see if he's willing to grass on his mates to keep himself out of the shit.'

'Don't forget,' Bill reminded them, 'that Creedon considers himself to be his grandmother's only carer. There's leverage in that situation you can use as well.'

'You'll need to be very careful how you use that, though. Any solicitor worth their salt will soon put a stop to any attempt to put pressure on their client by suggesting his grandmother could suffer if he doesn't co-operate.'

'It's got to be worth a try,' Pete agreed. 'And if he doesn't decide to talk about his mates at the very end of the interview, we can still introduce the blood found on the truncheon recovered at his home address. Let's see if he's got an explanation for that.'

'Sounds like a plan. Good luck.'

104

3.00pm, 26 September 1987
Custody Block, Mansfield Police Station, Nottinghamshire

Pete Hazard and Nick Grainger were now in an interview room with Sam Creedon and his solicitor.

Nick carried out the introductions of everyone present and said, 'You have answered bail today in connection with enquiries we are conducting into the assault of an on-duty police officer at West Bridgford in Nottingham on 31 July. This incident occurred following the football match between Nottingham Forest and Leeds United. Were you in Nottingham on that day?'

Sam Creedon stared at the desk in front of him and mumbled, 'No comment.'

'You'll have to speak up for the tape, Sam,' Pete said loudly.

Creedon looked up and said in a much more assertive voice, 'No comment.'

Pete continued, 'Did you drive to Nottingham that day in the Vauxhall Astra you own?'

'No comment.'

'Is that the same Vauxhall Astra we seized from outside your house when you were arrested?'

'When will I be getting that back, by the way?'

'We're still carrying out further tests on the car–'

Creedon's solicitor interrupted, 'Remember my advice, Sam.'

'Do remember that it is only advice, Sam. Be aware that you don't have to take that advice. If you want to answer my questions, you can.'

Creedon gave a sly smile before saying, 'No comment.'

'Did you take Dixie Bradder, Wes Handysides and Geoff Hoskins to Nottingham in your car?'

'No comment.'

'We've found evidence linking those three to the attack on the police officer and to your car. Can you explain that?'

'No comment.'

'We seized training shoes from the homes of Bradder, Handysides and Hoskins. We've since found the sole prints of those training shoes in the passenger footwells of your car.'

Creedon shot his solicitor a glance, then said hesitantly, 'No comment.'

'We were able to see those sole prints because the wearers had recently trodden in the blood of the injured police officer.'

Again, there was a worried glance. More reluctantly, Creedon said, 'No comment.'

'There was blood from the injured officer on the soles of their training shoes. Did you assault the police officer as well, Sam?'

'No comment.'

'I know how worried you must be about this.' Pete Hazard paused and allowed a long silence to hang heavy in the room.

'You must be worried about how all this is going to affect your grandmother?'

'What are you on about?'

Creedon's solicitor said, 'Sam, you don't have to answer that.'

Pete continued, 'I'm just saying, it must be a real worry for you, that's all. I saw for myself how much you care about her.'

Creedon said, 'I'm not worried about my grandma, and I'm not worried about me. You've got fuck all, copper. So what if you've got their trainers and there's blood in my car. You've got nothing that connects me to what happened.'

'Are you telling me it was just the other three who attacked the police officer?'

'Well, there's no blood in the driver's footwell, is there?'

Creedon's solicitor again interrupted, 'Sam, you really shouldn't be answering these questions.'

Pete pressed on. 'No, there isn't any blood in the driver's footwell. Were you there though, waiting in the car? Didn't you take part in the assault?'

'You know I was there. I didn't assault anybody; it was the others.'

'So let me get this right. You're telling me that the reason PC Warden's blood was found inside your car is because he was attacked by Bradder, Handysides and Hoskins. Is that correct?'

The enormity of what the detective was saying suddenly hit home for Sam. He didn't want to be a grass, but then he thought about his grandmother's welfare and decided that self-preservation was his best course of action.

'Yeah. That's exactly what I'm saying. It was them three. I was just the driver. I stayed in the car.'

'So you didn't take any part in the assault?'

'No.'

'Do you remember when we searched your house, that we recovered a decorative truncheon?'

'Yeah, that thing I brought back from Benidorm.'

'Did you take that to Nottingham.'

Creedon knew he had washed the weapon down thoroughly, so he said, 'No, I didn't. It's only an ornament. It never leaves my bedroom.'

'We've carried out extensive forensic tests on that truncheon. Can you explain how we found traces of PC Warden's blood on that truncheon?'

'That's bollocks. There's no blood.'

'How can you be so sure?'

'I made sure...'

Creedon's solicitor interjected quickly. 'I would like a further consultation with my client.'

Ignoring the solicitor, Pete pressed on, 'The reason you're so sure there's no blood on the truncheon is because you thoroughly wiped it down after the assault? Didn't you?'

'Bollocks! I'm not that stupid.'

'The blood was still there, Sam. It was underneath the leather strap. Hidden between the strap and the wood. You didn't do a good enough job cleaning it, did you?'

'Fuck off! I'm not falling for that shit!'

'That officer's blood was on the truncheon because you assaulted him with it. Then you and all your mates gave him a bloody good kicking, didn't you?'

'Prove it.'

'Forensics have proved it. And you've just helped us to prove it a little bit more.'

Creedon's solicitor cut in again. 'I insist that we stop this interview so I can consult with my client.'

'I've got nothing else to ask him. I'll stop the tapes. Interview terminated.'

'Have your consultation,' Pete Hazard said to the solicitor. 'I don't think we'll be needing a further interview.'

'I'm not happy about this, Detective.'

Pete smiled. 'But if your client wants to answer my questions, what can I do?'

105

4.00pm, 26 September 1987
MCIU Office, Mansfield Police Station

Pete Hazard and Nick Grainger were outlining to Rob Buxton and Bill Keenan the success of the last interview – that Sam Creedon had implicated the other three suspects and then himself in the assault on PC Warden.

Danny heard the four of them talking and came out of his office. 'Sounds like things are going well?'

'Very well,' said Rob. 'As you know, the forensic evidence tying all four defendants to the assault is overwhelming. Well, on top of that, Sam Creedon has just turned turtle and implicated the other three in the assault. He ignored his solicitor's advice and felt he was best served to distance himself from the training shoe evidence. Unfortunately for him, he hadn't counted on the blood evidence on the truncheon seized from his home address that is also compelling and ties him to the assault, as well.'

'That's great. Do you think there's anything to be gained

from reinterviewing the other three? Letting them know they've now been implicated by Creedon?'

'I don't think so, boss. I don't think they'll accept that Creedon has grassed them up. They'll assume we're trying to pull a fast one.'

'In that case, talk to the custody sergeant. I'd like him to accept a Section 18 Wounding with Intent charge for all four of them.'

'Will do, boss.'

106

5.30pm, 26 September 1987
Mansfield Police Station, Nottinghamshire

Sam Creedon was the last of the four men to be charged. Even after being charged, Bradder, Handysides and Hoskins had all stuck to their mantra of 'no comment'.

Now it was Sam Creedon's turn.

Rob Buxton cautioned him and said, 'Sam Creedon, you are charged that on 31 July, at West Bridgford in the county of Nottinghamshire, you assaulted Mark Warden, thereby causing him grievous bodily harm. Contrary to section eighteen of the offences against the Person Act of 1861.'

'What's going to happen to my grandma?' Creedon asked, looking panicked. 'You can't send me to prison. Who's going to look after her?'

As Creedon was being charged in the custody block, Danny was upstairs in his office, talking to Chief Superintendent Potter on the telephone.

'The last one's being charged now, sir.'

'Good work, Danny,' said Potter. 'Are you going for a remand in custody? Or bailing them to a court date?'

'Definitely a remand in custody. All four of them pose a massive flight risk. They know that if they're convicted, they'll all be looking at double-figure prison sentences.'

'They could quite easily have been looking at life sentences. They could've killed that officer. They're worse than bloody animals.'

'All over a bloody game of football. I don't know why they can't just enjoy the match. I'll never understand this insane tribalism. It's just nonsense and all so pointless.'

'I couldn't agree more. I'll let the chief constable know straight away. As you know, he's taken a keen interest in this enquiry from the outset.'

'I'm just glad we managed to track them down. Hopefully, the courts will see the job through now and put them all away for a long time.'

'It's been an excellent week for the MCIU. Your team have done some sterling work.'

'It's been a hard few months. The Solomon Peleg enquiry was like nothing I've ever worked on before. The challenges came in thick and fast, but my team met them all and, more importantly, overcame them. I just need to make sure that the paperwork and file preparation maintains that same quality. That's the only way we'll achieve the right results at the Crown Court.'

'I'm sure you won't allow anything else, Chief Inspector.'

EPILOGUE

4.30pm, 18 December 1987
Trentside Gardens, Ruddington, Nottinghamshire

It had been an hour since the verdicts had come in at Nottingham Crown Court in the trial of Bradder, Handysides, Creedon and Hoskins.

The jury had taken just over two and a half hours to return guilty verdicts on all four men.

As soon as the verdicts were read out and sentence passed, Danny had left the courtroom. He had made a promise to Don and Esther Warden, the parents of Mark Warden, that he would personally let them know what had happened.

The elderly couple had felt unable to attend the Crown Court in person. They just didn't want to see the faces of their only son's attackers. The police officer was now out of hospital and living at his elderly parents' home. He had only made a partial recovery from his extensive injuries. His speech was slurred, and his thought processes were slow, and his vision was slightly impaired, and he was profoundly deaf in his right ear. He would continue to recover, but it would be a painfully slow process.

He would never recover enough, physically or mentally, to resume his chosen career as a police officer.

Danny parked his car on the tiny cul-de-sac directly outside the Warden residence.

As he got out of the car, he slipped on his black Crombie coat. It was already dark, and a bitterly cold wind was gusting around the close. Thrusting his hands deep into his coat pockets, he walked slowly up the driveway and rang the doorbell.

Don Warden opened the door. 'Danny, it's good of you to drive over. Come inside, it's bloody freezing out there.'

Danny stepped inside and saw a worried-looking Esther waiting in the hallway. She stepped forward, fussing. 'Let me take your coat, Chief Inspector. Otherwise, you won't feel the benefit when you go back outside.'

Danny slipped off his coat, handed it to the anxious mother, and followed Don into the lounge. Noticing that Mark wasn't in the room, Danny asked, 'Is Mark around?'

'He's upstairs, listening to music on his headphones. Grab a seat, Danny. Would you like a drink? Tea? Coffee?'

'I'm good, thanks.'

He waited for the elderly couple to sit down on the settee opposite, and then said, 'It's good news. The jury found all four guilty as charged.'

Danny could see by the facial expressions of the couple that his words had brought a massive relief.

'What sentence did they get?' Don asked.

'Twelve years. They all got twelve years.'

With more than a note of bitterness in her voice, Esther said, 'And my Mark gets a life sentence. That's not justice.'

Don put a comforting arm around his wife's shoulders. 'Twelve years is a long time for them to reflect on what they've done. I must admit though, it still doesn't seem long enough when I see how our Mark struggles every day. The poor lad struggles to tie his own bloody shoelaces.'

Danny could see the tears welling in the old man's eyes. He didn't know what to say, so he just nodded in agreement. He hadn't the heart to tell them that the four men would probably only serve eight years of that twelve-year sentence.

'Would you like me to talk to Mark and tell him what's happened?'

Don shook his head. 'That's not a good idea, Danny. Whenever he hears anything about the trial, it seems to set him back a bit. It's the same when people talk to him about what happened; he gets agitated and distressed quite quickly. I think it's best that we tell him when the time's right.'

'Whatever you think's best, Don.'

'We really appreciate you driving all the way out here to tell us. You already know how grateful we are to you and your team for bringing those monsters to justice.'

'It's not a problem. I know that Mark won't be able to return to full duties, but I want you both to know he'll never stop being part of the police family. If you ever need anything, or if there's anything you think I can help you or Mark with, please don't hesitate to call me, anytime.'

Esther stood up. 'Thanks, Danny. You must be wanting to get home to your lovely wife and family. I'll go and grab your coat.'

Danny stood up and shook hands with Don. 'I meant what I said. You can call me anytime, day or night.'

The old man gripped the detective's hand tightly and said, 'Thanks, for everything you've done.'

As Danny walked back out into the frigid night air and made his way to his car, in his head, he could still hear the bitterness in the voice of Mark Warden's mother.

He said the old woman's words aloud, 'That's not justice.'

WE HOPE YOU ENJOYED THIS BOOK

If you could spend a moment to write an honest review on Amazon, no matter how short, we would be extremely grateful. They really do help readers discover new authors.

ALSO BY TREVOR NEGUS

EVIL IN MIND

(Book 1 in the DCI Flint series)

DEAD AND GONE

(Book 2 in the DCI Flint series)

A COLD GRAVE

(Book 3 in the DCI Flint series)

TAKEN TO DIE

(Book 4 in the DCI Flint series)

KILL FOR YOU

(Book 5 in the DCI Flint series)

ONE DEADLY LIE

(Book 6 in the DCI Flint series)

A SWEET REVENGE

(Book 7 in the DCI Flint series)

THE DEVIL'S BREATH

(Book 8 in the DCI Flint series)